■ □ ■ □ ■

THE FORTRESS

T0308957

Writings from an Unbound Europe

■ ◻ ■ ◻ ■

MEŠA SELIMOVIĆ

THE FORTRESS

Translated from the Serbo-Croatian
by E. D. Goy and Jasna Levinger

NORTHWESTERN UNIVERSITY PRESS

EVANSTON, ILLINOIS

Northwestern University Press
www.nupress.northwestern.edu

Originally published in Serbo-Croatian in 1970 under the title *Tvrdjava*.
Copyright © 1970 by Svjetlost, Sarajevo. English translation
copyright © 1999 by Northwestern University Press.
Published 1999 by Northwestern University Press. All rights reserved.

Printed in the United States of America

10   9   8   7   6   5   4

ISBN 978-0-8101-1712-9 (CLOTH)
ISBN 978-0-8101-1713-6 (PAPER)

Library of Congress Cataloging-in-Publication Data

Selimović, Meša.
    [Tvrđava. English]
    The fortress / Meša Selimović ; translated from the Serbo-Croatian by E.D.
Goy and Jasna Levinger.
        p. cm. — (Writings from an unbound Europe)
    ISBN 0-8101-1712-6 (cloth). — ISBN 0-8101-1713-4 (paper)
    I. Title. II. Series.
    PG1419.29.E43T913 1999
    891.8'2354—dc21
                                                            99-27539
                                                              CIP

To Maša and Jesenka

■ □ ■ □ ■

CONTENTS

TRANSLATORS' FOREWORD

THIS TRANSLATION ATTEMPTS TO PUT THE ORIGINAL INTO acceptable English-language form. To this end, sentences have been shortened and, rarely, lengthened. The many foreign names have been retained, since any attempt to do otherwise would appear ludicrous and would detract from the foreign atmosphere that conveys to the reader the strangeness inherent in the text's impact. All Serbo-Croatian names, be they of people or places, have been adapted to English spelling; the reader may thus comfortably scan them with full confidence. To aid the reader in negotiating these names and terms, we have added a glossary, which includes all terms appearing in italics in the text, as well as a few brief cultural and historical references.

E. D. Goy and Jasna Levinger

■ ☐ ■ ☐ ■

THE FORTRESS

■ □ ■ □ ■

CHAPTER 1

THE DNIESTR MARSHES

I CAN'T TELL YOU WHAT IT WAS LIKE AT CHOCIM, IN THAT FAR Russian land. Not because I don't remember, but because I will not. It's not worth telling of dreadful slaughter, of human terror, of atrocities on both sides. It's not worth the recalling, be it to regret or to glorify. Best to forget. Let people's memory of all that's ugly die, so children may not sing songs of vengeance.

All I'll say is that I got back. Had I not, I'd not be writing this and no one would know that all this really was. What's not written down doesn't exist; it's past and gone. I swam the swollen Dniestr and so got away. The rest were butchered. With me came Mula Ibrahim, our clerk, with whom I struck up a friendship during those three months of our journey home to our distant country. He came because, swimming, I dragged his holed boat out of the dangerous current and carried him, sick, half the way, dragged him, urged him on when he fell on his knees or lay on his back, staring, motionless, at the dull alien sky, longing for death.

When we got back, I told nobody about that Chocim. Perhaps it was because I was tired and confused, so strange did all that business of Chocim seem, as if it had happened in some other, distant life and as if I, myself, had been somebody else and not the I who looked, with tear-filled eyes, at his native town, scarcely recognizing it. I felt no regret, no bitterness, no sense of betrayal. I was just empty and confused. When I quit my post as teacher and left the children I'd taught, I set off for glory, for some light, and fell into the mud, into the endless Dniestr marshes around Chocim, among lice and sickness, wounds and death, into indescribable human misery.

Of that wonder men call war I remember countless details and only two events, and I tell of them not because they are worse than others, but because, do what I may, I cannot forget them.

The first concerns one among many battles. We were fighting over a fortification, constructed of wooden hurdles packed with earth. Many had perished, both ours and theirs, in the marshes surrounding it, in the black waters of the swamp, dark brown with blood. It smelt of ancient marsh roots and of rotting corpses left behind after the battle. And when we'd taken the entrenchment, blown it apart with guns and the heads of our people, I just stood there, tired: What senselessness! What had we gained and what had they lost? Both we and they were surrounded by the only victor: the utter silence of the ancient earth, indifferent to human misery. That evening, seated on a wet tree trunk in front of a fire that stung our eyes, I held my head in my hands, deafened by the cries of marsh birds, scared by the dense mist of the Dniestr marshes that stubbornly enveloped us in forgetfulness. How, that night, I managed to survive the horror both within me and around me and that deepest of all sadness, of defeat that follows victory, I'm unclear even to myself. In that darkness, in the cries and whistling, in the despair for which I find no reason, in that long, sleepless night, in the black fear that was not of the enemy, but of something within me, I was born as what I am, unsure of all that is me and of all that is human.

The second event is ugly and no way can I cast it from me. Often it's there inside me, even when I don't want it.

Everything brings it back, even what is its opposite: someone's merry laughter, the cooing of a child, a tender love song. And my memory always begins at the end, not as I tell it now, so, perhaps, some of it is inaccurate, but any other way you wouldn't understand. In Company 3, a dozen or so of us from Sarajevo stuck together from fear of an unknown country, an unknown enemy, and the other unknown soldiers. Each of us, for the other, contained something that was his, something intimate, one for the other we served as conductors for thoughts of home and family, dumb looks and wonder at what we sought in an alien land other than our own and others' misfortune. I joined them as if returning home. They were ordinary men, good men. Some had come to war voluntarily, some because they had to.

Ahmet-*aga* Misira, a tailor (I can't remember him ever sober), had long wanted to become an *aga,* but no sooner had he succeeded than he was immediately called to war, which he certainly didn't want. Grumpy old Hido, an ex–town crier, had fled poverty. The muscular Mehmed Petsitava, always bare-chested, cursed in rudest terms both war and he who had invented it and himself for volunteering, but never disclosed his reasons for doing so. Ibrahim Paro, bookbinder, with the split upper lip, which they say is the sign of a lucky man, had three wives in Sarajevo and joked that he'd run away from them. The two sons of the barber Salih from Alifakovats had wanted to escape the barber's trade, although one of them, the elder, had brought a razor from his father's shop, but used it only on himself and not for anything would he use it on anybody else. Hadji Husein, known as Pishmish, had fallen into debt and taken refuge in the army. Smail-*aga* Sovo, a coppersmith, joined others under the influence of drink and enthusiasm, but the enthusiasm quickly evaporated with the drink. Avdiya Suprda, moneylender in peace, *bayraktar* in war, was a good and honest man in both callings, and one can hardly say which one is the worse.

And they all perished. Ahmet Misira wasn't long an *aga*, and dearly he paid for it. Ibrahim Paro was freed forever from his wives. He was finished off by three Russians, one for each wife. Husein Pishmish paid all his earthly debts, his head thrust into a Dniestr marsh. The elder of the two brothers cut his throat with the razor one early morning in a Ukrainian village where we'd spent the night.

Apart from me, only Smail-*aga* Sovo and *bayraktar* Avdiya Suprda returned. Smail-*aga* fled home before the end of the war. He disappeared one night and after a few months, just as the war ended, arrived in Sarajevo, mad with worry for his wife and three children. He was hardly recognizable, and once he was recognized, which was immediately, he was hanged as a deserter. Avdiya Suprda, the *bayraktar,* who feared nothing, who survived a hundred charges and from a cloud of a thousand bullets emerged with a whole skin, took up fruit growing in his village, Lasitsa, when he returned, after the shattering of the army. He fell out of a pear tree and died.

So, there you are. I, the only one left, am telling you about those who are dead. But, to tell you the truth, I am glad it's this way, rather than that they live to talk about me, dead, especially since I don't know what they'd say about me, just as they don't know what I'll say about them. They've done what they had to do, and there's nothing left of them. All that will remain is what I, rightly or wrongly, say of them.

And so, these some dozen men from Sarajevo, like thousands of others, were possessed by something they didn't need, and fought for an empire, without thinking that the empire had nothing to do with them, nor they with it; a fact learned later by their children, for whom no one even turned their heads. For a long time I was tormented by the useless thought: How stupid and unjust that so many good men should perish for a nameless fantasy. What business had they in distant Russia, on the far Dniestr? What business had the tailor Ahmet Misira, or the bookbinder Paro, or the two sons of the barber Salih from Alifakovats, what business the coppersmith Sovo, what business the town crier Hido? And if they'd held on to that damned Chocim, if they'd taken somebody else's land, what would have changed? Would there have been more justice or less hunger, or, had there been, wouldn't people have choked on every mouthful won by another's suffering? And would they have been happier? No way. Some other tailor Misira would have cut cloth, hunched over his work, and then set off to die in some unknown marshes. Two sons of some barber from Alifakovats, tied by brotherly love, would rush off to vanish at some other Chocim and on some other Dniestr.

The wise Mula Ibrahim says it's neither foolish nor unjust. It's our fate. If there weren't wars, we'd massacre each other. So every sensible empire seeks a Chocim, to let out the evil blood of the masses and divert the accumulated discontent from itself. There's no other profit, nor loss, be it from defeat or victory. For who ever remained sane after a victory? And who ever gained any experience out of defeat? Nobody. People are wicked children: wicked in action, children in mind. And it'll never be any different.

I didn't agree with Mula Ibrahim, at least not entirely, and for a long time I couldn't be reconciled to the death of comrades in the morasses of Chocim. It seemed to me quite unacceptable, almost preposterous, as though some mindless and dread force were playing games with people. I couldn't free myself from the nightmare of memory, too abruptly had I fallen from the peaceful boredom of teaching into the cruel reality of killing. And Mula Ibrahim said it was not a bad thing that I blamed some irrational force. It would be dangerous had I sought an earthly culprit.

But neither I nor Mula Ibrahim, who knew everything, could explain the event I'm about to narrate. Indeed, people changed in the long months of war, grew coarser, more merciless, perhaps because of the endless space that separated them from their homes, perhaps because of the cruelty that war imposes and the constant proximity of death. Or, again, how can people change so much, that in a moment one stands dumbstruck and asks oneself in amazement: Who are these people? They can't be those men whom I knew two years ago. As though war had long plagued them, and the evil in them, concealed till now and perhaps unknown even to them, had suddenly broken out, like a scourge.

At dusk I'd returned from guard duty to my quarters upon a patch of firm earth between pools, where stood a hut in which a woman, still young, lived with her three children and with a skinny and mangy cow in a stall made of reeds. She cared for her children and the cow herself. Her husband was certainly on the other side of the marsh, against us. She didn't speak about him, she didn't speak about anything, nor did we ask her. She kept away from the soldiers and at night shut herself away in the hut with her children.

She resembled a pretty young bride in one of our richer villages by the Sava, and we'd watch her till she vanished behind the stall, into the reeds, firm, upright, but we said nothing. Perhaps for the children's sake. Or perhaps because of the *bayraktar* Avdiya, who would have cut the head off anybody for using dirty words about another man's wife. Or perhaps we were ashamed in front of one another.

That day, when all this happened, the *bayraktar* was absent on some military duty, and I had been on guard. They met me with scowling faces, with a certain threatening malevolence in their eyes. "Go into the cow's stall!" they said. And they just kept on repeating it, like an order, urging me and not replying to my questions. The children were crouched by the hut door.

I went round the hut and the stack of reeds and went into the stall. The woman lay on the ground. Ibrahim Paro, dusting off straw and spider's webs and tightening his belt, came out without as much as a look at me.

The woman lay still, her thighs bare, and, not even trying to cover herself, waited for it all to end. I knelt down beside her. Her face was pale, her eyes closed, her bloodstained lips clenched. The horror had passed over her. I pulled down her white petticoat and covered her and tried to wipe the blood from her face with her headscarf, upon which she opened her eyes and looked at me in terror. I smiled in order to comfort her: Don't be afraid, I shan't hurt you. As though this terrified her even more, her eyes flashed hatred. I took some army biscuits that I'd not eaten on guard out of my pack and offered them to the woman: Here, take them, for the children. She brushed the biscuits aside with a furious gesture and spat in my face. And I? I did nothing, I didn't even move or wipe my face. I was petrified by her suffering. For I grasped it all in a moment. Had I raped her, as the others had, she'd have borne it with clenched teeth and hated us, dogs, for the rest of her life. But human concern and pity, following on rape, which for her was a catastrophe, a plague, a fate sent by God for which there was no cure, suddenly within her awakened her pride and showed her the measure of her humiliation. From a victim of inscrutable fate, she had become a victim of cruelty.

I'd injured that woman, more than all the others. She got up and went toward the door, but changed her mind, took the biscuits, and went out, hanging her head.

The next morning we sat in front of the cow's stall, scowling, angry at one another, angry with ourselves and with the whole world, choked by the marsh fog and by the yet worse fog that rolled over our souls. The woman led out her children one by one and began to wash them on the hut threshold, and then she went into the stall, without looking at us, her face hidden in her headscarf so as to hide the bruises. She milked the cow and took the milk into the hut.

With a sigh Paro swore.

The others sat motionless, silent.

I got up, just for the sake of doing something. The silent tension and the woman's calm hatred were unbearable. I went up to the rotting woodshed and began to chop firewood with an axe I found there. The woman came out of the hut, tore the axe from my hands, and went back inside, bolting the door.

Suddenly space pressed in on us. We were gripped by a sense of threat. For certain she was standing behind the door with the axe in her hand. How did they get to her last night? By trickery, by force, by surprise? And all this, it would seem, she'd borne in silence so as not to disturb the children. I wondered at her, admired her, pitied her, but of the woman and of that which had happened the night before, I said not a word. Nor did anybody else. But it stuck in our throats like a bone.

The bolted hut and its hidden children were a silent reproach.

The elder of the two sons of Salih the barber from Ali-fakovats got up and went toward the reeds, no doubt to relieve himself. Since he was a long time gone, the younger brother went to look for him and found him dead. He'd cut his throat with the razor. It must have taken him quite a while to slit his throat from ear to ear, to sever the larynx and the rubbery tissue of the windpipe, blood pouring as from a tap, soaking the damp earth beneath him. The pain must have been dreadful, but he didn't even groan. We were only fifteen paces away, and we didn't hear a thing.

And while we were waiting for someone in authority to witness the death, for he had not died from a bullet or from an enemy's saber, we looked at the gaping wound on the neck, fearing what the younger brother would do. He kept staring at the severed throat, not allowing us to cover the body. All one could hear from him was a stifled groaning.

When Mula Ibrahim and his young assistant had recorded the details, quite unnecessarily, since the reason for the death was unknown and nobody mentioned last night's raping nor could his death be linked with it, the woman wordlessly pointed to a spade, and then locked herself back into the hut with her children.

The younger brother dug the grave himself in the wet

earth, placing a sheaf of reeds at the bottom, in the water, and himself lowered his brother into the grave, stubbornly refusing every offer of help. He spread another sheaf of reeds over the body and covered its face with a handkerchief. When he'd filled in the grave, and we'd all thrown a clod of mud on the wet mound, he signed to us to leave him.

For a long time he stood alone over the grave. Who knows what he was thinking or what he said to himself and to his dead brother, whom he loved more than he loved himself. We didn't hear it nor will anyone ever know. Then he went off. He neither bent down nor kissed the grave nor uttered a prayer. He just raised his eyes from the damp mound and set off toward the marsh. We called him, went after him, begged him to return. He didn't look back, perhaps he didn't even hear us. We saw him wade into the water up to his ankles, then up to his knees, and vanish into the reeds. What he was about, what his intentions were, whether he had lost his reason, is hard to say. No one ever saw him again.

Mula Ibrahim's young assistant, the student Ramiz, stayed the night with us so as not to return in the dark.

He talked with us all, listening more than speaking, yet he spoke strangely and as if he knew all that we knew.

I told him the whole incident, and he said, with a tired smile, "They kill them, and they kill themselves. People's lives are hunger, bloodshed, misery, bare survival on their own land and senseless dying on another's. And the rulers will return home, every one of them, to tell of glory and to suck the blood of the survivors."

Never had I heard such words from anybody. We were used to cursing both heaven and earth, God and people, but we never spoke thus.

"Why did you come here?" I asked him.

"To see this, too," he replied, thoughtfully looking into the dark night that surrounded us.

I've forgotten other events, more important, more striking, more shattering, or, even if I've not forgotten them, they don't haunt me like apparitions. I scarcely think anymore of battles, of wounds, of the cruelties men call heroism, of revulsion at slaughter, at blood, at shallow fervor, and at animal fear. I don't think of the vast Dniestr, swollen with the rains, when we were cut off from the rest of the army on the further bank, when thousands of soldiers perished or were taken prisoner and hundreds were drowned in that terrible river, and when I swam across it, dragging our clerk, Mula Ibrahim, in his holed boat, and he messing himself with fear, a fact he begged me never to disclose. I've forgotten a mass of other things which might well be remembered for the closeness of death, for the shame, but, there you are, I carry with me these two events which might easily be forgotten. Perhaps because I could neither understand nor explain them, and mysteries are remembered longer than the clear truth.

■ □ ■ □ ■

CHAPTER 2

SADNESS AND LAUGHTER

I TOLD ALL THIS, FOR THE FIRST TIME, TO A LITTLE GIRL; THE first time, from beginning to end, in some sort of order. In this way I put it together as a consistent story, one that had, hitherto, always lost itself in a confusion of isolated parts, in a fog of fear, in a sort of extratemporal occurrence. Perhaps it went beyond any defined meaning, like some bad dream that I could neither accept nor reject. And why to her particularly, and why this, is something I can't explain, even to myself. I felt she might have the ability to listen. For sure, she'd not understand, but, then, listening is more important than understanding.

Experience had taught me that what you can't explain to yourself is better told to another. You can deceive yourself with just one part of the picture that happens to impose itself with a feeling difficult to express, since it hides in the face of the pain of comprehension and flies into the mists, into the intoxication that seeks no meaning. For the other, exact speech is essential, and this forces you to seek it, to feel its presence somewhere within you, and to grasp it, it or its shadow, so as to recognize it in another's face, in another's glance, as he begins to comprehend it. The listener is the midwife in the difficult birth of the word. Or, still more important—if he desires to understand.

And she did. Even more than I'd hoped. As I told it, the innocent expression that perhaps had led me to begin this unexpected conversation vanished from her face and was replaced by something strangely mature and sad. All she said was, "Lord, how unhappy people are!"

And this didn't occur to me at the time, even though it seems—now—that it was just this I was thinking of. The thought is neither very profound nor original: It's what people have been saying ever since they began thinking. And it was not so much the thought that surprised me, even though I didn't expect it, but the assurance with which it was uttered. It was as if she'd opened her most secret drawer, laying herself bare to me, with a completeness never offered to anyone before. And I was happy to have come upon something, even if only something, for the first time in another person, and for my own sake alone.

Her name was Tiyana, the daughter of the late Micha Byelotrepich, a Christian killed by some unknown and undiscovered assailants two years before, on his way with a load of furrier's goods to the fair at Vishegrad. The powers that be made little effort to trace his killers, which would suggest they'd little longing for the truth, or that they knew them and left it all to be swallowed by oblivion.

All unusual, all as it should not be. But I didn't choose the circumstances, nor they me: We were like two birds in a storm.

When I got back from the war, I was met by bad news. My family had fared worse than if they'd been at Chocim: My father, my mother, my sister, and my aunt had all died of the plague. I couldn't even find their graves. Hundreds had died in one day, and the living had hastened to bury them wherever they could. Our rickety old family house had burned down, set on fire by Gypsies who'd camped there during the winter. They'd done it by accident, careless, since it was not theirs. Occasionally, I'd go to look at its blackened walls and the dead eyes of a dead building, in which I could no way envisage its former occupants, as though it had been empty from the beginning of time. Nor could I imagine myself as living there, as once I did. I didn't exist in my own memory, as though I were someone else. My garden was a wilderness, the fruit trees choked and overgrown, a miserable and pitiful sight. People wanted me to sell it, but I wouldn't. It was as if I hoped memories might return and that I might have a use for it. But I remembered all this later. At that time I couldn't have cared less. I was indifferent, indifferent in a particular way, without any profound sadness or great mourning.

I was wrapped in a quiet indifference, neither sad nor happy. I'd seen so much of death that my own survival seemed like an unexpected gift, how or from whom I knew not, yet not far from being a miracle. Perhaps my consciousness was still in confusion, faced with this unusual truth, but my body grasped it entirely. In fact, I was living my second alien, donated life; all the rest was unimportant, unimportant for the moment. This was a bonus, this was luck, luck that thousands of others didn't have and that thousands of others couldn't understand, since they hadn't traveled my road. Few people in the town, perhaps I alone, could say: I am happy to be alive. I didn't say it, but I felt it, powerfully, in every vein. Others couldn't, for they hadn't hung over the abyss.

Nothing else mattered to me. Not even tomorrow's possible pain. Nobody invited me anywhere. Nobody offered me anything. And I bore no one a grudge. To others I may have seemed strange, as if I'd lost my wits. I had no work, no house, nothing, and I couldn't have cared less.

For hours I'd sit on a stone in front of the Begova mosque and watch the people pass, or look at the sky, or look at nothing. I'd listen to the sparrows and their funny chattering, like good-natured argument or happy gossip concerning this or that. They seemed to me like small, ordinary people, cheerful, innocuous, inclined to be quarrelsome, superficial, peace-loving, satisfied with little, tough in adversity, ready to cheat in small things, without any great pride. They were tame, innocent as children. And I like children, their ringing voices, the rapid tramp of their bare feet, their joyful laughter, the harmless rudeness of their speech. Only when they fought did I shut my eyes and ears, upset.

I liked everything that was not war. I loved peace.

But then even peace disturbed me.

I used to be joined in front of the mosque by Salih Golub, a poor vendor of *sherbet* from Vratnik. He'd slip the heavy vessel of *sherbet* from his shoulders and sit down on the stone, breathing heavily. Once a bit rested, he'd start humming, half-aloud, to himself, leaning against the wall, eyes closed. He knew only a few words of one single song about maidens who mourned the departure of their young men to war. He hummed this over and over, beginning again when he reached the confines of his short memory. Pale, thin, with yellow eyelids, he resembled a man close to death. For thirty years he'd supported a blind mother. For her sake, he'd never married. For her sake, from morning to night, he'd hoisted the heavy, strapped vessel full of sugared water. Whenever he dozed off, the children would come, pour some *sherbet*, and drink it. I'd smile at them.

Salih Golub had a brother in Gorazhde, but they cared little for one another. This brother in Gorazhde owned woods and estates and rented other communal lands, lent money at the usurer's interest, and amassed a considerable fortune, which became known only after his death. At Glasinats, where he kept a large stud of horses, he was killed by bandits led by Bechir Toska, and, since his wife was already dead, his property came to Salih and his mother. So luck came to Salih Golub, overnight, such luck as he'd never dreamed of.

He turned up in front of the mosque on the following day, without a trace of happiness. He told me quietly what had happened and offered me money, either to start some business or to go with him to Gorazhde to help him deal with so large a property. It was as if he wanted to share some misfortune. When I refused, Salih showed no surprise. He looked at his place on the stone where he had rested and hummed for so many years, and went off, hanging his head. He died that same night, be it from joy or sadness. His mother soon wed the *hodja* Shahinbashich, who was more like a woman than she was herself. They were both seventy years of age. Neither deceived the other. She had no sight, and he no property. The only one whom life deceived was Salih Golub.

I no longer went to sit in front of the mosque.

I began to seek for water, flowing water, clear, shallow. Perhaps due to the marshes of Chocim, or the muddy Dniestr, vast as the sea. And perhaps also because I could look at the water in tranquility, without thinking. All was flowing, softly, with a murmur. Everything: thought, memory, and life itself, at peace. I was at ease, almost happy. For hours I'd gaze into the clear water, letting its small dense waves flow over my hand, caressing me, as though they were a living thing. And this was all I desired, all I wanted.

Out of this dreaming I was awakened by Mula Ibrahim. His shadow fell on me as I sat there on the bank of the stream, in a world of light.

"You're watching it?" he asked.

His voice sounded pitying, worried.

I smiled, but I didn't reply.

"You here every day?"

"Every day."

"What do you do?"

I shrugged my shoulders.

"And for how long?"

"Why?"

"What do you do for a living?"

Again I shrugged. I didn't know what I did for a living. Nor did I care.

"You'll go mad on your own like this."

"I won't."

"Winter will come, illness, you'll get old. What will you do then?"

"I don't know."

"Have you had a row with someone? Are you sad? Are you having bad dreams?"

"I'm not having bad dreams, I am not angry with anybody, and I'm not sad."

"You helped me when I needed it most. And I want to help you."

"You owe me nothing."

"I've opened a scribe's shop. You can work for me for as much as you like and for as long as you like. For sure your hand's grown stiff, but it'll ease off."

"You don't owe me anything, Mula Ibrahim. When I saw your boat I grabbed it quite unconsciously. Perhaps I thought it'd help me to stay afloat."

"I'm not repaying a debt. I need an assistant. You'll work, and I'll pay you. As much as I can and what's fair. You'll not get rich. But I like to work with somebody I know."

"I've got used to this water and to the silence."

"You can come here when you're not working or when we're not very busy."

"Well, all right. As you wish."

"I've got a nice shop. Real cozy."

The shop was in the bazaar, in the street called Mudzeliti, under the clock tower, tiny and insignificant, hot and stuffy in summer, cold as a dungeon in winter, close to the public toilets that stank unbearably, so that Mula Ibrahim and I took turns to light incense and *inulin,* as in a church, to appease the evil power of stench. But our use of incense helped not at all, and we had no choice but to grin and bear it.

None of this mattered to me. I laughed, "A man can get used to any smell."

Mula Ibrahim just gave a good-natured smile and replied,

without his usual mention of God's name, since we were alone, "I always say: Let it be no worse."

"Which is what the wise man said when they were taking him to the gallows."

"And rightly, too. They could have killed him then and there, and he'd have lost even those few, last moments of life. There's always hope, even on the way to the gallows."

"Pretty vain hope!"

"Still, hope. And that's better than nothing. But this stench, mind you, suits me fine."

"How can it?"

"Well, it's this way. Why do you think the public toilets are here? Because this is the center of the bazaar. And that's just where I want to be, under everyone's feet. Left to choose between pure air and paupers and a stink with profit, no wise man would hesitate. Two watermelons under one armpit won't go, nor can two good things come together. So, let it be no worse."

"Amen."

Mula Ibrahim was so pleased with this business that it was amazing he hadn't discovered it before. He'd gone to the army to escape the boredom of being an imam at the mosque and a teacher of children and, still more, to escape the pay of eighteen *groschen* a year. He was attracted by the thought of a clerk's fifty *groschen* together with free army rations and, secretly, he'd hoped for some luck, for somebody's favor when he returned, so that he might gain some position that would not pay too badly. But he had returned penniless, with no new clothes, without health, and without prospects of any work whatsoever, not to mention a well-paid job. At home he'd found two children fewer than he left—they'd died of plague—and thank God he'd not found more, as did some others with the selfless assistance of those who'd not gone to war. His wife didn't reproach him for his pointless wandering. She'd have been right to do so, only she thanked God he'd stayed alive, for, left with their remaining three children, she'd have gone through hell till the end of her life. All she said was, "Why go dragging yourself all over the world for all these years? Couldn't you have been a scribe here?"

It was as if he'd gone to war for the hell of it. A poor man doesn't choose, but does what he must to make ends meet.

And then Mula Ibrahim had got used to the thought: Why not give it a go? Why run to the ends of the earth to seek one's fortune? He went to the wealthy Shehaga Socho and borrowed the money to start his scribe shop. Shehaga lent him the money without a word and without a receipt and, more important, without interest. Mula Ibrahim found a shop (Ibrahim Paro, the bookbinder, had perished at Chocim), cleared it of rubbish and mouse droppings, tidied it somewhat, bought some furniture and writing materials, and sat down to wait for customers, praying to God to help him. And God did: Customers turned up in greater numbers than he'd expected, and he became convinced that a wife's scoldings can be very useful, if taken as advice and if fortune serves you well. And it did, as if wanting to recompense him richly for all the time it had stubbornly passed him by. But he realized (he told me this the evening of the first day, as we were going home) that there would have been no shop, nor customers, nor good fortune, had it not been for God's mercy and for me, Ahmet Shabo, who together had given him life. He thanked God for His mercy and began to search for me, the moment he'd got things going. And this he did not out of gratitude, but out of love. He'd adopted me in his heart, glad that such a man existed and that it was his fate to have met him. For it's easier to come upon a bad man, since there are far more of them.

And I knew this, which is why his kindness puzzled me. Perhaps he, too, felt the happiness of being alive; perhaps he, too, couldn't forget the death that had laid hold of him.

More and more, despite myself, unconsciously, I sank

into that strange occupation of which I'd scarcely even heard. Another side of life opened to me. Or was it its essence? All the sorrows of the world came together in that smelly little shop, all the sorrows and misfortunes, all the greed, the spite, the madness. We wrote pleas for outstanding pay on behalf of old soldiers; for the rectification of real and imagined injustices; for the bringing of legal actions regarding property, personal insult, fraud; for money seized, concealed, or unpaid; for some long-standing spite, whose cause was long forgotten, so that it seemed to me that the entire world was dislocated and stank as did the public toilets near our shop.

And Mula Ibrahim quietly pursued his work, conversed about passion, listened to greed, raised hope in the righteous and the unrighteous, satisfied people's needs, the human need to seek imagined justice, surprised at nothing, condemning nothing, taking all as normal because human, giving the impression he was above misery, even though he lived off it.

"Isn't this work of ours good?" he'd asked me cheerfully, pleased with himself, his customers, and with his young assistant, glad to have dragged me from lethargy and dangerous solitude.

True, he dragged me, freed me from a strange torpor. Yet I continued to be amazed at the life I'd not known. And when, again, soldiers were called to war, for the Russians took Bender, Braila, Ismailia, Kulia, and other towns, illiterate women flocked to our shop for us to write letters to husbands and sons, letters that would never arrive, since they'd be lost in the chaos of war or find those they were written to dead. Then I began to wonder whether my parents, too, had sent such letters to me: to mind catching cold and to come back as soon as possible. Did Salih, the barber from Alifakovats, write letters to his two sons—he had no other children—and was he still writing, addressing the letters to Company 3, of which only the name remained and nobody knew anymore that the two brothers from Alifakovats had ever fought at Chocim or that their father was angry at his sons' neglect, at their delay in replying, and I couldn't tell him the truth. What use would the truth have been?

For me Mula Ibrahim was a great mystery. I looked at him in wonder, not knowing where to place him—between nobility and cold business calculation. He would receive women and old men with care, listen to them routinely, unmoved, without emotion, yet somehow intimately assured, filling them with a faith that was hard to explain. I'd write, waiting for them to tell me what they wanted to say, and both I and he who spoke would get tied up; he wasting general, unnecessary words, useless, dead, unusable, or I'd hear a sob, at which I'd choke and my hand would falter over the paper, so that people thought me lacking in skill.

Mula Ibrahim well knew their inner being and their circumstances and read their every unexpressed thought, as though he saw into their minds. He didn't wait for them to say anything, saving them the trouble of stammering confession, himself writing, speaking aloud as he wrote: "My dear son, my darling child, I wrote to you a month ago . . . (Was it so long ago?) . . . and not a word from you. I know it's not easy for you in this horrible war, and that you've no time for writing to your mother, but at least let me have a word from you. Don't be angry with me for writing to you so often, you know what mothers are like, miserable and unhappy, once their child is a hundred stages from them. During the day it's all right, I've enough to do to take my mind off, but at night I can think only of you and your dear eyes, and I can't sleep. I wait for the sound of the knocker on the courtyard gate and hope, silly me, that it's you . . . (There, come on, don't cry, let's get on with it.) . . . or someone bringing news of you. Don't worry about us, we're fine . . . (I know you're not, but he can't help, and this won't upset him.) . . . and my breathing's better. Meyra asks after you every day . . . (Doesn't she? Oh, she's getting married.) . . . The girls ask after you every day. . . ."

I stopped writing to listen to the beauty of these words that reminded one of an old song. A sorrow, old a hundred years and more, could be felt in them, in these letters written, more for those who sent them than for the soldiers, dispatched into the wind, to the land of no return, and fated to be burned on some cookhouse fire on the first cold night.

And while I, saddened, scarcely holding back my tears, listened to this grief and comforting, suppressing the memories they awakened, Mula Ibrahim remained completely calm. He'd even notice my hand paused above an unfinished line and would draw my attention to it: "Come on, finish it!" And when he'd written a letter, full of love and beauty, he'd take the money and put it in his drawer with a businesslike gesture, politely inviting the customer to come again.

Of the two completely different men in him, which was the true one?

In the evening he'd note every penny he'd taken, thanking God for His mercy. Then I hated him. It's ugly to earn by another's misfortune, I thought. And I told him so.

"I didn't invent misfortune," he replied calmly. "And I help people. Don't I do honestly what they ask of me? I do. And I charge less than others. But there you are, many misfortunes mean bigger earnings."

But he didn't raise *my* pay.

"You're paid enough," he said, quite seriously. "When I was your age, I got only half as much. And was happier than I am now. Do you know what's best in life? Desire, my friend."

Indeed, he didn't rob me of a single desire. They were all there, unsatisfied, even unawakened. I didn't worry. Whenever I found the time I'd go to Dariva or Kozya chupriya and, seated on the riverbank, listen to the flow of the water.

Mula Ibrahim would say, "Why don't you fish? It may look like a damn silly occupation, which it is, but it can get hold of a man. And it keeps a man from greater follies. The world can go to hell, and you'll sit there staring at the water without a move. The greatest wisdom in life is to find a true folly. If the authorities had any sense, they'd decree 'Everyone take a fishing rod and off to the river to fish!' There'd be no riots or disorders. I tell you, Ahmet Shabo, go fishing!"

"I'm not thinking of raising any riots, and I don't need any folly. I am at peace, as you see."

"Too much so. That's what I'm afraid of. I'm afraid of what will happen when you wake up. Go fishing, Ahmet Shabo!"

I laughed, because I thought he was making fun of me. And then I remembered that he looked on everything not according to the rules and the law with suspicion, which is why he didn't like my spending too much time on my own. Isolation gives birth to thought, thought to dissatisfaction, dissatisfaction to rebellion.

I was far from any thought of rebellion; I was only a daydreamer.

One day he told me that some of the imam's relatives were coming to us from the village of Zhupcha. The imam had been strangled the night before, together with two villagers, because the people of Zhupcha had refused to contribute supplies to the army. Their relatives set off immediately to save them, but justice was swifter than family feeling. Only today had they heard what had occurred, and they wanted an application written for the receipt of the bodies. I was to write the application.

"Why did they strangle them?"

"Why? You're asking me why!"

For the first time since we'd been together, I saw that he was upset. His voice was quiet, but trembling and muffled, as though overcome.

"What do you want me to say? They've killed so many people, and you're asking why they've killed the imam and two peasants from Zhupcha! Go fishing, Ahmet Shabo!"

He went out into the alleyway, and I looked after him,

worried. In his state, he could have done something he might have regretted.

How many different people there were in that one man.

They came in a crowd: the imam's wife and the wife of one of the peasants (the wife of the other was giving birth, as they told me apologetically), brothers, sons, and relatives. They stood in our small shop, bunched together, holding on to one another, lost, but, to my surprise and relief, they neither complained nor wept.

See, they know what's happened, the imam's brother said, and all they ask is that they should receive the bodies so they can bury them in Zhupcha where all their relatives are buried. They'd like it to be immediately, tomorrow, there's no point in waiting. What he meant was: After all they're dead, they're no more use to them in the Fortress, and one doesn't want to keep the dead unburied, 'cause they'll stink. They've brought three planks, and they've come with a cart, so, if it's at all possible, they'd like to take them early tomorrow morning. They're in a hurry. They've a lot of work waiting at home. It's summer. There's loads to be done and, as it is, they'll lose a lot of time.

I paused, amazed, shocked more by the calmness of their words than by their disaster.

"Why aren't you writing, master?"

My hand scarcely moved to complete the plea to the *kadi*.

God! Life's harder than I thought.

Mula Ibrahim returned with some packages.

"Is it done?"

He told them how much they owed, got the money, and they left, jostling one another in the doorway.

I looked after them.

"None of them shed a tear nor uttered a word of complaint. As though it didn't concern them."

"The more it concerns you, the less you say. And they're used to suffering. Everything hits them, heaven, earth, and people. Will you help me decorate the shop?"

"Why?"

"Tomorrow's the sultan's birthday. Hold on to this!"

I looked at him in surprise: What sort of a joke was this?

It wasn't a joke. He was taking an unserious matter seriously, giving himself to it entirely, energetically, almost passionately.

With some scissors he cut a crescent moon, stars, and paper chains out of colored paper, and we stuck them on the windowpanes and frames, making a sky beside the public toilets. A mass of multicolored stars and pointed crescent horns adorned the hovel that was our shop, and in the window we stuck a picture of the sultan Abdul Hamid with the words "May God give you long life," together with a picture of a *janissary* unit departing joyfully to war, under which we wrote, "Allah has given us an unconquerable army."

I cast aside the thought that haunted me, that I, too, had been in that unconquerable army when it fled across the Dniestr. But what of that now? This isn't real, it's just a festival.

We put candles in the window and, since it was already getting dark, we went out into the alleyway to admire them.

Mula Ibrahim was pleased with his work. "Isn't it nice?"

"Very."

"No one'll think of a *janissary* unit."

"No one."

"And the stars? What do you think of the moon and the stars?"

"Wonderful."

It was pathetic, it was funny, it was ugly. It would have been no surprise had I wept or ground my teeth. Instead I laughed, both at my friend's enthusiasm and at my own disgust. Our friends from Zhupcha had completely unstitched me. There they were, sitting somewhere in a strange town, waiting to receive their corpses, and there was I looking at this colored marvel and laughing, laughing, laughing. I laughed till the tears flowed. Had I stopped laughing, there'd only have been tears.

"Stop it!" whispered Mula Ibrahim, looking around in fear. "What are you laughing at? What's so funny?"

I don't know, I thought, I don't know what's so funny or why I'm laughing.

Was that why we decorated our shop and lit candles under the colored stars and the heroic sultan, because the imam and two peasants from Zhupcha had been killed, because now their relatives were sitting silent in the darkness, waiting for the morning to take their dead ones home? Or was it because all my friends had perished at Chocim? Or because the barber Salih from Alifakovats was still waiting for his sons?

I don't know why I laughed.

■ □ □ □ ■

CHAPTER 3

HAPPINESS, NONETHELESS

I WANDERED DOWN THE LITTLE, DARK STREETS, AIMLESSLY, going nowhere, and found myself in front of the blackened walls of my house, nowhere.

Does every generation of us have to begin all over again?

That dead past and nonexistent future, those black ruins of all that had once been, upon which I thought to build nothing, still represented some sort of link with something. With what? There was the moonlight, as ever, just like that of my childhood, but now deceitful, covering the burned remains with silver. Did I see it from my room up there, which no longer existed, or under the fortifications at Chocim, imagining that I was here? For me time and space had long been mixed, and I did not know where I was, nor where what I was thinking of happened. There were no frontiers, as in the desert, as in the sky, and the memories floated by, settling where they might. They were like clouds, indifferent as to where they were, indifferent as to when they arose or when they vanished. This didn't worry me. I even liked it: I felt no need to find a solution for anything.

When I heard her voice, I was amazed. Could there be anyone there? Afterward I wondered how she could have recognized me. Did she know that only my shadow could visit this graveyard? Or had she seen me when I had come earlier?

I went up to the fence just to say hello. After all, we were neighbors. And I stayed till the clock on the clock tower struck midnight.

Tiyana, I repeated softly, in amazement. Tiyana. All the way down the stone steps, all the way to the bazaar. Tiyana. And nothing else, only this unusual name.

I was as if I'd lost my mind. What was that girl to me? What was that name that echoed within me like a sounding bell? But I comforted myself that I hadn't been any saner when I was making my way up to what had once been my house. The candles in front of the sultan's picture had gone out. The stars made of colored paper in the windows could no longer be seen. I'd forgotten the peasants from Zhupcha sleeping on some market square under their carts, waiting for morning and for their dead ones. I'd no idea why I'd come here in the first place.

I stood there numbly present, with a hollow echo inside me, as in an empty cave, when my childish step of long ago had led me to the ashes where there was no memory. And what could these memories have been? A cruel yet vague longing over a dear but hostile town. A boy's room peopled by imaginations, burning pictures that had neither aim nor foundation. My father, to me like the moon, who all his life flippantly lost everything he ever gained; my mother, who gave no thought either to her children or to God, only to him, my father, and who surely died of grief for him, and not from the plague; my sister, with whom I could never talk, so different were we; my aunt, who bored us all with her tearful love and her malicious stories about the husband, who, ungrateful, ran away, which did not surprise me in the least. Up there, above all the weeds, was my father's room. I was allowed to enter it only twice a year, at the two Bairams, to pay my respects and kiss his hand, that wonderful, white, aristocratic hand. Even this was like a dream.

I bore them no grudge, even though they'd left me not a single memory. They lived as they could, and for sure they didn't wish me to stand here, empty, on this graveyard, after their death.

I said nothing about this to anyone (Mula Ibrahim was right: It's hardest to speak of that which concerns you most), yet I told it all, the very next evening, to a girl who was once my neighbor, of whom, before our meeting, I had not for a moment thought whether she was alive or dead. The first evening I talked about the war, ostensibly not about myself, but it turned out to be all about myself. It was about me that she said, "God, how unhappy people are." About me, and about all people. About herself, too?

And that was all she said. She just listened, in silence.

Going down the stone steps (she smiled as the clock struck midnight), I was not surprised, although I was aware that it was strange that I should recount to an almost unknown girl what I'd never said to anybody and which only now, with her, had I put into words. I talked because of the moonlight, because those burned walls held no memories, because two slim, white hands gently touched the rotting fence, because a pair of dark, childish eyes of a mature girl tenderly looked at me, because she listened to me as no one ever had listened to me before. I didn't try to explain it, there was no need. I knew only that I'd stopped. A barrier had grown between us.

The following evening, without arranging, we met again at the fence between the two gardens. And the third evening, and the fourth, and the summer grew colder, and we hid in the darkness, not desiring that any should know how we'd become necessary one to another. But, of course, everyone knew.

I was more and more with her, even when I was alone. I'd take away with me her name and her moonlit shadow under the trees. And I was full of her deep voice, more beautiful than the rippling of water.

The paper stars and the sultan's picture remained on the shop windows for some other festivity, and they were no longer funny. I didn't notice them anymore. Absentmindedly I wrote complaints to the court or letters to soldiers and read them over to make sure I hadn't written "My dear love." It would have looked funny for the *kadi* to read that in a complaint for some debt.

In autumn I proposed to her. I truly desired it. I couldn't imagine anything different. Yet I told her honestly that I was a poor bet, having nothing and being without prospect of ever having anything, and that she'd gain little by marrying me. Perhaps it was unfair of me even to make her the offer, but love gave me the right to be unfair. I'd love her, and we wouldn't have a thing, would that suffice?

But she was even more mad than I. We'd love each other, she said seriously, and that was a great deal, indeed everything. She desired nothing more.

I said, jokingly, that at first everything would certainly go well and afterward, when I began to bore her, we'd manage the best we could. We'd refresh our love, as old Dzhezar did, who divorced and remarried his wife three times.

"He needn't have bothered either himself or her," Tiyana protested. "He should have found a wife he'd never want to part from, or live on his own. It's not worth mending a dress, never mind a love. It's better to leave."

"You'd leave?"

"I would."

"Because you don't love me?"

"Because I do love you."

This feminine logic was anything but clear to me, but I knew she was speaking the truth. I was glad she'd said it, even though it sounded too serious and irrevocable. At that moment, I wished for nothing else.

Soon after that, we were married. Mula Ibrahim and old Omer Tandar, the barber from the shop next door, were our witnesses. Tiyana Byelotrepich, the daughter of the late Micha and the late Lyubinka, became Tiyana Shabo.

Mula Ibrahim was not surprised when I told him, though

he certainly looked on it as a passing madness, thinking that I would not actually marry (a Christian girl and poor at that!), but made no objection. I saw his look of surprise, or perhaps I expected it and therefore thought I saw it, but what he said and did was correct. He praised the girl and her family, praised my decision, offered himself as a witness, invited the jolly *hadji*-Omer to go with us to the *kadi*, and then took us off to his house, where a real feast awaited us. Mula Ibrahim's quiet-mannered wife welcomed us warmly, and, for some reason, burst into tears when she kissed Tiyana. She showed us her three children (two had died; *hadji*-Omer laughed: Death takes them, the parents replace them), and she went on looking at us, constantly, like a mother, sadly and happily at the same time. Later I remembered that compassionate look of hers, and thought how she must have pitied us for all that life had in store for us. After lunch at Mula Ibrahim's, we went off to my ugly room and looked at one another in embarrassment.

"It went well," I said.

"Very well."

"They were very kind."

"Because they're good people."

"Are you happy?"

"Yes."

"You don't look it. Something's worrying you."

"I'm a bit confused."

"Why?"

"I don't know. It'll pass."

"Perhaps you're sorry that none of our families were there. Mine are gone, they're all dead, and yours are angry. What could we do?"

"Sit here beside me. Give me your hand."

She was silent, pressed against me, as though seeking protection. She was swallowing the fact that her family had deserted her. She was getting accustomed to me. Now that she and I had nobody, would we be sufficient for one another?

What had been her girlish dreams? What had he been like, the beloved she'd imagined? Had she ever, even in her worst dreams, seen this awful room that had suddenly become unbearable even to me?

Should I ask her about it, or should I leave her to get used to what was to be her life?

At that moment, somebody knocked on the door.

Who could it be? We were expecting nobody.

I opened the door. In front of me there stood an unknown man, strangely radiant, with moist eyes and a sad-happy smile, as though he'd escaped from his own funeral. He looked a bit silly, with his air of endearment, and so, undoubtedly, did I: staring in amazement at his face lit with a happiness of which I knew as little as I did of the man himself.

He said he was looking for me. His name was Ferhad, a close relative of my mother's, and that it was no wonder that I did not recognize him. Twenty years earlier, during the rebellion of the brothers Morich and Sari-Murat, he'd fled to Valyevo and had now returned.

I'd forgotten all about this relative of mine. I'd heard about him at home, but I'd forgotten him and why he'd run away and on whose side he'd been, on the side of the Morich brothers or of the town merchants. But I was glad that somebody of my family, indeed, even as if risen from the dead, had come to visit me, just as we were thinking we'd no one of our own in the world.

I asked him to sit down. He greeted his new "sister," remarked on her beauty, and said that he'd not had time to buy us a present since he'd only just learned of the wedding and had hastened to visit us and would bring us our gift the next day. He talked and talked and then paused, full of joy, an unknown happiness that seemed utterly remote to me, and I thought how strange it all was. Only twenty years had passed, and everything had been forgotten, the brothers Morich and Sari-Murat, and their misdeeds and the people they'd killed. Popular memory had failed, and a sad song was sung about the hanging of the two brothers, as though they were heroes and not the cruel ruffians they were. And perhaps that very song in which popular tradition made heroes of those who were not so, and that forgetfulness, as though it had all happened centuries ago, were what brought my relative to Sarajevo. That, and a longing for his native town. He spoke of this longing with tear-filled eyes. He could neither sleep nor eat. He thought he would die of sorrow. He'd sit for hours, picturing his town, step by step, house by house, fearing lest its picture escape him, like a phantom. Hundreds, thousands of times he'd pass down well-known alleys and think that nothing was more important or dearer to a man than his native country. And today he'd walked and walked through the real town, visited familiar places that seemed more beautiful than he'd imagined them there, in distant Valyevo, and tomorrow he'd do it again. He felt that his longing and his love for his hometown could never be satisfied.

And this madness surprised me. Had I had anywhere to go and were I not utterly indifferent, I'd have gone off anywhere in the world. And now? I'd just take my beloved wife, whom I'd so suddenly gained, with me.

Ferhad didn't satisfy his love. Nor did he bring me the promised gift. He was prevented.

The next day, the *serdar*-Avdaga recognized him, enthralled and stupefied as he was by his newly discovered town, beautified by twenty years of longing, and reported him to the *kadi*. He was taken to the Fortress and strangled. For something everybody had forgotten.

It was then, for the first time, I noticed in Tiyana a strange disquiet. She appeared afraid. For a long time she was silent, absent, gazing at a single point.

"If we let everybody's misfortune trouble us, where would we be?" I comforted her with a gentle touch and harsh words. "We didn't even know him. We didn't expect him, not him nor anybody else."

We soon forgot silly Ferhad who'd suffered because of his longing for his native town. Had he not loved it so much, he might have still been alive. But, who knows? He was so mad that, perhaps, he had preferred to die in his own town than to live in another's.

So we lost our one relative. A stranger to us, he'd emerged from the darkness, lived but a moment, long enough to see the town and us, and then returned to the darkness.

We wondered, afterward, whether he'd really existed or whether we'd imagined him, so much did it all resemble a bad dream.

A few days after Ferhad's death, Shehaga Socho mentioned him. Accompanied by his steward, the powerful Osman Vuk, who looked after his business affairs, he'd dropped into our shop for some deeds of gift to schools and libraries. He knew that Ferhad was my relative and asked me about him. And I could only tell him what Ferhad had told me.

"Bloody fool," growled Shehaga, frowning. "Bloody fool! That's his native town for you! That's his native land! He spent all day roaming the streets, you say? And what did he find? Stench and his own and our misery. He was born here, big deal! That's not pride, it's a disaster. It's a reason for a man to cry, not to get sentimental about. What did he spent twenty years longing for, for God's sake! For this poverty-stricken country, for the spite that lives in us longer and stronger than a mother's love, for our irresistible urge to do evil whenever we can, for our savage gloominess?"

"Countries are countries, people are people, the same everywhere," Mula Ibrahim ventured, timidly glancing at the frowning Shehaga and the smiling Osman Vuk.

"Neither is this country like others, nor are its people. The country's wretched. Haven't you noticed the names of our villages? Tell them, Osman!"

"Luckless, Mudville, Blackwater, Burnt Ash, Thornystake, Hunger, Fuckham, Wolf, Wolf-valley, Wolfsden, Thorny, Hopeless, Stink, Snake-hole, Misery . . ."

"There! All misery, poverty, hunger, bad luck. And the people? It makes me sick to talk of them. Why is it like that? I don't know. Perhaps we're evil by nature, marked by God. Or perhaps because disaster is ever with us and we fear to laugh aloud lest we anger the evil forces that forever circle around us. Is it any wonder that we bow and scrape, that we hide, that we lie, that we think only of today and only of ourselves and see our good fortune in another's misfortune? We've no pride, no courage. They beat us, and we thank them for it."

Mula Ibrahim was in a sweat, fearing the powerful Shehaga and even more so those whom his words would not please, and tried at least to stay out of it.

"One shouldn't look on the black side, Shehaga."

"That's what I say, Mula Ibrahim, and I lie to myself and others. But sometimes, not very often, when lies make me sick, then I speak the truth. It is black, Mula Ibrahim. We live in a hard time, and we live shamefully and miserably. The one consolation is that those who'll live after us will experience still worse times and speak of our days as happy."

These were the most pessimistic words I'd ever heard, and they weighed on me like funeral hymns, perhaps because he spoke them without rancor, quietly and with conviction, bravely yet helplessly. For certain, all that he said was not true, but the greatest truth was his sadness.

I couldn't help but ask him, to Mula Ibrahim's great horror, "Surely we're not all bad, Shehaga?"

"All. Some more, some less. But all."

"The peasants from Zhupcha, you've heard of them, aren't bad. The soldiers from Chocim aren't bad. Our misery isn't our fault, Shehaga."

But it seemed his passion was extinguished and his desire to talk had passed. He gave me a bleak look and went out. I followed him out onto the street, saying I'd like to continue our conversation. His words burned me like living coals.

No, he said limply, we'd not be continuing any conversation. If I was interested out of pure curiosity, then it was not worth talking. If something was paining me, why seek another's opinion? He didn't trust his own, let alone another's, and often even said what he didn't think, or what he thought only today and forgot the next day. And what good would that do me?

"Or do you want to report us?" said the frightening Osman Vuk, with a grin.

Mula Ibrahim also reproached me for getting mixed up in a dangerous conversation. It was all right for Shehaga Socho, he was stinking rich and held all the high-placed officials in his pocket by means of loans and bribes, and everybody pretended not to know what Shehaga said. But what was I? A poor clerk working for a pauper. Somebody more powerful had only to sneeze to blow us away like dust. Even more powerful people suffered while little people simply melted away like soap bubbles. And it was no business of ours to ask why Shehaga spoke like that. His worries were different, while ours were simply not to be drawn into this whirlpool of life. So, use your head!

I knew this, I'd heard it long ago, in the shop, on the street, in the bazaar: Use your head! As a final law, as the most effective defense against innumerable dangers. Therefore, in everything you did, in what you said, in your looks, in your thoughts: Use your head!

Fear everything, and be not what you are!

I could not assent to such despair. There must be some possibility for people other than fear, yet I couldn't forget that piece of wisdom, that dread common experience that poisoned life.

OK, then, I'll obey it: Use your head, Ahmet Shabo! At least so this new life may not be poisoned.

One afternoon I went to the bazaar to buy Tiyana a present. Mula Ibrahim had warned me, without any need, against accustoming my wife to expensive presents. This was a good habit that, if applied rationally, made for happiness and kept love going. But if irrationally used it would create greed in a wife and would become a burden. Nothing expensive! But something small and pretty, a bunch of flowers, or something useful like slippers, when her old ones were worn out, or a headscarf if she'd nothing to go out in, and, best of all, a loving word.

"And there, I'd been thinking of buying her a gold necklace."

"No way! That's not affection, it's madness."

I laughed.

"I'd be glad to commit such madness, if I didn't have to live on your twenty-five *groschen* a year. Where would I get the money for such a necklace!"

"How should I know? Your wife's got her share of the estate."

"She got such a pittance, I'm ashamed to mention it."

"Why did you agree to it?"

As though I could have cared less.

"Heh, it'll go hard with any wife of yours and with any children you have," he continued.

"We're all born with our own fate."

"That's what all flippant people say."

I didn't know whether I was flippant or just satisfied with my unexpected happiness, after the dog's life I had had during the war, but I took no offense at Mula Ibrahim's words, since I knew that this strange man wished me well. I set off happily to the Kuyundzhiluk to buy something small, a silver ring, cheap buckles, or a chain, to show goodwill, and to it I'd add a bunch of flowers and a loving word.

I was looking forward to going home.

I stopped in front of Mahmut Neretlyak's shop: There were a few pendants and other trinkets hanging behind the dirty glass window.

I didn't know he'd reopened his shop. When I was still

going to school, he used to make false copper coins in this shop and pass them off as real ones. For this he was beaten and expelled from Sarajevo. He spent ten years in exile, somewhere in the East, and had returned that spring, and there he was, back in his old shop.

I didn't see him through the window. But I heard voices coming from the little room behind, Mahmut's deep, hoarse voice, and the high voices of children. He was teaching them. But what? It seemed familiar. God Almighty, it was Arabic, broken and distorted, stuffed with Turkish, Persian, and Greek words and spiced with our own colorful swearing. What was he doing? I listened, amazed at that incredible mixture, at that no-man's language, that wanderers' lingo that could bear witness to the many lands through which the exile had passed and to the many occupations in which he'd engaged. But this would scarcely be of much help to the children. It would only sow confusion in their innocent little heads.

And while I was hesitating whether to call him or go on my way, he saved himself, me, and the children by releasing them from the prison of his ignorance and of their perplexity. They emerged stunned, staggering under the weight of nonsense with which he'd drilled their brains.

"They must be thinking they're stupid, or that learning is beyond them," I said cheerfully, watching them go.

"You're right on both counts," Mahmut replied reasonably.

I laughed. "I was listening to you teaching them."

"And what was so funny?"

"But you don't know Arabic."

"Sure I don't know. How could I?"

"Then why are you doing it?"

He stretched his hands out in front of him. The fingers were shaking.

"I can't work at my trade anymore. And I know nothing else. I don't make these trinkets, I just sell them. And I teach children. I don't know much, and they don't pay much, so no one owes anybody anything. What do they lose? Nothing. They'll learn it all in the *medrese*, if they need it. But it's my living."

"What if it gets about that you don't know anything? You can't hide a thing like that for long."

He shrugged his shoulders. "I'll find something else. Like making false copper coins."

I looked into his wrinkled wanderer's face, into the sly yet innocent eyes of a criminal with imagination, and laughed unconsciously. In my childhood his false copper coins had excited us, as had the cruel beating he received and his exile to far unknown lands. And now, in front of me, the hands that had created silver wire and forged coinage shook. Life had broken him, illness had drained him, but life had to go on.

"I'll help you," I said, without even thinking. "I know a bit of Arabic."

Mahmut frowned. "Find yourself some children. Why should you take mine away?"

"I'll help you for free."

He was shocked, not knowing whether to suspect me all the more or simply to pity me. "Listen, laddie, if you've only good intentions, then you haven't got much sense."

"OK, I haven't much sense, but I'm not hiding anything. It'll help me, too. It'll bring back to me what I've learned."

"And what if I'm having you on about being sick, if I'm just doing it to get drink money?"

"So what? It won't hurt anyone."

He still hesitated. "Then why were you listening?"

"Quite by accident. I wanted to buy some small thing for the wife."

"What, from this lot? You see, I didn't even ask you. Got out of the habit. Come and have a look."

With shaking fingers he took down some cheap jewelry and showed it to me.

"Would you like this? . . . And as for the teaching, if

you're serious I'll pay you just enough not to be doing it for nothing. If these boys don't come, and sometimes they don't, I'll find others. It'll be easy now. We could even get some real students from the *medrese*, only this room's a bit small. . . . Take these buckles and this little chain. If she doesn't like it, we'll find something else. . . . Can you start tomorrow? Anyhow, when you like and at what time you like. It's all the same to me. And if you're not serious, then you won't come, and that's all there is to it. . . . You'd better pay for these things now, in case you change your mind."

His confused reaction to my suggestion struck me as funny, his caution, his disbelief, his surprise at my offer of help, the hopes that opened up before his eyes, the doubts. What if this idiot comes to his senses? He could have thought I was mad or that I was a good man or that I was having him on or that I was pursuing some secret end of my own, but he left it to God's will, for he'd nothing to lose, even if I changed my mind. He'd be just as he was.

The next day I started teaching the children the real Arabic language, consoling them that their present mental darkness would soon be transformed into light. They looked at me in disbelief, and Mahmut sat there beside us, nodding his head like a real *muderis*, applauding my knowledge and frowning at the children's lack of it, although his own lack of knowledge was the equivalent of theirs. And he wasn't the least surprised at what I was doing, nor did he make any further mention of payment: He accepted my insanity as something that touched only me and had no wish to offer me what I'd not sought. He took over the task of summoning the children, of seeing to heating his little room with a brazier when it was cold, of collecting the money for the lessons, of extolling my learning wherever he could, while leaving to me the less important matter, that of teaching.

Of course he was right, he did drink, quite a lot, yet it was scarcely noticeable. He was only pleasantly cheerful and so happily disposed that I preferred it when he was rather tipsy.

Even his hands ceased to shake so much, and then I saw that the shaking came not so much from sickness as from drink. After the lessons he'd lead me to Idriz's coffeehouse to reward my labors with a coffee and himself with a *rakiya*.

"This is my scholar," he would say proudly.

He hadn't thought up this strange business simply for the sake of making a bit more money. I think what really attracted him was the desire to do something out of the ordinary.

He'd talk, with longing and even with envy, about a woman from one of the villages who was born without arms but who knitted and did other things with her feet so that her relatives displayed her at fairs and earned money. Or he'd talk of the merchant Hasan who bought two weird rams and earned a fortune with them because everybody wanted to see them.

All else, pertaining to the everyday, bored him as unworthy of human attention, as being petty and uninteresting, tedious, not leaving a man enough time for himself. But why he needed this time, I was unable to ascertain.

Did I resemble, for him, the woman who was knitting with her feet or was I like an ostrich from distant parts?

I said this to him with a grin.

He took umbrage.

"How can you talk like that! And who asked to do this, anyway, I you or you me? You said: It'll help me, I'll refresh what I've learned. And I did what you asked, helped you, gave you the shop, gave you the children. What's strange about that? I know, you'll say you know Arabic and I don't. Well, big deal! They'll remain idiots both with your knowledge and with my lack of it. And as for the ostrich and the woman without arms, don't think I don't know what you mean by that. I'm exploiting you, eh? Who offered to pay you? And you refused. I'll pay you now. You can take it all if you want. Only I won't stand for injustice. And let's be clear on one thing: Whether you can do without me, I don't know, but I can do without you, that's for sure."

However, the next day, at the appointed time, he was pacing slowly in front of Mula Ibrahim's shop. He greeted me humbly. "I was afraid you might be late. I don't like to keep the children waiting."

I told my wife I was helping an unfortunate chap who'd made every possible mistake in life, and that I was pleased to work with children, particularly since she'd told me she was pregnant, and we were awaiting a dear unknown being who would grow between her and me, as between two oak trees, protected, sheltered, and would not have to go to any Chocim nor learn Arabic with Mahmut Neretlyak. I'd teach him poetry and teach him to hate war.

She listened, touched, with tears in her eyes that became ever deeper and more lovely. A woman prefers a gentle word, even if stupid, to a wise one if it be harsh.

I told the real truth to Mula Ibrahim, namely that I was renewing what I once knew, in case I might need it.

"What have you got against making a bit of money?"

"He's getting so little from it that it wouldn't be worth dividing."

"You're making two mistakes," he advised me seriously. "You've joined up with a man nobody respects. Who'll respect you then? And you're taking no money in return for your honest work. How are people expected then to value your knowledge? They'll think you know nothing. And that you're refreshing your memory, that's OK. Until you get somewhere with it. Afterward, you'll forget it all. Some people, in fact, can achieve much without any knowledge. But you need it. You haven't got the cunning."

"Can cunning replace knowledge?"

"An experienced man would ask: Can knowledge replace cunning?"

"Cunning is dishonesty."

"It's not always even dishonest. Because you can't get on without it. It's like a coat in winter. Some would call it wisdom."

"How would you advise a man if you wished him well?"

"Not to challenge common opinion. If he does, he'll come to grief before he manages to do anything."

"These pictures in our window don't challenge common opinion."

"My second piece of advice to a man I wished well would be: Don't always say what you think."

"Have you ever done anything that was against your inner feeling? Cunning is surely necessary, but don't you sometimes feel ashamed?"

"Not at all. There are things that are above us and cannot be measured by our usual standards. The sultan is an almost supernatural concept that unites our many aspirations. He is the absolute who holds us together, like the force of gravity. Without him we'd fly off in all directions like a stone shot from a catapult."

"That'd really be fun!"

He looked at me in surprise, startled: He'd thought I'd recovered from the madness I'd brought back from the war as my only booty. I'd rid myself of the strange lethargy and quiet sadness and was resolved to take the well-trodden path followed by most people. But I felt suddenly that the possibility of the force of gravity disappearing was extremely attractive and that everything might begin to hover and fly in every direction, that old links would be broken, that the oppressor in his irrevocable flight would forget his victim, and the avenger launch himself upon a path either above or below that of him on whom he'd be revenged. There'd be no more guilty or righteous, there would be just a hovering. They'd fly away—the mosques, the streets, the graveyards, the trees, the houses—and I'd settle myself in one of the houses, alone with my wife, holding her in a tight embrace, lest the universal whirlwind carry her away, and we'd be happy, knowing that the evil forces, which could return us to an ugly life of crawling, were no more. And I'd grab hold of a tree, an apple tree or a cherry tree, so it could blossom for me, forever circling, and give fruit to our child who was to be born in that circling. And war would no longer be possible, excepting only if one managed to kick somebody or hit people in passing, and even then it'd probably be better if you asked after their health. And the education of children would be rather different than it is here and certainly less boring. One would just have to teach some rule at top speed to a flying pupil and, after a year or two, when you coincided with him, ask him whether he remembered it, or perhaps never encounter him again, if he were lucky. All I'd do would be teach my child everything beautiful that I knew, for no reason, just for the sheer satisfaction of giving him pleasure.

I laughed at this daft idea, like a reformed drunk at the smell of whisky, with a touch of nostalgia and irony. It would not have surprised me immediately after the war. Today I could do without it.

I wiped the dust off Sultan Abdul Hamid's portrait, stuck the dried stars back onto the glass, straightened out the upturned horns of the half-moon, and didn't find it funny. No doubt because of my wife, who was waiting for me as though I were going to bring her good luck as a gift, and no doubt because of the child whose growth I followed, with my hand on my wife's swollen belly, with an ear to the pulse by which the new life announced its emergence from nonexistence. I was no longer alone. There'd been two of us and now a third, yet unborn, more powerful than either of us, a link that bound me more and more with the burnt house of my parents. It was for their sake that I calmly reordered the constantly drooping and wearing heavenly vault, there by the public toilets. I didn't laugh at them anymore. Indeed I remembered my earlier laughter and thought of the peasants from Zhupcha who were seeking the bodies of their dead ones. Not particularly often, probably ever more rarely, for time stubbornly devours human thought till all that remains of it is a skeleton, a pale reminiscence, bereft of true content.

I was unconsciously conforming, and Mula Ibrahim was daily more contented with the banality of my thoughts. He'd said once, "Go fishing!" And he could have said, "Get married! Have some children!" For that, too, assuaged discontent by imposing obligations—the toughest there are—those of love.

Mula Ibrahim had a good knowledge of people. It seemed to him that the moment he'd been waiting for had arrived. He really wanted to help me, thinking I was worth more than stagnating in this pigsty.

"Get ready. We're off to dine with *hadji*-Duhotina," he said with pride.

I knew what this meant. This invitation was equal to getting an honor. And, moreover, it meant the possibility of meeting with people of influence. *Hadji*-Duhotina had once chopped salt but then grew rich and, every month, threw a party for well-known war heroes. He'd never been in a war, never fired a gun nor buckled on a saber, yet for some reason he loved soldiers and enjoyed gathering them together and entertaining them in his spacious house. His circle of guests was narrow, carefully selected.

I did not refuse. I'd got over the indifference with which the war had crippled me. I'd become like other sensible folk. I even thought myself lucky and Mula Ibrahim omnipotent.

The dinner went by, and we didn't go. And many months went by, and no invitation arrived. New guests, it would seem, didn't enter that house easily.

"Patience!" Mula Ibrahim consoled me. "It's worth waiting for."

And I replied that I couldn't care less for war heroes nor for old Duhotina. I could get on quite well without them. I entrenched myself in resentment, which became my defense. I began sincerely to despise those people separated by an impenetrable wall from those who had a better right to be of that company. Old Mehmed-*aga* who, during the battle for Banja Luka, was the first to attack the enemy and to leap into an enemy trench, Mehmed-*aga*, a famous hero and a famous drunkard who recognized no rank but only the man, he was not invited. Old Dugonya from Begovats, cut up by Austrian bayonets and scarcely put together again, peppered with bullets as if he'd been a target on a rifle range, and who afterward made rolling pins and pipe stems with his crippled fingers, they didn't invite him either. Nor did they invite the brave *bayraktar*, the last of a hundred *bayraktars* of the Banja Luka army, who stood without a word in front of the stone *han*, begging. And not one of the old heroes, not a single one, for the new ones didn't like to share their glory, and even the new ones weren't invited unless they had position and wealth. But they did invite to their table pretentious clerks who wouldn't have gone to war, not for their own mothers' sake, as well as polished dandies, pederasts, wine-bibbers, clowns, flatterers, these they did invite, these heroes who were no heroes. Defeat bears its victims, but victory has its own! But let them, let them enjoy their dead glory while they defiled it. I'd lived without them till now. I could live without them in the future. Better than with them.

Almost all winter passed, and then, one Thursday, Mula Ibrahim came into the shop, out of breath, excited and happy.

"We're invited!"

"Who by?"

"*Hadji*-Duhotina! Tomorrow evening, to the dinner!"

"You go. I don't want to."

He stopped in the middle of the shop, unbuttoned, hot, flabbergasted.

"You don't want to? What do you mean you don't want to?"

"What I say. I don't feel like it."

"Hang on, wait a bit. You clearly don't understand. We've been invited by *hadji*-Duhotina. To a dinner."

"I heard you, and I understood, but I don't want to go. What do I want to go there for?"

"What do you mean 'What do I want to go there for' for God's sake!"

His eloquence deserted him, all his determination, all his clever reasoning. He sat down and regarded me in amazement.

"So, you don't want to. But we're invited."

"No one will notice if I'm not there."

"And do you know what people do to get invited there?"

"I don't know, and I don't care. Personally, I wouldn't do anything."

"You're making a mistake. A big mistake."

"Are you sick of me?"

"Of course not, God forbid. I just want things to go better for you. I don't suppose you want to remain a pauper all your life?"

"To tell you the truth, I don't give a damn."

"I don't know what to say to you. We shan't get another chance like this. And we'll offend them."

He looked sad and frightened. Sad for me for not accepting his help, frightened because of them, since I didn't accept their invitation. I was ashamed of myself, and I thought how many words he'd spent, how many reasons he'd thought up, how many flattering smiles he'd given in order to open for me that inaccessible fortress. And how much time he'd wasted running from one person to another, all for my sake. While I rudely and ungratefully rejected all his efforts and goodwill.

For this reason I put it more gently, justifying myself. "We'll be bored. I don't know anybody there. I don't even know how one talks to such people."

"Just be silent and listen. That's probably the best way. Does that mean you'll go?"

He came to life. His good mood returned. I hadn't the heart to disappoint him yet again.

He looked at me suspiciously. "You're angry because they didn't invite you before?"

"I'm not. I'm sorry you had to humble yourself for my sake. It wasn't worth it."

48

"I didn't humble myself. And you were offended, I know you. And now you'd pass up a chance like this out of pure vanity!"

It was true I'd lost any desire to go to that damn dinner. I was still the man from Chocim. On the other hand, there was my wife and the child we were expecting and the need for some hope for something better than sheer poverty. I ought to go, if only for their sake. I still bore in me the dull mists of Chocim and from time to time the deep sadness for those who'd perished there. And now I had to become, all of a sudden, cunning and bow down before God knows whom for the sake of a position that would give me a better life. But what about my shame afterward? Could I put up with it? I was a pauper, but a beggar I was not. I'd accepted the first invitation, looking on it neither as an honor nor as a privilege. But when they rejected me, I'd cast them aside. I'd taken it as an insult and a humiliation (Mula Ibrahim guessed rightly) and answered them with a contempt that saved my pride.

Now, on the other hand, faced with tomorrow's certainty, I began to make a deal with my conscience. I'd not humble myself to anyone, but if the chance arose, I'd be a fool not to take it. I didn't see how such a chance could come, but I left it to chance to worry about my fate. If it didn't come, I'd be where I was, and nothing would be lost. I even hoped I'd pass unnoticed so I could return to my accustomed rut. How was I supposed to talk to these people and about what? After Chocim all I was capable of was looking at the water, listening to the sparrows, and burdening the unhappy world by writing appeals and complaints. I just didn't have the words, especially intelligent ones or pleasant ones, for anybody. Except for Tiyana, with whom, at night, I'd talk long and quietly, and the next morning I'd not be able to repeat what I'd said, so much was it the fruit of the night, ours alone, and so much did it issue from our coming together that the morning light pressed it into a pleasant but unclear memory and it was lost, till the following night, when it would reappear, like an underground stream.

And what words would I find for them?

In the evening I'd sit in our little room, the only one, except for the hall and the other secreted spaces, which, if I'd put on weight (which certainly wouldn't happen), I shouldn't be able to enter. That little room of ours had one or two advantages and a host of disadvantages. It was cheap, we were on our own, and, since it was above a bakery, it was always warm in winter and every morning we'd be awakened by the smell of fresh bread. Of course, it was not so good in summer. We were heated by the sun and the hot baker's oven, and the cockroaches scampered about freely as if we weren't there. We enjoyed the advantages and patiently bore the heat, opening doors and windows. We discouraged the cockroaches with some herbs Tiyana bought in the Bashcharshia. Or else we just ignored them and let them be. I wouldn't have minded the cockroaches if Tiyana hadn't hated them, especially at night when they began rustling about the floor and on the bed. Sometimes I'd wake up and find her sitting up in bed, embracing her knees.

"What's the matter?"

"Nothing."

"Are you in pain?"

"It's nothing. Go to sleep."

"You're in a funny mood tonight."

"I'm happy tonight."

I accepted her reason, because I wanted to go to sleep, but the next day I wondered: Does happiness keep one awake?

In that heated room of ours, I found it better than at Chocim, but for her it was worse than it had been at home. She wouldn't admit this, for my sake. We didn't discuss things. I wouldn't have liked it even if we could. All that mattered to me was that we should be caring for one another, and this we were, without any great effort. Except for the odd row over nothing, over something we couldn't even remember.

I told her I was going the next day to *hadji*-Duhotina's and told her how I'd refused his invitation and then changed my mind for the sake of Mula Ibrahim.

"Why shouldn't you go? You'll find someone to talk to. What's wrong with that? Will you be long?"

She was a bad liar. Never in my life had I met anybody so incapable of concealing what they were thinking. She gave herself away with her voice, with her expression, if not with direct words.

She'd agreed too easily. She was even urging me to go. Why?

"You don't want me to go?" I asked her.

She laughed. "I don't like your going! I never like you not to be with me."

"Perhaps you'd rather I didn't even go to work?"

"Of course I would."

Now I began to laugh, too. She was completely nuts.

"Who can live like that?"

"I'd like to live like that."

"OK, shall I not go to this dinner, then?

"No. You must go anyhow. Otherwise, later, you'd think you'd missed something."

"Then what are you angry about?"

"I'm not."

And then she added, as if in justification, "I'm a bit upset. Perhaps it's the pregnancy."

This slight cunning with which she masked her discontent, while averting mine, turned my thoughts to that third person, present yet invisible, who for months had held us in suspense and forced us to involve it in our life, to arrange our paths and desires according to it.

For its sake and for hers I had to get out of that room. For its sake and for hers, I'd go to that damned dinner. And I'd be smart, and I'd be cunning.

I put my hand on her belly and felt it with my fingertips. In silence.

In the street downstairs voices grew quieter. Beneath us someone was throwing logs into the big bakery oven. The cockroaches still crouched motionlessly in their holes, waiting for us to put out the candle. And I held my palm on the taut curve of her belly, on the secure body of the small being that was already alive in this safest and most comfortable of all the shelters in this world. I wanted to say something nice to this woman whose frail body was deformed by this unknown tadpole, to think something nice about that dear tadpole that would be what I'd not been. I wanted to, but I couldn't.

There were the three of us, in the whole world just us three: my fingers, her body, and its rhythmic pulsation, gripped in the unstoppable circulation of the blood. What was going on in the world or what would be tomorrow didn't matter. All that mattered was this moment of bliss without thought. Would he drive me out of the house, this third one, as his son drove out the sick Mustafa Puhovats? Or would we be proud of one another? Or would we just tolerate each other, as most people do? At that moment all this was unimportant.

There'd be a thousand such moments for others, but this one never again. A thousand other people's loves would be like this one, but this one could never be again. Never: the one finality.

For the first time I knew happiness, felt it, saw it, sensed it.

The whole world, the entire universe, the three of us.

And there is happiness. Could I retain it?

I wanted to say to her: My love! For tenderness warmly washed my inner shores, but she was asleep, smiling in her sleep.

"You sleep, too," I said to the third one and put out the candle.

The cockroaches had certainly been waiting impatiently for me to let them into the room. Perhaps they were late for some cockroach ritual.

Outside it was a spring night with a moon. And I couldn't sleep because of a happiness for which I sought no reason. Nor was I surprised that it was so.

CHAPTER 4

ENEMY COUNTRY

NO ONE ON EARTH CAN CAUSE YOU SO MUCH TROUBLE AS YOU can yourself.

What made me go to this dinner at which I'd be what I'm not or be such an I as I would not have people see: stupid, clumsy, boring, a nobody? I'd rather no one knew about it, or at least only those at home.

I wasn't even sure what time I should turn up. If I came late, after everybody else, they'd think me impolite. If I got there early, they'd think I was pushing in front of all the others. No matter how you look at it, trouble.

"Are we going to be late?" I asked Mula Ibrahim, who, by good or by ill fortune, walked beside me, for, left to myself, I'd have gone home. "Are we going to be late? Or are we going to be too early?"

"We'll wait till they come out of the mosque, and then we'll set off and take our chance."

"I'm sorry now I've come at all."

"Just follow me!"

At the crossroads, under a lamp, near the street where *hadji*-Duhotina lived, stood the old *bayraktar* Muharem, begging.

I gave him some small change, feeling ashamed: ashamed because I was giving him charity, ashamed because I was going to the dinner. It was his place to be there, not mine. Before and above all others.

"I hate to see a man like that begging," I said grimly.

"He's doing it out of spite, just because they've forgotten about him. That's why he's standing here, so people can see him."

"All the same, I feel ashamed."

"It's not your fault."

It wasn't my fault, but I still felt ashamed. Sorry you old bastard, I thought. You're doing this out of spite; I'm doing what I'm doing because I can't help myself. You want to have it as bad as you can; I want it as good as I can. You can't go my way, and I can't go yours. Neither's any good, as I see it.

We stood in the dark alley, like children, hiding like fools, waiting. It got embarrassing and funny. Was this the way honored guests behave?

I began to curse, both these old soldiers and myself, an idiot, who would be an ape among these mummies. I'd smile falsely and be genuinely frightened, while I could have been sitting at home with my wife, being what I wanted to be and how I wanted to be. Never can a man destroy his life so easily as when he desires to improve it and doesn't know either why or how. And I didn't even know whether it was to be an improvement or a worsening, particularly if it were to cost me my peace.

"There, they're coming out," Mula Ibrahim whispered, as though announcing the start of a battle. "Come on! And don't worry about your wife, that's easy. She'll wait. These people won't. And without their help you won't get anywhere."

As we entered old *hadji*-Duhotina's house, past servants holding candles and lamps, Mula Ibrahim said quietly, "Don't leave me!"

I looked at him in amazement: I'd hoped for support from him and not that he'd ask help from me!

"Are you scared?" I asked.

"A bit."

"Then what are we doing? Come on, let's go home!"

"It's too late to go back."

"OK, if we can't, to hell with them! Courage. Think we're going into enemy country!"

"What enemy country, for the sake of God Almighty!" he cried, shocked.

I gave a chuckle, relieved of fear and shyness, cured by his fear. My flippant words scared him, words I'd uttered to spite both myself and them, not knowing for certain from what I was defending myself, and, in his confusion, he stamped his feet on the stairs, scarcely bending his stiffened knees. And he looked at me as he might have looked at an arsonist, taken aback and angered at my pathetic protest. There was no point, for with such fear life isn't worth living and, if it once mastered me, I'd not even bother to live. For it's one thing to be afraid when there's a reason for it, in disaster, or in war, that comes to everyone, and another to be afraid constantly, of everything. The mighty Mehmed Petsitava said once, in the Chocim marshes, "Fear to sit, fear to shit, and when does a bloke get to live?"

And when do I get to live, Mula Ibrahim, if I'm forever afraid? When shall I live then, you gentlemen of the enemy country?

It was ridiculous, my show of bravado, and I knew it was, for I, too, a while ago had felt fear, and in my imagination I'd created both fear and danger. And this was the same as for real, and henceforth I entrenched myself in an attitude of cold aloofness.

At my first step inside this rich house I realized that my aloofness was ridiculous and my armor unnecessary. Our host, *hadji*-Duhotina, short, with a large stomach, like a stuffed turkey, greeted us with a beaming face, so ingratiatingly polite that I couldn't believe my eyes. What had Mula Ibrahim told him about me? Or was this splendid man so nobly hospitable that he showed such respect even to insignificant guests? "How wrong and unjustly grotesque was my idea of the world and of people!" I thought, both moved and puzzled, ready to exchange my aloofness for a tender cordiality, like a hunchbacked girl to whom someone addresses a kind word.

But, alas, the hunchbacked girl was better advised not to hope too much.

That splendid man passed us by as though we were shadows. His beaming host's face, the wide-opened arms, ready for an embrace, and the obsequious cordiality were not meant for us, but for the *kadi* who was behind us.

Mula Ibrahim and I were received by our host's sons, with formal politeness, of which one could neither complain nor boast, and who immediately separated us, placing Mula Ibrahim in the middle room and me in the front room near the entrance. Our host led the *kadi* into the last invisible and inaccessible room, reserved for the most prominent guests. These "most prominent guests" arrived last and passed into their secluded refuge, cloaked in a dumb respect and groveling silence, like dead men at a funeral.

And where were the soldiers?

In all, there were only a few. The rest were tradesmen, clerks, or craftsmen: This was the place where it was worth being seen. Perhaps many of them were like my Mula Ibrahim.

I grinned to myself recalling his "military exploits."

Beside me sat an elderly man, somewhat slovenly dressed, with a swollen face and, as it seemed to me, already drunk. And he was drinking now. He had a jug beside him and took a drink whenever he thought no one could see him. And he seemed to think himself invisible rather often.

"What did you come here for?" he asked, frowning.

"For what? For nothing!"

"Really for nothing? Have you no complaints? You want nothing? You're not asking for anything?"

"Nothing."

"You're rich? Or you earn a lot?"

"Yes, I'm rich all right, and I earn plenty."

"Eh, lucky you! Those who have, get more. Lucky you!"

"I'm an advocate's clerk. I get twenty-five *groschen* a year. Lucky me!"

"Pff, so that's what you are! You're pretty much muck, aren't you? Have some *rakiya!*"

"I don't drink."

"Not with me? I'm not good enough, I suppose?"

I took a drink, not to anger him.

"There you are, you do drink! Come on, have another! That's it, bottoms up!"

The second drink went down better than the first.

"And you don't drink, you said! I can see you don't drink. You're a funny man, I see. What were you laughing at a while ago? I like to see people laugh."

His praise pleased me. I began to feel good.

"I was looking for the war heroes. And I remembered a man I carried across a flooded river, and he shat himself. And perhaps, I said, a lot of those who are here shat themselves, and that's all the war and the rigors of war they ever knew."

He burst out laughing, like an explosion, splattering me with the *rakiya* he was about to drink, choked, coughed, came to, and went on laughing aloud, roaring, smacking his knee, jerking his whole body, shrieking, till I began to be afraid both for him and myself.

"Drink!" I said, offering him the jug to calm him down.

"Oh, brother, you say: shat himself and that was his war!"

His laughter was cut off only by coughing.

People began to look at us.

"Go on tell 'em, tell 'em all! They'll die of laughing!"

"No way! It's not for telling. And, anyway, perhaps I made it up."

"If you did, you did a good job."

"And you, what are you doing here?"

He didn't hear me.

"All their war and rigors of war, you say!"

"Heh, hang on. You don't seem to like talking about yourself. I asked you what *you* were doing here."

I wanted to turn the subject to him, to escape his embarrassing laughter. I asked him and thrust the jug into his hand.

And it worked. The laughter still came from him in bursts, but more quietly and less frequently. And we went on drinking. I'd abandoned any sense of caution, anything to make him forget what I'd said.

"I've nothing much to tell. Mine's a very normal tale."

"Tell me, all the same."

"I was in the war. The Austrians captured me, badly wounded. They healed me and then forgot about me. I was sent to cut wood in the Tyrol. I'd three shots at escaping, so they confined me to a tighter and tighter prison. It was all of nine years before they let me go. Off you go, they said, and try to forget it. I will, I said, I've been a prisoner of war, not a wedding guest."

He got back to home and wife, but there was another in the home and on the wife, and on his land as well. There were five children, not one of them his. He understood it and wasn't angry: She'd waited and waited, and then remarried. Now all he wanted was his own back, that is, the house and the land, and the man was welcome to his wife. Very simple. So it was, but that was where the argy-bargy began. Since nothing had been heard of him for some time and others had seen him fall badly wounded, the *kadi* had issued a death certificate, and his wife had inherited everything and brought it to her second husband. What was he to do now? He wanted only what was his. He hadn't sold it nor gambled it away; indeed, he left everything in the best possible order, and that he was not dead everybody could see. What more evidence did they need? But his wife's husband, his replacement, who had performed his duty as a husband well, claimed the following: It's true that the man's alive; that the lands were his, there's no question. But had it not been for the *kadi*'s death certificate, in the writing of which he had no part, he wouldn't have married the man's wife, that is to say, his own wife, nor would he have married her had she been without property, since he had none of his own, and even if he had been mad enough to do so, he'd never have produced so many children.

Was it his fault that the man had remained alive and that the *kadi* had proclaimed him dead? He agreed to strike a deal if there were no other way round it: He'd return the wife and two or three children and keep half the lands. Or the man could live with them, there was room for all of them. But our friend would have none of it, not wife nor children. He wanted what was his own, or at least half of it, for neither was he to blame for staying alive nor for the *kadi* proclaiming him dead, but he preferred it as it was, rather than that the *kadi* had proclaimed him alive when he was dead. As it was, he was keeping under the noses of those on whose decision the possible disentangling of this unnecessary muddle depended.

Now I began to laugh. The *rakiya* was having its effect.

"And this is what you call an ordinary story!"

"Well, it is! The land's mine, and the children are his. What's difficult about that?"

At that moment, Dzhemal Zafraniya emerged from the middle room. He wore spectacles that were not much use to him, but he used his ears as eyes and they served him excellently. When he got close, he checked them with his sight. He was attracted by our loud laughter, something rare in that place.

"You sound happy," he smiled politely.

He was always smiling, forever using pleasant words.

"It would seem it's always funny when you talk about real life," said my new acquaintance, surprising me with this remark. It was more intelligent than I might have expected from him.

Then he turned to me. "Do you know Dzhemal-*effendi*? One of the *kadi*'s clerks. A good chap."

"We went to the *medrese* together. Only he was younger

than I. I gave him a good beating for his logic. We know each other well," I said.

"I think I'm better at logic now than you are."

"That's for sure. My pay is twenty-five *groschen*. Just one of your smiles is worth that."

Dzhemal smiled approvingly, as though he'd heard a good joke.

"Why don't you drop in on me?"

"I don't want to waste your valuable time."

"Sit down, Dzhemal-*effendi* and have a drink with us," insisted the ex–prisoner of war. "I didn't know you were friends."

"Thank you, I don't drink."

"He doesn't drink; he doesn't smoke; he has no vices. Except for those he keeps hidden."

I didn't like Dzhemal. He always disgusted me with his false smile, his dangerous courtesy, with his sniffing, even when I was stronger than he. Now even more so. I didn't like people who worked for the *kadi*. If his spine had been made of iron, he'd have cracked it in a couple of months. He'd been two years a clerk but wouldn't stay there. He'd climb. There was no need to break him, he'd bend before being touched. He was like water. He'd no form of his own; he'd adapt himself to any vessel he was poured into. Nothing disgusted him if it was useful, for he had one and only one aim in life: to succeed, to escape the memories of a poverty-stricken childhood and of a father who was a prison warder, a drunk who'd spy for anybody, who died despised by everybody, and whose son turned even this family tragedy to his own advantage, begging the aid of the powerful against an unfavorable fate. And when everybody had forgotten, he hadn't. He remembered everything. His father was to blame for being nothing and nobody, to blame for being everybody's servant, to blame for not knowing how to profit from the evil he did. Had he been powerful, no one would have despised him, at least not in public. They would have bowed to him, even if they hated him. The wrong he'd done to people and the suffering he'd caused he might well have turned into money. He could have made them a ladder to climb, perhaps to some height. Many do this. But his father was a weakling. He sold his skills for peanuts. Dzhemal would not be a weakling. He'd do everything to put right his father's mistakes. He was calm, self-controlled, dangerous. He knew how much people feared him, and he enjoyed this with a smile of satisfaction.

I'd never spared him a thought. Like so many ugly things in life, he didn't concern me. But that evening I was more vulnerable, rather drunk, disturbed, rather restricted by the armor I'd put on as self-protection. For this reason, he bothered me. I recalled what was being said of him, half laughingly and half admiringly, namely that for a year he'd been the lover of the rich *haznadar* Feyzo, partly in order to have a powerful protector but mainly because he wanted to marry Feyzo's daughter, who would bring him a fair dowry. Was his aim first to please Feyzo and in return to ask to marry his daughter, or was it to go on playing two instruments at the same time? Which was the more likely, I didn't know.

But I knew one thing: He disgusted me. His smile made me sick. I wanted him to go, which is why I made my remark. He showed no anger, although he had a great sense for the innuendo and knew what I was thinking about when I mentioned his hidden vice.

Being drunk and mischievous, I wanted to see what he'd do. Could I shake him out of his apparent complacency, would he blush, get angry, shout? Would he strike with a contemptuous word? Or would he begin to talk against me, to pick an argument, no matter about what, merely to show his superiority? Just let him try! Neither his brains nor his position scared me. My arguments were stronger, because they were those of a free man; my speech was bolder because I wanted nothing. I was content with my poverty.

He was persistent in his polite condescension.

"And what vices do I hide?" he said with a smile.

"Those we don't know about. What man hasn't vices?"

"Clearly there are such men. I haven't a single vice, not one."

He looked at me calmly, lying in his teeth without as much as a blink.

"I didn't know there was such a man."

"What's strange about it? God creates us, and it's His will that I am as I am."

"Sinless?"

"Without sinful vices."

"You're not serious?"

"Very serious. Don't you believe in God's will?"

"To cast responsibility for good and evil upon God's will means to hide behind a principle. Very wise. Look, during the war a quartermaster lost the army's tobacco ration. They questioned him, and he kept saying he'd lost it and that this was God's will. But the witnesses stated he'd sold it for drink. So it was God's will that made him a drunk."

"And wasn't it?"

He kept his cool, rather sarcastic, not giving a damn for anything I said. I got really angry.

"Nonsense! The more holy refuges there are for people to hide behind, the more space there is for human evil. Man's forever thinking of a cause outside himself, so as to be free of guilt and responsibility. This merely encourages communal irresponsibility. Woe to mankind as long as this is true."

"You mean that everybody has the job of deciding what's good and what's evil?"

"Everybody! And no evil can become good just because the majority accept it."

"Is defense evil? Defense of one's faith, for instance?"

"Defense is often aggression."

Zafraniya didn't stop smiling even then. What was he made of? Was it strength or just insensitivity?

"Wrong, but interesting," he said without resentment.

He took me by the arm, leading me aside. We looked like the best of friends.

"It's as well nobody heard what you said."

"Do you think I'm afraid? I say what I like."

"You've nothing to be afraid of. But it's not nice. Nor wise. People might misunderstand."

"I don't give a damn."

"You should. These are our best people."

"Best? Did you see the *bayraktar* Muharem on your way here? The best people are probably those who are starving, or dying in prisons."

Then I noticed, by the look of delight that he tried to conceal with apparent embarrassment and by the sudden deathly silence, that he desired nothing more than that I should say this! That was why he'd led me into the middle room, without my noticing. That was why he'd encouraged me, counting on my drunken pride that I'd blurt it all out, like a fool.

They listened, offended, scowling, threatening, Mula Ibrahim wriggling his thin neck as if he'd swallowed a live eel.

But nothing now could halt my madness. This myopic rascal was making a big mistake if he thought I'd retreat in terror. I'd said nothing bad. And they knew it.

I went on speaking. Pride demanded it. I was not afraid, so I'd go on saying what I thought. Somebody had to speak up. We couldn't all be silent forever.

I didn't wish to upset anybody (I said, more gently), but I was shaken by the sight and by the fate of the old *bayraktar*. (But then I felt I was explaining myself out of fear. Pride prompted harsher words.) Is the *bayraktar* any worse than we people here? (And that was a compromise! What I wanted to say was: than *these* people here! Coward!) And how many are there like him? We care neither for the living nor the dead. (There! That's it! Tell them the truth!) The life of this people consists of hunger, bloodshed, suffering, miserable vegetation in their own country, and senseless dying in a foreign one. All my comrades at Chocim died like dogs, without knowing why, and thousands of other poor devils the same. And if they'd come back, they'd probably have had to beg, like *bayraktar* Muharem. It's not enough to think only of our own good."

Mula Ibrahim had swallowed his eel and was now hiccuping, quite purple in the face.

And I knew, as soon as I'd spoken, that what I'd said was utter stupidity, without need or reason.

Dzhemal Zafraniya could never have hoped that his sly revenge for my insult could have worked so perfectly. But there was no backing out. Being sorry wouldn't help now. To hell with them all! I'd made a fool of myself, but they'd heard what they hadn't heard for a long time.

So much for my effort to get something better out of life!

Some of them leapt at me, intent on beating me up, juniors of lower rank, insulted for their own sake and for the sake of their superiors.

Dzhemal Zafraniya calmed them down and led me out of the house.

"What did you need to do that for?" he asked, reproachfully.

"I didn't need it, you did. And now get out of my way or I'll give you a beating."

My reasoning convinced him, and he went back into the house, without further ado.

I was greeted by a night without a moon. It had not yet risen. My dinner had finished early.

But that's how it was.

Whose were the words I'd spoken there, in front of those scowling people? Perhaps they were mine, but I'd never expressed them so bluntly, not even to myself. Certainly they were mine, both the words and the thoughts behind them. Where else could I have got them? I shouldn't drink, I thought. Drink gets to me, and I can't control myself. But it wasn't the drink only. I did it to provoke, to anger

Zafraniya, and then didn't want to withdraw. But he'd made a monkey of me, led me like a puppet on a string. He'd directed me just where he wanted, and left me to make a fool of myself. And I'd been so sure I was cleverer than that half-blind dwarf! No way! It's always risky when anyone thinks they're clever.

And suddenly I remembered! From the fog of dormant memory arose the serious face of the student Ramiz and the words he'd spoken in the dark forests around Chocim. I'd remembered them without knowing and repeated them, in his very words and at a most unsuitable moment.

Well done me!

I was still slightly drunk with a drunkenness that does not make one stagger but that makes it hard to assemble one's thoughts. I decided to take a walk by the Milyatska to sober up a bit. Because of my wife. She'd say, "Oh honestly, you know you can't take drink!" as if she were talking to a child. And I also had to work out how to tell her that I'd let my tongue run away with me. Where she was concerned, I'd no secrets. Something gnawed inside me if I kept anything from her. And there was no point in trying. She sensed every change in me, even the subtlest. She could tell when I was lying, however innocently. So I'd tell her everything, no matter how bad I might feel about it. Well, you've made a name for yourself this time, she'd say when I told her. What should I tell her? That Zafraniya made a fool of me? That I'd spoken out intentionally, because it was burning me inside? That I was drunk and didn't know what I was saying? What was the truth? Or was it all true, more or less?

What I'd said was right, and I really believed it, but I shouldn't have said it. It gave me no satisfaction, for I was ashamed of it, and nobody would start to think differently than he had because of what I'd said.

Foolish, unnecessary, useless. And all because of Zafraniya.

Damn him for the bugger he was! He'd made an ass of me, as a whore would. Beware of pederasts, Smail Sovo used to say, or perhaps it was somebody else. I'd got to ascribing everything to dead comrades. And that somebody had also said: Those who don't hide it, they're not so bad, but those who do are the worst shit of all.

Why did I have to prove it on myself!

Anyway, to hell with it! Still, it might not be so bad. With my mean, frightened, kindly Mula Ibrahim I'd go on writing complaints and appeals for dissatisfied people and letters to soldiers. There would always be plenty of them, just as there would be wars. Even better than if I got some more important post. This way, no one depended on me, I was only a go-between, a means for the appeals of others to get to the ears of others, and I could sympathize with and comfort people in their disasters, real and imagined. This way I was always on their side, and there could be no greater misery than to have to pronounce judgment, no matter in what cause. Who could judge between an ex–Austrian prisoner of war and his inheritor? Everything human is complicated, and no one could say of anyone that they were completely right or completely wrong. (All that is obvious is the injustice that humiliates and kills men, but nobody ever touches that.) Well, OK then, I thought cheerfully, this evening I've passed judgment on myself: I'll never pronounce judgment on anybody. And thank God for it. But what I said was the truth. Indeed, the truth seen from below, but then from where else could I see it? Those from above saw it differently. And this way, damn its eyes, everyone had their own truth, and that was just fine. Only then I didn't know why it was called truth, because truth ought to be one. And then we'd die of boredom, so the best way was to call another person's truth untruth; it made life more amusing.

Having thus entangled my stupidities in a web of superficial thinking, thus relieving my pain, since I'd justified myself by adopting at least some sort of attitude and an attitude lent a sense of being in the right as well as a feeling of courage, I set off for home down the narrow streets. I'd greet Tiyana with a smile the moment she opened the door and I'd say . . .

I didn't manage to work out what I'd say. I suddenly felt my head burst open from a blow, and, as I fell, I vaguely heard the stamping of many feet like sticks on a drum. And then everything went blank.

I didn't know how long I'd lain there, nor how long the dreamless sleep, the gift of the blow, had lasted, but when I began to regain consciousness, I was vaguely aware of moonlight above me. I closed my eyes again. They were heavy, as with sleep.

Someone was coming down the street in my direction, I could tell by the footsteps, but whoever it was came to a sudden stop and hastily withdrew. What's happened, I asked myself with an effort, forcing my deadened brain into action. My head hurt. My back ached. My arms and legs hurt. A fire burned in my mouth. Once again unconsciousness relieved my suffering.

I was awakened by the sound of a voice and the feel of hands on me.

"Thank God, he isn't dead," said a husky voice. "Can you stand?"

"What's happened to me?"

I'd fallen asleep and awakened with the same question.

I could hear water flowing somewhere from a pipe. What I'd give for a drop!

"How should I know what's happened? I just happened to come this way and saw somebody lying here. I thought it was a drunk. When I got here I saw it was you. And it wasn't drink that knocked you down, my friend. Someone's had a right go at you."

I recognized him: It was Mahmut Neretlyak.

He was wiping something off me.

"They've shat all over you, poor bugger, from head to toe, shat and pissed. Phew, God, what a stink! I'm trying to get the shit off with this twig, but it doesn't work. Look I've messed my own hands. Were you fighting with someone?"

"I want to go home."

"Home, for sure. Let your wife give you a good wash, and you can see to the bruises later. Come on then, try and stand up."

I spat out blood and shit.

"Let me wash a bit here."

"You can a bit. But your wife'll have to wash the thick stuff off in lye. And you'll have to put another suit on."

I had no other suit. This was my only one. Tiyana had patched it and made it respectable for the dinner, and now she'd see me in this state. She'd get a shock.

He led me to the water pipe. I put my head under the stream, took a gulp of cold water and washed out my mouth, and passed deadened hands over my suit to brush off the filth. I didn't want Tiyana to see me like this.

"Leave it alone, you'll only rub it in."

Again I put my head under the jet of water, to lessen the pain in my head. Mahmut supported me.

"You're in luck! I was for going home. My friends wouldn't let me. What are you rushing for, they said, stay a bit longer. So you have a drink, you talk some more, and that's how I came to find you."

"Somebody came by and went away when they saw me."

"Nobody likes to get involved, my dear Ahmet. It's easier to run away than to help. Why should one waste time having to go to court and be a witness? To be honest, they're right. Come on, lean on me. There, you see, that could be another bother: taking those you find on the street home."

He didn't ask what had happened nor who had done it nor why. He wasn't even surprised. I told him somebody hit me suddenly, out of the dark. Not even this surprised him.

"It happens," he said calmly. "Perhaps they were thieves. There are more of them about these days than there are honest folk. Or perhaps it was a mistake. They were waiting for someone else and took you for him. You were lucky. It's not so bad when they beat you. The bad part's while you're expecting it. You look and you wait for it, and feel the pain beforehand. It hurts afterward, as it's hurting you now, but that's not so bad."

I knew he'd been beaten, almost to death, for his false coinage. They'd beaten me for telling the truth.

"Don't tell my wife anything," I said.

"What could I tell her? She'll see for herself."

Tiyana was awake. She'd have stayed up all night, for sure, and was shocked when she saw me. She froze in the doorway, petrified with fear. Managing a smile, I said one shouldn't walk at night in town. Someone had hit me and run off, but, luckily, it wasn't dangerous.

"My word, they did just about everything all over him and *then* ran off," Mahmut explained. "Anyway, let's get this suit off him. And you wash it, sister, while I apply some cold cloths."

They undressed me, washed me like a child, like a corpse. Mahmut put a cold cloth on the bump on my head. "It's quite a bruise," he said. "Pity you haven't any *rakiya*. It would bring the bruise out. And it wouldn't hurt us either."

And when Tiyana began to gather up my soiled suit from the floor, bending down with her swollen belly, he laughed. "Leave it, my dear, I'll wash it. You just heat some water."

"Why? I can do it."

"I know you can. But, just my luck, you'll do better to put your hand on this lump here, God bless us, it's as big as an apple. It'll make him feel easier. I'll do it in no time at all, I'm used to anything. You'll get used to it, too. But there's no hurry. And I see you're pregnant. You just sit down beside him. If he gets feverish, a bit from fear and a bit from the beating, don't worry, he's young, it'll soon pass."

I was really shaking with fever, and, as in a dream, through the reeling, in this coming and going of awareness, I felt her hand on me, like a balm, soothing, and with an effort, I sought it shakily to bring it to my split lips, to kiss my one sure support. I wanted it to keep me on the surface, to protect me from the awful dizziness that kept dragging me back to the events of that night. They kept returning, monstrous and distorted. I was being strangled by dwarfs with massive heads and by giants with heads the size of pinheads. I'd swim up out of suffocating depths and find her, bending over me.

"It's hot in here," I said. "They're feeding the furnace in the bakery tonight."

"Are you feeling better?"

"Don't leave me."

But I was leaving her, into the darkness, among the monsters, to find her again beside my pillow whenever I opened my eyes. She was a quiet harbor into whose peace I entered, battered by the storm, but happy to be back.

I was sorry for her having to stay awake, but I was afraid of her falling asleep. Who'd greet me when I emerged from my delirium?

"You'll tire yourself. Lie down. I'm feeling better."

She lay down, but I constantly felt her hand on me, on my heart, on my forehead. She watched over my agony.

"You're not letting me sleep," I said, with a pretense of reproach, yet I desired nothing better or dearer, ever in my life.

"Are you really feeling better?"

"I am. Go to sleep."

I closed my eyes, trying to drop off completely, so that my being calm might help her go to sleep too. Soon she began to breathe deeply, overcome by tiredness.

I leant over her face and looked at the long shadows of her eyelashes on her soft, oval cheeks. Her dear face drove away the phantoms of sleep and the threatening eyes of reality. I had her. They no longer mattered.

I lay back. My arm would no longer support me.

She woke with a start. "What is it?"

"I was looking at you."

Her big eyes were wide with fear, her mouth open, as if she were about to scream.

How beautiful she was!

I kissed her cheek, and she grew calm, her expression of fear turning to a sleepy smile.

And while the cockroaches crawled and rustled about the room, gnawing everything, the floor, the walls, and soon to begin on us; and while the moonlight waned, leaving her face in shadow (and I regretted it, for I wanted to thrust its silver light on her, so I might not lose her), I listened to the footsteps of passersby in the street, before dawn, and thought about her and about myself. She deserved better, but what would I do without her? I'd dragged her out of her world. My people didn't approve of her, hers didn't recognize her, and I was all she had, all she'd dreamt of having, love, tenderness, security, a shield. The thought helped me. In these girlhood dreams of hers, she still saw me as the man she'd desired. But what would happen when the storm of life broke that fragile thread, finer than a spider's web, and when the man of her dreams became what I was this night, pitiable and humiliated? So begin all human dreams, and so do they perish. She'd stand in horror. There'd be nothing left, not even illusions.

I don't know how it was that I recalled the Chocim marshes and the elder son of Salih, the barber from Alifako-vats, nor what link I could see between him and us. There were no similarities, at least not superficially speaking. And then I remembered. Suddenly it became clear why he'd killed himself. His younger brother looked up to him as though he were a God, based his actions on his, was brave alongside him, because he believed in his strength, wor-shiped his earnestness and purity. And then, that brother of his dreams, one night, became a thing of pity, like the rest.

And this man, in his disgrace, humiliated in his own eyes, reproaching both himself and those who'd involved him in an ugly act, surely suffered most at the thought of his brother. That he'd defiled himself he could have survived and got over. He'd have done it one day anyhow. But he'd destroyed his brother, taking from him everything, in a single moment, depriving him of both his past and his hopes of the future.

That younger brother had wept while on guard. They'd sent him there to avoid his seeing an ugly act, but he saw it all, and then, alone, he'd remained silent the whole night, suddenly bereft of support, utterly alone in the world, even without his naïve faith.

People are our thought and our concept of them. We dream life and the world. But how are we to preserve our dreams and those of others? Others see us, we see others, and everything is revealed, as at a merry game of masks. Only this is no game. One day we wake up and look at one another in bewilderment: What has happened to our dreams?

And would Tiyana also ask herself, "What's become of my dreams?"

I'd not promised her a star from the heavens, although people do that and are even believed, sometimes for a long period, but not forever. I'd obediently lit the candles under the sultan's flyblown portrait at every festival. I'd written letters and appeals, always the same, never complaining, even to her, at this boring job. I'd brought home all my small earnings to the last penny, earnings that would never grow, and I couldn't promise either her or myself that it would soon be any different. And yet I was happy: We'd not be rich in money, but we'd be among the richest in love; I feared neither life nor people, I only feared that you'd have enough of me; I was alone, now I had my own world, as though I'd conquered my own planet; I'd oppose any intrusion into our kingdom in order to secure our peace.

And now, tonight, this lord of this kingdom above the local bakery, full of cockroaches, rats, coughing and rattling, the lord of this, his own conquered planet of three meters in width, tonight had been pissed and shat upon. Not even the Russians would have done that to me had they captured me in their country. They'd have killed me but that would have been honorable. Our people had done it; it's always one's own people who do these things. And in such a way that would leave indelible traces. In vain had they washed me last night. In vain would I wash myself tomorrow and for years to come. I'd never wash out the humiliation.

I turned my head and buried my face in the hot pillow. What had they done to me?

And why?

Surely not because I'd been stupid, been drunk, provoked? Surely not because I'd said what I didn't think? That I'd said what I did think? If this is what they did to sparrows, what would they do to hawks? What were they? Arrogant madmen? Feebleminded bullies? Wild beasts?

I, a worm, tiny and unimportant, what could I do to them, the elephants? What possible harm could I cause?

I was a fist that hit a wall.

I was a blow that hurt the one who gave it.

I was sand beneath their feet, a bird that crouched silent when a hawk flew over the wood, a maggot that got pecked up by a hen when it ventured from its underground passages.

I was a small man who forgot that he was little. I'd insulted them by daring to think.

Why did they need to take such vengeance? To frighten me? To frighten others by my punishment? To triumph over the weak? To forbid thought? To forbid speech?

I could find no answer. I felt a horror at this senseless cruelty. Where were we? In what sort of a world were we living?

Or perhaps it was all a dream, for utter senselessness could not be reality?

But no! A dream is what's desired, but life is wakening.

And did you know this, too, my ten dead comrades from the Dniestr marshes? When you experienced sorrow and awakening? "It'll all pass, sir," the quiet Ibrahim Paro used to say. But what comfort is that? Happiness will pass, love will pass, life itself will pass. What hope is there in the fact that everything passes? All the same, this too will pass, my dear sir, this shame, this bewilderment, this torture for which I'd agree to die, without regret.

I cuddled up to Tiyana, so that a beloved creature might shelter me from my fear of a new day. She fitted herself to me, aware of me even in her sleep. I breathed in the smell of her hair and silently whispered, swallowing bitter tears of rage: This too will pass, my darling. Forget what you've seen. Don't wake up, not tomorrow, not ever. Forget what you know. We'll be happy again. I, too, will forget, if I can.

But perhaps I should try not to forget. I would not destroy my life, just because there were wild beasts. They'd humiliated me, by the hands of others. They had agents for everything, eternal servants without conscience or reason, just like themselves, with the single difference that they had the authority to pass judgment and the power over people, although I'd never understand how or why. Everybody sneered at them, despised them, but everybody feared them.

And I despised them, and I feared them.

They'd humiliated me, spat on me, defiled me, but break me they would not. They were from a foreign, enemy country, and I myself was to blame that we had ever met. We'd no common language, no common thought, no common life.

I, a stupid sparrow, went to visit a hawk and scarcely got away with it.

It wouldn't happen again. It was too big a mistake to bear repeating.

And if the hatred arising from this present agony of soul remained with me, they would be to blame.

■ □ ■ □ ■

CHAPTER 5

EMPTY SPACE

THE DAY WAS SPRINGLIKE, FULL OF SUNSHINE. I FELT IT ON my face like the gentle touch of waves. And I didn't want to open my eyes, nor leave the apparent night. While they thought I was asleep, I was not present, at least not for them.

I could hear them whispering, Tiyana and Mahmut. He'd brought strengthening herbs and ointment for my bruises. The herbs were good, he said, there was no doubt about that. He himself had been an herbalist and had lived off it in Turkey. Indeed, their herbs were not the same as ours, but then, once a man had the hang of it, he knew at once what was for what. He believed in herbs. He'd proved their healing powers both on himself and on others, and that was no wonder, for they consisted of sun, water, and all kinds of salts, and all this mixed and melted together in the capillaries of plants, and the result was something like *rakiya*, stronger or weaker, but all as pure as crystal. As regards the ointment, he couldn't say. The herbalist Fehim had made it. He hadn't told him whom it was for. There was no need to tell more than one had to, but he couldn't guarantee anything, because Fehim himself suffered from sores on his legs that he couldn't cure, yet still he was ready to treat others. Only she, Tiyana, had better not say anything to me about it. It was better that I should have faith in it; then it might help. Should it not help, the best thing for bruises was bear fat; only where could one get it? Rabbit fat wasn't too bad, and he'd get some.

When he'd gone, Tiyana was looking for something in the room, opening the door and peeping under the trunk.

"What're you looking for?"

"Your shoes. There were here by the door."

"Perhaps you've put them away somewhere."

"I haven't."

And where could she have put them in such a small space? No one had been in the room. Except for Mahmut Neretlyak. So . . . "Did Mahmut take them?"

"Why should he?"

"But where are they, if he didn't?"

She stood by the door, confused and ashamed. She always felt embarrassed whenever anyone did anything dishonest.

"No matter," I said, to calm her. "I'll wear my winter ones until I can buy some new."

"It's not the shoes."

"Don't think any more about it."

"How are you feeling?"

"My arm hurts. And my back."

She was so worried that I was ashamed at my lie.

"Don't worry, it's not too bad."

She brewed the herbs and rubbed me with the ointment. I let her fuss over me as she might over a child. I enjoyed being helpless, and she enjoyed helping, and it kept us both occupied, so we did not have to talk about what had happened. And all the time, I was expecting her questions. I wouldn't have answered them, or, perhaps, I'd have complained, in a martyred voice: Why couldn't she just wait until I'd got a bit better? Luckily, she didn't ask, but all the same I felt a sense of loss. It might have been a chance to relieve my tension.

I sent her to Mula Ibrahim to ask for some money and to tell him what had happened, that I'd been attacked the night before and wouldn't be able to come to work for a few days. And she was to buy what she could, so as to entertain him, since he was sure to come and visit me.

When she'd gone, I felt relieved. She, then, was the cause of my tension. I couldn't lie and pretend I was the victim of my principles. If they existed, then it was like some tiny particle flying above a desert, a seed borne on the wind, like vegetation concealed and formless under a fog. But then again, I was ashamed to admit that I was the lowest of the low, whom anyone could beat up on the street like a wretched chicken thief. For nothing! Without fear of anybody, without fear that anyone might ask them: What have you done to this man? I couldn't even take them to court. Whom? Darkness? Witches? And why? People would think, as Mahmut did when he found me, that I was drunk. They wouldn't even care. Were I to turn against them, they'd only laugh. I could think what I liked, but I could do nothing. In the world of today, we've only two possibilities: to adapt or to be our own victims. Struggle you couldn't, even if you wished; they'd make it impossible at the first step, at one's first words, and it would be suicide, without effect, without sense, without as much as one's name being remembered. You couldn't even say what was in your heart, even if it meant suffering. They'd beat you up before you could say a word, and all that would remain of you would be shame and silence.

Oh, wretched time that doesn't allow a man either to think or to be a hero.

So, being helpless, I used big words to wash away my shame.

I got up and walked about the room, my bruised legs bathed in the sunlight, and mindlessly counted the dark blue imprints on my body.

Martyr or fool, I desired to be neither. They looked on me as a common louse.

And perhaps I was. Out of all that I could think or feel, the truth was: I felt ashamed of myself. And somewhere there was a vague pressure of humiliation. I knew neither my offense nor my offenders. I'd no thought of revenge. I lacked a healing hatred. A certain dull anger flowed like a fever through my veins.

Tiyana found me in bed. She brought money and oranges for Mula Ibrahim when he came. He sent me his greetings and wished me well.

"He's not cross at my having to stay at home for a couple of days?"

"He says the most important thing is for you to get well."

"Didn't I tell you he was a good man?"

"And you were good to him."

"That's different. In war, or great disasters, a man does both good and evil, equally, one after the other. Because he's insecure. But in peacetime, evil takes over, and he thinks only of himself. But he isn't like that, you see."

She looked at me concentratedly, with large, intelligent, fearful, yet penetrating eyes, all in the same glance, and then turned away and busied herself with something or other.

What did her look mean? Did she think I was talking nonsense? Or that I was saying something that, for her, was quite natural? Or because I didn't speak about what had happened? Or because I was speaking at all, after all that had happened?

I'd grown sensitive. For, yesterday, I wouldn't have been surprised at any expression of hers, even the most astonished.

I knew it would be better to pass it over with a smile or a joke, but my tension was stronger than my good sense, and I asked her, "What have I just said that was so strange? You were going to say something and then stopped."

"Why should I? You know I always tell you everything I think."

"Have I said something stupid? Or something I shouldn't? Did you want to ask me something? Or to object to something?"

"None of those things."

"Are you cross because I haven't told you everything? OK,

I'll tell you. Last night, at the dinner, I said some stupid things to stupid people."

"I know all about it. So, you don't have to tell me."

"You can't know all of it. Not even Mula Ibrahim knows everything. And why shouldn't I?"

"You're just hurting yourself, that's why. We'll talk about it later."

"Why should it hurt me? I'm saying what has to be said, and I'm saying it now so we won't be silent about it. I didn't know until now in what a menagerie we live."

Only afterward did I notice that I did more swearing in anger than I did narrating, and that I cursed *them* more and more, rather than myself. I defended myself to her by attacking the others. I told her that last night a blind scoundrel and a drunken fool had come together and, in front of the worst scum of the earth, created such a spectacle as the fool would remember as long as he lived. Not because he'd said stupid things, that didn't worry them, but because he'd said what he thought. That was why I called him a fool. They took cruel revenge. Beat me up. Shat on me. Pissed on me. They wouldn't even do it themselves, but sent their servants to do it.

"They killed my father."

"They killed your father; they humiliated me. But OK, I'm grateful. I shall remember. I'll not forget so costly a lesson. But I'm not the only one who won't forget. They make a big mistake if they think Ahmet Shabo's a puppy they can kick whenever they like. I've been a fool once and that's enough! Enough for life! But someone will pay for the lot, one day."

I was preserving my pride before her and before myself, excited and embittered. Maybe it was funny (what could I do to them?), but it was no lie. It was my hurt that spoke.

She didn't think it funny. She listened to me with greater attention than my vague threats, which could harm no one, deserved. Suddenly she looked happy, opened-up, even proud at what I'd just said. She preferred my revolt, vain and false as it was, to my feeling of humiliation and helplessness. Even in the face of everything, she cherished me as I'd been in her dreams. Like a magician, she was putting me together from the broken bits, perhaps even without noticing the cracks.

She touched my hand with her soft fingertips, moved, full of faith.

"I'm glad you've told me all this. I saw how troubled you were, but I thought it was something worse than it is. Don't let what's happened get to you. You've nothing to reproach yourself with. You said what you thought, so what? You haven't stolen, you haven't hurt anyone, you haven't humiliated yourself, you just said frankly what all honest people think. They've beaten you. You'll get over it. They'll hate you. Well, we'll hate them. We need nothing from them. We'll go on living in poverty as we have till now, but with our heads high. You're better and braver than any of them. They're not worth your little finger. They're better than you only in doing evil. And yet, much as I love your bravery, it frightens me. You're a dampened fire. One can hardly see it, but when it flares up, it's hard to put out. Promise you'll be careful, for my sake."

"It's not bravery, it's anger."

"No matter. Promise me."

I didn't know where she found all these wonderful qualities in me, qualities which I neither dreamt of nor desired. But why spoil her naïve picture of me? Why shouldn't I appear to her as she saw me? I'd be her pride and her defense. Bad as I was, I'd uphold her faith in me, since this was her need. I'd pretend to be the mighty oak tree sheltering her fragile stem.

It would seem that our lives are truly a dream.

But, here's the wonder, I believed in her words myself. I'd no idea what I was before, but last night I'd matured, as if I'd lived through many years. I'd gained valuable experience, and I wouldn't fall into a trap again. And let others beware of me.

Without saying a word to her, neither telling her how healing her words were nor how much her unreasoning trust had strengthened me, I embraced her tenderly, as I used to do once, prior to the events of the night before, without fear or hesitation, washed clean, freed, filled with a new courage.

The days passed, and I neither left the room nor often even got out of bed. I felt ill.

Two days passed, and Mahmut did not come. Nor did Mula Ibrahim.

When I heard Mahmut coughing downstairs in the yard, I told Tiyana to put something on the trunk by the door, something she didn't need.

"I need everything."

"Put a glass."

"We've only got two."

"We'll drink out of one."

She put the cracked one, just in case.

Mahmut entered with a smile, as always, but his cheerfulness was unconvincing, his smile was there solely for us. He looked thin, his hands shook, and he coughed.

"Still in bed?" he asked cheerfully, not wishing to burden others with his problems.

"I don't feel well."

"Where's the pain?"

"Everywhere."

"When the pain's everywhere, it's not dangerous. Here you are, I've brought the rabbit fat. To put on your arm."

He examined my arm, my legs, head, and back, and stood over me with a bright expression.

"You want to have a good rest? OK. I'll take the rabbit fat back, you don't need it, thank God, everything's healing. You've got good blood."

"The thought of getting up makes me sick."

"Because you're not moving. And because you're afraid of

people looking at you if you go out. No way, man! They've plenty of their own troubles. I felt the same, at first. When I came back, they gave me blank looks. Some said, 'I don't think I've seen you for days!' Some not even that. And I'd been away for ten years! I was a bit offended—just like that, as if they'd seen a dog! Then I laughed to myself: Would I have done anything different? Why should I? It's better like that, each going his own way."

Had someone else said this, it might have sounded serious, even sad, but coming from him it was a joke. His clownish expression, and all I knew of him! He vulgarized and ruined everything; what he said, his actions, and himself. I laughed at what he'd said, but someone else, other than Mahmut, would have gained some serious wisdom from his bitter experience.

But when he'd gone, the cracked glass was no longer on the trunk.

Tiyana laughed, although she didn't feel like laughing. She seemed surprised.

"When I hear him cough, we'd better lock the door and keep quiet. This hamster'll take everything," I said, laughing.

But we did nothing of the sort, not once. We'd let him in. He pinched the odd thing, and we hid the odd thing, and we got used to this strange balance of caution and trust, and neither were we annoyed at his taking things nor he that we hid them. But we were taken aback when he brought Tiyana a gift of a gilded cup and a pair of nearly new slippers. God knows where he got them!

"They're from my wife," he said simply, "and she'd like to see you."

He stopped urging me to get up. Let each do according to his taste.

And I would sometimes get up, just in order to walk about the room, and then lie down again. I was really quite weak.

Ten days later, Tiyana said, "Isn't it time you went out?"

Mula Ibrahim did not visit us. No doubt he was too busy. We ate the oranges, when they were half bad.

"I'm still ill," I protested.

But she retorted with unexpected decisiveness, in that special female manner that doesn't hurt but doesn't give in. "You're not ill, you're just nursing your anger. But you *will* become ill in this heat. Go out, go for a walk, talk to people."

Angrily, I got dressed and went out, indignant as though driven from a bed of sickness. What a bitch she could be! Nursing my anger! And no doubt she was thinking I was scared to go out.

Unfortunately, she was right. That's what irritated me.

The spring air, full of the clinging scent of rising sap, intoxicated me. My head spun, as though I were drunk, as if I were back in that hateful night. My legs dragged. I was too hot in my winter shoes, and it was a long time since I'd been on my feet.

I was ill, but what of it! I'd fall down in the street, and they'd carry me home to bed, where I'd lie, with closed eyes, pale, exhausted, without a word of reproach or complaint.

But I didn't fall. The legs were ever firmer, and the breath came more surely. It was a fine day. I hadn't realized that spring was so far advanced. Nobody looked at me; there was no surprise, no questions.

Why hadn't Tiyana made me go out before?

A flock of pigeons occupied the whole street, not giving a damn for people, unafraid, refusing to run away, and I had to watch out not to trample on these feathered pests. "Bugger off, you little devils," I said without irritation. "Are you going to drive us off our own streets?"

And there were children there, too. They were surrounding old Mehmed-*aga* Chaluk. He, as usual, was wearing his coat of yellow fox skin. He was casting small coins around him, and the children were laughing, screaming, thrusting with heads and shoulders, like sparrows at grains of wheat, and then returning to follow the old man, and he, with a smile, with his white hand, sowed the worthless coins to his own and the children's joy. He was the ruler who gave, and they the subjects who received. But he lost nothing by his openhandedness, nor did they win by their desire for gain. And this colorful, crazy, childish suite offered cheap amusement daily to itself and to others who became part of the smell and light of the town, of its wondrous childishness.

Why had the old man and the children annoyed me once? Now I looked at them with a smile.

I stopped in front of our shop. In the window the sultan's picture was larger, finer, in a gilt frame. And the inscription was of a more serious nature, written in elegant calligraphy: "The beloved of Allah, our Lord."

I smiled and said to him, "Good morning, my Lord. From now on we shall meet every day."

He, too, smiled, I thought, being neither severe nor ridiculous, as he was before.

Now I understood how dear this shop was to me and how necessary. Miserable as it was, narrow, low-built, cramped, poor, it was my own. I sniffed it: It stank. Everything was the same and would always be so. Here was my security.

Mula Ibrahim greeted me kindly, like a friend, though with an expression of gloomy seriousness, as at the funeral of a close relative for whom he had little regard. He was glad, he said, that I'd recovered and that I'd dropped in to see him. He'd asked about me and hoped I'd been told of it.

Yes, thanks, I'd heard. And as to what happened at *hadji*-Duhotina's dinner, I was not to blame. I was rather drunk, rather angry, and, there you are, I said some things I shouldn't have. I regretted it because of him, myself, and because of certain honest people.

"What can one do, these things happen," Mula Ibrahim said sadly.

"Everything's a bit dolled up here, quite festive, in fact." I was trying to be funny: Seriousness had passed by on heavy feet, leaving behind it an awkward silence.

He didn't take the joke. "We've changed a bit," he said, "done some repairs, added some space. As much as we could."

The other half of the shop was partitioned off with boards. I peeped behind them: Two beardless youths pretended to be bewildered and scared.

"I had to take them on," Mula Ibrahim said, "for the sake of the work."

"Is there as much work as that?"

"Thank God, there is."

I laughed, reminding him of his words "Many misfortunes mean bigger earnings."

"Something like that."

"And I? Where shall I sit?"

He blinked his little eyes and swallowed, placing his hands on his narrow chest, as if in pain.

"You? I'm afraid there won't be a place for you."

"What do you mean? I don't understand."

"Well, you see how it is. You were away a long time, and I employed these two. I thought you'd found another job."

"What other job? You knew I was ill."

"How could I know? You didn't come, you sent no word, and customers crowded in, as if they knew I was shorthanded."

Suddenly, it was all clear. I realized what the situation was. Like that clever chap who, when they took his pants down, laid him on the floor, and took up some rods, immediately realized he was going to be flogged!

I could have realized before: He didn't visit me or ask after me, nor did he send for me. It had all been decided long ago, perhaps even the very same evening when it all happened. And I said, quite needlessly, "So, you're sacking me?"

"I'd no intention of sacking you. You can see for yourself how it is."

"It's just as others wanted it to be."

"You didn't come, you didn't send word, customers crowded in."

"As if they knew you were shorthanded. You've said that. I quite understand."

"I'll pay you a week's, no, I'll pay you two weeks' notice, until you find another job."

"Thank you, I don't take charity."

"I'm doing it out of friendship."

"Friendship, don't give me that!"

He held out the money. He'd clearly had it ready.

"Please, take it. You've earned it."

His voice was quiet, strangled, sticky. His wrinkled face strove to retain its calm; his glance lost its confidence. His thin lips drooped as if he were about to cry.

I took the money, and I was free to go. But I still stood there. I stood there and looked at him. My look perturbed him in anticipation of angry words. But I had none. I knew he feared other words, weightier than mine. And I thought: God, what's going on in this man, and what's been going on all these days? He'd been ordered to sack me and didn't dare disobey. Another might have dared, but he didn't. His fear of those stronger than he, no matter in what way, was almost irrational. Like fear of thunder, of earthquakes, of fate, a fear that can neither be explained nor averted. When that fateful word, the command and desire of someone unknown, reached him through the mouth of another, naturally of less importance but still not to be questioned, he must have immediately agreed to my sacrifice. The thunder broke from on high, and distant memories went to the wall. But night came and with it sleeplessness, or was it the day after, or two days, and then, from the tangle of thought, God knows how, God knows where from, I emerged. Perhaps he saw me here, in this narrow shop, bent over appeals and complaints, perhaps leaning over the water, deep in thought, shattered into a thousand pieces, perhaps in the waves of the angry Dniestr, madly dragging at the shell of a boat and the shell of a man, without thought of whether I could save myself.

I'd been anything you like, mad, empty, helpless, cynical, embarrassing, but never his enemy. And now he knew he had to leave me to the current, not daring even to stretch out a hand to hold me. And he knew I was a victim of injustice. And he was the one who was carrying out that injustice. And it wasn't easy for him. No doubt he'd shed no tears about this, but he'd toss in his bed, torturing himself in vain, for all was decided, and he could change nothing, nor did he think of doing so for one moment, not even for the sake of his conscience. But, alas for him, he could not forget me, nor make me out blacker than I was. His hope for justification and consolation was threefold: fate that is stronger than we, his well-timed warning to beware the devil in me, and the hope that in the end I might use insulting words. He'd keep them in his heart, like a magic charm, preserve them in his memory as a cure, in his conscience as a justification, in case he might feel remorse, for man is not master of his actions. Or perhaps it would serve him as an excuse for feeling offended. It would be worth gold to him, those insulting words, that firm ground in which he could entrench himself.

I'd leave him the justification of fate, even though that fate had a name and a surname, and despite the fact that a part of that fate was his own cowardice. I'd also leave him the consolation that he'd warned me beforehand to watch myself and that I hadn't listened to him. Here, indeed, he was in the right. But I wouldn't give him the satisfaction of cleansing himself by my insulting words. He'd not deserved it.

It would seem that I'd greatly disappointed him. All I said was, "I don't believe this was all your doing, Mula Ibrahim."

He looked first at me, then at the partition, behind which other, curious ears were alert. He was really unhappy, not daring to express regret nor to summon enough courage to add a word of wisdom, although a reproach to my stupidity or advice that I should never repeat it might well have earned him recognition from those to whom he gave importance. To myself, I gave him silent credit both for his bravery and for his sacrifice.

"Thank you for everything," I said finally. It sounded pretty spiteful.

And he accepted this quite seriously, thanking God that he'd been able to help me as far as it was in his power. And then he came to a sudden halt, perhaps realizing how comical his words were, and whispered uneasily, "Sorry!"

This was the best his cowardly sense of honor could offer.

And thus, happily, he cast me from his conscience and amicably saw me off into his past.

But for me, it was my first step into the future, a future unknown and, until then, unimagined.

I'd imagined it in this dark shop beside the public lavatories, and now here I was cast out from my pauper's paradise in which the evil stench of the toilets reminded me we were in the center of town, in a good position, and that here I'd always find my miserable twenty-five *groschen* a year. Now they seemed to me as though they were gold pieces.

I'd have to find something else; what, I hadn't a clue, but I'd find it. It was a large world, there was a mass of possibilities, and I was strong enough not to be discouraged by a single failure. We'd manage somehow. And why did my future have to be linked to the scribe Mula Ibrahim's stinking little shop? He'd have left me to the mercy of the current when things were worse for me than now, so probably it was better that the tie between us was severed, when I was not hanging over an abyss.

Good luck, my dear fellow, whom fear makes such an untrusty friend. Hard luck on those poor kids you've employed. You'll be merciless to them: They haven't dragged you out of the flooded river. But perhaps you'll get on well. Nothing holds you together, you mean nothing to one another, and you, Ibrahim, will not be tormented by the memory of another's sacrifice, nor will you live in fear of their possible unreasonable acts. OK, good, they ordered you to kick me out. And you can easily reproach me for all that I did, and it'll all be mad, it can't be anything else, you see that now, even if you did hope that your wise advice would divert me from the wrong path.

And when you're in a good mood, when there's plenty of business, when you've no fear inside you, you might whisper to yourself insecurely that it was all the fault of the devil, the war, and my interrupted youth. And it's a good thing I wouldn't be near you, for I'd give you a rude answer, and that would serve as a belated justification for the injustice that you did me.

But may God forgive you, your petty soul was none of your choosing, it was given to you. You were last in the queue when there were no other, better ones left. Fare you well, man like all other men, who does evil without intending. May God preserve both you and me from those others who plan evil and assign it.

At the water pipe I felt an urge to put my hands under the cold stream. At the mosque I envied the students of the *medrese* who, in their wooden slippers, were going to wash before prayers, merry, full of desire, stupid in their inexperience, happy in their dreams of the wondrous life they believed awaited them. At Morichs' *han* I left the shade of the walls and the tall trees and bathed in the spring sunshine.

"Spring, sun, brightness, weightless thought.
Happy thought lightening the heart,
Happy for no reason,
Thought that has no object . . ."

I whispered these senseless lines. I heard the cooing of a dove in the branches of a tall poplar. Children's laughter filled me with joy. I was sorry for a bird that, frightened, swooped over the roofs. I was a part of all I saw, and I was happy and felt as light as if I were made of air.

Flippantly, or was it cunningly, my heart rebelled against its suffering.

Smiling, I went into the *bezistan*, like a rich young prodigal, and asked them to show me a woman's headscarf.

"For what sort of a woman, young or old?" they asked me.

"Young and beautiful, the most beautiful in town."

Were we courting?

Yes, we were still courting, although she was my wife.

The middle-aged tradesman looked at me pityingly and said, "Come back in a year or so, and let me ask you about courting then."

"I will," I said, and laughed.

And he laughed, too, God knows why. Because of my naïveté or because of his experience?

I took the headscarf to Tiyana to enjoy her pleasure.

"Aren't you at work? Why are you home so early?"

"First have a look at your present, and then we'll talk about it."

It was an eternal pity that I couldn't buy presents every day, all sorts of presents, just to see her eyes gleaming with delight like a child's.

At first, she had no words, then she had too many. She said I was wonderful. Then she said I was mad, and that, perhaps, I was wonderful because I was mad. How could we afford such expensive presents? It would certainly look nice on her. She'd never dared tell me how much she'd wanted just such a headscarf. How did I guess what she was thinking? But really, I hadn't any sense. I ought to have bought myself shoes. One must have shoes, but one can do without a headscarf, though she had to admit she loved it.

And so she went on in a circle, going from delight to common sense and back.

I laughed.

"And now let me tell you why I'm home so early. It's because I missed you, because it isn't early, because it doesn't matter even if it is early, and if it's early for you and important to you that it's early, then you're not glad to see me."

She laughed too.

"OK, I know you're daft. And now tell me what's happened."

I told her that nothing had happened today. It had all happened earlier, only we knew nothing about it. And so, why should we worry about it when it had all happened anyway?

Imitating Mula Ibrahim, his long neck and hunched shoulders, the blinking of his tiny eyes and his timid withdrawal of his thin hands from his long sleeves, like two young weasels peering out at the world, intently sniffing and withdrawing at the first sign of danger, I said, in Mula Ibrahim's quiet voice, "You haven't been in for such a long time, I thought you'd opened a shop, or that you'd found a better job."

And I replied that I hadn't made up my mind yet. They'd offered me several positions but nowhere stank as much as in his shop, and I'd got so used to it that I should always pass by there, to inhale it.

"Well, all right, it means . . . ," she said laughing, but not so happily.

"It's not all right, but it does mean," said I, laughing too.

She stopped playing, looked at me uncertainly, and said in a serious voice, "But what are we going to live on?"

"If my abilities aren't sufficient, I'll carry water to the ghetto! Why worry about what we're going to live on?"

Unfortunately, her absent smile, with which she hid her fear, told me that my cheerfulness had in no way deceived her. But I wouldn't give it up, that cheerfulness of mine: We would live! What was so great about that?

And I lifted her up, as one would a child, gently shackling her with both my arms, feeling her warm and rounded form close to me. I caressed her with my chin and cheeks: She was so young. I smelt her, as I would a flower: Her smell was pure and loving. The most beautiful woman in town, I'd said. And so she was, and not only in this town. And I knew I could do anything in life. How could life be hard, with her? And I whispered incoherent words of love.

And she clung to me like a frightened puppy to its mother's teats, hiding her face from life, from fear, tiny like a toy, silent, like a dream.

Was she thinking of her murdered father?

I held her in my arms, her and that third one that was living off her blood like a small vampire. I rocked her, ever so slowly, to separate her from the world, from fear, from ugly memories, so that there was only me, all around her, infinitely, like the sky, like the sea, to swamp her with the tenderness that boiled within me like water in a spring.

Don't be afraid, I said.

I love you, I said.

Who can hurt us, I said.

And I felt myself Lord of the earth, holding a pregnant woman in a hot room above the local bakery.

This feeling of rapture lasted for days, not, indeed, as surely as that day when I laughed at the misfortune that had overtaken me, for I didn't know what else to do, but at least sufficiently for me bravely to seek some solution, some way out, among all the possibilities that existed in the world. And that they did exist, people were a living proof. Somehow, they managed to live. And that's all I wanted. I knew the old sayings:

> There's nothing a man can't do.
> For every sorrow there's a consolation.
> The last deed counts.
> It's all a nine-days' wonder.

These and a lot more. And I believed them. Everything depended on me.

At first, I even managed to find the odd person who could help me. But it all ended absurdly.

Mula Ismail, a local leader, who represented the people of our *dzhemat*, received me so politely that I thought he'd taken me for someone else. But then I realized that he hadn't taken me for anybody, he didn't even know who I was, nor could he have heard of me, no matter how hard I'd tried. For him, politeness was a habit, his job. And so he was polite to all, since he couldn't know everybody, nor did he need to, while politeness would be remembered, even if things failed. What also surprised me was that he didn't ask me why I'd come nor what it was I wanted. He said he was glad to see me and that he'd always be glad to see me, although I could no way unravel why he should be so glad. And then, without pause, giving me no time to say a word, he went on to speak of various "issues." The issue of the war that couldn't be waged without unity. And the fact that we were losing in Romania and Russia; this was not due to the weakness of our Muslim army, but to disunity among our generals and the absence of God's aid. And then he addressed the "issue" of lack of respect for the faith, the authorities, and for people of rank. For instance, people didn't even respect *pashas, ayans, ulemas*, nor even *kadis*. Such debauchery was a sign of the plague to come. Indeed, as the Book says, a red sunset, when it appears from the north, foretells both plague and war. And snow, when it falls out of season, as it did last year when it snowed on the twenty-fourth of August, that also foretells plague. And when the dogs howl a lot while the *muezzin* calls from the minaret. And when the children shout abuse at Jews and Christians. And when too many children are born. And when people become too greedy. And so, everything points to plague, to war, to disasters, which wasn't so silly, for disasters constantly happen, and even if they can't be averted, at least they can be explained, and that solves half the problem. And the other half scarcely depends on us.

Neither wars, nor the disunity among generals, nor the causes of plague interested me, and I began to lose my cool: How long would this mindless blather go on, a day, a month, a year, an eternity? Would he, even as a skeleton, go on rattling his dry jaws before another skeleton, mine? Would he, if I didn't stop him?

Perhaps he didn't even realize I was there. Perhaps he thought I was somebody, God knows who, who'd been listening to him yesterday, last year, always, always the same one, only with a different name, faceless, insignificant, like a string of prayer beads.

All that mattered was what he was saying, careless of who was listening.

"Forgive me for interrupting," I said, gathering my courage, which had begun to desert me. "I've come to ask a favor."

"By all means," he replied politely. "And disobedience is a symptom of plague."

I knew this already: Love, hatred, life itself, were all symptoms of plague.

I felt sick.

"I'll come back tomorrow, if you're free. To see whether you can help me with your advice or recommendation."

"Yes, there are things the human mind can grasp only with difficulty. When the brothers Morich were strangled there was an earthquake in Sarajevo, and when the grand vizier Sirhan-*pasha* died, a large meteor flew over the town."

God help us, this representative of the people dwelt in a worse wilderness than a Bedouin. The desert was not only around him but inside him.

"Mula Ismail, it would appear that I've not put things clearly. I'm in trouble, and I'd be glad if you'd hear me out."

"And I recall numerous such omens. They occur by God's will and we cannot understand them."

Merciful God, this Mula Ismail was utterly deaf!

But the real trouble was that he was unaware of it. Or didn't wish to be aware of it. All he wanted was to hear himself speak. What could he hear from other people? Troubles, complaints, reproaches. What good would that do him!

I felt like making a joke, if only to have my own say, whatever came into my head, so he could have his say and I mine, and we'd chatter on happily about nothing in particular, like human beings. But I was afraid he might appear in my dreams, as a nightmare, at a time when I was least prepared for jokes, and that I'd go mad with fear. The humorous and the dreadful can be close relatives.

He fell silent as soon as I turned away. It would seem that his speech stopped the moment he ceased to see surprise on another's face.

Then I got the sort of opportunity I wouldn't have dreamt of in my wildest dreams. Mysteriously and importantly, Mahmut Neretlyak announced that the *defterdar* of Bosnia, Bekir-*aga* Djugum, would see me. I thought he was having me on or making up the whole thing so as to boast of his nonexistent connections. It seemed to me as fantastic as if the grand vizier himself had summoned me.

To reassure me, he said in a whisper that this was no great wonder. His wife had once been married to the shoemaker Titsa, but, when Titsa died, she'd married him, Mahmut. While he was in exile, she was helped by her former brother-in-law, Salko, also a shoemaker and a good man. This Salko, the shoemaker, had an aunt, Almasa Mechkar, and her son, known as Little Husein, worked as an apprentice to the barber Ahmetaga Choro, and Ahmetaga Choro used to shave the *defterdar* Bekir-*aga* Djugum. And so from one to another my name reached the *defterdar* and he said that he'd see me. So it was really quite simple.

After this complicated account, which I couldn't repeat twice the same, and I'm sure I've got it wrong now, it all looked less likely than ever. And even if it were true that a barber could persuade such a great man to receive someone unknown to him, it was laughable to imagine my name passing through so many ears and mouths, and God alone knows in what guise it reached the *defterdar*.

Given that each one added his mite to the story, I might

end up as the well-known scholar Birgivi. And what the *defterdar* would get would be the insignificant scribe Ahmet Shabo, who wouldn't know how to string three words together properly, so that both I and the *defterdar* would find ourselves in a quandary: I, because I'd betray my false reputation, and he, because he'd quickly see that I was unworthy to be even the servant of one of Birgivi's apprentices. Luckily, this was certainly a product of Mahmut's imagination, and I'd no need to tremble at the thought of such an unthinkable encounter.

But when Mahmut told me that the *defterdar* expected me in two days' time, following afternoon prayers, and recommended that I be on time, since Bekir-*aga* was a busy man and who knew when he might find time to receive me again, I once more realized that I knew nothing of life.

Unfortunately, or fortunately, for I'm not at all sure whether all this would have led to good or evil, the following day the old and sick vizier Muhsinovich died. And only some two hours after the vizier, the *defterdar* Bekir-*aga* Djugum, till then healthy, strong, and indefatigable, died also. He died of grief for the vizier. There could hardly be a greater proof of a subject's loyalty. I might mention in passing, however, that such loyalty, moving though it may be, may prove dangerous, and the event that I recount shows how harmful it would be were the people to follow the example of their leaders.

Thus failed my appointment with the *defterdar*, which he made, not supposing that the day before it his master would die, so I've no right to feel aggrieved, since duty comes before courtesy. We did, indeed, meet at his funeral, and that's better than if he'd come to mine.

His successor, who came with the new vizier, was not shaved by Ahmet-*aga* Choro and so the unlikely chain could no longer carry my name anywhere.

The rich merchant *hadji*-Feyzo also offered hope, but I ruined that myself. Several times before this, he'd met me with a smile and a kind word, but now he stopped me on the street and told me he knew all about my situation, and invited me into his warehouse for a talk. Behind the warehouse, which was crammed with rich fabrics newly arrived from the East, he led me into a room covered in carpets, with settees along the walls and with thickly curtained windows. He didn't open the curtains to let in the daylight, but lit some candles in silver and copper candlesticks. At once there was a pleasant scent, for the candles, it appeared, were impregnated with aromatic oils. He also lit a grain of incense.

"I love fragrance," he said. "It wards off evil smells. It's the true soul of things. Even the human soul has its fragrance. What is yours?"

"I've no idea."

"Give me your hand."

I stretched out my hand.

He examined it slowly and carefully and, lifting my palm to his nose and widening his nostrils, inhaled the invisible exhalations of my skin. Then he turned my hand over and almost sniffed it, tickling me with his yellow beard.

"Sensitive," he said, without letting go of my hand. "Introverted, good-natured, cheerful. Perhaps at times impulsive."

I pulled my entrapped hand from his soft palms.

He asked me what I'd like: a drink, *lokum*, fruit? I took some *sherbet* to disperse a drowsiness and a strange feeling, as though I had a slight fever. It was due to the heavy scents, to the silence and the half-darkness, to his soft whispering.

"And now you're looking for work? The best thing is state service. You don't need any special abilities, you don't have to work too hard, you've no worry about making a loss, and you get as much profit as you've the wit to acquire. But there's a problem. You've offended them."

"I know."

"They've a long memory. They don't forgive insults. They've no mercy."

He spoke of them without hatred, but with an ironic contempt. And not because they were coarse and stank, but because they didn't know how to live. With their pretentious grandeur and their stupidity, they spread around them fear and boredom, repellent both to themselves and to others. Stiff in their torpid clumsiness, they resembled elephants and, like elephants, they could suddenly fly into a fury and destroy everything around them. So he'd always thought of them, with their thick, stiff legs: ill disposed, stupidly vain, ruthlessly vengeful, utterly deaf and blind to everything that was beautiful in life. He compared them with elephants, since elephants were the ugliest of all animals, totally lacking in sense. So when they died it seemed like the end of the world, yet nothing happens. All that happens is that they're replaced by a new set of pachyderms. The world should be ruled by people who know how to enjoy themselves in everything. It would be better for everyone. But that would never be, since such people disliked struggle; it was not enjoyable. There was only one single exception among them, who was not a pachyderm, and that was Dzhemal Zafraniya.

I disagreed. "He'll become worse than all of them. Very soon!"

"You're wrong. He's a wonderful chap. Wonderful! It's a pity you've quarreled with him. In some ways he's rather like you, only you're more beautiful. Do you realize how beautiful you are? They must often have told you."

"I'm as beautiful as an emptied pocket."

"You really are handsome, a real man. There are fewer and fewer of them, unfortunately. How do you like it here?"

"I like it."

"You can come whenever you wish. I'll give you a key, if you like."

From a low table he took a small bottle of scent and put a few drops on his beard and on his hands. He sprinkled me, too, and a heavy oriental perfume almost entirely cut me off, like a wall, from the rest of the world.

"Does Dzhemal Zafraniya come here too?" I asked.

"He does. Often. We're great friends."

"Was it you who got him the job with the *kadi?*"

"I like to help people. Especially my friends. And I'll help you."

"And does Zafraniya know how to enjoy himself?"

"He does. Indeed, he does!"

And it was then, only then, as God's my witness, such a fool, such a dope was I, it was only then that I realized what I'd got myself into. And at that, not because of my shrewdness, but because it had become obvious. He spoke more and more quietly, in a muffled voice, bringing his face so close to mine that I felt his breath damp and hot, and his hand sought mine and stroked it ever more softly.

I saw that things were getting serious, and they were none of my making, and I thought: Should I strike him across his trembling chops, so he'd remember the day he brought me into his stinking lair? Or should I get out of it without a quarrel, safely? I'd had enough of hatred and conflict.

I got up and asked him to unlock the door, I had to go and see Mula Ismail.

Hadji-Feyzo gave a smile. "He won't help you."

"Isn't he one of your friends?"

"God forbid!"

"And these . . . friends of yours, are there a lot of them?"

"You'll see."

"And do you all help one another?"

"Come and see for yourself. We don't desert one another. Why don't you drop in after you've seen Mula Ismail?"

"I shan't have the time."

"Then tomorrow. By all means. I'll be expecting you."

I glanced around me, fearful lest anyone saw me coming out, yet I'd gone in without a worry.

I looked at the clear sky, to free myself of the flickering twilight, and inhaled deeply, once, twice, thrice, to rid myself of the oily smell. Ugh, I felt dirty. I'd never forget his sweaty palms trembling on my hand. I spread my fingers, letting the air dry them.

But to hell with him, it had nothing to do with me.

Tiyana immediately caught the scent of rose oil. I was spreading it around me as if I were an open bottle. She frowned.

"You smell funny," she said suspiciously.

"Let it be, woman. I nearly got raped."

"So I see."

I told her what had happened and tried to make a joke of it. She looked at me in amazement. You must have dreamt it, she said. She couldn't accept that such things happened, and no way could I make her believe me. She knew I wasn't lying, but it sounded like a lie or like a bad joke. My efforts were in vain. She suspected that the source of the perfume was no *hadji*-Feyzo with his beard, but some unknown girl called Feyziya. "Unfortunately, that's not the case," I said, laughing. But my statement of the truth seemed to her to be far-fetched, even though my far-fetched truth might well have seemed easier for her than her imagined truth. I didn't need either. Only it was wrong that honest folk should be suspected just because others were bad. One might well have thought that it was better to be suspected for something one had done wrong than to be suspected for nothing. But Tiyana rejected even this intelligent conclusion and said it was better to come home not sprinkled with perfume.

And there you are, those were my only three opportunities, which, in fact, were not opportunities at all, but just false hopes, about as reliable as a cloud in the sky. Afterward, I didn't even get this.

I went from office to office, from one man to another, but I got nowhere. Nobody was ever available. Minor officials heard me with boredom and disinterest, with blank looks, without even malice.

I spent hours sitting in waiting rooms, but those for whom I was waiting never appeared. They'd either crept in through the window or flown in like birds or were invisible, or perhaps there was some secret underground entrance that defended them from those of us who existed in a state of waiting.

My words sounded tired, my story tedious. People were bored at the sight of me. I'd become a man asking a favor, the lowest form of life on earth. There's nothing lower.

Gradually, despite my efforts to avoid it, I began to feel a wall around me, invisible but impenetrable. It stood there like a fortress, without exit or approach. I was constantly beating my head against a brick wall. I was battered, bloody, covered in lumps and bruises, but I didn't cease trying. For there always seemed to be a way round it. There had to be a crack somewhere; it couldn't all be wall. And I wouldn't give in to being walled up like this, as if I were a living shadow whom none could see but who saw all. Who talked in vain, shouted in vain, unheard, a nothing. It didn't need much before they'd begin walking through me, as if I were made of air, or wading through me, as if I were water.

I felt fear. How could they have killed me like this? I was not wounded, no one had killed me, I was not dead, but I didn't exist. "For God's sake, people, can't you see me?" I'd say. "Can't you hear me?" I'd say. But my face did not enter their vision, nor my voice their ear.

I did not exist.

Or was I dreaming this impossible situation that defied experience? For I was alive, I moved, I knew what I wanted. I refused to be nonexistent. They could beat me, shut me away; they could kill me; hadn't they killed enough people for no reason at all? But had they made a ghost of me? Why had they deprived me of my ability to fight?

I wanted to be a man! Let me fight like a man!

Useless!

The empty space around me grew ever emptier, my ridiculous rebellion ever quieter.

CHAPTER 6

A STRANGE SUMMER

SUMMER CAME HOT AND HEAVY.

It was as if the sun were melting, madly belching fire, casting hot sparks upon the earth.

The bakery furnace downstairs also went mad, turning our little room into a hell.

Around noon, it seemed as though both heaven and earth would burst into flame and everything would become a fiery desert.

At night, we'd lie on the narrow wooden veranda facing the courtyard. The shadows of our strange neighbors moved in the insecure darkness. The stamp of horses' hooves came from the stall at the bottom of the yard, which was like a *han*.

Unknown people came and went, going about unknown business, leaving behind them a sense of unease.

"Don't be afraid, go to sleep," I'd comfort Tiyana when she woke.

"I'm not afraid," she'd whisper, but her eyes followed the faceless night shadows.

One morning, we noticed that the withered leaves of a wild apple tree, the only tree in our yard, had been attacked by some caterpillars. During the day, they'd spun a web over its stumps, but the local children, with the aid of stones and sticks, had removed this decoration from the dead tree.

In the neighboring gardens the caterpillars had multiplied

to such an extent that they'd covered, with their webs, both the yellow and the black plums, as well as the dried grass on the parched earth. It looked as if the fruit trees had blossomed anew or that there'd been a fall of snow. Within a few days the web covered yards, streets, windows, and sofas. An infinite army of caterpillars had begun to occupy the town.

People were leaving their houses and fleeing, laden with their household belongings, as though from a fire or a flood. They'd halt at the first caterpillar-free spot, as if in a refuge, and, sighing, look back at the ashen orchards and ravished homes.

Is there any disaster that man does not have to bear!

The caterpillars bred with incredible speed, as though intent upon a rapid conquest of the whole earth. Before our eyes they grew in clumps of tiny, voracious animalcula, which constantly gnawed, chewed, destroyed, enmeshing trees in their fine web, sealing up houses, covering the ground. People retreated to the bare rocks, to die of hunger and fear.

A miserable lot, we people, helpless in the face of everything, I thought fearfully, hiding my feelings from Tiyana. But after a day or two I was surprised at my fear: The caterpillars perished, almost at the same time, every one of them, as if by agreement. All that remained were their dried corpses, which the heat turned to dust, and all that was left was our amazement.

People returned to their homes and, disgusted, removed the withered webs.

And then the forests around Sarajevo took fire.

Mahmut Neretlyak invited me to climb a hill, above the town, so we could witness this wonder too. For this he had two main reasons: first, to stretch his legs, since of late he had been increasingly troubled with cramp in his calves, and, second, he'd thought up some new business, namely to write prayer-charms for the peasants of the village of Podgrab, since they had no *hodja*.

"These bugs have frightened everyone," he said, explaining his reasons, "and they'll need prayer-charms against everything. And I happen to know some charms against fear, spells, and sickness. It won't hurt them, and it'll help me."

We climbed slowly, taking long and frequent rests, because of Mahmut and his ailing legs, even though he said he felt better when he took a walk and slept the better for it. It was all the same to me. I was young, healthy, used to walking in my pursuit of nonexistent work, and the change was welcome. I'd get tired in a different way from down there in the town and forget my troubles.

We stopped by every spring and under every shady tree or anywhere else, whenever Mahmut's legs began to give in.

But if his legs betrayed him, his tongue didn't. He talked constantly, picking up what he'd begun, the moment we'd sat ourselves down and got our breath. He talked of all and sundry, of the people we'd met, of Tiyana, of me, of his wife. He talked to make up for the time he'd been silent, during his exile, and here, while he was on his own, for now he had a friend to listen to him.

His talk was not without interest. He'd been through much and his words were ripe with experience and suffering, but it was all jerky, patched up with fragments of stories that in no way held together, but intruded one into the other, each with its own flow and its own motive. His memories did not present a linked chain, but came in bits and pieces, a broken and scattered mosaic, nor did he make any effort to assemble them. And he sought no meaning, no message, no rounding of his story. For him the event, such as it was, was sufficient. What more could one want?

Strangely enough, he was most coherent when he spoke about his wife. He returned to this subject several times, at several of our stops, without any digressions. It was the first time he'd ever spoken to me about his wife. At first I laughed, it was so unwonted, but then I listened in wonder to this very strange statement of love.

"She's ugly now," he said, "but when she was young, she was even uglier, only in a totally different way." Once her large teeth had protruded under the skin of her thin face; now all she had left were a few stumps, between her double chin and the fat of her cheeks, so that she looked as if she were always smiling. One knew she wasn't, but her teeth, sticking out as they did, didn't let her look nasty, even when she was belching poison. And she didn't like showing them, for she knew they weren't exactly beautiful, so that most of the time she kept quiet. So it was, for as long as he wanted, but should he wish to see her involuntary smile, all he had to do was make her angry so she'd talk. Then she'd make up abundantly for her silence, without a care for her beauty, and he'd listen with enjoyment to her juicy words, ever dominated by the three thrusting surfaces of her upper teeth, resulting in a form of cheerful abuse. What she said rarely made sense, but this didn't matter, because this didn't put him to shame. And then again, he had to admit, she was smarter than he was, and that was usually the case, only he admitted it where others didn't. Whatever they were, women were wiser and better than men. One shouldn't tell them that, but, between ourselves, men were stupid, vain, conceited, worthless. It was amazing how women put up with us. This he knew from his own case. What had he not got into, but she was there waiting, always, as if he'd just been to the mosque. There were no two ways about it, they were better than we. For example, I was intelligent but, no offense, Tiyana was more intelligent than I and in every way superior. Indeed, his wife was not like mine, but then I'd been luckier than I deserved, but still his was not too bad. She wasn't very tidy, but then what had she got to be tidy with? Nor was she very good at saving, but then what had she got to save? She was bad-tempered, but then he was often not at home, so it didn't worry him. She was bad-tempered if he went out or if he stayed at home, so he chose to do what he liked. And no matter what he did, he knew he'd find her at home, waiting for him, useless as he was, for them to continue the life that God had given them. No, truly he wouldn't replace her with any other woman.

His conclusion was somewhat unexpected, or perhaps it wasn't, for it stemmed from his recognition of her modest virtues as much as from his own imperfections.

I was cheered by this clumsy, yet calm acceptance of what life offered.

Was it wise not to expect much either of ourselves or of other people?

Was it a loss or a gain were we to learn truly to evaluate both ourselves and others?

The loss lay in our demanding so little, but the gain lay in our not asking more.

I said, "The world's made up of imperfect people."

"What did you say?"

"I'm thinking up a poem."

"How do you do it? Can I hear?"

> "The world consists of imperfect people.
> All else is lies.
> Or death.
> The perfect people are in the grave.
> But they are no longer people."

"Is that about me?"

"About everyone."

"My God, that sounds marvelous! Even I know that people aren't perfect, but when I say it it's as if I've said nothing. But in a poem it sounds, somehow, sad. And beautiful. 'The perfect people are in the grave. But they are no longer people.' But with the living, there's either rather more evil or rather more good, and at times there's more of the one or more of the other. Most often more of the evil."

"Look!" I cried, pointing to the smoke and flames. "Everything's on fire!"

"Yes."

We'd already been aware of smoke and a heavy smell of burning, but now we saw that the forest was on fire as far as one could see. For some distance, across the broad valley, one could hear the fire hissing and crackling, angrily bursting out of the huge skein of smoke that enveloped both forest and sky.

"Sad," said Mahmut.

Why sad? Dreadful, perhaps, but sad? No.

I watched, entranced, this senseless fury, mindless power, enmity without hatred. I wondered in horror at this distraction, as though it were a game, due to an excess of energy, and I felt no regret, perhaps because it wasn't human.

Yet, perhaps, it was not very different from human. The dread raging, its devastating destruction without malice, as in a war with weapons, or a war without weapons.

The fire was senseless and destructive, like hatred.

And so, my thought descended to earth, like a tired bird.

"Sad," said I, too, thinking of the dead forest of blackened trees that this madness would leave behind it.

As my comrades had been left in the woods of Chocim, like all innocent people, in the flames they, themselves, had not kindled.

So, tired, I sat down beside Mahmut, whose legs had long ago let him down.

And then I noticed that he was no longer looking at the fire.

Turning in the direction of his surprised, bewildered, and frightened gaze—I don't know how to describe it—I saw on the road, near the forest, an armed horseman. He was watching us in silence.

"Who's that?" I asked Mahmut.

He didn't answer, but stared intently at the horseman.

I got up so as to get a closer look at the stranger.

Slowly, he drew a pistol from his belt, leaning on his saddlebow, without aiming the gun in our direction.

I stopped.

"Are you enjoying this?" the horseman asked, pointing toward the flaming forest.

Mahmut gave a timid smile. "People were talking about it, and my friend said let's go and see."

"There's plenty to see."

His voice was calm, almost quiet, somehow absent, as though we were of no importance, yet still he looked at us intently.

And I looked at him, amazed at the richness of his equipment and at the beauty of the horse he was riding.

"Is that an Arab horse?" I asked admiringly.

He made no reply to my friendly question, but merely continued to examine us with his severe gaze.

"And you've climbed up here just to look at this catastrophe?" he said in the same calm voice. "I don't believe you're such fools."

"So, my friend," I said angrily, "no one told us we had to ask permission. But if you want to be insulting, it's no great problem, you've got a pistol."

"I'm insulting nobody. And it's all the same to me why you've come here."

"We were on our way to Podgrab. To write out prayers for the villagers," Mahmut explained humbly.

"Well, you'll not be going to Podgrab today. You'll be going back to town. And tell the *serdar*-Avdaga not to send any more spies after me."

"What spies, for God's sake!" Mahmut cried.

"Such as you."

"And who sends him this message?" I asked.

"Bechir Toska."

"You are Bechir Toska?"

"I am. You've heard of me?"

"I've heard."

"Good or bad?"

"Good, Bechir-*aga*," said Mahmut with a polite smile, showing his yellow teeth.

Here the luckless Mahmut exaggerated, and all three of us knew it.

"There, you see," Toska said to Mahmut, even then without anger. "Your friend's more honest than you are, even if more of a fool. At least he said nothing, while you, my brother, are lying. Now go, and don't look back!"

We didn't wait for him to repeat his command, which freed us from his presence. Mahmut had quite forgotten the cramp in his legs and leapt up like a youngster, and we both hastened in the opposite direction, seeking to put as much distance as possible between us and Toska and his pistol.

By the time Mahmut began to breathe heavily and to stumble on the uneven path, Toska was far behind, yet still we seemed to see his threatening eyes.

Fear gripped me only after we'd left him.

Toska, the cruel bandit, who neither feared nor spared anyone, had let us go without so much as a threat!

And while Mahmut was catching his breath and calming the rattle in his chest, I began to laugh. Mahmut looked at me in surprise and, more with signs than with words, inquired what the matter was and why I was laughing.

"Just think," I said through my laughter, "what a miserable pair we are. Even the terrible Toska took pity on us. He was careful not even to raise his voice in case we shat ourselves with fear. The man looked at us and nearly wept with pity. And all you could say was 'We've heard only good of you!'"

Mahmut began to laugh too.

"Well, what was I supposed to say? That I'd heard bad things about him? No way!"

"I know you couldn't say that, but it's still funny."

"Funny, yes. But then again, it isn't."

"And what do we say to the folks in town? They'll laugh at us."

"What shall we say? Nothing. I don't give a damn if they laugh at us. Who cares about that? I'm only scared they may suspect something different. Who'd believe we met Toska just by chance and that he'd let us go without a word?"

"It sounds a bit strange to me, too."

"So don't say a word about it. We saw no one and we've nothing to tell anybody. Mum's the word. Such are the times."

I agreed that this was the wisest course.

Yet it's one thing to know what is wisest and quite another to do what is wisest.

Mahmut knew it was best to keep silent, so at once he went and told the whole thing to the *serdar*-Avdaga.

Avdaga sent for me.

I could have crossed myself in amazement, sought for any rational explanation. I could have been angry, but none of this would have helped me understand it. It seemed Mahmut always did the opposite of what he thought. Or he was incapable of not saying what he knew. It was too important for him to keep quiet about, even if it brought him trouble.

Mahmut couldn't enlighten me.

"I don't know what came over me," he said in a scared voice.

"And what did the *serdar* say, when you told him?"

"He told me to go home."

Why had the *serdar* sent for me?

I didn't know much about Avdaga. Nor did any of the people I asked. Or they didn't want to say. They shrugged their shoulders, waved the question aside. There was a sort of mystery surrounding him, one it was better not to mention, as with some great evil. A name and a mystery, that was Avdaga. So it was better not to mention his name at all.

A man is bound to land in trouble if he's friends with such hopeless people as Mahmut, I complained to Tiyana, seeking thus to put my unknown guilt upon another, but she didn't back me up in my effort. I knew what she was thinking: You've been messing about without any need. No one forced you. You couldn't wait for Mahmut to invite you, and I've been sitting at home alone. Don't put the blame on others!

So Mahmut's lack of discretion plunged me into a sea of trouble both with the *serdar*-Avdaga and with my wife and God knew with whom else, if ill luck deigned to take its teeth to me. And the easiest way was to take it out on Tiyana, who was completely innocent, though I could blame her and fall into a hurt silence, pitying myself at finding no sympathy even with my nearest and dearest. But, fortunately, she averted both the anger and the storm. She laughed and at once dispersed my mood. Her laughter was more intelligent than either of us.

"Come on," she said, "what are you worrying for? He heard it from Mahmut, and now he wants to hear it from you. What matters to him is the bandit. What does he care for two idlers who went into the hills to watch a fire!"

This, her ironic encouragement, warmed me all the way to Avdaga, but, faced with Avdaga, I felt a chill in my heart. And not so much because of him, as because of his mystery.

Everything about the man was usual, an almost empty room with whitewashed walls, a floor grease-spotted from the droppings of candles in cheap candlesticks, uncurtained windows, only the most essential and roughest furniture of heavy wood. And he himself was ordinary, quiet, polite, his look bore no menace, as I'd imagined, nor did he scare me with threatening words. He even seemed unsure of himself, thin as he was, with a worried expression and fluttering eyes, which, most of the time, he hid by looking to one side or straight in front of him. And yet, I was uneasy. I felt there was this *thing* of his hovering about him, hidden from me, unknown yet ever present. And this alone mattered. All the rest was unimportant, of no significance, like the clothes he wore.

He didn't ask much about Bechir Toska. He'd heard it all from Mahmut Neretlyak. All he said was that we'd been lucky. We'd had more good fortune than good sense, for

Bechir might well have taken us for spies, and we did well not to quarrel with him, for it might have cost us our lives.

"I didn't quarrel with him. I just asked him not to insult us."

"No matter now. Only thank God you're still alive and light a good thick candle."

And just as I was thinking he surely hadn't summoned me just for this, and a chill pierced me to the heart at the thought of his real reason, which I was yet to hear, something happened that belonged in the naïve stories for children, or even more fantastic than that, as if the wolf had begun to sing like the nightingale. He referred to the poem I'd been thinking out up there on the mountain.

Good God! What would that Mahmut not blurt out!

He said Mahmut couldn't remember all of it, only the first line. The rest of it he muddled up so much that he even laughed himself. It seemed like a complete tangle. "The world consists of imperfect people." What comes next?

It's not a good poem, I replied, scarcely getting hold of myself. Rough, unfinished. Verse shouldn't sound like ordinary prose. Perhaps "People are imperfect—such is the world" would have been better. It needs time to ripen.

"No matter," said the *serdar*. "Let me hear it."

I repeated the poem, even though I thought to do so was ridiculous. What interest could he have in a poem?

Even stranger was the fact that he listened devoutly, with an expression of gratitude, almost with delight.

"Please, let me hear it once again."

Silently he moved his lips, repeating the lines after me.

"Would you like me to write it out for you?"

"I'm no good at reading other people's handwriting. I'm not much good at writing, myself."

Soon he had it by heart and recited it slowly, incompetently, once, twice, three times, with an enjoyment I couldn't fathom.

I asked him, "Do you really like poetry so much?"

"This one I liked, the moment I heard the first line."

And again he began to roll the words over his tongue, listening to their sound, tasting their sweetness, voluptuously sucking the sense from them as one would marrow from a bone. This unusual and unexpected enjoyment of verse raised him in my eyes, especially when the verses were mine. If they could have such an effect on him, it meant they were good. And if he could feel their beauty, then there were values in him that he didn't show to everyone.

I forgot his *mystery*.

"Is that all you do? Write poems?"

"I can't find any work."

"That was your choice. Why complain? You want to say whatever comes into your head. Well, get on with it. Did you expect a medal? You're not such a fool as that."

"I was drunk."

"*In vino veritas*. Being drunk, you gave yourself away."

"Words are just air. What harm can they do?"

"Words are poison. They're the source of every evil."

"Better, then, be silent."

"No need to be silent. There are plenty of things to talk about, without giving offense. One should help, not hinder. It's a matter of the state, of man, of a thousand worries and troubles. You can't arrange your own affairs properly, never mind the affairs of so many people. And then somebody starts to grouse: This is wrong, that is wrong, and all hell's let loose! Of course, it's wrong. It's amazing that anything is ever right: so many people, and everyone out for their own interest. Do you think it's easy for those who rule?"

"It isn't."

"That it isn't. And you attack them! That part's easy, my friend. Let's say, for example, somebody comes to your house and says: You've got everything wrong there. What would you do? You'd be angry and throw him out. And you'd be right."

"That's different. What is mine concerns nobody."

"Oh yes, it's different, the moment it's yours. And what's yours concerns nobody: It does. There, you see, you're wrong. You have to live with people and one shouldn't go against them."

"How do you mean go against them?"

"Well, there you are, you attack them. Why? Everyone will think: He's married a Christian girl."

"Is that a sin, for God's sake?"

"Her father was an enemy of the state."

"If he was, then he paid for it with his life. But I've never even met him. I've never exchanged as much as two words about him with my wife."

"If you're not lying, then it means your wife is hiding things from you. A father can't be forgotten so easily."

"Good Lord, had I died before meeting you, I'd never have guessed what I was guilty of."

"You wouldn't be guilty, if you hadn't upset people. Everyone should look for a small portion of guilt in himself."

"Then I shall be guilty eternally. I can't remove that dead man now, as though he'd never been. Or should I leave the wife I love?"

"Who's asking you to? Only, when a man's at fault, he should watch what he does. Particularly when he is not alone. Why should others suffer because of your foolishness?"

"Is that what you called me for, to tell me this?"

"No. I summoned you because of the poem. All the rest is just by the way, talking, and won't hurt either you or me. A man seems different, until you see him and talk with him alone and without witnesses. I thought you were more dangerous."

And I you, I almost said, so quiet and soft was his voice.

What was there about him that could be so dangerous? Mahmut Neretlyak met me outside on the street, as if by chance, and I knew he'd been waiting for me. He looked at me, furtively testing my mood and expression, trying to guess what had taken place with the *serdar*-Avdaga. I kept silent, as though worried.

"What did he call you for?" he asked, as if by the way, pretending he was asking merely out of politeness.

I stopped and looked at him, frowning.

"He called me because of you. He asked me what you talked about with that bandit."

"What bandit?"

"Now you pretend you don't know. The one for whom both you and I will have to answer. Bechir Toska. And you told me we should say nothing. Now we'll be accused of being Bechir Toska's spies."

I wanted to get back at him, to make him feel the fear I'd felt in front of Avdaga's door.

But I immediately repented my rough humor.

Mahmut regarded me in horror, as if he were drowning.

"I told him what happened," he said in a scared voice.

"But why did you have to tell him?"

"Well, it was Avdaga who sent me to the village to find out whatever I could about Bechir Toska. So how, my dear Ahmet, could he say I was Toska's spy!"

Will wonders ever cease! I'd played a stupid joke, and gained, for my pains, an ugly reality. So that was the meaning of the fire, of the prayer-charms for which we went to the hills!

"Did you really make such an ass of me, Mahmut? And I, like a fool, followed you and your filthy doings!"

"I kept wanting to tell you, but I couldn't, I just couldn't. And I had to go. He didn't ask me what I felt, but just said: On your way! You're the right man, he said, for this job, nobody'll suspect you."

"And he was right. Not even I suspected you."

"So how can he accuse me of being Toska's spy?"

"Are you afraid of the *serdar*-Avdaga?"

"How should I not be afraid!"

"Did he beat you, for that other business?"

"Avdaga doesn't beat anyone."

"Then what does he do?"

"He kills."

Now it was I who began to gasp for air and open and shut my mouth like a fish out of water.

Mahmut washed himself at the water tap, cooling his hands and taking a long drink, trying to regain his lost breath. And, by God, I, too, could have done to have put my head under the water tap to recover.

So this was Avdaga's mystery that drove people to be silent and to dismiss it with a wave of the hand. And I'd recited my silly verses to him, urged on by his polished kindness and understanding, stating that all people were the same, imperfect, and that there was no difference between him and others.

What had my poem achieved? It had served to mask an executioner. And he used it to conceal his bloodstained soul, allowing a fool of a poet like Ahmet Shabo to be his witness and guarantor!

But perhaps there was something else. Perhaps my poem served to confirm his belief that perfect people were to be found only in the grave. While they lived, they were evil.

Oh my poor poem!

Shame and repentance helped me not to be too angry with Mahmut Neretlyak. He'd done an ugly thing because he was forced to, while I'd done one of my own free will.

And so, because of this *serdar*-Avdaga, I began to contemplate what no one had ever solved, but which no one, achieving maturity, ever completely dismisses from their thought: What are we, and what is life, in what webs are we entangled, into what traps do we fall by our own will or against it, what depends on us, and what can we do with ourselves? I was not good at thinking, I preferred life to thinking about it, but no matter how I turned it all over, it seemed to me that most things took place beyond our will, without our decision. Chance decided my fate and the path my life took, and most often I was faced with a fait accompli, and fell into one of the possible currents; only a different chance could cast me into another. I didn't believe in a foreordained path, which I would follow, since I didn't believe that this world had any particular order. We didn't decide, things were decided for us. We were cast into a game full of numberless changes, at one definite moment, when only that situation awaited us, the only one that could await us in the dealing of the cards. You could neither avoid it nor refuse it. It was yours, like the water you fell into. And you'd either sink or swim.

Such conclusions didn't satisfy me, but I could find no other answer. What then was this chaos of ours? Something had to be mine.

I'd not sought the *serdar*-Avdaga. I didn't even know him. He'd turned up at a given moment, without any act of mine, and become a part of my life. I couldn't refuse him, and nobody had asked my consent. It had happened, like everything else happened.

Only how could we consent to such an injustice?

The groove into which I'd fallen didn't please me, so I tried to change my life's path. Every morning I left the house with the hope that one day the stars would be in a favorable position, and I'd come upon someone who would help me. Surely fate had not destined only the *serdar*-Avdaga to cross my path, without the slightest advantage for me.

But I hoped in vain, for the inexplicable punishment continued, and I remained just air, voiceless and faceless. The only people who saw me were those as much in need of help as I, or even more so. The only other to see me was the *serdar*-Avdaga, and I'd rather that I'd been invisible and inaudible to him.

In the early afternoon I went home, like every working man, and found lunch, such as it was, prepared and a wife who was happy and smiling, as though she hadn't a worry in the world. I, young and healthy, was being supported by the sick Mahmut Neretlyak and by my pregnant wife.

Mahmut was teaching Greek to some merchants who'd begun to trade with Salonika. I thought this was another of his games, but his pupils seemed satisfied. They certainly couldn't have expected much, for Mahmut hadn't much to give them. When he brought us money or provisions, he'd make a note of how much we owed him, simply not to offend us.

Tiyana had got some work in the house of the rich Muharemaga Taslidzak, the brother of the *serdar*-Avdaga. (I was to learn later that it was Avdaga who'd found her this work at the request of my former employer, Mula Ibrahim. I didn't know which fact surprised me the more.) Tiyana helped Muharemaga's wife, Rabiya-*hanuma* to dress, spending hours applying creams, trying to make her beautiful. Her years demanded it, and wealth made it possible. Tiyana assured me that, for her, it was more amusement than work and that she found it not at all tiring. She even enjoyed it, not only for the money that she received for doing little, but because it meant she was not alone the whole morning. And it wasn't even far to go, for Muharemaga's orchard was next door to our yard, and one could reach it through a side gate.

Tiyana had been at this strange job for a month or more and then, rather embarrassed, told me something almost unbelievable: Rabiya-*hanuma* had begun an affair. It was neither strange nor unbelievable that Rabiya-*hanuma* should be having a love affair, but she must have forgotten being young: She'd been forty years married to Muharemaga. What was strange and unbelievable was that she'd fallen in love with a young lad who lived with his father, Ibrahim Pakro, in our yard, above the stables. The young Pakro was only twenty-five years of age; Rabiya-*hanuma* was not far off sixty. Her lover might well have been her grandson.

I laughed: Love makes a woman young.

"Only God preserve the man from going mad," said Tiyana disgustedly.

"You and love together have made her young."

"She puts so much powder and rouge on her face that you can't see her skin."

"Lucky for her!"

"And she dyes her hair black."

"What's that to you?"

"All she talks about is him. She's lost all shame, as if she's lost her head. And how can he, a kid like that, do it?"

"She's too old even for his father."

Nobody knew anything about these Pakros, father and son, nor how they made their living. Indeed, one might have said the same thing for most of the people living in our yard, including me. It was said they came from Belgrade, where they'd committed some violent crime, but this was no doubt mere guesswork, since they had nothing to do with anybody. All that was known about them was that they'd been at Chocim, in some unit I'd never heard of.

Tiyana decided to give up going to Rabiya-*hanuma*, since she could no longer bear to see such shame and disgrace. And I immediately agreed with her, first, because I always agreed with her decisions and, second, because I felt one should not tempt the devil by allowing a handsome young man (suddenly I'd come to think of the young Pakro as being very handsome!) to compare a young and attractive girl with an old and bent woman, a painted corpse. Were he blind, this would make him see. Were he a rogue, he might take both the one and the other, each for what they were worth.

I didn't care if he cast an eye on the *hanuma*'s jewelry—in any case she'd give him anything he'd ask for—but I'd have torn his heart out if he touched a single eyelash of my wife's. But eyelashes didn't interest him.

When I said this to her, Tiyana grew angry at my stupid thoughts. How could I imagine such nonsense, and did I think that a man had only to show himself willing to have a woman come running? Men were conceited and dishonest, and there were far more honest women than dishonest ones, and so on and so forth until I admitted that she was in the right, while, in myself, I was happy that I didn't have to worry about what might or might not have happened. I trust you as I trust myself, if not more, but you stay here with me, that will be best! For anyone would have laughed and rejected the idea of an old woman falling in love with a young man as nonsense, but, all the same, that's what had happened. What she'd never done before, she'd done at a time when one could have least expected it.

With people anything can happen.

A few days later the *serdar*-Avdaga met me on the street and asked me why my wife wasn't going any more to Rabiya-*hanuma*. And was it true what people were saying about young Pakro and his sister-in-law?

It would be dishonest of me to say anything about something of which I knew nothing, I said. And how could I know? How could anybody know? It was so unlikely that one would think one was imagining it, even if one did see anything untoward.

"A lot of things seem unlikely, but still they happen."

"I really don't know."

"I'm afraid in case they commit a crime. If you were to say they're dangerous, that they've attacked you, insulted you, or threatened you, we could either lock them up or exile them."

"Who should say this?"

"You and Mahmut."

"They've never given me a dirty look or spoken an ugly word. How could I accuse innocent people?"

"To prevent evil. And they couldn't care less where they live."

"Why don't you talk to your brother?"

"I will."

Is the husband always the last to find out?

But Avdaga didn't find time to talk to his brother. Perhaps he was embarrassed, or perhaps he was sorry for him. Perhaps he hoped the whole business would pass over. Perhaps he was late by a single fateful day.

His sister-in-law's stupid madness brought about a host of disasters, and our humble yard fell silent in fear of a crime, and we held our peace in our small darkened rooms, looking out fearfully at dark windows and thinking of the flitting shadows that passed through.

That night, a Thursday (we always added that whenever we talked about it later—that Thursday night—perhaps because that night was supposed to be dedicated to prayer and quiet contemplation), Rabiya-*hanuma* decided to take care of her husband.

She let her lover and his father, Ibrahim Pakro, into the house and led them to the room where the old Muharemaga was sound asleep. Father and son together stabbed him over and over again, rendering him the mercy of dying in his sleep, without waking even for a second, without, in his last moment of life, seeing either them or his wife and thus feeling neither fear nor hurt, and perhaps not even pain. It remained unclear whether they'd acted in this way for his sake, to save him suffering, or for their own, to stop him crying out, which would have caused trouble both for them and for him, or for his wife's sake, lest Muharemaga die without forgiving her, when forgiveness was no longer possible. They'd been happy together for forty years, so why spoil it at the end? Then they wrapped him in a sheet, so as to leave no trace of blood, and then in a shroud so that he looked like a bale of goods, which they flung across a horse's back, and dumped the body in a well on his estate at Goritsa. When they'd arranged everything, they stabled the horse and returned to their flat over the stable, for they were pretty tired after dragging the heavy Muharemaga.

Rabiya-*hanuma* did not go to sleep immediately. Since

she was a cleanly and tidy woman, she first put Muharema-ga's room in order, putting new pillows on the bed and burning the bloodstained pillowcases in the kitchen stove. After that, she had a bath, said several prayers for her husband's soul, and sat down by the window to wait for the dawn. She was of a sensitive nature and couldn't sleep. She thought and she thought. She'd wait for a month, two at the most, until people forgot Muharemaga, and then, then who knew what sweet dreams she had, this brave lady who, for her love, didn't hesitate to sacrifice her husband's life.

It's none of my business, but I'd like to know what her thoughts were, waiting for that fateful night to pass. Did she think of her long life with Muharemaga? Did she recall all the ugly moments? Had she hated him before? Did she repent? Did she fear discovery? Did she consider that, with his being her husband, she had a right to do with him what she wished? Or did she rejoice at a stone fallen from around her neck, at her liberation from prison, that she'd removed an obstacle on her way to a new life? Or did she think of that new life, which offered her everything that had seemed to have passed her by? The magic of love brought back what had been lost. And she dreamt of her handsome lover who loved her so much that he was ready to kill for her. For such a love and for such happiness, it was worth doing anything, perhaps the deranged woman whispered, frantically clutching at the life that was fading.

The next day she told the servant who came in the mornings and left in the evenings, for the *hanuma* would not have anyone sleeping in the house, that Muharemaga had gone to his estate in Brezik. She repeated this to the lads from Muharemaga's shop, when they came for the keys, and also told them to bring all the day's takings before nightfall, showing yet again how determined and capable she was and how she thought of everything.

The following day in Goritsa, a peasant, a certain Misir-liya, was looking for water, since all the springs in the neighborhood had dried up. He peeped into Muharemaga's well and first smelt and then saw Muharemaga's corpse and rushed headlong to the courthouse to report that he'd found what he was not looking for, and that he'd have preferred to have found water than the dead Muharemaga, and that he was sorry about Muharemaga, he was a good man, and, as for the cattle, he didn't know what to do with them, they'd die of thirst.

The whole courtyard knew at once who the murderers were, as did the authorities. The two Pakros and Rabiya-*hanuma* were arrested and immediately confessed everything.

The father and son stated that they'd nothing against Muharemaga, but there was no other way of getting at his money and, as for the murder, it was like in war, you charge, either to perish or remain alive, and there you are, neither they nor Muharemaga had had any luck. As for them, ill luck had haunted them ever since they came back from the war and that was that.

Rabiya-*hanuma* spoke calmly. It was due to fate and to love, she said, looking at the young Pakro. Perhaps, like so many people, she really didn't feel any guilt.

They stripped her naked and beat her with wet ropes and then, half dead, they hanged her. (I would wake in a sweat, dreaming night after night of her aged body and its leathery, faded skin cut into bleeding furrows.)

The father and the son were strangled, so ending their last charge.

It was strange that the murderers made no attempt to escape, which they could have because of the commotion when the *serdar*-Avdaga and his two assistants, completely by chance and completely unexpectedly, ran into an unknown and armed man in their room. In the chaos and confusion when the man ran off down the stairs, the two of them calmly waited for it to finish and to be led off to the fortress. As for the unknown man, they said they'd known him from Belgrade and that he'd come to them the night before, seeking shelter for a few days. They'd said nothing to him of what they'd done, since they did not want to put themselves into his hands.

It happened at midday.

■ □ ■ □ ■

CHAPTER 7

THE DEAD SON

IT HAPPENED AT MIDDAY.

I was returning home to an unearned lunch, as I did every day, tired from the useless effort I'd put into seeking a way out of the isolation. I'd grown used to seeking and not finding. The one depended on me, the other on I know not whom, and I'd nothing to reproach myself with, and I couldn't be angry at refusals. Once, in anger, I'd have threatened the world with a hatred I didn't feel. I didn't feel it even then. And thank God.

Were I different, were life a burden to me, were I embittered, I might have begun to lose my way, to drink, to hate. I might have become a troublemaker who turned against the whole world.

But I couldn't do this. Despite everything, I lived as did others, who were not branded as I was, happy and sad over ordinary things; happy for the good people who were only slightly bad, sad for the evil ones who were rarely good, happy in a wife who made my life easier and in the child she was carrying. With the child, things would, indeed, be harder, but somehow we'd manage.

That's one of the mysteries of this world: So many people have a hard life, one can't imagine how and on what they manage to live, yet no one starves. I know it's not fair to greet this little creature with the consolation that it won't die of hunger, yet I also know that we never believe in anybody's bad luck and that one always hopes for better things.

I'd been unable to make either great suffering or great thought out of my troubles. It would seem I'd been born for trivialities, like most people, and I wasn't sorry for it.

I was as honest as I could be. I wished nobody any great harm. I'd have preferred to love people more than pity them, and I prayed to my good fortune that everything that didn't concern me might pass me by.

My prayers were not answered.

That day I was returning to the one place on earth that was mine, carrying a carnation that I'd found on the street, crushed and soiled, but I'd washed it at the water tap and carefully smoothed its petals, so as to delight Tiyana with a cheap gift.

No sooner had I left the sunlight and entered the shady carriage way that led into our yard than I saw a strange man leap from the staircase of the house in which the Pakros lived and run into the stable under the house. He led out a horse and mounted it at full gallop. A police guard rushed to get in the horse's way but quickly leapt to one side, and he acted wisely, for the horse would have crushed him.

The horse galloped for the carriage way and the rider, bent over in the saddle, drew a pistol from his belt.

I clung close to the wall, thanking God that I was thin and that I'd probably not be crushed. And then I forgot the clatter of the horse's hooves and the pistol in its rider's hand, for guns began to fire from the yard, aiming at the runaway, and I was seized with a fear that I alone would be the victim of this reckoning that was not my concern. Bullets whistled in front of my nose, like angry, invisible bumblebees, missing both me and the rider. And never had I been so glad at anybody's incompetence as then, not for the rider's sake, but for my own.

The police guards ran toward the exit, trying to make up

for their errors, but the *serdar*-Avdaga called them back. No doubt this was because of the two Pakros, to make sure they didn't run away as well.

I saw the unknown horseman had got away and the police guards returning, and I knew it was all over, yet I still stood there, hugging the rough wall.

It was rather shameful, that mental and physical paralysis, that fear that drove the blood from my heart, but of this I thought only later, not then. For God's sake, who wants to be killed?

Detaching myself from the wall that sheltered me to the side where there was no danger, I went into the yard.

The Pakros were still standing on the stairs, and the police guards were approaching them to lead them off, as though they didn't know how to walk without their help.

Why hadn't they run away?

The unknown man had run away. Fate hadn't been on his side. He'd been overtaken by events not of his making. What didn't concern him was near to costing him his life (no doubt he was not without guilt), but he'd spat at fate, shattered the chain of coincidence that had pressed him.

I would think about all this when I'd more time.

Avdaga stood in the middle of the courtyard, deep in thought.

"And you didn't want to tell a lie," he said, as I came up to him. "And look what disasters you'd have prevented!"

Was he putting the blame on me?

His voice was rough, more sad than reproachful.

It seemed to me he was right! I'd never thought that a lie could avert evil.

But what if there hadn't been any evil? The shame of a lie would have remained, as well as repentance for the evil done to people who'd done no evil.

The *serdar*-Avdaga saw evil everywhere, and he was often right. I didn't, and I was right, too. But what is to happen cannot be prevented. If they put everybody in jail, there wouldn't be any crime. But no life, either. I hated crime, but I preferred life, even with crime, to a living death.

But how was I to say this to him, when it wasn't even clear to me? Nor could he, struck by the death of his brother, which had confirmed in blood his grim thoughts about people, accept any other reason than that of hatred.

I said, feeling really sorry for him, "I'm sorry, Avdaga. Truly sorry."

Without a word, Avdaga followed after the guards who were leading the Pakros away.

At that moment Mahmut Neretlyak came up to me in a state of agitation.

"Didn't you hear me calling?"

"What's the matter?"

"It's all right now, but your wife's lost her baby."

"How can that be all right, you fool!"

"It's not all right, but it could have been worse."

"How's Tiyana?"

"The women are with her."

I hurried home. When I'd entered the yard, I'd been carrying the flower as a gift; now I didn't even know where it was. I'd lost it long ago, looking at the disaster of others, ignorant of my own.

Mahmut gave a muddled explanation of how he'd come to look for me and how Tiyana had suddenly been seized by pains and he'd run off to fetch some of the women from the neighborhood and how, when they'd driven him out of the room, he'd seen me in the yard and called to me, but I'd been staring at what didn't concern me and so didn't hear him. And, perhaps, it made no odds; the women would have driven me out, just as they had him.

"Why didn't you come for me?"

"I was afraid of the shooting."

When I knocked, one of the women peeped through the door and snapped at me, "Wait!"

We waited, I looking at the door beyond which my wife

was suffering, Mahmut at the yard, where he daren't descend because of the firing.

Now, after the event, he seemed excited at all that had happened and spoke in bursts, scarcely linking one thought with another, or so it seemed to me, for my own thoughts were in no great order.

"There you are, that's life for you, my dear Ahmet. Some sow tares and get wheat, others scatter pure seed and get nothing. . . . Those two were led off like lambs, why they didn't make a run for it, God knows. . . . But you mustn't let it get you down. You're both young. Whether you'll always have bread, I don't know, but I do know there'll always be children. . . . But then, you know, not even bread's the most important thing. Look at that Muharemaga Taslidzak, he'd loads of it and of everything else, but his wife didn't even let him have his daily bread, while we, God willing, will eat ours, even if there's not much of it. . . . Ah, God help both the hungry and the full. . . . And Avdaga gets hit by good luck and bad, losing a brother and getting such a fortune. I don't know whether it'll make it easier or harder for him that he hardly ever exchanged a word with his brother, but the money'll relieve his sadness, as far as he has any. . . ."

At that moment the all-powerful women let us into the room.

Tiyana lay on a clean, newly changed bed, her hair wet with water and perspiration, pale, with sunken eyes, looking small and exhausted, as one who has suffered a serious illness.

And the floor had been washed. Of her blood?

You're both young, there'll be more children, Mahmut had said, comforting me. No, there'd be no more children! She was more important to me than those unknown, dangerous beings.

I touched her transparent hand with my fingers, not daring even to kiss it. She tried to smile, for my sake, but immediately shut her dark blue eyelids as though even that weak smile had exhausted her.

She was all I had, and I wanted to tell her, yet I feared to disturb her. She'd lost a lot of blood and sleep was more necessary than my stupid words, which could not express all that I was feeling. I'd forgotten the war, the injustice, the humiliation, become incapable of hatred, all because of my love for her. They'd taken everything from me (I said to myself with feeling), but you've made up for it. If I hadn't found you, I'd have been angry at life and would have had nothing, as now, but I wouldn't have known what happiness was. Because of you, I feel neither defeated nor do I think of revenge. I think only of you. I desire only that the smile return to your pale lips and the healthy color to your cheeks. What was I looking for in the town? Why did I stare in fascination at madmen chasing each other, while you were writhing in pain? It wouldn't have been any easier for you, but it would have been harder for me. That would have been fair. I'll never leave you alone again. Whatever happens to us, we'll face together.

She didn't hear me. I whispered her name, I spoke stupid words, "Sleep darling," hoping that sleep would restore her, but I was only doing harm, waking her from her uneasy sleep.

While I was kneeling, bent over her, sorry that I was unable to share at least some of her pain, Mahmut came in, holding a glass of lemonade in a trembling hand. Who knows where he'd got it, but I had to admit that his practical effort was of more value than my pointless sentimentality.

"Give her this," he whispered, handing me the glass.

He gave me the opportunity to appear caring at his expense.

Gently I raised her head, trying to get her to drink.

She drank it, in short gulps, greedily, as if it were extinguishing a fire somewhere inside her, and smiled at me gratefully.

She didn't even look at Mahmut.

And again she closed her eyes.

"She'll need some better food now," Mahmut warned me, when we went out onto the veranda.

I nodded, yes, she'd need nourishing food, but how was I to get it?

"And the child has to be buried."

It lay there, that erstwhile child, wrapped in a blood-stained towel in the corner of the veranda.

We buried this bit of meat at Alifakovats; this former third of our family that didn't desire to be born. In the funeral procession, which consisted only of Mahmut and myself, I carried him on a board under my arm, covered with a bit of sheeting, and we dug him into somebody else's eternal resting place, among some old bones.

"He died without even being born," said Mahmut, and that's all the eulogy this nameless creature, whom I no longer even regretted, received. He'd been the joy of my thoughts, while he was expected. Now he was nothing.

I remembered the two sons of the barber Salih, who lived there in Alifakovats, and I thought it was better to lose a son like this than to lose him in the marshes of some Chocim, when he grew up. For then you knew him, had learned to love him, and the sadness was the harder to bear.

"You're right," Mahmut agreed. "Only Salih is still waiting for his sons to come back."

"Surely he doesn't think they're still alive?"

"A man can believe in whatever he likes. Have you been to see him? You should."

"Why should I? What could I say to him?"

"You could tell him they were alive when you last saw them, that's what you'd tell him. Whatever else he wants he'll make up for himself."

"Perhaps I will, then."

"It would be a kind act."

I asked Mahmut to go to Tiyana, to replace the woman we'd left her with. I'd go to Mula Ibrahim to borrow some money.

"Get as much as you can. I haven't any either. The merchants haven't paid me yet."

I laughed. We'd be lucky if he gave us just a little, for anything more we hadn't a hope. That Mahmut was a strange one. He gave as easily as he took, caring nothing, either for his own money or for other people's. He stole from me, but he also helped me, but his thievings were petty while his help was great. It had saved both Tiyana and myself.

And that was the truth, I knew, and yet, for a wonder, I was not particularly grateful to him, nor did he expect gratitude. Perhaps it was due to the fact that I couldn't get rid of the thought, hidden though it was, of his guilt and exile, and even of his inferiority. That others considered him in this light, he knew, but that I did, luckily, he did not. To be honest, I'd never given it a thought, unconsciously accepting him as he was, as though it were his stamp, his smell, and I was ashamed when I became aware of his trust and my own stupidity. But then I'd never really given it much thought.

I never offended him. I enjoyed meeting him. I felt that there was a certain unusual freshness in this childish man. Yet in myself I did him an injustice.

Mula Ibrahim was not surprised to see me. It was as if he knew I would come and was neither glad nor sorry.

"You look as if you were expecting me. You're not surprised."

"We haven't quarrelled. Why shouldn't you come?"

"But you're not pleased."

"You're not in a good mood today."

"I was in a good mood once, and a lot of good it did me."

I myself was well aware of my unpleasantness. Was it because of the betrayal of our friendship, which I still regretted? Or was it because of his kindness: Man's nasty by nature, and it's easy to take it out on one who offers no resistance.

He showed no anger, but merely changed the subject. "How's Tiyana?"

"Bad."

"Why? What's happened?"

"Everything's happened. Send your assistants away," I hissed like an angry gander.

"I can't turn them out. We've nothing to hide."

"If you haven't, then I haven't!"

I put it to him as nastily as I could, and nasty it was that a man could find himself in the mess in which I found myself. I'd become, thank the Lord, a bogeyman, a black sheep, more dangerous than a criminal, only I'd no idea to what I owed such a fortune. Did the people in power require a scapegoat and choose him at random to justify their existence and their cruelty? It was of no importance what anyone did, only what they say he did. Now it was my turn. OK. I could bear it. It was even better this way, I'd neither master nor friend; I owed nothing and was grateful for nothing. I wasn't even afraid anymore. I'd learned how the birds live, and I could tell him it was not bad. I should be deeply grateful to him for having sacked me, since otherwise I'd never have learned this, and I'd have remained everybody's slave to the end of my life, thinking that this was the only way. After the experience of war, I'd have remained like a blind man and never regained my sight. As it was, injustice, thank God for it, had taught me that life is beautiful when it's free, even when it's hard. And dearest to me of all was to have realized what a treasure my wife was. Misfortune is like fire, it melts everything but gold. Sometimes, however, I thought I'd lost by it, for had she been ill-natured, and she'd have had every right to be so, I'd have had somebody on whom I could vent my feelings and gain relief when troubles oppressed me. But how could I take it out on her? She, poor girl, suffered too, put up with hunger, patched old dresses, and still consoled me, as though it were all her fault. She carried a child that she didn't bear, but lost it. I fed her on bad news and empty love, which had never nourished anybody. Now I had to feed her on something better, and it was solely for her sake I'd come to ask him to lend me some money. Those who'd helped me had nothing themselves, nor had I any idea how they'd managed to help me so far. Their generosity was wonderful, for I'd in no way deserved it, but it was fragile, since they were poor themselves. Now I was in a fix and forced to come to him for a loan. It wasn't easy for me, but one loses one's pride in trouble. And I was doing it only for my wife's sake, since it hurt me to see her suffer without any fault or blame. But I wouldn't even have come to him if we hadn't once been friends.

"We're still friends," he said with feeling.

"No longer, Mula Ibrahim. It's no use. We were, and I thought we'd always be, but we're not any longer. I'm sorry, but it's not my fault."

"Nor mine."

"Then it's the fault of fate. What can we do?"

I was resentful, bitter, and unpleasant and placed the burden of my troubles on him, yet I knew he wasn't to blame. His fear was stronger than all else within him, and he was certainly ashamed, yet could do nothing against it. He was a good man and, in other circumstances less brutal and less callous, might have been worthy of every respect. But where were those better circumstances, and would they ever exist? I didn't know. I didn't believe they ever would. But today I see clearly that he was a victim, just as were many others.

"Forgive me," I said more gently.

He looked at me with gratitude. I'd absolved him as easily as I'd accused him, and his good and cowardly soul felt relief.

He wanted to say something, something kind and sincere, or so it seemed to me, judging by the softened expression on his face, but changed his mind, not wishing to bind himself with words that could do no one any good and might do him harm.

I was sorry. Both he and I would have gained by his careless, yet human words. He'd have removed a goodly part of the canker in his soul, and I'd have been comforted by the knowledge that he was a man, despite everything. And I'd not have told a soul, so he'd have taken no hurt.

He took the easy way out and opened a casket, counted out money, adding more than he'd at first intended.

"I don't know when I can return it."

"No matter. And come back if you have trouble."

"I shall long have trouble, I fear."

"I don't like to hear you say that. It means you won't do anything to make things different."

"Is it my fault, Mula Ibrahim?"

"If not your fault, then your bad luck."

"Where is my fault? Why have I bad luck?"

He whispered so quietly that I had to go right up to him to hear what he was saying. He didn't want his assistants behind the partition to hear, yet he didn't want to be alone with me, so difficult was our relationship.

"I don't know. I don't rightly know, since I don't understand you. I well remember the peasants from Zhupcha and your laughter when we put the sultan's picture in the window. I'm all of a sweat now when I think of it."

"The two things came too closely together."

"Everything in life comes too closely."

"Yes, I know, both good and evil. But crime and servile obedience?"

"How can you change everything that's bad?"

"I'm not thinking of changing. But I do see what is bad."

"Is that why you have to destroy yourself? That's what I don't understand, you see. If you were a rebel, you'd clench your teeth and go on struggling. You wouldn't gain anything, but you'd have an aim in life, even if a wrong one. The way you're going, you want to say anything you like, but you don't accept the consequences. You're surprised, hurt, and offended. Which means you're no rebel. Rebels give and take blows, without grumbling. Maybe you're so fond of things as they are that you don't like it when something nasty happens? I don't think that's it. No, I don't understand you. I don't know what you want, but I do know that you're destroying yourself. Why?"

"I was drunk and said things I didn't even mean. Is that such a great sin?"

"Hang on, don't lose your cool. I'm not accusing you. We're just talking. Do you think it was easy for me?"

"Who ordered you to sack me?"

"It doesn't matter who. You babbled what you didn't think, you say? No one's asking what you thought, they're asking what you did. Your thoughts are your own, actions belong to everybody."

"What action? I didn't steal, I did no physical harm to anyone, I hurt nobody. Can empty words be called action?"

"Not so loud! Why do you always want everybody to hear you? And speech is an act. And what an act! Had you stolen, hit anybody, or done anyone any harm, they'd probably have forgiven you. But you had to go and talk about things any sensible person keeps quiet about. That's what they don't forgive."

"I said the truth!"

"So much the worse. Speech is gunpowder: It explodes in a second. There's always discontent, of all sorts, but it never bursts out on its own. It's speech that sets it alight."

"Why, then, don't we use this gunpowder speech? Why should this accumulated discontent not burst out?"

"No, come off it, you're not as naïve as that. You didn't say what you didn't think when you were drunk! I can see that now. And you'll destroy yourself, and I'll never understand why."

"Is honesty such a mystery to you, Mula Ibrahim?"

"It's not honesty that's a mystery, it's your behavior. I've thought a lot about you. I'm trying to make sense of you."

"And have you succeeded?"

"I told you, I'm trying. You went to the war when you were quite young, without any experience, honest like most young people. You came back just as naïve as when you went. Only muddled, because you didn't believe people could be so cruel. But you were even more confused by the cruelty in life without war. You thought war was dreadful, but how could life in peace be the same? And you thought people didn't see, and that it was your duty to tell them."

"Wasn't it?"

"If you hadn't gone to war, life would have knocked you into shape, molded you, sharpened you, and you'd have entered into its stream without noticing it, adjusted with no thought of it having to be any different. There, that's my explanation: The war robbed you of your years of apprenticeship to life."

"I learned a lot in war. Too bloody much."

"Not what you needed for peace. War's a cruel but an honest struggle, as between animals. Life in peace is a cruel struggle, but a dishonest one, as between men. There's a great difference."

"I'm learning slowly."

And then, suddenly, he changed the subject. I was amazed that he'd said as much as he had.

"I'm sorry for Tiyana. I'm sorry for you, too. I'll try to help you."

"How?"

"I don't know yet. I'll think about it."

We'd hissed at one another like two ganders long enough, trying to keep to ourselves what others would like to hear, and those two pimply-faced clerks behind the partition must have thought us selfish and unjust. They'd have little to say to those who'd ask them about our conversation.

All this wise talk had told me nothing, save that Mula Ibrahim had thought more of me than I'd supposed. And that was something, if not much. His explanation was interesting, but of little use. I'd been in the war, and that I couldn't change. I'd lost my time of apprenticeship, missed the good fortune of having life smooth me as a river does to a pebble, and now I appeared strange to others and was a mystery to myself.

Who was I, where was I, how did others see me, to what did I belong? What sort of a man was I, good or bad, superficial or painstaking? What did people and life mean to me, what was I aiming at, what did I expect from myself and others?

I seemed perfectly ordinary to myself. Why, then, was I different from other people?

Did I put myself apart from others, or did they put me apart?

I was fond of people yet didn't know how to deal with them.

Who'd understand my constant reminiscences of my dead comrades in the woods around Chocim, and what did they mean to me? Was it guilt or pain?

Who could I tell and who would care about my petty pleasures, at which people would laugh but which I would not give up for anybody else's: listening to the night and its deep rustling, gazing in rapture at moonlight reflecting on leaves, listening to my wife's breathing as she slept.

And how could I explain to anyone my pity for the two Pakros, for Mahmut Neretlyak, for the barber Salih from Alifakovats, for the old soldiers begging in front of the mosque, and for the young ones setting off to war, not knowing what awaited them?

What could I do with this, my pointless thinking, which offered neither harm nor benefit to anybody, of no use to anyone except myself? Pointless, mad, useless, yet it seemed to me that, without it, only half of the world, or even far less, would remain, and that that little would be of no value, and that without it I'd not be I, but somebody else, deaf and crippled, a stranger and hateful to myself.

In front of Siyavuz-*pasha*'s Jewish quarter, where the Jews of Sarajevo lived, as in a fortress, I met Asim Petsitava. He was carrying water from the water tap at the Begova mosque to the inhabitants of the ghetto. At the gates, through which he passed from morning till night a hundred times or more, angry with himself and everybody, he'd put down his two large metal water-pots so as to take a rest. He looked exhausted.

Two large water-pots full of water for somebody else, that was his life.

"Is it hard going?" I asked needlessly.

Asim looked at me in surprise, as though he hadn't understood or as though he thought I was mad. Be it the one or the other or both together, he answered in his usual manner: He began to swear abundantly and violently.

"You're right," I said, "especially if it makes you feel better."

Mahmut Neretlyak was waiting for me on the veranda. He was rubbing the calves of his legs to relieve the pain of the cramp that gripped him more and more often. He made a sign to me to speak softly since Tiyana was asleep.

"Did you get it?" he asked in a whisper.

"No. He refused."

"I knew it! By God, I knew it! That Mula Ibrahim has a petty-minded soul. As small as a grain of millet."

"How did you know he wouldn't give it?"

"Because I tried it, for you."

"When did you, you idiot?"

"What do you mean when? When you needed it."

"And you didn't tell me. Nor did he."

"If I'd got it, I'd have told you. And he'd nothing to boast about."

"And what if I say that he did lend it?"

"Did he?"

"He did."

"There you are. I knew it! By God, I knew it! Why shouldn't he? He owed you."

"So you see, he's not so petty-minded, after all."

"Sometimes petty, sometimes broad. Like the rest of us."

This time he'd been very broad: I counted out fifty *groschen*.

I gave Mahmut half, which he took without saying it was too much or too little. He just looked at it, as it lay in his hand.

"If one just had a bit more of this shit, a man would sleep easier."

"As far as sleeping goes, you're better off as you are. You're not scared of being robbed."

"Yeah, you're right. I don't even lock my door. What for?"

He shook the money in his hand before putting it into his pocket.

"Did you always hope to be rich?" I asked him.

"Everybody does."

"And now?"

He waved a hand and went off, smiling mysteriously.

Here was a tale of a man who dreamt of being rich all his life but had lived in poverty, who'd suffered more from hoping to get rich than he had from being poor. And now, at last, he'd had to abandon his dream. If that were possible. For, before this, he'd had no more reason to believe in his miracle. Now, in his old age, this madness of his was more necessary to him than ever.

He was soon back with some lamb's liver, wrapped in clean paper.

"When she wakes up, fry it for her. Not before, or it'll be hard. Do you know how to do it?"

"Do you mean to say this needs skill?"

"No, of course not."

I had to throw the first lot of liver away. The second, which I had to go and buy, got burned, so I ate it myself. The third Tiyana ate but, I thought, more to please me than because she liked it.

In a few days' time, she got up and began, slowly, to busy herself about the house.

So, my clumsiness, not only with the liver, became a humorous memory, and Tiyana laughed her heart out at my being so useless.

"You surely wouldn't like your husband to be good at women's work?"

"I certainly wouldn't."

"Then why are you laughing?"

But I dropped the subject, feeling that she might ask: What are you any good at? I recalled her generosity for not having asked this, even though it was an obvious question. It would have hurt me had she spoken the truth.

What was I any good at, after all? Nothing, it seemed. I was so hopeless that I couldn't even find a job I could do. As it was, it was as if I knew nothing. Yet, damn it, it was not my fault, and it would have been unjust to blame me.

And there you are, even such trifles as these could bother me.

I'd have felt hurt, had anyone reproached me, but I was unhappy just because nobody blamed me for anything. It would have been easier if I'd had to prove that I was not to blame. In this way, everything seemed to echo inside me, both the imagined reproach and the imagined defense echoed inside me like the sound of a rock in a cave that works loose and falls. Faced with opposition, I might have justified myself. Alone, I had grave doubts. There was something wrong with me or with the world, or everything was right both with me and the world, but we couldn't somehow relate. Does anybody relate, or do people lie about it, pretending there's no breach, or didn't they care and merely kept up an appearance? Was any link possible between a man and the world, other than through necessity? I didn't choose what I had. Indeed, I didn't choose anything, not birth, family, name, town, nationality; it was all imposed on me. Still stranger was that I turned this necessity into love.

For something had to be mine, for all else was alien, and I'd adopted the street, the town, the country, the sky above, which I'd looked at since childhood, out of fear of emptiness, of not belonging to the world. I'd taken the world by force, imposed myself on it, and my street couldn't care less and the sky above me couldn't care less, but I rejected this indifference, I offered them my feeling, I breathed my love into them in the hope they might return it.

I couldn't breathe my love into people, and they couldn't return it. They regarded me coldly, suspiciously, weighing up the danger they saw in me, and, already shut away, they shut themselves up still more at the first unexpected word, at the first unusual gesture. Or else, they attacked at once, defending themselves, for they preferred to kill rather than to feel fear. The truth is people are afraid, which is why they're cruel. Attack is a defense dictated by caution, and so there's no cure for cruelty, for there's no cure for man's insecurity.

But what was wrong with me? I couldn't attack, I couldn't even defend myself. I was a drum on which others beat, but a mute drum that neither sounded nor summoned.

CHAPTER 8

THE FEAR OF ISOLATION

WHENEVER I GREW TIRED OF HOPELESS EXPECTATION THAT, by some miracle, the walls surrounding me might fall, whenever I got bored with aimless wandering about the town, when talking to people lost its interest, since I knew little of practical affairs, or when talking grew painful, since I was seized with a fear of becoming a ruin, just like the majority of those whom I met, I'd go off into the old library that smelt of paper, dust, and ink, and for hours would sit with the books and with Seid Mehmed, the librarian.

Most often, there was just the two of us. Sometimes a senior student of the *medrese* or a rare-book lover would drop in, but after that all would grow quiet again, and the old manuscripts would be silent on the shelves as before, peaceful, wise, youthful in their centuries of age.

Here I found quietness, a quietness greater than usual. I felt that time was not just a flow, but a presence. The visible trace of a hand that had written those uneven lines defied death, and the words and their meaning lived on, like a spring that never dried up, like a light that never went out.

So all human effort did not perish.

I grew so used to Seid Mehmed that I could sit beside him for hours without saying a word. He himself was silent, even with other people. At first, I found it strange to sit in silence with a living man in the empty space of the library, and I tried to engage him in some kind of conversation, no matter on what subject, testing him, feeling out what interested him. I came to the conclusion that absolutely nothing interested him, not God, not life, not death, yet he had a considerable knowledge of many things.

Sometimes I was almost stunned by his knowledge of life, of philosophy, of literature, or by some wise remark that only he could have said. But alas, whatever he said was short, like a flash of lightning in a long night. For, both before and afterward, Seid Mehmed was completely absent, in some far world of his own that had neither link nor bridge with ours.

Until I got to know him, I tried to awaken him, to bring him to life through words, no matter on what subject. Later, I gave it up.

He'd sit motionless, staring at the wall, at the floor, at a beam of sunlight, seeing nothing, floating down the quiet stream of his unfathomable musings, from which my talk was unable to return him to this world.

Whenever his absent, yet happy, restrained smile began to vanish and his face grew tense, troubled, as if in fear, he'd get up with an effort and unsteadily go into the other room. He wasn't long away, just long enough to take opium, and then he'd return, enlivened, soon to float off into his world of dreams.

So the most educated man in town was also the most pathetic. In him lay a vast treasure unexploited, worse than if he'd known nothing. Or perhaps he was the happiest of men, for he needed nothing, cared for nothing, and it was all the same to him whether he knew anything or not. Yet I didn't know whether the pictures he conjured up in his imagination would have been more vivid had he known less. Or did his knowledge make them gentler? I'd ask myself the question merely for its own sake, for had there been an answer, it would have had no significance. Surely, no one would study or gain knowledge just so that his opium dreams might be the richer.

Everything about him was a mystery. He was entirely walled in within himself, as in an unmarked grave. You saw nothing in it, and it told nothing of itself.

Once, before I'd discovered his many-faceted nirvana, it happened that I recited one of my poems to him, for some reason thinking that he'd understand it. The thought came to me suddenly, at a time when he appeared unusually benign, open to confidences, or so it seemed to me.

I recited my poem concerning my sense of being lost, following my return from the war:

In living, in suffering
The heart grows pale,
The heart fades,
A shadow follows
The former me,
In suffering, in living.
I have lost myself in seeking.
I was,
I still am now.
I was not,
Nor am I now.
I have lost myself in seeking.
In wanderings, in dreams
Night hems me in,
The day returns me.
The day is lost,
Life is shortened,
In dreams, in wanderings.
In hope, in waiting,
I dream life,
Yet live by dreaming.
I hide my heart,
I blame my heart,
That I do not live,
That still I dream,
In waiting, in hope.

He listened attentively to the end, seeming, I thought, surprised, even displeased. I gathered from this that he was dissatisfied with the poem, which seemed very bad to me, too. And then a smile appeared on his thin, pale face. "Ah! A poet, I see! Erring and wayward."

"Why 'erring and wayward'? Is that what you think of poets?"

"It's not what I think, it's what the Koran says."

"I don't remember."

"I'll remind you. What does God say of Muhammad? 'We have not taught our messenger poetry. Poetry does not become him.' And you remember the *sûrah* Ash-Shu'arâ: 'It is the erring and wayward that follow poets.' 'See you not that poets stray in the valleys and speak madness?' 'Their aim is to scoff and to debauch. They shall receive punishment that shall humiliate and destroy them.' Since when have you strayed in the valleys and spoken madness?"

"Since I came back from the war."

"Ah yes. 'A shadow follows the former me,' the shadow of war, of course. So, my friend, I can see you haven't looked at the Koran since that time. Otherwise, you'd have seen that what you were doing was sinful."

I laughed. "I'll take the sin on my soul. All right, then, since you've condemned me, can you, at least, explain to me why? What harm is there in a poet's words?"

"It's not I who've condemned you. The Koran says: 'In defense of the faith, advance in ranks! Allah loves those who fight in tight ranks, firm as a wall.' But Allah does not love you, for you advance alone, you break ranks, you undermine the firm wall. And not only do you not defend the faith, you're against it."

"As bad as that!"

"'The Faith is the Law that governs the whole of life.' Poetry is outside that law. It doesn't recognize it. It seeks freedom of speech and thought and rejects the perfection of God's world. To live in dreams, in hope, in expectation, means not to accept what is. It means rebellion."

"God preserve me from having you as my prosecutor! What, then, isn't rebellion?"

"Prayer."

"Do you pray? Are you a defender of the faith in a rank as firm as a wall?"

He smiled sadly, or with a gentle irony. And didn't answer.

It was time for one of his silences. He withdrew into his dreams. His eyes grew dull, turned somewhere inward, into himself, to something more important and more beautiful than were the muddled verses of an Ahmet Shabo.

He was clearly scoffing. But at whom? At me or himself? Or at everyone? When he spoke, he appeared wide awake, yet, both in his artificial sleep and out of it, he was far removed from this world of ours and from people and cared nothing for how things arranged themselves. He rejected everything that was not the vortex of his fantasies, which no order of human making could disturb.

I looked at him in bewilderment, almost in fear, as though he were dead.

The things I cared for were just the things to which he was utterly indifferent.

Then I heard a movement behind me.

I turned: In the doorway stood a young man. I knew him by his thin face and burning eyes. The student Ramiz!

I'd tried to avoid him; clearly I'd not succeeded.

For the last month, he'd been preaching in the evenings in the Ali-*pasha* mosque, speaking to the poor from Crni vrh, Berkusha, Bjelave, Koshevo, saying what no sensible man would ever say in public. I'd listened to him once, because I'd heard people quoting him in whispers. I could hardly find myself a space by the door, yet I'd left before he finished. I'd fled in terror!

I recalled what he'd said that dark night in the woods around Chocim. I'd repeated his words at a bad time and to my cost, and I knew that one could say anything, but not this, in this way!

Never from anyone had I heard so many cutting words, so much contempt for people in power, so much mad freethinking, as I did listening to that passionate student of Al-Azhar University, who didn't know what fear was, or, rather, didn't know what authority was. He said —I remember even now my astonishment—that there were three great passions: alcohol, gambling, and power. People could be cured of the first two, but of the third never. Power was the worst vice. For its sake, people killed, people perished. For its sake, people lost all human resemblance. It was irresistible, like the magic stone, for it gave might. It was the genie in Aladdin's lamp, who served every fool that owned it. On their own, these three passions represented nothing; together, they were the fate of the world. There was no such thing as honest and wise government, for the lust for power was limitless. A man in power was encouraged by cowards, backed by flatterers, upheld by rogues, and his idea of himself was always better than the reality. He considered all people stupid, because they hid their true opinions from him, and he took to himself the right to be all-knowing, and people accepted it. No one in power was wise, for the wise quickly lost their reason, and no one was tolerant, for they hated change. They immediately created eternal laws, eternal principles, an eternal order, and by linking their power to God thus affirmed their might. And no one would overthrow them did they not become a hindrance and threat to others in power. They were always overthrown in the same way, accused of oppression of the people, yet all of them were oppressors, and of treason to the ruler, but nobody ever thought of this. And no one had learned from it; they all flew headlong to power like moths to a candle flame. Weren't all the Bosnian governors impris-oned, exiled, or killed? And all their followers. And always came new ones, bringing their own followers and repeating the stupidities of their predecessors, since they couldn't do otherwise. And so it went on, in a circle, forever. The people could live without bread, but not without power. The pow-erful were a disease on the body of the people, like boils.

When one burst another grew, perhaps still worse. You couldn't do without us, they told us, robbers would increase, the enemy would attack us, there'd be chaos in the country. Yet who made this country, who fed it, who defended it? The people. Yet they fined us, punished us, imprisoned us, killed us. And, moreover, they forced our sons to do so. They couldn't do without you. You must do without them. There are few of them, there are many of us. Were we only to lift a finger, so many are we, this filth would no longer be. And this we will do, my downtrodden brothers, the moment we have real people who will not allow vampires to sit on their necks.

It was then that I left the mosque, in my confusion stepping on the feet of shocked neighbors in torn socks who, holding their breath, listened to these fiery words of rebellion.

Where did he get such courage? On the way home I kept tripping on the cobbles, like a drunkard, scarcely believing my ears. How had he dared to say what he'd said, and how did people dare listen to him?

Amazed and bewildered, I told Tiyana about it. "My word, he's brave," she said admiringly. Yet, all the same, she warned me not to go to the mosque anymore. Perhaps she was afraid I'd be sickened by my own silence.

And now that same young man of whom I'd thought so much in waking and dreamt of in dreaming was standing there in front of me, with a book in his hand, and looking at me attentively.

"Do I know you? Have we met somewhere?"

"I heard you talk once in the mosque."

"I mean before that?"

"I don't think so."

I avoided mentioning our former chance meeting, since I feared possible dangers.

"You write poems?" he asked, changing the subject. "For whom? And why?"

"For myself. For no reason."

"Like the nightingale singing?"

"How else should one write poetry?"

"But you're a man."

I couldn't give him any easy answer, for all his thought was aimed at rebellion, and everything had to serve this end. I well recalled everything he'd said in the mosque, and I'd gladly have turned to this. I thought how his enthusiasm was more seductive and his courage more attractive than anything he'd said. I wanted to ask him whether one could really attain freedom through violence. Could one really employ evil against evil? And who would uproot that second evil? And how could one forget its existence?

But were I to say this, he'd have hated me, despised me.

I'd stick to poetry. But what should I say?

Here, too, I was alone. Here, too, I was guilty. Here, too, I was breaking the tight ranks, firm as a wall.

Drawing closer to his theme, yet holding myself apart at the same time, I said that we all felt crushed and restricted, even if we weren't rebels. It was enough that we thought. But a man felt the need not only to think but to speak, a greater need to speak than to think. In this way one relieved tension. Speech was like being bled. It gave an outlet to suffering and the appearance of freedom. The powers that be should nurture and encourage it and not repress it. They should arrange festivals of speech or, even better, of swearing, as they do for singing or prayers, as a means of cleansing. Some tribes in Africa did it, and in this they were much more sensible than we, in this and probably in much else. They should give rewards and medals for swearing. And for poetry, too, since it was the same thing. And they should order as many people as possible to take part and listen. It would help them carry their inevitable burdens.

"Are they really inevitable?"

I wanted to develop my amusing picture, make a joke of

it, imagining what one could make of such a marvelous coming together of swearing, shrieking, and derision, to the accompaniment of *gusle*, *tamburitzas*, and drums, walking around, sitting, crying to heaven, thudding on the earth, but Ramiz interrupted me in my hyperbolical indulgence, at a moment when I couldn't have agreed with him, while I myself felt no great attachment to what I was saying.

"Are these burdens really inevitable?"

"I'm afraid they are."

"No, they're not. People will throw off these imposed burdens and cease to deceive themselves by trying to make them seem easier. And the day is coming ever nearer as the burdens grow heavier and as there are fewer words of consolation."

"Who will do this?"

"The people."

"The people are just an empty number, a scattered force. They've no aim, nothing in common, save their immediate needs and their fear. We're divided. One village will not help another in the face of danger. Each hopes the danger will pass it by."

He shook his head in disagreement.

"The people is a scattered force only if it sees no common end, nor lasting gain. If they come to realize it, if they're once assured of it, they can do anything. But first those in power must be driven off."

"Suppose that's possible. But somebody has to lead the people, free them from their fear, prepare them for sacrifice, so as to lead them to victory."

"Is that impossible?"

"In that case, the leaders would gain honor and recognition. And what would happen? They'd begin to live off their reputation, and with every day they would grow greater and their reputation would turn into power. In this way, instead of the old government, we'd get a new one, perhaps worse.

That's the history of government from time immemorial. Everything repeats itself, from enthusiasm to force, from nobility to tyranny, always and forever."

He laughed, rather reproachfully, I thought.

He didn't agree with my pessimistic views, believing in the people's ability to arrange their lives themselves, as was best for them, and to break the vicious circle in which heroes became tyrants. Without heroes, nothing could be done; they were the lump of snow that starts an avalanche. Only they must not be allowed to besmirch their glory. The ancient Romans sent their heroes into exile and so preserved them for immortality. If that was too cruel, we could return our heroes to the position from which they'd come.

Nor did he agree with me that the word should be a consolation and a relief, since this was a final recognition of defeat. The word should be a rebellion, a summons to battle, as long as there was evil in the world. Otherwise words were just lies, opium, and people would dream rosy dreams, like poor Seid Mehmed, and let everything go to the devil.

Where did he get this firm faith that contradicted all probabilities? So many had hoped in vain. Yet the new generations still went on believing. Man's hope was stronger than experience and couldn't be shaken by the failure of others.

Or was he reconciled to anything that might happen, even to death? I didn't know how one could be reconciled to death, but perhaps his fervor accepted it as part of action. Or perhaps he didn't think of it. He could do this, too, for he'd the willpower to make himself do anything.

Did he ever think of anything else? Did he have a family that he sometimes missed, a friend with whom he talked about ordinary matters, a girlfriend to whom he whispered words of love? Or was he a constantly lit fire that burned and burned itself out, forgetting the other warmth that was closer to him?

I asked him this, to get away from a conversation on matters that I respected but didn't understand.

He took me by the arm and led me into another, empty room. He was unafraid to say things aloud in the mosque, which others wouldn't dare even think, but, when it came to talking of himself, he could only whisper, avoiding being overheard, lest the sleeping Seid Mehmed happen to wake up.

He had friends, he said quietly, and not a few. He was glad when he gained them and sorry when he had to leave them, and he never forgot a single one of them. He felt safer with them. And we, too, could become friends, but he wished that I would change, become a man, as indeed I was, only that I lacked the courage to show it. He could get to like me as I was, kind but helpless, but he wouldn't be able to respect me, and that would be only half-friendship.

He had a girlfriend he loved very much, and he was sorry to have to be away from her for long periods, so that their love had become a constant waiting. But were it not for this, he'd not be what he was. And were he to leave everything and return home to be a teacher and grow roses and set potatoes in his garden, he'd no longer be capable of true love and, perhaps, would even blame her for his having abandoned his dream. He'd said all this to her and left her to choose. She'd chosen to wait. It was hard, yet right.

In the evenings, when he came back from the mosque, he'd close his eyes and, imagining her sitting in her miserable room, he'd tell her what he'd said to the people and how eagerly they'd listened to him. (Although his tale of youthful naïveté touched me, I thought, mischievously, that that distant girl, tired of waiting, might well exchange whispers at night with a closer and more ordinary young man, concerning closer and more ordinary matters than a hopeless struggle for the good of the poor.)

He also had a family, a widowed mother, a married sister, and a brother who was a blacksmith and lived with their mother. His father was killed in the battle for Dubitsa, and he'd kept himself in the Al-Azhar University by giving lessons to rich and stupid students. It was then that he'd swallowed his fill of bitterness, endured much humiliation, seen enough of the extravagance of the rich and the sufferings of the poor to convince himself that the world was badly arranged.

Indeed, he'd been aware of this before, for it didn't take much intelligence to know it, but he'd realized his path in life suddenly, in a moment, as though lit by a flash of lightning. This had all been made clear to him by a dervish from the Hamzevian order. Authorities were unnecessary, neither ruler nor state, all that was oppression. It was sufficient to have people make all decisions by common agreement, ordinary people who went about their business without desiring to rule others and without allowing anyone to rule them. And sufficient was God's mercy that would aid them. The dervish had been killed, but his words had remained. All of them, save those regarding God's mercy. People could arrange whatever they needed among themselves.

He was happy, as far as it went. It wasn't always easy, but he'd grown used to difficulties. He cared nothing for abuse, prison was an accepted hardship, beatings were unpleasant, but he was young and could stand them. The worst was when he thought of his mother, his brother, his girlfriend, of the warmth of the home fire and of the small talk that he hadn't experienced for years. But he'd cast these thoughts aside, not allowing himself such weakness.

He'd like to find a friend here; not a supporter, not a follower, those he had, but a true friend with whom one could converse and be silent in a different way than with the rest of the people, no matter how dear they might be. Friendship could not be made; it happened, like love. He'd be glad if we could become friends.

I gave him my hand, touched by his fear of isolation and by his need for ties with another man. He'd never betray his belief, but life with it could be cold and empty. My friendship would be of little help to him, but it could serve him as an inner refuge.

We went out onto the street.

I invited him to drop in at my house. We were simple folk, I said, but we'd do our best to make him feel at home. What I didn't say was that we'd invite him to lunch. He needed it. I didn't think he ate often.

So, because of a quite normal conversation, I forgot the caution with which I'd first approached him.

A strange lad. He'd be a fine man as long as he didn't succeed in his aim—a terrible one, were he to succeed. He'd remain proud of his pure ideals even afterward, when they'd long been corrupted. Today he was against force, yet he'd bring it to bear in the name of freedom. Today he was for freedom, yet he'd crush it in the name of power. He'd fight fiercely for his principles, thinking it noble, not knowing that they'd become inhuman. He'd be the most ruthless enemy of his former self and would cherish, like a talisman, the coarsened image of his erstwhile enthusiasm. And if he didn't succeed, as so many others, and if the present erstwhile fanatics stood in his way, his suffering would do more than any victory. People would preserve a touching memory of his sacrifice and of the thought that never became reality. And, for a wonder, this was the best that a man might ever do: to attempt and not to succeed.

In this way, the desire and the belief that one day the heaven of dreams would come remain. And with such a desire, life is easier. If prophets disappoint, dreams grow dark. Prophets need to die before they achieve anything. It's enough that they should have, once again, revived an old hope. Why should they extinguish it by action that disillusions? Perhaps a long time needs to pass before enough of that unsullied beauty accumulates in the souls of men, that, purified, they may realize their ancient dream.

I was sobered by the rain that was beginning to fall and

that drove from my head the muddled thoughts that I'd used as a defense against another's enthusiasms.

I was hurrying home, without taking shelter. But I repented when I saw the *serdar*-Avdaga standing under some eaves. I thought of retracing my steps. This was a meeting I didn't want, and I didn't care if he thought I was avoiding him.

I stopped and then went on. I was so confused that I went to him like a hypnotized frog to a snake.

He greeted me politely.

"You're often in the library."

"*Merhaba*, Avdaga."

"I see you there every day."

"I've plenty of spare time. So have you, it would seem."

"I didn't know you were a friend of Ramiz."

"We met for the first time today," I lied.

"The first time! What did you talk about?"

I told him about Ramiz's family, about his girl, about his desire for real friends, about everything that Avdaga would consider utterly stupid.

"Is that all?"

"And what else should we talk about?"

"Did he mention what he'd been saying in the mosque?"

"I've no idea what he says in the mosque. Why do you ask?"

"Just chatting."

The rain was dripping down his nose, and mine, too, no doubt.

He looked funny, and this put me at ease. I lost my fear.

"Avdaga, do you have to get wet through like this? Your brother left you a large estate, and I thought you'd retire. I can't believe you like doing what you do."

"I like doing what I do."

"Hmm, I don't know. It's hard work."

"I'm strong."

"And ugly work."

"Ugly? Why ugly?"

"All right, let's say strange work. Because you concern yourself with what other people do."

"I do concern myself with what other people do. There are a lot of rogues about."

"Are there more rogues than there are good people?"

He looked at me as though my question surprised him. He was so surprised that I could guess his thoughts without his saying a word. Of course there were more rogues, and without him they'd conquer the whole world. He had to know what people did, what they said, what they thought, whom they met, but it would be better if they didn't talk, if they didn't think, if they didn't meet. It would be best if everything were forbidden. Why did people travel? Why did they go to other towns? Why did they sit in coffeehouses and talk and whisper? Why did they leave their houses? Were he able, he'd stop it all. But since he couldn't, all he could do was to watch over life, distrusting everything in it that lived and moved. He was the most concerned and responsible man on earth, and his conscience troubled him because of everything that he couldn't foresee and forestall. And were he to put everybody in prison, he'd prevent all evil. Alas, no one understood him.

But there was no point in his explaining this to me. All he said was, "If you see Ramiz again, remember what he says."

"I won't see him!"

"I said, if you see him. He'll look you up, for sure. You're the same sort, only you're afraid."

"You know what he says, you know who he'll look up, what do you need me for? Is this on the orders of Dzhemal Zafraniya?"

"It doesn't concern you on whose orders it is."

"Tell me one thing, Avdaga. If you were ordered to arrest me, you'd certainly do it, even if I were innocent?"

"No one's innocent."

"And if they ordered you to kill me, you'd obey. Why, Avdaga?"

"And why shouldn't I obey?"

"*Allahemanet*, Avdaga."

"I asked you about Ramiz. Why don't you answer?"

"I ask you: Why? You ask me: Why? And we just go on asking and wondering. *Allahemanet*, Avdaga. May God help both of us."

"By God, you'll need help more than I shall," he said thoughtfully.

We both got wet to the skin, holding this absurd conversation.

CHAPTER 9

A TALE OF
CHILDREN'S FLUTES

I WASN'T DYING OF DESIRE FOR WORK, BUT HOW ELSE COULD one live?

I required work more than ever. Tiyana embroidered women's blouses and so supported us, but I was ashamed that she was the only one of us to be working.

Mahmut's merchants had deserted him. It seemed that the Greeks asked themselves in amazement what strange language these people were speaking when his merchants proudly began to speak Greek in Salonika. Mahmut explained to them that he spoke a different dialect, that of Antioch, and so got away with it, but lost his source of income.

Tiyana assured me that the work was simple, that embroidery calmed her nerves and paid well and that the worry about where the next meal was coming from no longer hung over our heads. And it would all have been fine if I hadn't been without anything to do. This way it was all wrong. I was living off a weak woman, and she was bearing the brunt of my errors.

"It's not your fault," she'd comfort me. "And I'm not working for somebody else, but for us."

Or she'd scold me whenever I hung my head in depression. "Oh dear, how terrible, his wife has to feed him! Come on, don't be silly. It's not as if I'm doing something bad."

She wouldn't let me take the finished blouses to her customers. She'd get angry if I cleaned the room. She kept me clean and tidy, preserving my male dignity and her pride as a merchant's daughter, as though in our poverty nothing mattered more.

She received some money from her sister, as her share of her father's legacy, much less than it was worth, but we hadn't expected anything, and so we were satisfied, feeling, for a wonder, more secure with this insignificant heap of silver.

As though we were forever safe from troubles.

Mahmut Neretlyak immediately got a whiff of the money and talked excitedly in whispers with Tiyana, thinking up extraordinary ways and means of doubling it, increasing it tenfold, until, in his imagination, it became a real fortune. Tiyana would shake her head distrustfully but didn't interrupt his building of castles in the air. I just laughed at this game, in which Mahmut, as so many times in the past, pursued his everlasting dream, but she listened to it as she would to a pretty fable, yet determined not to take any risks, for she was no gambler.

Mahmut even knew how we'd invest our newly acquired wealth. The merchant Shabanovich was selling his house: four rooms, an entrance hall, a balcony, and a vine, surrounded by a garden with rose trees and a crystal-clear spring.

"We'll wait a while for a house like that, or even for a smaller one," said Tiyana dryly, but her eyes gleamed nonetheless.

Suddenly, however, we had a chance not exactly to achieve wealth, but at least to double our money.

Through his connections, always complex, Mahmut heard from the relative of his next-door neighbor that the young merchant Husaga, the brother of the coppersmith Abid, was going to Constantinople to buy merchandise. And Mahmut suggested we give Husaga money to buy merchandise for us. The young man was honest and capable. He'd acquired a fine shop and a still better reputation. The year before, he'd brought a whole caravan of goods and sold them all. It would be best if he were to buy us some expensive fabrics, as much as he could. There was a big demand for them, and they could immediately be sold to the merchants of the bazaar. When we'd paid his expenses and given him something for his trouble, our money would still be doubled. Finally, he said that Husaga had already agreed to do us this favor. There was no problem.

So we realized he'd already spoken with Husaga and arranged everything, leaving the job of convincing us to the last. It seemed rather strange and a little too like Mahmut, and this time I, too, shook my head suspiciously. But Tiyana refused it out of hand, saying there was nothing to it, and money didn't come as easily as that.

All the same, we agreed to talk to the young merchant and thank him for his kindness, and we would tell him that, unfortunately, we'd spent the money and, in any case, there hadn't been much of it.

We didn't tell him anything of the sort. Husaga dispersed all our doubts and fears. He was young, but with a seriousness more suggestive of long years of life and experience. He resembled rather a learned teacher than a young merchant. He'd be glad to help us, he said. It was no big deal, just to purchase it and see it loaded. He'd do it for anybody, and he had a still better reason, since his father and Tiyana's had been friends. And he'd do it for me, because he knew what had happened to me and how I'd suffered innocently. He needed no money, he'd plenty of his own, and we could pay him when he brought the goods. We'd have no difficulty in selling them. He'd only assist us, for it would be embarrassing if he were to buy it from us. It would be against every mercantile custom and would look as if it were an act of charity. This way it would all be above board.

Naturally, we gave him the money, and he gave us a receipt with his seal on it. We wished him bon voyage, and we parted as the best of friends.

"Pity we hadn't more money," Mahmut sighed. "You might have gone to Constantinople."

Tiyana interrupted. "Constantinople! For two whole months! And what would I be doing!"

"Other wives stay on their own," I said, defending my right to my imagined journey to Constantinople.

"Others do, but I couldn't."

"Don't say that, dear, perhaps one day he'll go. Just imagine: Constantinople, with its shops, its caravans, its hostelries, all sorts of people! Don't talk like that, it's wrong."

"And it isn't wrong that I'd have to stay alone!"

Ignoring the excitement with which he imagined this unattainable good fortune, she treated me to angry glances, as though I, there and then, were preparing to set out.

And I sulked, as if she were really preventing me from going, selfishly depriving me of the freedom to make my own decisions. Why shouldn't I go, like the rest of the people?

Mahmut left without noticing the sparks that were flying between us. He'd get drunk, for sure, thinking of the journey to wealthy Constantinople.

And our anger immediately collapsed, becoming ridiculous, as was its cause.

Our protests had been short-lived, so short that they hadn't been worth starting. Especially since I knew, no matter how angry I was, that for me nothing could replace her, just as she was, narrow-minded in her love, intolerant toward everything that could deprive her of even the smallest part of me, her property. I quickly returned from my flimsy rebellion and apparent desire for freedom to the firm fortress of her love, like a humble fugitive who had not got far from the gate.

Life was not on our side, and we ourselves created our own small community, our cosmos, in which we supplied each other with all we lacked.

When I was under threat, I thought only of her, taking

courage from her presence. When things went badly, it was her name I spoke, as in a prayer, finding relief in it. When I felt happy, I'd run to share it with her, thankful to her, as if my happiness were her gift.

She was a good person and a beautiful woman, but what she was for me was my own creation. Even if she had great faults, I'd not have noticed them. I needed her to be perfect and couldn't allow her to be anything less.

I attributed to her everything I didn't find in life, but without which I couldn't live. I even belittled myself to her, so that she should appear greater and I, too, only through her. I gave to her generously, so I might take. Where I was frustrated, she was realized, and this was my compensation. She returned what I'd lost, and I gained more than I thought to gain. My desires had been obscure and disparate, now they were united in a single name, in a single character, more real and more attractive than imagination. I recognized in her everything I was not, yet in rejecting myself I lost nothing. Weak and helpless when faced with people and the world, I gained significance through my creation, which was more valuable than either. Uneasy before the uncertainty of all things, I was sure in the love that was self-creating, for it was need transformed into feeling. Love is both sacrifice and violence; it offers and demands, it begs and scolds. I needed this woman, my entire world, to admire and to feel my power over her. I'd created her, as a savage creates his idol, to stand above his cave fire, his defense from thunder, enemies, wild beasts, people, the heavens, and loneliness, from whom he might seek the usual things but also demand the impossible, feel ecstasy, but also bitterness, whom he might both thank and scold, ever aware that, without it, his fears would be unbearable, his hopes without foundation, his joys without permanence.

Solely because of her, even people seemed closer to me.

Husaga returned from Constantinople sooner than we'd expected. He invited me into his empty shop and, a changed man, crushed, grown thin and pale, informed me with regret that he'd lost all the money in Constantinople, both his own and other people's. And to add to this, he'd run into debt. He hadn't lost in trade. No one had robbed him or held him to ransom. He'd drunk the lot. He'd never done anything like that before. Now he had.

What had come over him he'd no idea. It happened one evening. It came of itself, suddenly, like an illness, like a madness. He drank, paid the singers, threw money on every side, ready to fight the friends who begged him not to ruin himself, and in several days and nights was left with nothing, so that he had to borrow in order to get back home. He was sorry for us and his brother Abid, but what could he do, if he killed himself, it wouldn't help. If we wished, he'd borrow the money and return it to us. But if we were not in immediate need, he'd return it to us with interest in a year's time.

We were not in immediate need, I told him. We could wait. It could happen to anyone, and we didn't wish to add to his troubles, he had enough of them as it was. He could return it when he was able.

What else could I have said? Why add to his misery by asking for the money? We were fated not to have money, and I agreed generously, with a smile, to a loan, until a distant and probably nonexistent "next year," as if we were rolling in wealth. He was grateful to me for this madness and, what's even stranger, I, too, felt a satisfaction, as if I'd completed a good bargain. Had I got the money, it would have been a hollow victory. I would certainly have felt guilty. And the fact that we'd made fools of ourselves would soon be forgotten. And we'd find it easy to forgive ourselves.

Both Tiyana and I were unfitted for life, but in a light-hearted way that caused us no worry. Tiyana did not reproach the merchant nor anyone else. She didn't even say that she'd had a foreboding of misfortune, as she usually did. She laughed and said cheerfully, "There, you see what wonderful businesspeople we are!"

Mahmut, too, reacted differently from what I'd expected. I thought he'd reject all blame, since he'd only been thinking aloud, and we were the ones who'd made the decision. He hadn't even said a word when we gave Husaga the money, which was true.

I was wrong. He didn't defend himself. He came to face us, admittedly, only two days later when our anger had had time to abate, and took all the blame on himself.

"If you think I've been able to sleep, you're wrong," he said repentantly. "I haven't slept a wink. I've let my best friends down. You've lost your last chance of anything like security. I've even damaged myself, because I, too, felt more secure because of your bit of money. I could have said: Who'd have thought it of Husaga? But I won't. You can expect anything from a Bosnian. He's lived like a sensible man for years and then he goes and does his best to prove himself a fool. You were probably not aware of it, but I was more experienced. It's my fault. I'll make up for your loss."

"Don't talk nonsense. Where would you get the money?"

"I'll sell my shop and give you the money."

"Then you'll be without a shop."

"I wasn't born with a shop."

"But why should you do that? You're not to blame."

"I am. You know nothing about business."

We went on like this, competing in our generosity, until Tiyana firmly put an end to our childish arguments, saying that it was all stupid and a waste of time. And she'd have no more of our nonsense, and we were to stop dreaming about easy money and getting rich. She didn't need wealth. She was used to being poor. And we two didn't need it either, for we were about as good at business as she was at walking on a tightrope.

So she gave us both a thick ear: Mahmut, indeed, by insulting his merchant's vanity and freeing him from responsibility, and me, for no reason at all. Angrily, I thought that

Mahmut had been certain that she'd say what she had and therefore had insisted, as it were, in compensating us for the lost money. His generosity had cost him nothing, since he had no fear of any loss, and it would have been amusing had we accepted his sacrifice, albeit as a joke. How he'd have squirmed and twisted like a worm to take back his words!

So it all ended happily, and we were all satisfied with our roles. The wheezy old rascal had bet on the certainty of Tiyana's good nature. He left pretending to be hurt that we hadn't accepted his sacrifice.

And in less than two days, he was nagging me with a new idea.

Tiyana took the finished blouses to her customers, and I went to the library to continue reading Mevli's verses about Sarajevo. He might have been talking about me and the people of my day, as though a whole century had not passed. Did time stand still, I asked myself, not knowing whether this was a consolation or a source of bitterness. Didn't people ever change?

I asked this of Seid Mehmed in one of his short intervals between two ecstasies, when one was passing off and the other had not yet begun. Only then was he aware, and only then did he not have his smile that was both sad and cheerful at the same time.

"People change," he said, "but for the worse."

"Impossible," I replied with some heat. "If people aren't better, then they're more intelligent. They know they have to arrange things between themselves, otherwise the devil will take them."

"The devil will take us anyway," Seid Mehmed concluded dryly.

I'd have asked him why he had such a low opinion of people. What had happened to him? What had they done to him, why was he hiding, what was he running from? But he didn't allow anyone to get close to him. He'd croak like a bird of ill omen and fly off.

He went off into the other room, leaving me, feeling bitter, to answer my own questions.

I couldn't believe him. My gut revolted at his pessimism. It was against life and against people. All people. If only one person were different, I'd believe in him more than in all the others. But there wasn't just one. There were more good people on earth than bad. Many more! Only the bad ones made more noise and made themselves felt more. The good were silent.

Could this not be turned round?

I'd have liked to have discussed it with Ramiz. He'd certainly say that people would change for the better. Without that certainty, his whole life would be senseless, as would everything he did. Even if it sounded unconvincing, I'd believe him. For his sake and my own.

Mahmut was waiting for me on the street, as wet as a dishcloth. It had been raining all day.

"What are you doing?"

"Nothing, I'm just standing here. I was in the coffee-house. It was stuffy in there. People were sitting on top of each other, because of the rain."

"Shall we go to my place?"

"What's the matter with here?"

We stood in a doorway under the eaves, watching the rain fall and the drops bouncing off the cobbles. My feet were soon wet through. It didn't matter anymore whether I remained there or not.

What would people be like tomorrow, better or worse?

"Rotten weather," Mahmut said, wiping his face with a handkerchief. "I don't like rain, I don't like wind, I don't like cold. It makes one miserable, you cough, your back hurts, and you feel like hell. I don't like the summer heat either. It makes you feel like nothing on earth. Isn't there anywhere on earth where it's always spring?"

"I don't know. Perhaps there is."

"I haven't seen it. But if I knew where it was, I'd go and live there. Like this, it's bloody awful. Either the sun bakes you or the cold cuts you to the bone. Rotten. Especially when it's humid. It's enough to drive you mad. For instance, last night I was in bed, and it got so heavy that I knew we were in for a change of weather. I couldn't breathe. I couldn't sleep. And it was too late to go out into the street. The wife was groaning, puffing, and turning over. 'Lie still, for God's sake,' I said to her. 'Every time I nod off, you wake me up.'

"'I'm tossing and turning,' she said. 'It's the weather, I can't breathe.' As for me, what could I do, I saw there was no chance of sleep. My eyes were wide open, my brain was going round and round, so I let my thoughts wander, since there was no way I could get rid of them. And I thought how many people in this town, at this moment, were looking into the darkness, sleepless, like me. How many slept, how many, forgive the expression, were busy doing 'you know what,' how many were departing this life, how many were being born? And how many, indeed! So I got to reckoning how many inhabitants the town had a year ago and how many there'd be in two years' time. My thoughts became muddled and tangled like threads. There was no way of disentangling them, so I got up, lit a candle, took a pencil, and began to calculate. And this is what I came up with: In our *kasaba* there are, roughly speaking, six thousand households with three children each. Children gain about nine *okes* in three years. Eighteen thousand children times three *okes* is fifty-four thousand *okes* of human flesh.

"My bewildered thoughts came to a halt at such a huge mass of human meat that grew in just a year."

I laughed. "For God's sake, you're calculating them by weight, as if they were lambs!"

"They're not lambs, they're children, that's the whole point! And every year they grow, and every year new ones arrive. The harvest can fail, but human breeding never does. There're eighteen thousand of them at this moment. See what I mean?"

He shook the rain from his beard and from his wet sleeves

and shook his head, disgruntled by my failure to understand.

"This is what occurred to me: There are more children than adults. And parents tend to spoil their children. Now, look here: If anyone had the cash and bought something for children and then sold it, they could earn good money."

"If, if! Stop dreaming, for God's sake!"

"This is no dream. There'll be a fair soon in Vishegrad, and one could buy several loads of flutes for children. A penny a piece. If one got three thousand, or, let's say, two thousand, that would be two thousand pence pure profit. Who wouldn't give two pennies to please their child?"

"There are more important things than buying children flutes."

"Ah, but if they can't afford anything better, people will buy their children flutes."

Would he spend his whole life thinking about trade, about profit and business? And this thing about children's flutes was the sort of thing only he would think of. It was sensible and stupid, pathetic and funny, all at the same time.

"Only you could come up with something like that. What the hell made you think of flutes!"

"It's not the flutes, it's the pure profit. You'll sell them to the shops and pocket the money."

"And where are you going to get the money from?"

"The money? Yes, that's the problem."

He looked downcast, wiping the raindrops from a nose blue with the cold.

Laughing, I said, "That's the old gypsy saying: If we had as much cornmeal as we haven't got fat, we'd have made some good corn cakes."

"But it's not quite as bad as that. We could find both the cornmeal and the fat."

"How?"

"You've got it."

"I? I'll give you all I have."

"If you'll give it, then there's no worry. I'll go off to Vishegrad and get the flutes."

"I've got nothing, man. Where should I get money?"

"You've got your father's house."

So that's what he was thinking about! He wouldn't have a moment's peace till he'd parted me from the last thing I possessed. It was like a disease with him.

I said nothing. He began to urge me. "What do you say? It's doing you no good just standing there."

I said nothing. My mind was blank. It certainly wasn't doing any good just standing there. And this flute business wasn't such a bad idea. It was mad but quite well thought out.

"Are you sorry to part with the house?"

I wasn't sorry, not in the least. Nothing bound me to it, save a few vague memories that I rarely thought of. I hadn't been near the ruins for ages. There was no point in returning to vain memories, to feel the pain of emptiness. It was time to break a useless tie and forestall all possible pain. My childhood was long gone. Why preserve this seat of spirits, where not even the bones of the dead were resting? I didn't even feel pain, only an emptiness. Why not bury it?

"What do you think?"

"I'm thinking how it would be if you drank the money, as Husaga did. You can expect anything from a Bosnian."

"A Bosnian gets wiser as he gets older, when he no longer needs wisdom. I'm beyond doing mad things. Do you agree then? I know someone who'll buy the house."

"We won't say anything to Tiyana, she'd be angry. Then, if the money's lost, only you and I will know about it."

"It won't be lost."

He said this decisively, as though taking an oath.

"You're forever thinking about deals. Why haven't you ever pawned your house and shop?"

"You see," he said gloomily, "they're the wife's."

I wasn't surprised at anything coming from him, that he'd

lie, cheat, steal. I was certain that he was only pretending when he offered to replace our lost money, but I never thought he'd play a trick like that on us.

"I see," I said angrily. "In other words, you were lying when you said that you'd sell the shop to give us our money back. You knew we were fools and wouldn't agree to it. Thank you, Mahmut, for your friendship."

"No way, for God's sake!" He waved his skinny arms, as if defending himself from a blow. "I wasn't lying! I talked to the wife about selling the shop, and she agreed. Honestly she did! And I'd have sold it, if Tiyana hadn't got so angry. And there'd have been some left over for me to spend on the flutes, so I wouldn't have had to ask you. What do you mean I was lying?"

To hell with him. No one on earth could guess when he was lying or when he was telling the truth. And everything with him was so muddled, such a tangle of plans, ambitions, calculations, lies, and who knows what else, that he himself must have had a hard time keeping track of it all. He was both true and false, honest and dishonest, real and unreal, with no middle state between them, and this was his sole integrity. But let him be! I couldn't choose people as I would wish, nor choose only that in them which was good. I had to accept or reject the people life sent me and everything that inseparably went with them. And I'd probably have made a big mistake if I'd accepted only saints, given that there were any, for they'd surely have been unbearably boring.

But when I saw misery dulling his aging and watery eyes, due to his fear that his plan, so long dreamt of, might fail, or because he truly believed his own lie, I repressed my pettifogging anger and gave him back his flippant hopes. Let the old fool have them! If I don't gain anything, I lose nothing, and what you gain or lose is not for me to decide.

My agreeing returned his dream unshattered. It also returned his self-confidence instantaneously, as though there were no trace of doubt or sorrow in him. And only a moment before, he'd been looking dismally at misfortune. This devotee of his own folly never doubted his luck for long. It would come, one day, no matter when, and he was always ready to adapt even to its shadow, as though it were waiting for him on some corner, on some turn of life.

And I realized that he wasn't deceiving me. He was going his own way, following his own desires, without reference to me.

Down the street, under the chestnut trees, strode the *serdar*-Avdaga, as though the rain weren't pouring, as if it were the perfect weather to take a walk. He was walking up and down, stopping every now and again, always at the same place, at the same distance from us, patiently watching and waiting.

"He's waiting for somebody, you or me," said Mahmut.

"You, for sure."

"Why me?"

"But why me?"

So did we generously pass the *serdar*-Avdaga from one to the other, lacking the ability to have the devil remove him from our eyes and from that wet street.

"Let's find out, then," Mahmut suggested.

He couldn't bear the uncertainty.

As we approached the *serdar*, we greeted him cheerfully, hoping that would be the end of it.

"Where were you going, Ahmet?"

"He was waiting for me!"

"You, Mahmut, you can be on your way."

It was an order.

Mahmut looked at me, smiled in embarrassment, as though sorry to leave me with Avdaga, or glad that such luck was not his and, politely taking his leave, thin, hunched, wet, but certainly relieved, went off down the street.

"Have you found a job?"

"No."

"No? Why not?"

I was silent, thinking how abruptly he'd got rid of Mahmut, not caring for the fact that he was rude, perhaps not even aware of his rudeness. This he didn't soften with even a smile, never mind a word. People didn't even expect anything different from him and were neither angry nor offended. An example was Mahmut's self-abasing smile and ingratiating manner; he was scared and took no offense. And I was scared, too! I should have said, "Mahmut's my friend. We were going on business. Why did you drive him away?"

I didn't say it.

It was my duty to defend Mahmut from humiliation. And myself, too. But I didn't. I'd swallowed Avdaga's insult, perhaps I'd even smiled, and now it stung me like a wound. I was ashamed of my cowardice, but still I thought, "It's a good job I didn't say anything to make him angry." I thought both things at the same time! Inside me two men were living simultaneously and with equal strength, totally different, entirely opposite, the one glad not to have exposed himself to danger, the other profoundly unhappy that he was a shit, and both equally sincere and both fully justified. And only a moment before, under the eaves, I'd been thinking of the double nature of Mahmut Neretlyak as being a wonder. We're all the same wonder, the same misery.

The *serdar* had no inkling of my torment. "What are you living on, if you're not working?"

"My wife works."

"That's not good. She'll take over. The man must do the work."

"I can't find any work."

"I'm sick of you and your 'I can't find any work'! Why not be a librarian? They'll sack Seid Mehmed. He's no good for anything anymore."

"I don't want to rob anybody of their living."

"Others will, if you don't."

"Then, it won't be my fault."

"You're a fool. But there are other jobs. Would you like to be a scribe for the *kadi?*"

"Are you seriously offering it?"

"I am."

"If you're offering anything, that means you want something in return."

"Nothing much."

"Let's hear it!"

"That student Ramiz is saying all sorts of things in the mosque. I trust you don't agree with him."

"If he's saying all sorts of things, as you put it, and those things are nasty, then I don't agree with him."

"The *kadi* wants everything he says noted down."

"And I'm to do the noting?"

"He'd recognize the *kadi's* scribes and change his tune."

"Look here, Avdaga, I've had a headache for the last three days. I shouldn't be able to remember a thing."

"You don't have to remember. Write it down."

"And besides, Dzhemal Zafraniya isn't keen on me. He won't like it if you give me the job."

"Dzhemal-*effendi* is the one who ordered me to approach you."

What sort of a fool had they sent to trap me? I'd guessed it, and now he'd confirmed it.

"Why didn't he come and tell me so himself?"

"I don't know."

"Then you can tell him I can't do it."

"You can, if you want to."

"All right, then, I don't want to."

"You don't want to?"

"I don't."

"You say you don't!"

"I said I don't. I've never been mixed up in that sort of thing, and I don't want to be now."

I'd dodged and look where it had got me!

For a wonder, I wasn't afraid any longer.

Even his look was not threatening, as I'd expected. He looked surprised, almost flabbergasted. It was probably the first time he'd ever heard or experienced anything like it. People weren't like this; he knew well that they were different. So what did this mean?

I'd bewildered him without intending, indeed, without any intention at all. He looked at me as though I were a stupid child, a madman, an apparition. He even smiled in disbelief, as though it were a joke, some strange misunderstanding that would soon pass, something he'd misheard, that I'd say I was joking, that I'd apologize, and he'd tell me off, and the world would be back in its familiar order. But nothing passed, the disjointedness remained, the disturbance was lasting, and he'd no remedy for this unknown state.

All he could find was an old, worn phrase, well tried, but it sounded hollow. "You'll regret it, Ahmet Shabo!"

"I'd regret it still more if I did what you wanted."

He clearly could find nothing more to say. He was silent, staring at me with a lost expression, and, had he come to himself, he could only have either killed me or gone on his way.

I went on mine, leaving him dumbstruck, standing in the rain under the chestnut tree, and I didn't turn back to see whether he'd dropped dead of a stroke. No such luck! He'd have been fine if he'd turned to stone and remained eternally there, under the chestnut tree, motionless, like a monument to loyalty that understood nothing. It would have been wonderful, it would have been my saving, for an icy cramp gripped my heart as soon as I'd left him.

Standing in front of him, I'd felt no fear. Left on my own, my legs felt like giving way beneath me.

Well done, you've behaved like a hero, and now you're going to pay for it.

Yet I didn't regret it, I couldn't, no matter how afraid I was.

I couldn't be dishonorable, yet I couldn't be brave either.

So I'd suffer in my fear, but honorably. I didn't even know whether it was possible.

Mahmut was waiting for me at the end of the street.

"Awful weather. Luckily."

He'd no idea just how awful the weather was, but why luckily?

"Because you didn't talk long."

"It seemed a long time to me."

"What did he want?"

"He offered me a job."

"That's good."

"But it was to note down everything Ramiz says in the mosque."

"That's not so good."

"Dzhemal Zafraniya sent him."

"And what did you say?"

"I said I wouldn't."

"You were wrong. You should have said: I can't, I haven't the time, I'm ill, I've got a cold, my wife's on her own, I've got a swollen hand, anything but 'I won't.'"

"I said what I said. I can't alter it."

"You could. But don't. You were right."

His conclusion was, as always, unexpected. He explained it thus: "It was stupid, but it was honest. They'll have it in for you, but let them see we're not all cowards. I've never dared say anything like it, but I've wanted to, I can't tell you how much I've wanted to. It's hard to spend one's whole life as a coward. True, you'll live longer, but is it worth it? It's worth it to me, because I can't do anything else, and I don't even try. I talk back, swear, say 'I won't,' say 'I will,' just to spite them, but all to myself. I daren't say it aloud. I say it to myself so as not to burst with rage. But it's not the real thing, if it doesn't come out. With you it did. It'll damage you, that's for certain, but, my friend, you did well. Had you had any sense, had you thought about it, you'd never have said it, and you'd have slept peacefully, while, this way, you'll be expecting a knife in the back, and I, too, since I was in for it in any case. Now they'll think we're both the same. So what, let it be, I don't care. Whatever happens, I'll share it with a friend."

He was making a big thing out of it. All the same, he was brave.

I said, jokingly, "Better be friends with a mufti than with me!"

"Thank you very much, to hell with it. I don't say it might not be useful. It might even help. But, when I think of it, you're just the friend for me. Not much, but still a good chap. All you do is cause me trouble and scare me half to death, but it's worth it!"

I recalled how he'd spoken about his wife. He'd probably say the same sort of things about me, such as: mad, useless, he couldn't be trusted with three sheep, hasn't a bent farthing, now he's a fool, but he was an even bigger fool before that, he'll mess up any chance he ever gets, he'll fall into every known trap, he's trouble to himself and all around him, no, indeed, I wouldn't ask for a better friend.

But now he didn't have time for such an expression of affection, which made me think: Who needs enemies? The *serdar*-Avdaga's threat worried him, and my reply worried him even more, but he didn't forget business. He hurried to sell my burned house. "Before something happens to you," he said soberly.

We completed the deal, agreed the sale, settled the necessary administration, all in a hurry, as though I were preparing to flee the town. And this because I suddenly felt regrets, for no reason. After all, this ruin was of no use to me, but, there you are, I was breaking a tie, parting from something that didn't even exist anymore, but once had, perhaps. What else could I do? Should I hang on to ghosts? In this land of ours, ties are often broken and little remains from generation to generation. Yet, for a moment, I felt an urge to preserve my ghosts. Later I regretted not having followed my weakness. But I'd have regretted if I'd obeyed it. Why should I let a nonexistent past haunt me?

Mahmut waited anxiously for me to get the money, luckily not having an inkling of my doubts, for, had he known how much I hesitated, he'd probably have had a heart attack.

When everything was finished, he became a new man, relaxed and radiant, cheerful and eager, while I withdrew into myself, depressed, but his happiness prevented him from seeing it.

The purchaser looked at us in amazement and the scribe at the courthouse did the same, taking us for two fools, which we certainly were. One madman had sold cheaply the only place that held possible memories of his dead ones in order to give the money to another madman for the daftest thing on earth, for a thousand worthless children's flutes.

Mahmut left early the next day. How he'd managed to sleep that night, because of his impatience, his plans and dreams, I don't know. He returned the following Friday, thin, sleepless but happy, with fifteen hundred flutes. The journey, hunger, and economizing had nearly killed him, but hope restored him to life, and so the wheezing victor, at the end of his strength, scarcely dragging a cramp-stricken leg, triumphantly entered the *kasaba*, shaky as a rotten fence, yet more self-assured than ever.

He sold the goods to the shops, not quite as profitably as he'd thought. He brought me an ordered account of his proceedings, agreeing only reluctantly to take expenses for his journey, so happy was he at this first business profit he'd ever made in his life.

But in the town, in the market and everywhere else, in the houses, fifteen hundred of Mahmut's flutes squealed from the mouths of children, making such a row that the pigeons fled in terror, and people held their heads in torment.

Mahmut walked about the town, happy to have presented it with such deafening music and the children with such a maddening enjoyment, while I laughed and felt rather ashamed, keeping to myself the fact that I, too, was to blame for the uproar.

I laughed, but I also felt sad.

What had become of the seat of my memories? They'd become the shrill sound of children's flutes!

I shouldn't have done it. I needed those ruins. They linked me to my childhood and to the life from which my own life came. I should have preserved those shadows, so they didn't remain just empty thoughts, without trace or basis, sadness for a lost past. Mine and theirs.

Now, left on my own, I had to begin all over again.

■ □ ■ □ ■

CHAPTER 10

A PURE-HEARTED
YOUNG MAN

I STAYED IN THE COFFEEHOUSE LONGER THAN USUAL AND much longer than I intended. I hadn't the heart to leave, for Mahmut Neretlyak's sake: He was celebrating his success in trade and treated everyone who came in. It was getting dark, and the call to evening prayer could be heard from the Begova mosque, but Mahmut went on drinking and treating. For days he'd been carried away with pride, unable to get used to his pathetic achievement. He talked incessantly, boasted, laughed good-heartedly at the ever more blatant and poisonous sneering, which he didn't even notice, and generously spent the money he'd earned with the flutes.

I was angry at him for what he was doing and amazed that he took the ridicule for a joke. They pretended to praise his cleverness. How could he have thought of children and flutes, when the idea hadn't occurred to a single merchant before! They asked him what new deal he was thinking up, so they could keep away from it, since it was hard to compete with him. They urged him to sell his shop. A man like him was not for small enterprises, and they expressed surprise at his having hidden his abilities for so long.

Sweating, heated with drink, carried away by his luck, he confided to all, as if they were friends, that he'd long suffered misfortune, and that when misfortune takes one between its teeth, cleverness and ability get you nowhere, nothing goes right. But he'd come across a good man who'd appreciated him, and it seemed that the spell had been broken. Now he was on his own feet, not very firmly perhaps, but still on his own feet. He'd found a support and hoped his ill luck was at an end, because a man had trusted him. Nobody knew, perhaps he was the only one who did know, what a help it was to be trusted by somebody. It strengthened the heart and gave power to the backbone. He'd thought of several enterprises. He'd planned them well and hoped they'd succeed. He'd be no threat to anyone's affairs, let no one worry on that score. As far as he could, he'd help anybody with advice or money, for he wanted to be friends with everybody and to live at peace with his neighbors.

In the smoky coffeehouse people were laughing aloud, smacking him on his thin shoulders, so that he bent like a reed in the wind, and mockingly thanking him for his goodness and generosity.

I felt sick.

"Let's go," I said. "That's enough of it."

"It's not enough. I can't leave these people now."

Then he whispered, with a knowing wink, that these people were necessary to him, for business. He'd help them, and they'd help him, and so they'd make money. It wasn't the money that mattered to him, but other things. What things? All sorts of things. Everyone has a secret burden. But we were friends, as they say, so why should he hide it from me: He had to get money to shut that dog's mouth. What dog's? His son-in-law's. May the devil take such people! When his daughter got married, Mahmut had promised her a pearl necklace and a string of ducats. It had happened before that business, while he still thought he'd spend his entire life in the town and get rich. It was his son-in-law who'd made him promise. If I'm to take an ugly girl, at least I don't have to take a naked one, he'd said openly. And she wasn't ugly, God was his witness. She was like her mother. He'd bought the pearls, but he couldn't get the ducats because of *that* business, and his son-in-law was giving him hell. He cursed them and swore fifty devils that he'd married into a pauper's family. He beat his wife. And how could a father look on at a daughter's misfortunes? He felt like killing him, but this would only have brought unhappiness on himself and his family. If they hadn't had children, he'd have brought her home to rest and live like a human being. But they had, three of them. How they'd got them they didn't know themselves, all in quarrel and bickering, and she wouldn't run away, because of the shame of it. But he'd get those damned ducats! Let the bastard be satisfied, and let his child have some peace. No illness, no weakness, not death itself would stop him from paying this debt!

His story took me aback. Could there be such a serious reason for his folly? In that case it wasn't folly, but deep trouble. I'd been unjust to him. I couldn't have helped him, made it easier for him, but still I'd been unjust.

And then I began to doubt the truth of this touching story. How could Mahmut have kept such a trouble secret? Wouldn't he have used it to engage our sympathy? And why hadn't he ever said he had a daughter? Where did this daughter come from?

And what use was this lie to him? And if it wasn't a lie, then perhaps it was once true, but had turned itself into self-deception.

He'd made up this daughter and son-in-law, or, at least, the troubles he'd had with them, and it was no use trying to look for the truth.

It was just as vain to get him to put an end to his celebrations. This was his moment of glory, long awaited.

I didn't know whether he'd thought of it in the years of hardship, whether he'd prepared the words he'd say and the satisfaction he'd feel, when once he'd succeeded in life. He hadn't succeeded, we all knew that, he knew it, too, but to wait for true success was too long for him, and he saw this poor beginning as a step toward his long-desired aim. It wasn't the aim itself, he knew that. His aim was far greater.

But it was a first step, success, free and full of promise. The spells had been broken. Fate had mercifully left him in peace. The *sheitans* had tired of trying to trip him up, and now all that remained was his faith in himself and his abilities to obtain a conceivable happiness. Not because of the money, God was his witness. But for what he'd have found it difficult to explain. Perhaps it was for the right he was paying for that evening, to speak about himself as others did, to listen to their sarcasms and take them for a friendly joke or for praise, to feel or to imagine their respect. He was taking it all, touched, grateful, all of it, perhaps even the sarcasm, only let it not be as on other evenings, let him not feel like one of the benches, like one of the walls, like a dog.

But if his triumph this evening was only a make-believe, tomorrow it would be a reality, and he'd have nothing to regret. Sitting with people shoulder to shoulder, in good fellowship, that was no make-believe. And if tomorrow there would be nothing left of it, at least there'd be the memories.

But Mahmut was not thinking so far ahead.

Perhaps he was right. It didn't matter what was. What mattered was what it was to him. And thank God for that. This evening he was a different Mahmut Neretlyak, the desired one, the one he'd dreamt of for years, without a wheezy chest and cramps in his legs, without a hidden sorrow in his heart.

A pity the illusion would not be longer lasting.

He wasn't angry when I said I was going home. He didn't try to detain me but generously dismissed me with a wave of his hand. Tonight he wasn't alone. Till then I had, for lack of anything better, replaced these people, this talking, this warmth. Now he could do without me.

Good luck to him. He'd look me up again tomorrow.

I hurried home. It was getting darker and colder. The streets were dark and empty. People had retired to their homes, like birds at dusk.

Tiyana was waiting for me, alone in the empty room. It wasn't fair of me to leave her on her own. I'd tell her I wouldn't do it again, even though what I did was for the sake of others. But what had others to do with me, Mahmut Neretlyak, and his madness? We have understanding for everybody, except for our closest ones. We consider that their affection is ours by right, like our own skin.

I hoped she'd not be angry, for then I'd refuse to admit my guilt, and we'd go on sulking till bedtime. It would spoil the enjoyment of my being generously repentant and my heady pleasure at my own good nature and at her forgiveness. It would be fine if she showed a bit of sense and didn't reproach me for my lack of consideration. If she should insist on her rights, I'd deny them, and I'd refuse to admit my fault for the very reason that I was guilty. But this only I could admit, it was not for her to say. And we'd quarrel. She'd cry and give a list of all my many shortcomings, and I'd get mad and call the gods to witness that I was the unhappiest of men for whom nobody had any understanding. After that we'd make it up, suddenly, and all would be well, like after rain, or after a thunderstorm.

It would be all right, no matter how she greeted me.

In front of the entrance to our yard I was met by Mula Ibrahim, the advocate, once my friend and employer. He was strolling, as if taking a pre-bedtime walk for the good of his health, and he must have been straining his eyes in the darkness to recognize my shadow, so he wouldn't miss me.

"Go on in," he whispered and disappeared into the darkness of the entrance.

"You must have been waiting a long time. I usually come home earlier."

I said this merely for the sake of something to say, to hide my surprise at seeing him there and at such a time. I felt a wave of fear. What had happened? Was I in some sort of danger? But I dismissed this, realizing that he wouldn't have come anywhere near my house if there'd been the slightest hint of danger. You could follow him across an iced river, as happily as you might a fox.

"Is anyone following you?" he asked cautiously, without replying to my clumsy remarks about being late.

"Why should they?"

"I was talking today . . ."

My neighbor, the drunken Zhucho, a street cleaner, went by.

Mula Ibrahim pressed himself to the wall and grew silent, hiding behind me.

I laughed. "What are you afraid of? He's drunk. He wouldn't recognize himself in a mirror, let alone you."

"I had a talk today about you with Shehaga Socho. It was his idea," he admitted frankly.

"Why should Shehaga be asking about me?"

"He said he might be able to help you. He asked you to get in touch with him."

"How could he help me?"

"He could find you a job. He can do most things."

"What would he want from me in return?"

"Nothing. He happened to mention you. We talked about you, and I told him everything I knew, and then he said you ought to visit him. I'd advise you to go."

"Maybe I will."

"Not maybe, but definitely."

"All right, definitely."

"Have you any money?"

"I have, thank you."

"That's all right then. Don't tell anyone I was here."

He peeped from behind the gatepost, to make sure he was not seen, and vanished into the dark.

I looked after his shadow that was melting into the night and felt an urge to run after him to ask him why he'd come, hiding in the dark and half dead with fear. This fear of his, of everybody, of nothing, was ridiculous, but it was no less fear for him just because it seemed ridiculous to others. It had cost him considerable courage to come anywhere near my house and to talk with me, an outcast, whose very existence was unrecognized, even if so briefly, as if he'd merely waved a hand to me in passing.

Why was he worrying about me? Was it because of his memory of the Dniestr, when I'd saved him from death, without thinking of my own? I'd already told him I didn't do it out of any kindness of heart nor out of pity nor through any conscious decision of my own. It was an impulsive act, as though I'd lost my head and didn't know what I was doing. I could have just as well left him to the torrent, without thought or conscience. So he didn't owe me anything. I'd told him that long ago. But reasons are forgotten, only the act is remembered. All he recalled was my action and his moment of terror when he'd messed himself out of fear, shattered by the death whose icy presence he'd already sensed. And a madman had stubbornly pulled the boat through raging waves for his sake, a stranger's (while I thought that I'd merely been clinging to a plank, so as not to sink). It was certain that he'd then prayed most sincerely for the life of another man, at least until we reached the bank, and for victory over death, both the man's and his own. And he'd never wished anyone so well as he did that man, for everything had depended on him. He remembered everything, the raging river and that mad moment before death and that mad youth, and afterward, even when he came to himself, he couldn't forget that he owed his life only to him and to chance. He'd first received life from his father in Sarajevo; his second life he'd received from me, on the Dniestr. The first life he hadn't even wished for; for the one I'd given him he was prepared to give his soul. He had to remember his parent, particularly the more important one. Of course, he could have forgotten, many do, but it was his misfortune to be a good man who wished to return good with good. But he'd been forced to return good with ingratitude. And perhaps it was harder for him than for me. It must have been harder. He hadn't forgotten. He'd come this evening, even though he was afraid. He didn't dare send a message by anyone else. He'd come himself. For him this meant the same as charging a fortified trench.

There'd been times when I'd wished him to wake in the middle of the night from shame and repentance from his ingratitude, and now, perhaps, he was more sensitive than I'd thought and even struggled against the fear that rampaged through his blood.

May God forgive you, I'd thought then when he deserted me, lacking the courage to save me, out of fear of others. May God forgive you, I repeated now, only more gently and warmly than before. He couldn't have left his dreaded fears at home, but bore them inside him the whole way, like a smoldering shirt, like a snake round the neck, like a fever in the body, and, for sure, that fear grew worse, certainly not better, as he approached the forbidden spot. Still he came, scorched with the fire, covered in bites, in stab wounds from within himself, came like a soldier to bring me news of aid.

May God forgive you, honest man, whom people did not allow to be so: You did your duty, though dying of fear. I was beginning to value that type of courage. It was probably greater than when fear was absent.

I'd tell Tiyana the strange tale of the hero who became such out of fear and of a sense of honor that was born of shame. Now, returning after having done what was not wise but honest (as Mahmut would say), his fear would be the greater, but he'd have a feeling of satisfaction. Or perhaps not. Perhaps he was already regretting his thoughtless action, but I'd not know and would continue to remember only his act of bravery.

When I entered our room, I stopped in the doorway, surprised. Tiyana was not alone. On our trunk, the *serdar*-Avdaga sat calmly.

I'd have rather seen a wolf.

Did Mula Ibrahim know that Avdaga was in the house? Then his courage was all the greater.

I looked at Tiyana questioningly: What does he want? How should I know, her smile seemed to reply.

I greeted Avdaga, waiting for an explanation for his visit. But he was in no hurry to say anything, as though it were quite natural to drop in to a person's house, unexpected and uninvited.

But it was not natural, even for him. I thought he looked embarrassed, which explained his silence and the meaningful clearing of his throat, sitting there stiff and frowning. He said he'd hoped . . . to find me at home. . . . It was well after dark. . . . And I had to explain, more for Tiyana than for him, that Mahmut was celebrating his business success, and I couldn't leave him.

"He's rubbish," Avdaga said shortly.

"No worse than others," I said.

Tiyana, liking neither Avdaga's remark nor my answer, said that Mahmut was a good man, only unfortunate. That was her greatest justification for anybody.

For Avdaga, this was the worst thing you could say about anyone. He surely thought: If he were worth anything, he'd have succeeded in something and not remained a miserable wretch. He couldn't be a good man if he was a thief. And he was unlucky because he got caught. All people were potential criminals, and those who were condemned as such could never be considered honest people again. In fact, he said nothing, but simply slid his oily glance from me to Tiyana, as though not understanding what we were talking about. And still worse, he couldn't quite make us out; we were neither criminals nor respectable folk. So what were we then?

"You're a strange pair," he said thoughtfully, huddling himself on the trunk, as though there were a weight pressing down on him.

I knew he was summing us up, and I thought it better not to worsen my position in his thoughts and to do nothing that might turn him against me. Better for us to be strange and obscure than suspicious.

His own people despised him, yet they left him to strike fear into all around him, and this he did with great diligence, as much in obedience to his strict conscience as to his masters. He preferred to punish a hundred innocents than to let a single guilty one go free, and, in his view of things, he could find everyone guilty according to his judgment. So I left his sluggish thought to rest quietly, undisturbed by anything that might set it alight.

But Tiyana didn't agree with me. She was incapable of not speaking out against an unjust word, even if, afterward, she nearly died of fear, and she never learned her lesson.

"Why do you say we're strange?" she asked sharply, and I knew that now there was no way of stopping her. "Are we strange because we've never done anybody any harm, because we've never caused anyone any trouble, because we've never done anybody an injustice? Or are we strange for calmly putting up with the injustices that are done to us? And what do we have to do, Avdaga, so as not to be strange? Do we have to swear, to curse, to complain, to hate people, to intrigue against them?"

"You exaggerate."

"Are we strange because Mahmut Neretlyak, whom you all despise, comes to our house? You say he's rubbish. But look here, when misfortune hit us, I say misfortune, for I've no other word for it, nobody as much as turned their head, nobody helped us, only he. God knows what would have happened to us without him. He brought us food he could ill afford, and that I'll never forget. And now he's rubbish, and we're strange! Where's your heart, Avdaga? What do you want from us?"

At first her sharp words scared me, but when I saw how taken aback he was, I enjoyed both her outburst and his embarrassment. He became flustered as soon as someone showed no fear. It was the second time I'd seen it. Perhaps because he hadn't figured us out, hadn't yet placed us, for, faced with those he considered criminals, he'd certainly have felt no embarrassment. Or perhaps the presence of a woman made him uneasy, he, an old bachelor who'd exchanged scarcely more than a few words with women, that mysterious species, now knew the force of the female tongue, especially coming from one so beautiful.

Looking at her in surprise, Avdaga turned to me, as though seeking help. But no help was forthcoming. I enjoyed watching him burning in the fire of her eloquence, and wished him even greater torment.

And she, angered by his insults, carried away by her own speech, waited for him to utter a single word, to resume her litany and to make him pay for all the bitterness of the last months.

"I thought . . ."

I wouldn't say he thought anything; everything in him was turned upside down. Perhaps he repented having dropped in (for what I still didn't know), or perhaps he wasn't even capable of that, due to his surprise that she felt no fear in front of him, as others did, that she didn't choose her words as others did, that she gave no thought to his bloodstained calling as did others. And without that terror that he unfurled above him like a banner, that hovered around him like a cloud, without that sword that severed people's courage, he was disarmed and helpless. May God be merciful to him, but now even those two single thoughts were stuck in his head like two bones in the throat.

I decided to come to his aid, for fear lest he seek refuge in cruelty, to save himself from humiliation. It was high time I did this. Perhaps I'd even left it till too late.

"Aren't you being a bit unjust, my dear," said I in a conciliatory tone, hoping she'd get the point. "Avdaga meant no offense."

"I don't know what he meant, I know what he said. But if he doesn't want to help us, why insult us?"

"But he's not insulting us, so leave it."

At this Avdaga found his words. "I was thinking of something else, not what you were talking about. I was thinking that you weren't exactly rich."

"Why don't you say we're paupers? Is that a sin?"

"No, it's not. But I offered him a job, and he refused."

"I don't want to be the ruin of another man, Avdaga."

"He's been the ruin of himself."

"What do you want from me then?"

"Nothing. Only I can't understand it. How can a man be in such poverty and refuse a position?"

So that was what was bothering him! But how could I explain it to him? I couldn't act dishonestly; I was no wild beast. The man had done nothing to me. Whatever I might have said might have seemed to relate to him, Avdaga. And I felt he was asking more for his own sake than anything else. He was a killer of people, convinced that he was acting honestly. I don't know whether I killed anybody in the war, but whenever I saw dead bodies after a battle, I felt a cold shiver at the thought that one of them might have fallen to one of my bullets.

Were I to have said this to him, he'd have thought I was lying or that I was an absolute weakling. He'd have disbelieved me also, because he knew plenty, indeed many, unscrupulous people.

He found it impossible to understand how I could have rejected his offer. I'd have got a job. They were asking very little in return, and no one would even have known that I'd done anything ugly. Only I'd have known, and he couldn't believe that this would have worried me!

Had I mentioned my conscience to him, he'd not have understood. His conscience was a state conscience, which didn't recognize the existence of the individual.

"Look here, Avdaga. The simplest things are always the hardest to explain," said I, trying to find a hole in his armor. "For instance, would you kill a man just in order to take his coat or his horse or his land?"

"Never! God forbid."

"Then why do you think I would?"

He was silent for a moment, then shook his large square head.

"That's different."

"Or don't you think it's wrong to throw Seid Mehmed out of his job?"

"Seid Mehmed is no good for anything anymore."

"Then you surely think it's no sin to destroy Ramiz?"

"That's for others to decide."

"But you don't think it is a sin. But why? Because somebody said that he's a danger to the state."

"He's against the state."

"Some state, when it's in danger from a single man," said Tiyana aggressively. "And he's not a danger to the state, only to those who think they represent the state."

This time not only Avdaga was taken by surprise at her words, but I, too.

I gave her a sign with my eyes to stop, to calm down, for she'd gone dangerously beyond the bounds of what was permitted, but she didn't see my signs, for she'd gone beyond caring for boundaries.

"Was my father a danger to the state?" she continued bitterly, revealing the cause of her anger. "No, he was no danger to anybody. But they killed him. They gave someone an order, and he obeyed it. Perhaps it was just because he said something when he'd been drinking, or it seemed to somebody that he'd said something. Another's life is cheap, Avdaga. There are plenty of people who'd pity nobody. So why try to make criminals of honest people? Leave them alone, if only as freaks."

"Like rare animals," I added, laughing, since this was all I could do.

"But thanks anyway for your visit. But if you came to persuade Ahmet to do something wrong, then you've wasted your time. And now it's time to go to bed. It's late."

So she got rid of him, not in the least politely.

I'd no idea what Avdaga would have done had I spoken to him like that. He didn't as much as frown at her. He merely fidgeted with his long legs and arms, as though he couldn't find a place for them.

I had the impression that he'd wanted to leave earlier, but didn't know how to do it so as not to appear either defeated or too easily offended. He chose the worst method of all; he looked at me, nodding toward Tiyana, with a clumsy smile, as though to say: So that's what she's like, is it! And since he thought he'd got well away with it, he got up, slapping himself on the thighs and said, taking his leave (I thought he was being sarcastic, but no, he was quite serious): "We've had a very pleasant conversation. Hope I've not upset you."

We'd certainly had a pleasant conversation, as if we'd been beating the hide off one another!

But I wouldn't say that he left hurt. Who knows what his stubborn head had taken in and what had fluttered past his ears.

And then it occurred to me that he might even respect us for not agreeing to a base action and for saying what we thought. Perhaps, for Avdaga was cruel, but not dishonest; he knew no mercy, but had no guile. He was an inverted, deformed example of a simple man who plowed and dug in a manner different from that of his father, yet still some human qualities remained in him: some grain, some deposit, some pale memory. Of course, this was only guesswork, for I'd no idea what took place in the mind of an executioner.

I accompanied him out onto the street, not knowing what to say. I wanted neither to soften nor to reinforce what had been said.

"That wife of yours is a terror," he said, only when we'd reached the bottom of the staircase, making sure she didn't hear him, I thought. "Now I know why you didn't take the job. It was because of her."

"What do you mean because of her? I gave you my answer immediately, without asking her."

"You wouldn't have dared face her, if you'd agreed. And I

was wondering why. Now I see why. Thank God I was never married. But I haven't told you why I came."

He managed to remember the reason for his visit, even though belatedly.

"Dzhemal-*effendi* wishes to see you tomorrow in the Begova mosque at midday. And he asked me to tell you that you're wrong. He's not angry with you."

"Why should I come to the mosque?"

"There's a meeting of the *ulema*. They're discussing that student, Ramiz."

"What's there to discuss?"

"Ah, that I don't know. But Ramiz has been arrested and put in the Fortress. Hadn't you heard?"

"When?"

"At dusk. The people he was addressing grabbed him and delivered him to the authorities. So that's it. And make sure to come."

He set off, but turned back.

"When I came, your wife wasn't alone."

"Really?"

"She was with Osman Vuk. He left as I arrived."

"He must have been looking for me."

"Perhaps he was. I thought you should know."

He trusted no one, so how could he trust a woman? And so he warned me to be on my guard, but I'd no worries in that quarter, thank God.

Avdaga went off into the darkness, leaving me shattered on account of Ramiz.

He'd told me how he thought of his home and family. Now he'd be thinking of them even more. He hated all the Avdagas of the world and still more their masters. He'd summoned the oppressed to struggle against them, while thinking of the warmth of a friendly conversation. And he was thinking of a girl, too. No doubt, in one of the Fortress cells, with eyes closed, he was speaking to her now, telling her how cruel people had seized him that evening, not his own people, for they were waiting for him in the mosque as they did every evening, telling her how he was thinking of them and of her, since all they'd left him were his thoughts.

Now he was alone, terribly alone, and perhaps he remembered the friend he'd wanted, perhaps even me. Perhaps his thoughts were hovering about my head, and I didn't see them, only sensed them.

I couldn't guess how he was feeling, empty and desperate. Perhaps only empty darkness surrounded him, on every side. He'd thought of everybody, now no one thought of him. He'd be lying awake, in fear, while others slept.

But perhaps I was mistaken. Perhaps his kind heart was satisfied that he'd done all he could. Perhaps he believed people lay awake because of him, that the seeds he'd sown had taken root. Perhaps he believed that another Ramiz would take his place to fight for human well-being. Not all people could be selfish and frightened.

I saw him as being like a dot of light in this night's darkness, and I felt as if this unknown youth was the closest being to me on earth.

But it was no use, for I could help neither him nor myself. No matter what I did, the dot of light would dissolve and vanish, and all my sadness for him would become only a nostalgic memory.

But now tears choked me at the thought of the world's fate.

Only let me keep it to myself. I couldn't trouble Tiyana, already disturbed as she was, with yet new worries.

"Did he say anything?" she asked, referring to Avdaga.

Yes, I'd think of him, rather than think of Ramiz.

"He said you were a terror."

"Perhaps I overdid it. I shouldn't have talked like that."

"Why shouldn't you? What you said was the truth."

"No, no, I overdid it. It was stupid."

In vain I assured her she'd been in the right and that she'd got the better of Avdaga. And it occurred to me, only too late, that I was wrong: Had I objected to her speaking her mind, she'd have argued the point. But needing no defense from me, she began to reproach herself. She accused herself while, at the same time, hoping for me to defend her, and, deep down, she'd remember that I'd stood by her.

And then she confided what I already knew. The cause of it all was her father. To her shame, she'd begun to forget him. She didn't even know where his grave was. There'd been a time when she felt she'd die of the pain and sadness, yet now she scarcely ever gave him a thought. It was Avdaga who'd brought it all back to her. People said it was he who killed him.

"Calm down. Don't think any more about it, and we'll inquire about his grave. I'll ask around."

"Why? He used to say: When I die it doesn't matter where they bury me."

"We'll talk about it later. Now try to sleep."

"I can't. I feel awful for having spoken like that. It'll just be another stone round your neck."

She wept in my arms, tortured by fears of the future, her tears easing her pain. I consoled her with the flippant thought that fears do not always bring disaster and that evil comes most often unannounced. And good, too. Troubles came to us when we least deserved them. Why should they not avoid us now, when we thought we might be at fault? And then, there's always more trouble than there is fault, and those who are most at fault usually have the least trouble, so it was a pity we weren't more at fault than we were. But the world was not ruled by reason. Nor did people reap what they sowed. It was ruled by the maddest of mad coincidences, and we'd expended our bad luck, so that only good luck remained for us.

And while I was busy unwinding my tangled defense of our right to happiness, seeking by words to avoid thinking, she fell asleep, breathing deeply, her cheek on my shoulder, her fear forgotten in sleep.

Only I and the youth up there in the Fortress remained awake.

■ □ ■ □ ■

CHAPTER 11

I'LL NOT THINK OF RAMIZ

AND I WOKE UP THINKING ABOUT RAMIZ, A MAN I DIDN'T know, yet whom I seemed to know better than anyone else on earth. He stood out because of his suffering, as though he were redeeming all our evil. No, not a single evil would he redeem. Everything would be the same, untouched, and his sacrifice would be without purpose. What could one man do? What could a hundred do? One cockerel and a million sleepers. Why had they arrested him? They could have left him in peace to go on shouting. No one would have woken. He knew what was waiting for him. Did he want to suffer?

Did he hope to raise people by his suffering?

I wouldn't think of him. It was pointless.

I went to the bakery to get some bread. The men in the bakery were cheerful, talking, joking, and laughing.

"You're laughing, I see. Have you had some good news?"

"We haven't. That's why we're laughing."

"What's new, folks?"

"Prices have gone up, if that's anything new."

"You work all night, and it's at night that things happen."

"Drunks stagger, thieves lurk, watchmen doze, lovers hide, but for us nothing happens."

"Haven't you heard anything?"

"What happens in the night is heard about in the day. We will hear then."

I would not think about Ramiz.

I found Tiyana awake.

"Why did you get up so early?"

"It's not early, lazybones. The bakers had emptied their second oven."

"Are you ill?"

"Why? Do I look ill? Aren't I allowed to get up early when I feel like it?"

"You were restless. I heard you tossing and turning."

I sat down beside her on the bed. Her black hair was spread over the pillow. Her eyes were moist with sleep, her lips swollen like those of a child.

"How lovely you are when you've just woken up!"

"And only then? Only when I've just woken up?"

"Only then. Only when you've just woken up. Can't you see, I want to make you angry?"

"You won't manage."

"Then I'll tell you the truth, just to spite you. You're always beautiful, and I always know it, but I don't say anything. Now I have to. I feel it in every pulse."

I would not think about Ramiz.

"And what else do you feel?"

"I want to smell you like a flower. I want to fill my eyes with your picture so there's no room in them for anything else."

I would not think about Ramiz.

"And now tell me, what's happened?"

"Aren't I allowed to tell you how much I love you?"

"You're avoiding something. You're thinking of something else."

"I'm thinking how happy I am."

"Why this morning in particular?"

"I often do."

"Happy, in spite of everything. How's that?"

She always drove me into a corner. I could never hide anything from her. It was useless trying.

I told her about Ramiz, how he was shut up in the Fortress, as Avdaga had told me the night before.

"Why did you keep it from me?"

"I didn't want to worry you."

"I saw at once that you were hiding something."

"How did you see it?"

"You're never so loving as when things aren't going well. You're like a child trying to hide."

"I don't even know him well, but I'm sorry for him. No one will lift a finger to help him."

"Who can do anything?"

"Nobody. But perhaps he's hoping that the people will protest and demand his release."

"I doubt it. He himself knows they won't."

"What if I went to Zafraniya and asked him?"

"Why you? It's the first thing he'll ask: Why you?"

"We're not friends, but I feel as if we are. He has nobody else."

"You can't help him; you'll only harm yourself."

She said this reluctantly, for she understood my motives, but she said it to restrain me. And she said more than this: "What can you do? He's guilty. He spoke against them."

"It would be no good; they'd not let him go."

"Don't think about him anymore."

"I won't. There's no point."

No use, no sense, no point. They'd scared us. We didn't dare ask mercy for anybody. No one would say a word for him.

But what could I do?

I had nothing behind me, no name, no achievement, no wealth, no family. In whose name could I speak? In the name of pity? What did my pity mean to anybody?

And what for? For the sake of a nonexistent debt of conscience, for a man to whom I owed nothing, for the sake of a crime they would not pardon.

I would not think about the impossible.

I would not think of Ramiz.

I ate my breakfast without knowing what I was eating.

Tiyana looked at me as if I were ill, hiding her anxiety with a sour smile.

I said I was going into town for a walk.

"Why don't you stay at home?"

"There's some meeting or other in the mosque at noon. Zafraniya has invited me."

"Why you?"

"I don't know."

"And what's the meeting about?"

"It's to do with Ramiz. I don't know."

"Don't say a word, please, not a word! Promise me."

"I won't. What have I got to say? I wouldn't even turn up, if I dared."

"Oh God, this is all we need. Come straight home, immediately after it's finished. Oh, by the way, Osman Vuk was looking for you last night. He wouldn't say what he wanted."

I'd completely forgotten about him.

Wet roofs, wet fences, wet streets, chill air, a blue sky, a morning sun.

I don't know why, but, suddenly, I forgot everything. I felt I was walking through dew, through fresh water, through a leafy wood. The blood in my veins sparkled. A quiet and reasonless joy obsessed me. Everything was clear and bright, like a mountain stream.

I would not think of Ramiz.

What time was it?

I wouldn't think at all, till noon.

Till noon.

I sought possibilities beyond those that oppressed me. Perhaps the body revolted against the nightmare that thought had imposed on it. The body is cleverer than the mind. It knows all about itself, what it needs and what it does not need. It even knows what we don't know. The body's like a plant, like a roe deer. Whether it be a good thing or a bad thing that it can't be entirely so, I know not.

But at noon I'd not be able to avoid anything. And the moment I recalled all this, I again felt a sluggishness in my limbs and a confusion in my thoughts.

And again I was a man tormented, a man who knew nothing.

I was not thinking deeply, nor was my torment particularly acute, but sufficient for the morning to loose its brightness.

I would not think of Ramiz, but I was thinking. I couldn't help it.

I'd fled from him into a blessed paradise of emptiness, but I was a plant, a roe deer, a healthy body, for but a moment. I would not have wished to remain so. I'd rather be a madman, thinking of something that didn't concern him, that he couldn't correct, but that was as far removed from him as a star in the heavens.

I could do nothing. Yet I thought.

That much I could do. I'd torment myself with the thought of a good man awaiting death in the Fortress. I'd think and I'd forget. Like so many other things. I was slowly becoming a repository of decomposing sorrows, pity, shame, defunct promises, and to all this stench I'd give the name of experience. I'd already sensed it, I still sensed it, later I'd feel indifferent.

I'd left the house in the hope of meeting somebody, no matter whom, to hear some news, to talk with somebody, to learn what I could. But I'd met nobody, heard nothing, talked about nothing. Whom could I have met, what could I have heard, what could I have talked about? Nobody knew anything, nobody cared, nobody would say anything. Or they'd say what I already knew, that it was best to mind one's own business.

In one of the courtyards I came across a wedding party. The gates were open, the yard full of young people. There was a sound of an invisible fiddle, a *kolo* was in full swing, there was laughter, singing, and chatter.

None of them knew anything of Ramiz. Nor of the meeting in the mosque. Nor of any other depressing matters. And they'd live out their lives without knowing.

I saw them in the entrance and couldn't get them out of my mind. To hell with you, I said. It's all right for you, I said.

Why wasn't I like them? Why did I take no care of my own life? Why did I concern myself with what didn't concern me?

Perhaps one day I'd be cured, grow up. One day. God knows when.

I would not think of Ramiz.

Now I was not thinking of Ramiz, but of what they'd say about him. It was close on midday.

I entered the mosque without looking at who was in the yard and sat down at the back, by the door.

As the mosque began to fill, I watched, thanks to my detached position, unnoticed, for everybody was looking at those who came in last: the *muderises*, the more important *imams* and *vaizes*, the more important scribes and the leading *kadi*, escorted by Dzhemal Zafraniya. Dzhemal was smiling at everybody, without seeing anybody, while the *kadi* passed by, scowling, his eyes fixed on an imaginary spot in front of him.

Mula Ibrahim was among the last to enter. He came straight toward me without looking and, when he saw me, stopped and started to look for a better place, pretending he hadn't seen me.

He was right, for, indeed, what business had I in such a gathering? Everyone would think I was a gate-crasher or that I'd been invited by mistake.

These people were the brains and power of the town, and if, by some miracle, the vault of the mosque collapsed, the town would remain without brains and significance. Despite all the sorrow I'd feel at such an event, I'd be glad to be a survivor, even if the only one, for it would not be right to figure in the list of casualties with such important people.

This was not spiteful but simply muddled thinking. I'd eaten nothing since morning. I felt sick. My stomach rolled, my hands burned. If I had to run, I'd dash through the crowd to the door, to find some suitable place. They'd think I was running away.

I began to have the most fantastic thoughts. Avdaga would stand up and announce how he'd summoned me to bear witness against Ramiz and how I'd refused. He'd recall the dinner at *hadji*-Duhotina's, mention that my wife was a Christian, and, were he to mention all she'd said to him last night, everyone would turn to gaze with piercing eyes at the monster that was called Ahmet Shabo.

I knew it was absurd. The *serdar*-Avdaga himself or Dzhemal Zafraniya or the lowliest policeman could do what they liked with me, without having to bother so many of the high and mighty. But the brain, once excited, is like a frightened animal seized by terror that thinks everything is against it.

Why had they summoned me?

Right up at the front Dzhemal Zafraniya got to his feet and began to speak. Closing his myopic eyes—and it seemed as though he were looking directly at me, smiling politely, yet determinedly, politely in his own name, determinedly in the name of the *kadi*—he stated that by order of the honorable and worthy *kadi-effendi*, whose reputation, honor, and wisdom were famous beyond the confines of our town (he bowed to the *kadi*, who calmly listened and appeared quite unembarrassed at such shameless praise), by an order that he was proud to announce, he'd invited the most prominent people to this meeting, for which he, on his own behalf, thanked them for coming. The reason for the meeting was unimportant and trivial, but the real reason was of great importance, and he, with the permission and at the command of the honorable *kadi*, would explain it as briefly as possible, so that those wiser than he might state their opinion. There'd been in our town a certain ne'er-do-well Ramiz, a well-known good-for-nothing who claimed to have been a student of the Al-Azhar University, which was certainly a lie, but even if it were true, the shame was his and not that of Al-Azhar University. No one objected to his living in our town. Our hospitality and openness were known to everybody. Nor had anyone anything against his giving speeches, speech is free to all, but this non-believer, this ignoramus, had dared to express in public such dreadful things, such as no honorable man could repeat. (And then he went on to repeat them, as though he'd forgotten what he'd just said, as though he thought of himself as not being an honorable man, which was surely an error made in the heat of rhetoric and not to be taken seriously.) This maniac had attacked our laws, our faith, our state, and even the sublime sultan himself. But although this was dreadful and scarcely comprehensible, we would not have been summoned simply because of this. There was a more important and serious matter at stake. This criminal had been spreading poison for a whole month, night after night, to a mosque full of people. And no one, no one, for a whole thirty days, had stood up to refute such blasphemies, to stop him from speaking, to report him to the authorities. (It was not the people he was speaking to who'd handed him over to the authorities, but others, employed by the authorities themselves!) And now, he asked, where were the true faithful? Where were the authorities and what were they doing over such a long time? We've been deaf and blind, I have to say it, and allowed our worst enemy to say to the people whatever came into his head. And the authorities, whose duty it is to know what suspicious people are up to, didn't lift a finger. Can we tolerate that every criminal, whenever he feels like it, should spit upon what is holy? Can we leave the people to be poisoned by sinister enemies who hate them?

"No more!" said the *kadi* ominously, interrupting Zafraniya's beautifully embroidered speech, which was clearly unfinished. There were still many ornaments and turns of phrase remaining in the speaker's throat, to his and our great detriment, but he took the *kadi*'s rudeness for praise, as though it were the perfect end and conclusion to his words, like the *kadi*'s signature to everything he'd said. So he glowed like a young bride at a wedding.

"You will say what you like, but I'll have no such criminal acts within my jurisdiction, nor such slackness. I hope you will say all you think, regardless of what I think. And now, the floor is yours!"

When the *kadi* had thus generously given the floor to the meeting, there followed a short pause, most probably to draw breath, but those present quickly recovered and hastened to declare themselves. Too long a pause might have been interpreted as hesitation or even disagreement, and from that let God preserve them!

The first to get up was my undestined benefactor, the deaf political leader Mula Ismail. I don't know how he'd grasped that the subject was an enemy of the empire, but he made no mistake. Before us, he said, was a question of disrespect for authority, for the law, and for the faith. And this smacked of the plague. For we, too, were disunited, and for Muslims disunity smacked of the plague. All this month the dogs had been howling, and that smacked of the plague.

Nobody stopped him. Nobody even smiled, as he spoke exhaustively of the causes and symptoms of the plague. Somehow this seemed to fit into the discussion of Ramiz. He who brings the plague is surely dangerous. Indeed, this scarcely required proof, but it needed to be said.

The *muderis* Rahman explained the root and causes of the rise of Hamzevian teaching, which rejected all authority and preached disorder in which everyone should take care of himself. From the many facts, dates, and names, I drew the conclusion, God knows how, that this teaching appeared, when and where I don't know, as a result of the poverty and dissatisfaction of the peasants for whom life was difficult. Today such teaching was senseless, for everybody knew that the peasants of today lived well and respected the sultan's government. He considered it was necessary to acquaint the ignorant and the erring with these scientific facts, even though such people were few in number, so they might not fall victim to deceivers.

Muderis Numan based his speech on the statement that any teaching not founded on the faith was erroneous. The faith was infallible, since it was God's law, and to stray from God's law was a sin and a blasphemy. He firmly supported freedom of thought, without it there was no progress or prosperity, but freedom of thought within the framework of the Koran, since thought outside the Koran was not free but retrogressive. He who committed a great sin and was our enemy considered freedom to be freedom from God's laws. That was not freedom, but the worst slavery, and slavery to Satan and darkness was a mortal sin against which holy war should be declared.

Ilijaz-*effendi* said that he felt regret and shame that we gave so much freedom to those who did not deserve it. It was as if we'd lost our heads, condemning ourselves to an evil fate, inviting disaster. It was our duty to be alert, to know everything, to resist. In his *dzhemat* he carried out this duty. He was alert, knew what was going on, resisted the enemy. The young people had taken a wrong road. They sang near the mosque during prayers, used indecent language, had contempt for distinguished people, and laughed at sacred things. He reproached them, shamed them, tried to bring them back to the right path, but he could do little on his own. What was the *muselim* doing? What were the police doing? They didn't seem to care. He would not give in. He'd go on struggling while there was breath in his body. But he begged the *kadi* to help, when those whose duty it was to do so did nothing.

Himzi-*effendi*, the *naib*, saw the aim of the meeting as the necessary intensification of the struggle against the enemy. As a judge, his hands were tied, if others did not do their duty. Things had to become completely obvious, as in the case of this Ramiz, for us all to take action. But was it really necessary to allow things to go so far? Surely prevention was better than cure. Was it not better to sleep securely than to wait till bad became worse? And Ramiz was not the only one. It was easy to deal with him. There were hundreds of young Ramizes, one had to say this, who were constantly sabotaging us, thwarting us in our efforts to carry out our sacred task, to strengthen the faith and the empire. And this at a time when the enemies on our frontiers were keeping a firm watch on us and were awaiting a chance to attack us. Such people were the open allies of our enemies, and allies of our enemies were also our enemies, and they should be shown no mercy. They should be shown no mercy, neither they nor those who supported them.

They then began to compete in their severity, in the rigor of their comments, in their attacks on various culprits, of whom there seemed to be ever more. No one wished to be outdone, and not lagging behind required yet greater severity and determination. They groaned, shouted, snarled, listed crimes, demanded punishments and extermination: It was better to have a few of us who were good than many who were lacking; better to have the enemy on the other side of the trench than among our own ranks.

They all burned with hatred and anger.

Ramiz was forgotten. He'd been condemned beforehand.

And then the white-bearded *hafiz* Abdulah Delaliya rose to his feet, Shehaga's best friend, whom I'd always respected for his gentle smile and good words for everyone.

Surely he'd not add his voice to this mad howling? Couldn't he have kept silent? Was he afraid they'd accuse him of freethinking were he to say nothing? Was even silence suspect? Or was he purchasing his peace at the price of a few words that meant nothing to him, since he needed nothing else?

I felt sick.

At first he repeated what the others had said, and they listened to him with a bored expression. But then he began to play his own tune, and the look of sleepy politeness vanished all of a sudden. My legs gave way in terror. Was the man mad?

He said he was against everything that Ramiz was saying, for he hated disorder and violence. And that this young man had been saying all sorts of things for so long a time was the fault of all of us. The *kadi* was right. But the *kadi* hadn't said why we were at fault. It was because we were indifferent. Nothing concerned us but ourselves. We thought too much of our own interests and of the goods of this world. We were surprised when no one said a word and when people sheltered the student. But he was not surprised. Why should they have informed us? What contact had we with the people? Little and ever less. There was a barrier set between us and the people, and across that barrier we sent only policemen. This was not one state. We were creating our state and the people theirs. Between those two states there were few friendly relations. The fault lay in us, in our pride, in our selfishness and arrogance, in the thousand foolish habits without which we could not imagine living. We reserved to ourselves the right to think, to point out the way one should go, to determine crime and punishment. Yet the Koran says: Make decisions together, in agreement! We had betrayed the Koran. We'd betrayed even common sense, since we took no care to do well what we had proclaimed to be our right. Our thinking was at fault, because we were detached from the people. We pointed the way to impassable thorn thickets and not to the broad pathways. We unjustly defined punishments and still more unjustly guilt. That was why a rebel could go on talking to the people for so long a time and we know nothing of it. The people sheltered him, surely that was obvious. And we are now seeking greater stringency, demanding greater cruelty, attempting to establish order through fear. Has anyone ever succeeded by this? Have you ever thought how the people will remember us? By the fear we've spread? By the arrogance with which we've defended ourselves? By their hardships to which we give no thought? By the empty words we scatter? You've competed here: Who shall offer the greatest threats, who shall demand the greatest violence, who shall propose the most stringent law? And nobody gives a thought to our errors. Nobody mentions the deeper reasons for our troubles. Nobody even expresses surprise that such things have not happened earlier and that there were not more of them. And why? I do not think that you all believe what you say, were that the truth it would, indeed, be terrible. Nor do I believe that you do this out of self-interest, for that would be unworthy of the positions you hold. "Is it then because you fear to offend somebody who is above you? If this is so, I can only pity you. But, in God's name, do not spread fear beyond this circle! Do not seek satisfaction for your own humiliation! Punish the criminal according to justice and the laws, and, if required, punish him with the greatest severity, but do not invent criminals among those who are not criminals. You'll drive them into becoming criminals. And do not use big words and vast reasoning to satisfy your own petty interests. We bear a greater responsibility before the people and before history than we think. I ask the *kadi* and all of you not to take offense that I speak so openly. I've too much respect for you all and for myself that I should be silent while I thought differently, or that I should speak differently from what I thought."

When he sat down there was silence.

Oh, honorable fool, I thought in terror, not daring to look around me.

While he was speaking, some people rose angrily to their feet, shouting words of protest and exasperation, but the *kadi* hushed them with a determined gesture, and calmly listened to *hafiz*-Abdulah to the end. Doubtless he was neither indifferent nor gratified, but his frowning face gave nothing away.

Why had he let him speak? Was he really so liberal? Did he wish to show that everyone had the right to say what he liked? Or did he wish to let the unfortunate man dig his own grave?

Had they invited me in the hope that I'd say what should not be said?

I recalled the dinner at *hadji*-Duhotina's. Hadn't *hafiz*-Abdulah said just what I'd said? And even worse. I felt a chill in my bones listening to him in that agitated and angered mass. Had it not been for the *kadi's* authoritative gesture, the *hafiz* would have fared worse than I, and we'd have gathered his aged bones into a bag.

Without getting up, the *kadi* closed the meeting, saying that, leaving aside a few isolated erroneous opinions, it had showed a high rate of awareness and justified his expectations. There had been no real difference of opinion, and that unity would urge us to greater efforts for the strengthening and preservation of all that we held sacred. If this were not done by those whose duty it was, then it would be done by people who put the general good above their own and who were ready to defend the truth from all enemies. Having informed us that he'd report on the meeting to the *vali* and to all other authorities, he thanked us for our presence and dismissed us.

As we came out, Mula Ibrahim gave me an imperceptible nod of the head, blinking his eyes, and immediately turned away. Wasn't it more dangerous for him to recognize me after so many threats? Or did he think that at that moment I was in greater need of his attention?

I considered whether to go after him and ask him what he thought of the meeting or whether to leave him in peace, since whatever he thought he'd not dare say and probably was so frightened that he didn't think anything. Yet, strangely, the fact that he'd nodded to me gave me courage.

I decided to wait till everyone had gone rather than jostle in the narrow doorway with those broad people.

In front of the mosque, Dzhemal Zafraniya took his leave of the *kadi* with a low bow. He waited for me with a smile on his face. He was clearly satisfied with the outcome of the meeting, though I couldn't see how he could have expected anything different.

"What did you think of the discussion?"

"There are some wise people."

"There are, indeed. But, you know, I was scared in case you got up."

"Why should I?"

"You must be sorry for Ramiz. You're a bit of a do-gooder."

"I'm sorry for everyone. Although I don't agree with Ramiz's ideas."

"I'm glad to hear it."

"What'll happen to him?"

"For what he's done, the penalty is death."

"Couldn't there be an appeal for mercy? He's only twenty-four years old."

"No one can help him now, not the *muselim*, not the *kadi*, not even the vizier himself. Only one person alone could save him."

"Who's that?"

"You."

"I? What do you mean?"

"That's what I summoned you for."

I thought he was playing a joke on me and on Ramiz.

Perhaps he saw this by my fixed expression and startled eyes, for he hastened to explain: I was friends with this student. All right, not friends, but he trusted no one as much as he trusted me. There was no need for me to be afraid. He knew that we'd discussed only the most general human questions, and this was exactly what he had in mind when he remembered me. (All this the *serdar*-Avdaga had told him, which did not surprise me. What did was that he'd believed what I'd told him.) Ramiz had expounded his convictions to others, to me he'd shown only his feelings. That made me closer to him than others, so that I could say to him what another couldn't. He knew that I didn't agree with Ramiz. He knew that, in fact, I had no opinions. I only regretted that people were not angels and that paradise did not rule on earth. And that we didn't agree was also a good thing, since, faced with one of his own persuasion, Ramiz would be firm and inflexible. Hadn't I noticed that sometimes people who didn't think the same, provided they were not enemies, often found it easier to talk? Surely, we two, Dzhemal and I, were a proof of this. And this was what I had to do, if I were to save Ramiz. He had had a considerable influence in the town. He spoke well, it seemed, or skillfully, which was the same thing. He promised much, since he didn't have to do anything; he was convincing, because he bore no responsibility; and people listened to him as if he were a messiah and wanted him to speak more often and in more places. That wasn't surprising, for it was easier to persuade people to evil and hatred than to love and virtue. Evil was attractive and nearer to man's nature. Goodness and love required maturity and hard work. Evil we carried within us, like an original passion, but, if presented as the one good, it could become disastrous. People had remembered his words, and now they'd pass them from one to another, repeat them like prayers, oppose them to every difficulty and to every misfortune. His glory would become the greater because, in the eyes of the people, he was a victim and not a criminal. He must not remain as a martyr nor must his words be like sown seeds, even though time would bring most of those whom he'd misled to their senses. We had to remove his martyr's halo. We had to crush the seed of his words, so that no harmful results would arise from them. How could this be done? Simple. Let he himself refute everything he'd said. It was up to me to persuade him. I was the only one who could do it.

He came so close that his lips were almost touching me, as if he were whispering into my nose. I smelt his sour breath and his powerful oriental scent. I felt giddy. I could scarcely gather my thoughts, holding them together, so they didn't fly out undirected, like frightened birds.

What should I say? How could I get out of it? They always required an answer immediately, without giving me time to collect myself. I knew what I ought to say, but how could I say it without harming myself?

"I don't believe he'd agree," I said, putting off answering, as though striving for breath.

Zafraniya was not like me. He had an answer ready for everything: "Fear of death is hard to bear, my dear Ahmet. Let him go to the mosque and tell the people that he was mistaken to have spoken to them as he did, that he was personally affronted and spoke in revenge, but now he'd thought about it and, as an honest man, regretted having directed them down a wrong path. If he said this, or something like it, we'd let him go. Only he won't be allowed to stay here. He'll have to go away."

"You mean to exile?"

"Alive."

"And if he doesn't agree?"

"He'll remain here. Dead"

"Will you kill him?"

"His crime is serious. Or don't you think it is?"

"It is."

"Then, do you agree?"

"Can I have time to think about it?"

"Why? You're not doing anything bad. You're saving his life."

"It's not bad, but it's not what one does every day."

"And it's better for him like this. I don't like cruelty. I really don't! It's a primitive way of resolving conflicts between people. I don't like killing. Nor do you. Nor, probably, does he."

"I don't know. It's hard to make up my mind."

"It seems that your humanity doesn't go much beyond words. And to tell you the truth, it was you I wanted to help as well as him."

"To help me?"

"You yourself said you were very close. Who's going to believe you that he talked to you only about his home and his girl?"

"You don't seem to believe it either?"

"I believe it, as long as it's necessary."

"I'll let you know tomorrow."

"I hope you'll be wise."

Oh, unjust God, what more will you unload onto my head, which is neither the most sensible nor the most stupid? So many, guilty and not guilty, live their lives in a constant yawn. Why have you chosen me, of all people, never to be bored? And I always have to solve the insoluble, like the proverbial third brother. But I'd like a bit of monotony, to live easily and smoothly, to sleep the summer day away peacefully till noon and to awaken without thought and without anxiety and not to think of the morrow with fear.

I'd defended myself to the *serdar*-Avdaga, telling him the touching story of the young man's home and of his girl, and all I'd done was to give them just what they wanted.

I'd sure found the right man to move with nice sentiments!

What should I do? If I refused Zafraniya's suggestion, it wouldn't save me. He'd said himself that he'd involve me in Ramiz's guilt. They knew he hadn't talked to me just about his home and family, and they'd do everything to squeeze the truth out of me. If I told them the truth, I'd be both an accomplice and a guilty person, since I'd not reported him. What I'd told them would be enough to incriminate me.

But how could I face him with the suggestion that he should refute everything he'd said? That he'd refuse, and he surely would, was not the worst, nor the fact that I'd once again be at Zafraniya's mercy. This was bad, but not the worst.

I couldn't bear it, in no way could I bear it, and this was where, in my imagination, I came to a halt, where my thoughts could go no further, where I could find no way out: I couldn't bear his horrified look if I were to do this.

What could I say to him?

"I'm sorry, they've forced me to do this."

But suppose we weren't alone? Suppose they left a guard with us? I wouldn't be able to say this. I wouldn't dare.

"It would be the best for you."

But he didn't want the best for him. His look, insulted and ashamed, would be more terrible than anything he might say in reply. Ashamed for my sake. Insulted for his own.

"What, you, too, the poet who sings just for himself, like the nightingale?" his contemptuous look would say. "I thought you were a man. I thought you understood. You're offering me life and shame. I could make a better thing out of my life than that. They're better than you are. They're offering me death with honor. They're offering me to be remembered by the people for the good I did. You're offering me to be spat on by the people whenever my name is heard. And what would there be left of me if I did what you ask? You ought to be scared of it yourself! I could become anything, except anything good. A loafer, a rogue, a murderer, an executioner. If I'd kill myself in this way, what would stop me from killing somebody else? If I'd have agreed to them breaking my back, why should I spare another's? What would stop me? Without honor and conscience, everything would be permitted. No, I'll accept their punishment. It's more honorable than your offer. And I chose this possibility long ago, when I first set out on this path."

How could I ask him to betray his ideals? And I, too, after that, could become anything, except anything good.

I'd thought that people were separated, and they were, but here, again, unbreakable ties could be formed between them. Our ways cross, like tangled threads. How could I ever have imagined that I'd experience such torment, all for the sake of a young man I hardly knew?

If I betrayed him, I'd destroy myself; if I destroyed him, I'd betray myself.

I could do neither one nor the other, and there was no third way.

When things are difficult, I tend to take refuge in being on my own. When things are more difficult still, I tend to seek good people.

I dropped into Mula Ibrahim's shop. He was getting ready to go to lunch. There were no assistants behind the partition. Yet once again I whispered, out of habit and because of all I'd heard in the mosque.

"Who was the *kadi* thinking of as not having fulfilled their duty?"

I was afraid he'd not answer, but I couldn't help asking. He did answer, all the same. Perhaps because of my obvious depression.

"He was thinking of the *muselim*. They can't stand one another. He was putting the blame on him."

"He was threatening others as well."

"Allegedly law and order have been threatened, and this was the fault of the *muselim*. But a lot of people will pay for it, too. Two birds with one stone."

"Why do they always threaten? Aren't people scared enough as it is?"

"The more fear, the more order."

Judging by him and his fear, order must have been perfect. And, by God, judging by me too.

"Advise me, Mula Ibrahim. They want me to talk to Ramiz. To persuade him to refute everything he said. If he did this, they'd let him go."

"Talk to him, by all means."

"He won't agree; he'll refuse."

"You can tell them that he's refused."

"How can I face him?"

"Easily. Just say to him: It's my job to make you the offer, it's yours to decide. They'll kill him in any case."

"You think so?"

"They've made a scarecrow of him. How can they let him go?"

"I'd rather go back to my river, Mula Ibrahim."

"They'd find you there, too."

They'd find me anywhere. There was no escape.

At home I found Mahmut. He'd spent all the money and was as repentant as ever.

I told him and Tiyana everything, at once, before getting through the door, so I didn't burst.

Their reply was the absolute opposite of what I'd expected.

"How could you insult the man like that?" Mahmut said bitterly.

"He'll be alive, that's the main thing," Tiyana said.

Mahmut scratched his bristly beard. "Indeed, not even death is a solution."

Agitated, Tiyana thought for a while. "He knew what was waiting for him, and he wasn't afraid. How can you tell him to be what he isn't?"

So we came back to the beginning: nowhere.

"Oh God," Tiyana sighed.

"Troubles again," Mahmut groaned.

But his restless thought couldn't be satisfied with lamentation, it had to find a way out.

"How about your falling ill? Eat a raw potato. Your temperature'll rocket up like a real fever. I'll bring Avdaga to see."

In my despair even this seemed a good idea. I'd fall ill without the raw potato, from worry, fear, from the sense of utter helplessness.

But it wouldn't help. I'd gain nothing by it. Why a fever, today of all days? And even if they believed me, they'd just wait till it passed. I couldn't go on eating raw potato forever.

Mahmut expressed the view that they'd leave me alone with Ramiz and that I should say to him: So on and so forth, brother, save me, I'm in great trouble.

He forgot that Ramiz was in even greater trouble.

So we chewed over our threadbare ideas and came to no solution. I could have done just as well without them, but it was better not to be alone.

CHAPTER 12

THE SORROW
AND THE FURY

THE NEXT MORNING I STILL COULD FIND NO WAY OUT AND stopped looking for one. I was stupefied by pointless thinking, and my brain was freewheeling. I was waiting for them to come for me, to take me whenever they were going to take me. Perhaps on the way I'd make up my mind whether to be humiliated or destroyed.

When someone knocked at the door, I was sure it would be the *serdar*-Avdaga sent by Dzhemal Zafraniya to take me. He was appointed my guardian angel, and only death could part us. I didn't know whose death, but I'd have preferred it not to be mine. But what could I do? Let it be, if it couldn't be any different.

But it was not my expected dark angel that entered; it was the unexpected Osman Vuk, Shehaga's steward.

He bore into our room his handsome, fair, and windswept head, his laughter, his flippant and superficially silly personality. But I remembered him as being different.

"What's the matter with you? As if you're in mourning for someone!" he cried laughing.

"Something like that."

"So what of it? Is that a reason for looking so down?"

"We were waiting for somebody."

"Are you sorry I'm not he?"

"No way. I wish the devil would take him!"

"Who is it? What does he want?"

"It's a long story. Are you here on business? I heard you were here last night."

"I am. Shehaga sends his greetings and asks you to come to see him. For a talk."

I was surprised. He said this to Tiyana.

"Who is it Shehaga's inviting?"

"You, who else? That's what he said: He sends his greetings and invites you. He also warned me to come straight here, meaning not to drop in to the coffeehouse, and to find you at all costs. And I was hurrying, like a fool, afraid I'd not find you, like last night."

"I'm always at home," I replied cautiously. "And why do you say: 'like a fool'?"

"Because I'm not smart. A man's never smart enough. As if it mattered, if I hadn't found you!"

The fascinated look he turned on Tiyana told pretty clearly why he'd have been glad not to have found me at home.

How had he looked at her last night? What had he said to her when she was alone, when he talked like this in my presence?

"It wouldn't have mattered if you'd missed us altogether," I said angrily.

"Why, my friend? What have I done to deserve such words?"

"You know very well what you've done," Tiyana interrupted calmly. "I don't go for that sort of humor."

"What's the matter with you people? What have I got into? I meant no harm, I swear by my children."

"You swear by your children because you haven't got any."

"And who knows that, sister! But I meant no harm. I know I'm all sorts of things, but bad I'm not. Except when I'm angry. And why should I be angry with you? Nor should you be angry with me. There, are we all right? So, shall we go and see Shehaga?"

"I don't feel like going."

"Why? If you're angry with me for nothing, what's Sheha-ga done wrong? Come on, give us a smile and give me your hand. I've had enough trouble for one day."

"You bring it on yourself."

"Not at all, man! I was gambling last night. A merchant I knew came to me. I'd done him well the night before last. He told me: 'A chap from Brchko came this morning. He grows plums. A rich aunt's died and left him a large legacy. And the silly fool's come to Sarajevo to get rid of it. If you've nothing against stripping him, go after him.' I don't mind, I said. If I don't, others will. So I went to find Muharem Pyevo. He's some gambler; I'm just a child to him. I told him how it was. 'Bring some cash, at first we'll lose a bit, to keep the plum-grower happy. And then, may God help him! You won't leave him enough for his fare back to Brchko.' 'He can walk,' Pyevo said with a smile. 'We'll share the profits.' 'OK. And we'll meet at the Stone *han*.' And the man from Brchko was a pushover. 'Do you often play?' I asked him. 'I don't play often, but whenever I have played, I've seen it's a matter of luck. If my luck holds, as it has lately, look out! And if I lose a bit, it's no big deal.' It's not a bit you'll lose, by God, I thought to myself, but everything you've got. And he said, as if he'd read my thoughts, 'I've got a hundred ducats, that's all I've brought. How much have you got?' We were shocked. A hundred ducats, a fortune! I could see that Pyevo couldn't wait. He gazed at the pile of ducats, scarcely saying a word. 'Come on,' he said, 'what are we waiting for!' 'Steady,' said the man from Brchko, 'let's discuss this like men. Let me see how much you have.' We could hardly scrape together some fifty ducats. Pyevo went to borrow from the *han*-keeper, fair-ly running, and we began to play with Pyevo's dice.

"I saw at once this was a simple chap, good but stupid. He began to lose immediately, but this didn't bother him, he just laughed and even ordered us food and drink. 'Nothing's wasted on good people,' he said. But I was even sorry for him. I like winning money, but I like to have to play for it.

But this would all be over in no time. And it was all over in no time. Suddenly there was a change, and the man from Brchko stopped losing and we took his place. 'What's this?' the plum-grower asked cheerfully. 'The luck's turned!' And indeed, it had! No matter what we threw, he threw higher. 'It's a miracle!' he kept shouting. And every time it came up for him. No matter how we blew on the dice, turned them round our heads, shook them. The man from Brchko simply nodded and encouraged us: 'One's got to try everything.' And he took the money. He finished me in half an hour and Pyevo in an hour. In the end he left us some small change— 'for drink,' he said—and asked when we could meet again. And Pyevo and I looked at each other, in amazement. What was it? What had this stupid plum-grower done to us? Pyevo gnawed his lips and turned up his eyes. He didn't mind losing so much as he did that people might get to know about it, while I just laughed like a drain. 'What is it? What are you laughing for?' Pyevo asked, surprised. 'Why shouldn't I laugh? Can't you see we've been made fools of? What aunt, what legacy! This is a real gambler, better than we are!' 'Oh, I do a bit of it, sometimes, for fun,' said the plum-grower, with a friendly smile. 'All right,' I said. "You've done us well and truly, but let's, at least, have something in return. How do you manage always to throw what you want?' 'To tell you the truth, I spotted at once that the dice were leaded and fell on the larger numbers. Until I rumbled this, I lost. The main thing is, there was no cheating.' So, the plum-grower took us, and, what's more, admitted that the merchant had offered to lead us to him, like game to the huntsman. We begged him to keep it quiet, and we didn't tell a soul about the way we'd been had. Why should only we end up as the fools? That's why I said I've had enough trouble for today."

"Serves you right," Tiyana said. "Aren't you ashamed to take a man's money?"

"I thought I'd said, sister, he took the money from me, not I from him."

"You took it from somebody yesterday, he took it from you last night. Fair enough."

"Fair enough, if you like, but I don't like it. So, Ahmet, shall we be going?"

"I'll come tomorrow. Perhaps."

"Not tomorrow, but now, right away. Shehaga's expecting you!"

"Then go, if he's expecting you," Tiyana agreed, "but don't stay long."

Osman took this in his own way: "Thanks, sister. And he'll be back quickly. He's not daft enough to leave you on your own for long."

There was no point in reproaching him; he couldn't help being stupid.

Out on the street he gave me a confidential nod of the head and said he wanted to tell me something, for my information, before I saw Shehaga.

He led me into the forecourt of the mosque, and we sat in the porch, to shelter ourselves from the wind that was blowing the leaves from the plum trees. He told me a strange story.

Shehaga had not summoned me. It was true that he'd talked about me with Mula Ibrahim and had said that I should come to see him, by all means, but he'd not said today. It was Osman who decided it should be today, since no one had mentioned a definite time, so it could be whenever we decided, but he, Osman, would like it as soon as possible. For this reason he'd come for me, to help him and to help Shehaga. Perhaps to help myself, too, for no one repaid a favor better than Shehaga. Should Shehaga forget, he, Osman, would help me, for he knew what I needed, which was not difficult, since I was without work. And that wasn't a good thing. When a man had such an attractive wife, he couldn't afford to be a pauper. He himself would commit murder just so his wife might have everything she could desire.

Good God, what a pain in the neck!

"You're at it again!"

"What's the matter? That's just by the way. Don't get mad! Let me tell you about Shehaga. Shehaga's in great trouble: He's stopped drinking milk for the last two days. That means he's about to start drinking *rakiya*. And when he begins drinking, it's not like with other people, but all hell breaks out. If he just drank at home, that wouldn't matter so much, but no! He goes off somewhere, so no one knows where he is, to some village or other place, throws his money right, left, and center, drinks, sleeps, and drinks again, eight days on the trot, eats nothing, just vomits and drinks, then sleeps three days and nights like a dead man and comes home a wreck, so you can't recognize him. He does this three times a year and never more. Otherwise he never touches a drop. And no one can stop him, not his wife, not his friends, not anyone. And one day he'll croak from all this poison. It's a wonder he's survived as long as he has."

"Why does he drink?"

"Why indeed! People drink without a reason, but Shehaga has plenty. He never speaks about it. He suffers, keeps it all bottled in, but when he can't bear it anymore he takes to drink to forget. This happens three times a year, at regular intervals, like infrequent changes of the moon, rarely more often. But now is out of time."

He seemed to be avoiding an answer, putting off saying why Shehaga drank.

I asked him again. "Why does he drink?"

"Because of his son. His only son."

"I didn't know he had a son."

"He had one. When his son was eighteen, he asked his father to let him join the army and go to the war. Some of his friends were going. They were older than he, but then he always went with those who were older. But his friends weren't the only reason. There were other reasons; youth, the drums, the banners, the speeches, the ideal of holy war, and the boy almost went berserk. Flames seemed to start from his

eyes. Shehaga tried to reason with him. War was not the firing of guns at Bairam, but mud, filth, hunger, cruelty, blood,
and death. But it was all in vain, the boy wouldn't hear a
word of it. 'I'll stand everything,' he said, 'even death, if God
so wills. If so many others can, then so can I.' But his father
grieved. He was his only son. For him he'd felt the joy of
gaining wealth, for him he felt the joy of living and never hid
his love for him, he couldn't. The young lad lived a pam-
pered life, spoiled, overfed, not knowing the ugly side of life,
not knowing hardship, and somebody filled his immature
head with big words and drove him to lose the one thing one
has only once. No one values their life less than a young
man, and then later, the older he gets and the less reason he
has for living, the more he clings to life. 'And I'll die, if need
be,' the stupid lad said. Shehaga grew angry and lost his tem-
per. 'That you won't,' he said, 'foolish boy. If I can't make
you see sense, then I can make you obey my orders! Today
you're all enthusiasm, but tomorrow you'll cry, when you
feel the lice crawling on you. A silly young fool like you
doesn't care for his life. But I care for my son, even if he is a
fool.' And he shut him up in the house. But the lad got away,
jumped from a window and joined up with the army that
was setting off. The next morning they found his room
empty. Shehaga was like a madman. He wanted to beat his
servants for not seeing the lad, for not hearing him when he
jumped over the wall. We rushed all over the place. Shehaga
even demanded the return of his son from the *vali*, since he'd
gone without his father's consent. And they'd have returned
him, because the *vali* owed Shehaga a thousand ducats and,
in any case, respected him. But the lad was nowhere to be
found, as if he'd run off to some foreign army. They went
through all the army lists, but his name wasn't there. Later
we learned that he'd been at Baba-dag in Bessarabia, but had
changed his name, so his father couldn't find him and bring
him back.

"Very soon what Shehaga had foreseen happened. The

boy soon had enough of war. Its cruelty sickened him. He was horrified at the killing and persuaded some ten soldiers from here to desert with him. They wandered, hiding by day and traveling by night, avoiding army units and bypassing towns until flight became one long torment. At Smederevo, three of them ran off and reported to the authorities, unable to endure the effort and fear any longer. The authorities seized the remaining fugitives and locked them up in the Fortress. And they, to a man, accused Shehaga's son of persuading them to desert, saying they regretted having done it. The boy confessed everything and took the blame on himself, begging that the others should not be punished. He added that he regretted nothing, for war was the greatest human filth and the most dreadful crime. He was condemned to death. He then told them his true name and asked that his father be informed that he'd died in battle, as though, for his father, one death were easier than another. The rest of the fugitives were given lashes and returned to the war. The young man they shot and informed his father that his son had been executed as a deserter and traitor to his country. Shehaga almost died. And it was as if he went a little mad. He reproached his dead son: 'You silly lad, why perish, why lose your silly head! If you'd been fighting for your own pleasure and someone had killed you, good luck to both of you, if it had been for the mythical golden apple or for the girl in the poem, or for the sake of a friend, I'd grieve, but I'd understand. But what have you done, my wretched son! For the sake of garbage, of robbers, for the sake of grabbing other people's land. And how could such a stench madden your pure heart? And why didn't you run off by yourself, once you came to your senses? How could you have relied on such people? You could have trusted a snake, a jackal, a sparrow hawk, never a local man. He'll betray you when you do your very best for him, kill you when you've given him your last bite of food. All right for you to kill yourself, you selfish son, but why me!'

"We tried to calm him, in vain. He didn't want to see anybody. Then we went to Smederevo to find his son's grave, but nobody knew where it was, and all our inquiries were useless. 'No matter,' Shehaga said. 'Perhaps it's better that we don't return him to this cursed land. I wish to God I'd never seen it either!' When he got back, he began to drink, eight days at a time, to the point of complete unconsciousness, paralysis. When he came to himself, he was silent, kept himself to himself, hated people, and, if he spoke at all, cursed everything around him, not thinking what he might say or do. He made everybody sick of him, especially those in power who also hated him but didn't dare do anything to him. He was too influential both here and in Constantinople. People owed him too much money, which he didn't hurry to ask for, and so he held them in his power. I'm afraid for him when he starts drinking. They'll arrange some accident. It'd be too easy, and no one would know. And now, he's off on the drink again, and it's not even time. And we'll all be mad with fear until we find out where he is. And why now, out of time? Last night his best friend, the only one he has in the town, *hafiz*-Abdulah Delaliya met with an accident. Some blackguards set on him as he was returning from the mosque, after evening prayer, and beat him to death. He was alive when some passersby came on him, but he died while they were carrying him home. This morning Shehaga went to the *kadi* and to the *vali*, too. They expressed regret and surprise, but knew nothing about it and promised they'd seek the culprits and bring them to trial and just punishment. They'll do that when I become the grand vizier! Such empty promises didn't make Shehaga feel any better. They'd killed his friend. A day never passed without their meeting, and now he has nobody. He shouted at the *vali*, threatened the *kadi*, but now he sits silent, drinks no milk, preparing to run away and forget."

This strange story came as a surprise, and even more the dreadful news that accompanied it. Were the implied threats beginning to take shape? Or was it but a continuation of the old cruelty?

Yesterday, when the old man was speaking, I thought by chance of *hadji*-Duhotina, but was it by chance? It was the same people who'd done this who did it to me, for the crime of speaking out, only with *hafiz*-Abdullah they'd gone too far, or perhaps his age was not so able to withstand the beating as was my youth.

"He spoke in the mosque yesterday," I said quietly. "Against the demands for stricter measures."

"Well, he won't do it anymore. Now he'll agree with everybody."

Then he told me why he'd come for me. He'd heard Shehaga talking about me with Mula Ibrahim. It turned out that I was the same age as Shehaga's son, that we'd been in the war at the same time, and that I was the same silly fool as he was. He wanted Shehaga to see me, so he'd remember his son, feel the pain of the past, and not think of his friend's immediate death. Nor of strong drink. And I was the right person for this: naïve, helpless, a slug, vulnerable to the slightest blows, without work, the victim of others. He, Vuk, certainly knew how stupidly I'd suffered, but Shehaga knew nothing of all this, nor was he interested, but it could happen that he'd get involved with me and become my protector. It would be good both for Shehaga and for me. I'd gain from his weakness, and he'd be inspired by his own generosity.

To think that I could be a cure for anybody's pain was just funny, but if so, let it be. Osman Vuk was no fool and certainly knew what he was doing. He was probably just trying it on, but then it was worth the effort.

I went with him, hoping Shehaga would help me, while Osman was hoping I'd help Shehaga.

"Talk about the war," Osman suggested, "and how old you were at the time. Don't mention *hafiz*-Abdullah."

When I knocked on Shehaga's door, he appeared and

invited me in, but he didn't seem pleased to see me. I even felt that my visit at this time was unwelcome, when all that existed for him was his own sorrow. He sat there on a settee, looking at me palely and sorrowfully, not even attempting to concentrate on my presence.

I told him I'd come at his request, through Mula Ibrahim, whose scribe I'd been, and that my name was Ahmet Shabo.

"I know," he interrupted.

All the same he grew more attentive and offered me a place beside him.

"Forgive me, you find me in a bad state."

"I'll come another day, if you like."

"You want to escape from my gloomy face? Do you really give up so easily what you've started?"

"I don't want to be a nuisance."

"You don't want to be a nuisance, you don't want anyone to dislike you, you don't want anyone to be rude to you. Then how do you expect to live?"

"As a pauper."

"That's not hard to achieve."

"It's not easy either. One has to make a choice."

He looked at me in surprise.

"One thinks of you lot as children. And then one's surprised at what you carry in your heads."

"These children have gone through war."

He looked through the window at a slender poplar that was bending in the wind. And then he turned. A shadow passed over his face. Was he gritting his teeth to resist a memory?

"Say something. Anything."

"Why, Shehaga?"

"No reason."

"About the war?"

"It doesn't matter. No, it does matter. Not about the war!"

"Shall I tell you about my looking for work?"

"All right."

Did I have to wet-nurse this fifty-year-old, to talk him out of his fear? Or was he trying to get rid of me so as to be on his own?

I looked at his hands: long fingers, strong joints, large veins, yet fragile and nervous. Their restlessness betrayed his tension. He constantly moved them, on his knees, on his chest, over the settee cover. They kept in motion, clenching and unclenching. Or else he brought them together in an inextricable knot and pressed them powerfully, as though he were strangling somebody, as though he were giving himself pain. I wanted to touch those joints that were red with pressure, to quiet him, to bring him back. Perhaps a friendly touch might liberate him from the inner cramp, help him to relax, to weep, to release his constrained heart from its prison.

I refrained, for fear of doing yet more harm.

He was too hard, his pain was full of fury. He hated his pain, denied it, rejected it, felt humiliated by it. He drove it out, yet it remained.

How many dreadful nights, how many savage struggles did that room remember, when he wrestled with his pain, as with the devil, and how many dawns had he met, defeated and unreconciled? Perhaps, sometimes, there was a moment of happiness: I've beaten it! But the pain would appear again, plunging, like a pike from the dark river of memory.

Perhaps these were the moments when, three times yearly, he benumbed his senses so as to remain alive.

If time had eased one pain, the new death had doubled it, reviving memories of the old one. Now both pressed on him; he'd lost all he wanted to preserve, and now he was tormented by the unbearable pain and by fury at his human inability to oppose misfortune.

Had he sobbed last night when he heard about it? Did he cry, curse, shout? Did he bang his head against the wall?

He'd paid for one death with sorrow and fury. Now was he to pay for another in the same way?

And had he faced his pain, had he not angrily rejected meeting it, raising his head threateningly to heaven, looking on people with hatred, seeking comfort in the troubles of others, would it have been easier for him, or harder? Had he accepted his loss as inevitable, grieving, for he was neither God nor made of wood, and given in to his sorrow, perhaps that grave and that dead man would have helped him to ennoble his sorrow with good deeds. For the sake of his son's memory. So many were in need of help!

As it was, he was possessed by an irreconcilable fury. And by constant thoughts of vengeance.

Not about war, he'd said. It was too painful.

I'd not speak of war. I'd spare him that.

I talked to him of what didn't concern him and wouldn't hurt him, about Mula Ismail whom God had endowed with a wondrous handicap, valuable for one of his calling, for he didn't hear what people were saying and was never in conflict with his conscience. He didn't know what hurt people, what they lacked, what they desired, and so was the most innocent and the happiest of men. He never changed his opinion, for he could always repeat the same thing. He was not petty, since he spoke of human unhappiness. He caused neither argument nor resentment, for what he said could be neither confirmed nor disproved. He didn't know his business, nor any other, yet it was as well he was in the position he was, since others would have done worse.

And I told him about the *defterdar* Bekir-*aga* Djugum. I chose him from among others, because he'd agreed to see me, despite his high position. Indeed, they'd probably got my name wrong, or he didn't know who I was, or had mixed me up with somebody else, for this would be the first time in the history of the human race that a *defterdar* had received such a nonentity as I, simply to listen to the tale of his misfortunes. But this was all the same to me, he'd agreed to see me, and I was grateful for that. And he'd have helped me, I'd no proof that he wouldn't, and I preferred to think what was pleasant than what was likely. It was my bad luck that I had to run across such faith and loyalty as were his, for other state servants do not usually die of grief at the death of their masters. But perhaps they ought to bring in an excellent custom based upon the example left by Bekir-*aga* Djugum: that all should die with their master, as Indian women do with their husbands, for it is dishonorable to end one's devoted service by betrayal, serving another. Of course, it might have had some bad results. For instance, nobody might agree to accept important posts, by which the people would suffer a heavy loss, but one had to sacrifice something for the sake of a good principle.

I told him a bit about the merchant *hadji*-Feyzo. I said he was a good man who'd offered me an opportunity, as he did to all young men who were not squeamish or petty-minded and accepted the attention and intimacy of *hadji*-Feyzo, which was no small matter in this cold and heartless world. Feyzo was a soft and broad man who asked little and offered much, but I'd lacked understanding either for his breadth or for his intimacy, which was my fault and not his.

And then I got tired of this sort of humor, forcing myself to encourage him with a taste of satire. I noticed that he scarcely listened. He'd led me to talk so he might remain alone with himself.

I stopped.

He showed no surprise, nor asked why I'd stopped talking. He just slowly turned toward the tall poplar in the courtyard, and his face once more expressed pain and tension.

Why should I not confront him directly with his sorrow? I'd followed his wish and talked about anything that occurred to me, so he could crush his pain, and put it aside. And I was mistaken, just as he was.

I'd mention his dead ones, make him get used to living with them.

"Did *hafiz*-Abdulah sit there?"

He looked at me in surprise at my having guessed his

thoughts. But he made no reply. He got up from the settee and began to pace up and down the room, clenching his fists together behind his back.

I didn't give in.

"I'm sure he liked to look at that poplar tree?"

"How do you know?"

"I can see it in your face. You're thinking of him all the time."

He stopped by the window, his back turned toward me. "How do you know?" he said. Did he want to go on talking about his dead friend, remembering him as he was when he was alive, or continue mourning for his death?

But Shehaga was hard to get at and didn't give in easily. Once again, he avoided facing the facts.

Without turning, he changed the subject to me. That was why he'd invited me and why I'd come. And he used this as a defense against admitting me to his world.

"What do you live on?"

"I've no idea myself. On love, perhaps."

He found this subject easier, since it had nothing to do with him.

"It's a good life. Only usually it's short."

"Which is better, a good life and short or a long life and an ugly one? The raven lives for three hundred years."

"The raven doesn't even know it's alive."

"We do, that's our fate."

"That's our bad luck."

"Both our bad luck and our good luck."

I saw where his thought was heading. He'd got to the edge, would he cross it? Would he mention the cause of his despair?

No, he didn't dare.

Once again, I'd served him as a get-out.

"What made you do what you did at *hadji*-Duhotina's?"

"To tell you the truth, I've no idea. I'd just returned from the war. I was upset, bitter. I don't know."

"Is that why Mula Ibrahim sacked you?"

"It wasn't Mula Ibrahim's fault. They forced him."

"Mula Ibrahim's a coward."

"It's not his fault. It's as if he'd been born deaf, or with a crooked nose."

"Do you really think that, or are you just being dishonest?"

"Unfortunately, I've never managed to learn dishonesty. I've no gift for it."

"How old are you?"

"In May I'll be twenty-five."

"In May?"

"Yes, why?"

"No reason, I'm just talking, for the sake of something to say."

His son was born in May, too. It had hit him, but still he wouldn't talk of it.

Then he began again pacing up and down the large room, his eyes fixed on the carpet.

The clock in another room struck something. Time was passing, and we were silent as if we'd forgotten each other's existence.

No, we'd not forgotten.

In his thoughts he was comparing me with his son. We were born in the same year, in the same place. We'd been in the same war. That was what we had in common. He was dead, and I was alive. That was what we didn't have in common. And what was he to do with me? Help me, which would remind him, or get rid of me, which would spare him the pain?

Nor had I forgotten him. This silence between two men made me uneasy. His rhythmical movement from wall to wall irritated me. I became angry: Why had he invited me? To be a witness to his withdrawal and isolation? Why had I come, to waste my time, simply to see how I could not gain his attention even for a moment?

Should I now leave, with a bitter feeling that I'd paid a vain visit to a proud man?

No! I couldn't. If I left now, I'd never return. Perhaps he needed my help. He was drowning. How could I refuse him a helping hand?

I decided to break into his stubborn silence by taking him by surprise.

"Do you know why they killed *hafiz*-Abdulah?"

"I don't."

"I do. I was in the mosque yesterday."

This brought him to a halt.

"They were all attacking the student Ramiz. He defended him."

This wasn't quite the truth, but I put it this way intentionally.

He sat down suddenly, discarding his armor, lessening the distance, emerging from his trench, drawn at once into the conversation.

"What happened? Tell me! All of it!"

I told him briefly about the others and in more detail about the *hafiz*, concealing the fact that he'd sacrificed the young man but had defended the truth. I didn't lie, but I didn't tell the whole truth, wanting to retain the dead man as a link between me and Shehaga. The day before, I'd held it against him that he demanded punishment for Ramiz. I knew that people weren't perfect, but I was disappointed when I found this to be so, and now I was putting right his error, or rather, misjudgment. Yet perhaps it was neither a mistake nor a misjudgment. He sought justice in place of force and put a mirror before all of them, so they might see their own deformity while attacking the deformity of others. He acted bravely and honorably, sparing no one, for which he suffered. I'd made no mistake in choosing him as a witness.

"Then they murdered him!" Shehaga exclaimed angrily. "Him, too!"

Him, too! Both his son and his friend. The two whom

he'd loved most in life, both murdered. He saw nothing else. Nothing else concerned him.

I wanted to tell him they weren't the only ones to have suffered. His was not the only tragedy. The world was full of it. Yes, we were concerned only with our own, but surely those of others were also ours?

"They've killed many, and they'll kill still more," I said, thinking of Ramiz.

But it was as if he didn't hear me. He held his fists together on his chest, as though suppressing a pain, pale, his face distorted, occupied with a single thought.

"Murderers!" he hissed between clenched teeth. "I'll pay you! I'll find the culprit! I'll search every corner, but I'll find him!"

"And if you take revenge, it won't raise *hafiz*-Abdulah from the grave."

"I'd die of shame if I forgot a friend!"

"Do something more practical. They're going to murder young Ramiz."

"They'll kill all honest people, and for that they deserve a thousand deaths!"

"You couldn't save your son. Save him."

He was not expecting that. Nor was I.

He stopped and looked at me in amazement. I'd broken mercilessly into his suffering heart.

He clenched his fists. His whole body tensed. For a moment it looked as if he were about to throw himself at me. How dared I say that to him?

He made no move toward me. Something restrained him. Perhaps it was the thought, which had never occurred to him, that for the sake of his dead son he might help a living one. The possibility disturbed him. Perhaps it seemed, at first, unjust, unacceptable to his fury. Yet still he couldn't easily reject it.

Was he thinking: If only someone had tried to save my son. Had he, in the fog of bewilderment, glimpsed a way by which he might give greater meaning to his son's memory? Had his natural kindness stirred within him?

I tried to lead him on. "He'll die innocent."

He still resisted me. "Wasn't my son innocent?"

"That's what I mean. You'll understand better than anybody else. He hasn't got a father. He died in the war. All he has is a mother. What can she do to help him?"

"And how can I help him?"

"I don't know. Ask the *vali* to release him."

"He wouldn't dare. They're afraid of one another."

"Then there's no hope for him."

"He's got a mother you say. Why didn't he think of her? Children think only of themselves; their parents don't matter."

"For God's sake, Shehaga, can't you even forgive your dead son for thinking differently from you?"

This was too much for him. I'd hit him where it hurt. How, I didn't know myself. He shouted, looking as if he'd have liked to have killed me, "Son of a bitch! What do you want of me!"

And then he looked down and began wringing his hands. For some time he just stood there.

Then, without looking at me, he said quietly, "You didn't have to say that."

"I said it for your sake. Make peace with him. He's dead. Accept him with sorrow, not fury. Young people often do silly things, because they want the impossible. Like your son, like Ramiz."

"Are you a friend of his?"

"No. I hardly know him."

"Why are you worrying about him, then?"

"Because no one else will. Because he's alone, because he's an honest man."

"You need help, too. I thought you were going to talk about yourself."

"I'm in danger of poverty; he's in danger of death. He's worse off."

"You're a damn fool! Everything that's worth anything is mad. My son, you, that Ramiz."

"He's mad because he thinks of others and not himself. Does he have to die because of that?"

"Do they think he's important?"

"They do. What he said stung them."

Suddenly he changed and a look of malice came over his face. "What if we were to rescue him? They'd go mad!"

So, no sooner had I thought I'd driven the devil out of him, than he began all over again. His pain was the fault of others, and its only cure was the suffering he could inflict on others.

"They certainly wouldn't like it," I agreed, glimpsing an unexpected chance of saving Ramiz. Shehaga's motives didn't concern me.

It was amazing how suddenly he'd changed. His expression was no longer threateningly dark but calmly determined. A thin smile about his lips betrayed an imagined triumph. His hands lay still, one beside the other. His whole body straightened up. This was another Shehaga, one who planned revenge.

This was the moment when he surely forgot his pain. But this malice of his would not be just vengeance. It would help another.

Now nothing could stop him. And had I by chance succeeded in awakening kindness in him, it would have been a limp rag.

How much is evil the more vital and industrious! God help us!

He clapped his hands. They performed their function with ease, without difficulty or tension.

A young girl came in.

"Tell Osman I want him!"

Osman came in at once, as though he'd been waiting behind the door, and perhaps he had, standing there with the young girl. Both their eyes shone brightly.

Shehaga rubbed his hands with renewed vigor.

"Sit down! We've got to rescue a man from the Fortress."

"There are several ways," Osman replied, without hesitation. "I'm for the most expensive."

"Good," Shehaga agreed.

And that was all!

Osman Vuk glanced at me cheerfully and inquired of Shehaga, "Shall I bring you some milk?"

"Later."

It was time for me to go, so they could plan things on their own.

I'd stayed longer than I'd intended and certainly longer than Tiyana would have liked.

She'd ask me why he'd sent for me. He hadn't.

She'd ask what we talked about. We hadn't said a word about me.

She'd ask whether he was going to help me. We'd neither of us given this a thought.

She'd ask why I was so satisfied, if that were the case. And I wouldn't be able to tell her why.

CHAPTER 13

THE RESCUE

THAT NIGHT, THE EVE OF BAIRAM, WAS STORMY.

Osman Vuk celebrated the end of the final day of the fast in Zayko's inn, sober, calm, almost solemn. The inn was not closed to other guests, as Osman was wont to demand, but everybody knew it was one of his private celebrations, of the beginning of Bairam, of the long period of Ramadan, or of nothing whatsoever. No one ever sought a reason for Osman's bouts of madness, for to do so would have been a regular and too-often-repeated labor. He knew how to celebrate as no other man in the town, turning it on its head and disturbing its sour silence. Fathers of grown sons and husbands of young wives would be worried, for the sons became restless, and young wives lost sleep and, complaining of headaches, would sit at their windows and sigh far into the night, which for many brought on a real headache from the gentle fists of their husbands, who, as a precautionary measure, drove the madness from female heads that were always full of dangerous dreams.

The guards would gather round him and follow him in the streets, fearing what he might think up. But they always remained at a respectful distance, scared of his inhuman fury.

That evening, at the first sign of dusk, a prepared feast with food and chilled drinks awaited him. Zayko, important and tightly buttoned, and his two lads dressed in their best, silently and hurriedly completed the final preparations for this mad liturgy. The old gypsy Ramo, the best player and singer in the world, and his five sons waited in readiness, gazing in religious awe at Osman and his friends: roisterers, gamblers, rakes, and drunkards, the biggest rowdies in town.

When the gun on the Fortress battlements fired, announcing the end of the fast, Osman got up, symbolically marking the end of the fast with a bite of bread and a glass of *rakiya*, and wished everybody a happy Bairam, for God knew whether the next day he'd know whether it was Bairam or not, and then the celebration began.

The guards and night-watchmen crept about like shadows outside the inn, but all night they heard only songs, music, shouting, and no one came out.

I was told all this by Mahmut Neretlyak, who'd spent the whole night drinking with Osman and his company, had slept a couple of hours in the morning, and then rushed out of the house, as yellow as a lemon, but happy and blissful, as if all his life's dreams had been realized. He'd been drinking with Osman Vuk! He boasted to everyone.

He'd never have got to Osman and Zayko's inn, which were as far removed from him as was the *pasha*'s dwelling. It was pure chance that led him to this unexpected good fortune. Osman Vuk had come to invite me to his celebration of Bairam, but Tiyana's ominously knitted brows killed my every desire to take part. I'd never done so, why should I now, I consoled myself, for want of a better consolation.

Mahmut had listened, as if in an ecstasy, and surely thought me a poor fool who didn't know what true male merrymaking was, nor ever would, when I refused an invitation that any real man would have accepted. So I, not being a real man, suggested to Osman that he take my friend Mahmut with him in my place, since he liked such things and was more sociable than I was.

Mahmut looked at me thankfully and at Osman hopefully, as excited as a girl who hoped to be proposed to, and, when Osman agreed, Mahmut gurgled, as though he almost choked at the honor, but he quickly recovered his balance and accepted the invitation with dignity.

To tell the truth, I was surprised at Osman's inviting him, but this wasn't my greatest worry. I went out with him to ask whether he wouldn't try to rescue Ramiz that evening, since it would be a good time, with everyone celebrating, but he just laughed, "I'll be celebrating, too."

I was left wondering, but Osman went off laughing.

The next day Mahmut told me that it had been a most glorious booze-up: No matter what one said, for a good drink-up you needed the right people. They were good, there was no doubt, especially Osman, but it was a good thing they'd invited him, Mahmut. He showed them how to drink, slowly, in long swallows, from the tongue not the throat, not at one gulp, that was vulgar and couldn't be kept up for long. True, later on, he, too, had drunk in gulps and sucked it out of a plate as if it were soup, but that was at dawn, when everybody but Osman was completely mindless. Mahmut had even taught them how the musicians should play, quietly, elegantly, so that it could not be heard outside, so the music got to the heart and choked you, without your knowing why. Osman Vuk appreciated his know-how, said the celebration was all the better for his presence, and kept putting his arm round him as though he were his brother or his best friend. And that Osman Vuk, the wolf, was no wolf but a lion. He could do anything anybody could, but what he could do not everyone else could. For him, Mahmut, it was all new, manly, merry, both what Osman said and what he knew. He, Mahmut, had nearly dislocated his jaws with laughter and wonder, and had he died yesterday he'd never have known such people existed. Osman was the most cheerful, interesting, best, most intelligent, and bravest man he'd ever seen.

And what there was in him was hard to believe. He played on the *shagiye* and Ramo sang, then he sang and

Ramo played, and then he did a Circassian dance. Mahmut had never in his life seen anything so beautiful. And then Osman did a Romanian dance with Zayko. Around midnight some rowdies came in and threatened to spoil the party, demanded that Ramo should play to them, and ordered the dancing to stop. But Osman told them: Sit down and drink, don't spoil our party, leave us alone, and we'll leave you alone. But nothing touched those bastards. They'd buried their schoolmaster long ago, and if he didn't like it there was the door, he was free to go, and so on and so forth. Enough to make you vomit. They were threatening, too. And I saw that anything could happen. But with Osman there, nothing nasty could happen. He just got up, slowly, unhurriedly, with hardly a gesture, as if he'd all the time in the world. He went up to one of the rowdies, a huge man, he'd scarcely got through the door, and hit him first on the right and then on the left cheek, with a backhand and forehand, and the rowdy simply staggered. He then went up to a second and knocked the hell out of him, and at every punch the rowdy's head flew back and would have fallen off if it hadn't been fixed to his neck, and then flew to the other side. It rocked through a whole two feet and then returned to its natural position. Osman's fist was like a bludgeon, and the rowdy neither knew where he was nor what was happening to him. And then Osman ordered one of them to open the door and both of them to get out and never again show their faces. And, by God, they cringed, obeyed him as children obey a *hodja*, and slunk out into the darkness. And Osman came back to the party. "Where were we?" he said, as if nothing had happened. Then Muharem Pyevo, full of enthusiasm, ordered a song and wanted to pay for it. Osman opened his eyes wide. They were frightening to look at when they flashed. One's heart withered like a sorb-apple. And then, a second later, the sun shone out of them, and he said to Pyevo, "Don't put your hand in your pocket tonight." How much he paid Zayko, how much the musicians, how much the waiters, he alone knew. He settled it all on his own, like a real gentleman, but it was quite a sum, one could see that in their ingratiating smiles, in the way they bowed to him. They'd all have been prepared to spend three days and nights on their feet, if he'd so wished. But when he heard the *muezzin*'s call to dawn prayers, he got to his feet and said: "Happy Bairam, brothers. And thanks for doing me the honor." And sober, quite as if he hadn't spent the whole night drinking, he took his leave of Zayko, requesting the musicians not to follow him far down the street: "It's Bairam, a holiday, people are on their way to prayers, we mustn't get in their way." The music accompanied him as far as the bridge. On the bridge they played one more song, and people, on their way to the mosque, stopped to listen, and Osman bowed to them, with hand on his heart, and wished them a happy Bairam. Then he kissed the whole company, including Mahmut, on both cheeks and went off home. Mahmut was too excited to sleep long. He poured two large jugs of water over his head to cure the effects of *rakiya* and of his delight, and long afterward told of Osman and that unforgettable evening.

For me none of this sounded much like Osman Vuk. I'd never seen him throwing a party, and this restraint and level-headedness were quite unusual and totally unlike him. Either Mahmut was somewhat mistaken or I knew nothing of Osman Vuk.

Afterward, it all became somewhat clearer when I heard what had happened that night in the Fortress.

That same night, on the eve of Bairam, someone had rescued Ramiz from the Fortress and hidden him.

Sometime after evening prayers, some unknown mounted men appeared in front of the Fortress gates and knocked loudly, ordering the sentry to summon the commandant, since they were the bearers of important orders from the *vali*. When the commandant arrived, they showed him a letter, and he let two of them in while the rest remained in front of the locked gates.

What happened after that nobody knew exactly. One could only guess, like those to whom it happened. The two strangers overcame the commandant in his turret, hit him on the head with a club, and left him bleeding on the floor. They overpowered the turnkey in his room by the entrance to the underground dungeons. Then the two of them went up to the sentry at the gates, as though they were leaving. He opened the gates and then, as he turned, a club struck him, too. He was the first to come round, perhaps because he was the youngest or because he had the hardest head or they'd not struck him so hard. He closed the open gate, raised the alarm, wakened the sleeping sentries, and then they found the turnkey, who had regained consciousness but scarcely knew what had happened, and the commandant, who had come off worst of all. He remained unconscious the entire night. They massaged him, poured water over him, all in vain. Then they held *rakiya* under his nose and even poured a few drops into his mouth. On this, the commandant came to, but was unable to get to his feet. There was a large lump on his head and a sick feeling in his stomach. He felt very weak and had only a dim memory of what had occurred.

Ramiz was gone from the Fortress.

People were to remember that Bairam by this event.

They spoke of it everywhere as a miracle, as heroism, as the end of the world, depending on who it was who spoke. There was a rumor that it was the work of Bechir Toska and his bandits. Others stated that it had been done by the heretical order of dervishes, the Hamzevians; others merely expressed their wonder, for Ramiz was the first prisoner ever to have been rescued from the Fortress. Some saw in this a reason for thinking people had got worse; others that they were braver. And perhaps both were right.

The authorities were alarmed. It was a great disgrace that they'd allowed bandits to gain entrance to the Fortress, and an even greater disgrace that they'd not only informed the *vali* of Ramiz's crime, but also Constantinople. How were they to report now that he was missing? What sort of Fortress was it, what sort of sentries, and what sort of governors were in charge?

They questioned the commandant and the Fortress garrison, but none of them knew any more than what they'd already stated and which was known to everybody. The commandant, scarcely able to speak for the pains in his head, stated that the letter really was from the *vali* and bore his seal. True, he hadn't read all of it, because the bandits struck him on the head the moment he began to read. All he remembered was the opening sentence: "To his Honor the Commandant," and that was all. And it would have been better for him if he hadn't remembered even that much, for they showed him the letter that the bandits had cheekily left in his room and asked him how he could have thought that it came from the *vali,* when even a blind man could have seen that the seal was a forgery and not a very good one at that, to which the commandant replied that he could see it now but hadn't then, because he'd had no suspicion and because of the bad light.

It was known that the authorities also asked the commandant why he'd admitted strangers into the Fortress, why he hadn't left them outside the gates while he read the letter (which demanded that Ramiz be delivered up to them) in his room? He replied that they'd been dressed in police uniforms, which the others confirmed, and that they'd said that they had orders to convey to him by word of mouth, and, most of all, what deceived him was that they ordered the gates to be locked while they were in the Fortress. And how was he to suspect anything, when there were only two of them, while in the Fortress, apart from himself, there were ten armed sentries? And what deceived him most of all was the inconceivable effrontery of those people. "Most likely what deceived you was your own stupidity," was the authorities' kind comment.

And so, nobody knew exactly what had happened. Not

even I, although I knew how it had all begun. But more than that, I knew nothing.

When I went to wish him a happy Bairam, I asked Shehaga where they'd hidden Ramiz.

He gave me a sharp glance, as though I were an enemy, and a contemptuous one, as though I were a fool.

"How should I know? Why ask me?"

I saw at once how stupid I was and how naïve I'd been.

And I wouldn't have even asked Shehaga had Osman Vuk not avoided me as if I had the plague, as if he'd never met me, or as if he considered me the lowest of the low.

I worked it all out for myself. OK, then, Shehaga had provided the money, and Osman had paid the people. Who could say who they were: ex-soldiers, brave but poor, or brigands from the forest or bandits or other outcasts who feared nothing if it meant money. And then he'd arranged the drink-up in Zayko's inn, with a large company, with musicians and with Mahmut who would tell everybody about it, and with the constables who kept coming and going all night to have a drink, with watchmen, drunkards, and night owls, and had remained there from dusk till dawn. Everybody could confirm this and clear him of any suspicion, should it occur to anyone to suspect him.

But whom had he bribed in the Fortress? The sentry? But the sentry was unimportant and might not even have been on duty that night, and, even if he were, he'd not have dared to admit anyone without the commandant's orders. No, it couldn't have been he. And he got the bang on the head free, gratis.

Then was it the commandant? His sparse pay and monotonous service, for he was never allowed to leave the Fortress, must certainly have palled on the old soldier, and he could have agreed to anything if a decent reward might enable him to be rid of the Fortress in which he was confined as much as were the prisoners themselves. And it might have let him get married and sample the things other people did and he couldn't. He didn't have to know the men who came, and he was surely speaking the truth when he said he didn't know them and had never seen them. In his bargaining with Osman, he probably wanted the rescue to be convincing and agreed, indeed insisted, that the rescuers hit him, not too hard, just a bit, to give him an alibi. But then, why did they have to hit him as hard as they did? Was it that they didn't know how to hit gently, or perhaps they wanted his alibi to be as convincing as possible? Or perhaps they were paying off who knows what old scores? As it was, the commandant barely got away with his life, and, had he realized the weight of a bandit's hand, he'd probably never have agreed to the plan. Or perhaps he would, for what's a heavy blow and a rather bad headache compared with the bliss that they would earn him? I don't believe he could have earned as much in his whole life as Osman probably offered him, and it was high time he realized that one couldn't earn any significant sum honestly. Indeed, when he finally got up, and he lay in bed for a whole week, his head ached whenever it was cloudy or damp, or whenever he tried to think of anything. But his head would not have ached because of other things that were, after all, more important than headache. And he didn't miss thinking, for it was truly unnecessary, and he recalled that thinking had never been much help to him. Some months later he resigned, when an uncle died and left him an inheritance, or so he said, although everyone was surprised that his uncle had so successfully hidden the fact that he had anything to leave. But who can swear that they know everything about anyone? The commandant purchased a small plot of land by Kozya chupriya, married a young and childless widow, and by dint of working the infertile soil and relying on a fertile wife, gained little money and many children. And putting a slice of raw potato on his forehead whenever his head ached, he thanked God that, for once in his life, fate had remembered him favorably, as pay for his long and honest service to the country and to the sultan.

Tiyana had learned from local gossip about Ramiz's flight, and I told her all I knew. Her first reaction was to be worried. "What if they involve you?"

"Who'd involve me? What have I to do with it? And how could they? I don't even know how it happened."

"Are you sure you're in the clear?"

"I'm sure. It's the game of people greater than we."

"The greater play, the lesser pay."

"This time you're wrong."

"I wish I were. Only don't tell anybody what you know."

"I'm not mad."

Then she remembered Osman Vuk and began to express her admiration. "He looks like a brigand. Only he could have done that."

This disturbed me. I wanted to change the subject.

"You like that brigand. Simply because he said you're pretty."

"Don't be silly."

"He says that to all the women!"

"What do I care!"

"The rescue was none of his doing. He was drinking all that night."

"Perhaps he went out and came back."

"He didn't move from the inn until sunrise."

"Who did it, then?"

"I don't know."

He'd not rescued Ramiz from the Fortress, but he'd planned it all. I didn't want to tell her, because I was hurt by her enthusiasm. But it was true. He did what he wanted, took from life whatever pleased him. He was intelligent enough to plan anything he needed, but too flippant to care about causes and effects. Had the rescuers got killed, it would have been all the same to him. He thought only of himself. For him life was just pleasure, enjoyment, and adventure. He was like the wind, like the afternoon sun, like spring rain. He did what he wished. He lived, like nature itself. Others took from him what they could, what he allowed them. He took no notice of anyone, but followed his own way that led nowhere. He was no dreamer, but ever wakeful and hungry for everything. He didn't desire, he took. He didn't defend himself, he attacked.

But had he done this?

He'd managed it all, he'd shielded and protected himself, had made sure that a hundred pairs of eyes were on him that night, and everything happened just as he wished. Nobody would ever think of him. He didn't even know Ramiz, so why should he have exposed himself to danger?

Yet it was indeed a dangerous undertaking. If the rescuers had been caught they'd have been sure to have betrayed him, and then not even Shehaga could have helped him.

Why had he agreed to do it? He was getting nothing out of it. Ramiz meant nothing to him, and I couldn't believe he'd sacrifice himself for anyone. He obeyed only his own thoughts and followed only his own wishes. Perhaps he'd entered into it out of defiance, out of his sense for adventure, to do something unusual and dangerous, to delight in the bewilderment of the pursuers, laughing at them and leading them on a false trail. Not on any trail! Into darkness. For there were no tracks, as though a ghost had passed by.

I knew a little about heroes, cowards, rogues, bullies, dreamers, rescuers, frightened officials, vain clerks, but of this urban brigand I knew nothing. All I thought of him seemed unsatisfactory and incomplete and could always be refuted by a second thought.

That first morning of Bairam, I woke late. I'd spent much of the night tossing and turning, wide awake, listening to the bakery workers singing, drunk for certain, and to the wind blowing from Trebevich Mountain. I'd been unable to sleep for thinking of Ramiz and Osman. I'd been certain that he was joking, having me on, when he said he would spend the night celebrating. He would begin drinking and then leave the company in order to carry out the task given him by Shehaga. And then he would return, and everyone would swear he hadn't been anywhere. Later, Tiyana was of the same opinion.

I tried to decide at what time Osman would arrive at the Fortress gates and, imagining a hundred obstacles, moved it further and further into the night. Now was the time! But then voices and singing sounded on the street, forcing me to postpone the beginning. At midnight, I heard a call to prayer from the Begova mosque. It was Salih Tabakovich, out of prayer time, and for no reason. Strangely, as though wailing, he cried his fear and desolation into the dark night. He was howling like a dog because of some horror of which only he knew, and this he would do some ten times a year, just as Shehaga would drink. He conjured up in people thoughts of disaster, of the emptiness of living, of death. That terrified shriek, together with the wind that moaned in gusts, distinguished this night and this moment from all others. Now is the time, midnight, wind, darkness, empty streets, fear over the town. Would Osman knock on the heavy gate? I shivered at the thought of that sound, the only human one at that time of night. Was the sentry warned of his coming, or did Osman have to overpower him?

From that moment, in my half-waking brain, there began to form a tangled ball of dangers, of the trample of feet, of shouting, alarm, acts of courage, but out of all this muddle, which I didn't dare to unwind, Osman and Ramiz somehow emerged, disappearing into the night, galloping on horseback, hovering on a cloud, vanishing into the dark.

And then I'd go back to the beginning. The sentry gave the alarm before Osman could do anything. Lights were lit in the Fortress. In the town, a desolate man cried his fear to the dark sky. . . . And I drifted into sleep, taking with me only the happy image of two brave horsemen.

When I woke up, I remembered that Osman had done nothing for Ramiz last night; he was more interested in his celebrations.

And then I realized that the rescue had already happened!

I'd hardly begun breakfast when Mahmut arrived. He knew nothing of Ramiz or of his escape from the Fortress, nor was he greatly interested when we told him. He'd more important things to think about. Most of all the party in Zayko's inn. Did Osman leave? No, he didn't go anywhere. Why should he?

I was completely at a loss. I'd spent all night worrying about Osman, and he'd spent the whole time in the inn. It was a pity Tiyana didn't hear this, but she'd just left the room to receive two baskets of goodies brought by some of Shehaga's lads. She returned the baskets, but kept the dishes.

"Shehaga sent them," she said in amazement, perhaps at the unexpected attention.

Mahmut shook his head appreciatively, but showed little interest.

"I bet it's Osman's doing," he said and went on to talk about Osman Vuk yet again, what a man he was, what a friend! He'd repeated several times how glad he was to have made Mahmut's acquaintance, and they'd kissed each other on both cheeks, on both cheeks!

It seemed to me that as he went on talking and repeating himself he grew ever stranger and sadder. He had a thoughtful expression and spoke quietly.

"Are you tired?" I asked him. "Or are you feeling sad?"

"Sad? What do you mean? Why should I be sad?"

"One can feel sad after a big party."

"One can, I know. But I'm not."

He even laughed to show he wasn't sad, and at once, without stopping to draw breath, told us how that morning he'd gone to wish Osman a happy Bairam, but the servants wouldn't let him in.

"Tell Osman it's Mahmut Neretlyak," he'd demanded.

One of them left and quickly returned.

"Osman's not here," he said.

"What do you mean not here? I can hear his voice."

"He's not here. He's not at home."

"You're an impudent lot of bastards," he told them angrily, "and I'll report you to Osman. I'll let him know what sort of servants he has who have no respect even for his friends!"

It was all in vain. They wouldn't let him in. They even sneered at him, the bastards!

He walked up and down in front of the gate, up and down the street, waiting to see Osman. He was frozen, but there was no sign of Osman.

People went in to deliver their good wishes. The servants greeted them with their hands on their hearts. He heard Osman's voice from somewhere in the house, but he couldn't see him.

He had another try. They turned him away.

He'd come back, aggrieved at the servants' impudence.

He was sorry because Osman would think him impolite, that he'd forgotten his friend, but what could he do, it wasn't his fault, he'd explain to him, he'd apologize, perhaps Osman wouldn't be angry.

So, I wasn't mistaken, he was sad after all.

He didn't seem to understand that it was Osman who'd turned him away! He didn't want to.

Would he be a child all his life and long to be accepted by people who were way out of his league? We weren't enough for him. Our poverty was a constant reminder of his own. Osman, the resplendent, the master of life, till yesterday could have been only a dream to him. Last night they'd become friends. What had gone wrong this morning? He assured himself, checking his every memory: It had really happened, he hadn't imagined it, it wasn't an illusion. Osman had embraced him, called him his friend, and kissed him on both cheeks. And this morning the servants had refused to let him wish his friend a happy Bairam and had cruelly insulted him out of jealousy, malice, enmity, which servants feel toward everybody.

Only it wasn't Osman's fault!

To anybody not infatuated, it would be immediately clear that it was his fault and, if they'd even a modicum of pride, they'd send him to the devil. But Mahmut was infatuated by what he imagined and by his own wish that what he wanted so desperately should be the truth. And he didn't need pride, he needed friendship.

And why did he have to find Osman who bewitched people, used them, and then cast them aside when he no longer needed them?

Osman was a cold cave wall; Mahmut was a beaten kitten seeking warmth. The one never remembered, the other never forgot. One was indifferent, the other bled.

What could I say to him? Idiot, pull yourself together! Or: You poor bloke, forget it!

He was both funny and pathetic, and I didn't know whether to feel sorry for him or to swear at him.

"As long as Osman isn't angry," he said in a worried voice.

He left apparently cheerful, but this didn't fool me. He felt the sting of a vague doubt, even though he rejected it.

Would his misery last, or would he soon forget it? His life had been a long series of failed expectations, and perhaps he'd grown accustomed to disappointment.

"I didn't do him a favor last night," I said to Tiyana when he'd gone.

"He's mad, and he'll die mad," she snapped angrily. "Do I have to cry just because Osman chucked him out? He's got a wife at home. Why doesn't he stay with her?"

There was no doubt she was in a shocking mood!

I thought it was best to leave her to get over her irritation by herself, so I said I was off to wish Shehaga a happy Bairam. Without saying anything to her, I'd be doing what custom demanded, and at the same time avoiding the storm breaking over my innocent head. For I saw the lightnings were flashing.

"Will the servants shut the door on you too?" she asked bitchily.

"Shehaga invited me. I can't refuse to go. And if they don't let me in, I shan't grieve like Mahmut."

"You can't wait to see them! You ought to be ashamed of yourself."

I didn't ask who they were. Perhaps brigands, like Osman, or the rich, like Shehaga. If she thought that, then it was an insult. Or perhaps they meant all those outside our room, all those who were not she. If this was so, then it was love.

I accepted the better of the two conclusions, kissed her on the cheek to show that her words had not offended me, and went out unhurriedly.

At Shehaga's, there was quite a crowd. The house was as full and noisy as an inn. At the front door I ran into Osman. He was seeing Zafraniya out. He pretended not to see me, or perhaps seeing me was a matter of indifference.

I met Shehaga in the hall. He was just taking leave of the *kadi*. Did everybody come to pay their respects to him? They didn't like him, but they still came. He didn't like them either, yet he thanked them heartily for their visit and invited them to come again, saying how delighted he'd be.

I knew just how delighted he'd be!

It occurred to me, and I laughed to myself with enjoyment: If they but knew that last night's rescue took place on Shehaga's orders, would they have smirked so kindly, concealing their thoughts and what they really wished for each other?

When he was alone, I went up to him and gave him my good wishes, kissing his hand. I'd thought we might kiss one another on the cheek, like equals, even though we were not, but I sensed in his rigid attitude that he desired no familiarity. Perhaps it was because we held an important secret between us and a different relationship from that of others. Or did I take the illusion for reality, as Mahmut did?

No, our case was different after all. (In vain, man is incorrigible and, more often than not, lies to himself without knowing it.)

Not wishing to be passed over immediately, I asked him what had happened to Ramiz, where was he.

He replied unsmilingly, "How would I know? Why ask me?"

"Whom should I ask?"

"Nobody."

And he gave a smile, belatedly, and led me into a room among the younger people, the younger and the less important. My place would always be known, even when I grew old, like Mahmut. Luckily, I didn't care.

And I had more pressing worries: I thought of Shehaga's reply. I was both ashamed and angry, ashamed for myself and for my stupid question, angry both at myself and at him. Perhaps he was right, I shouldn't have asked, especially at a time when there were a hundred ears that might hear, but he could have said it differently, less sharply, less offensively. Did they always have to show that they were superior to us?

What was I doing here, anyway? Why hadn't I just given him my good wishes and left immediately? I'd persuaded Shehaga to save Ramiz, wasn't that enough? I'd done more than I could have ever imagined, what more did I want? Did I want us to discuss a good man, to admire ourselves for having done a good deed, to gloat over a lot of unscrupulous people? What nonsense!

Theirs was another world, far removed and incomprehensible. They'd done it and that was that! They'd done it, so why talk about it? We ordinary folk liked to chew over and savor our experiences. They acted and forgot it. I admit, their way was wise, mine was stupid. I was proud and inspired by a brave action. They'd carried out the brave action and kept quiet about it. We didn't achieve many small acts, let alone great ones, and so we didn't easily relinquish them from our hearts and mouths. And God knows how many acts of all kinds and secrets they had. Everything for them was secret. We had no secrets. Perhaps this was just the difference between us and the great. Nothing significant could be accomplished in public. In public one lied, one spoke high-sounding words; in public one showed the facade, one committed violence. Important matters, good and bad, were done secretly. They were prepared while we, the weaklings, slept, and when we woke we'd be amazed at how they'd occurred so suddenly!

Tired of my naïve speculation, against both them and myself, I began to listen to the talk of those minor officials.

They were talking about last night's rescue and making a joke of it. Not even the Fortress was the fortress any longer, one of them said. It used to be tighter than the grave, now it was like a public house. You could drop in, as that Ramiz did, stay there a while, sleep there if you liked, have a rest, and then, when you'd had enough, out you'd go. The only difference was that you had to pay in a public house, while in the Fortress it was free and it was a pity that the Fortress was high up on a hill and it was a hard walk up there or else it wouldn't be bad to drop in, when you were tired of work.

Another said the Fortress had become unnecessary. The more important criminals could leave whenever they liked, while there was no point in imprisoning the less important. Wouldn't it be better to turn it into a storehouse for potatoes or for grain? There was plenty of space, and it was dry, so nothing would rot.

A third one asked who could have carried out the rescue. He didn't believe Ramiz's mother, old as she was, could have ridden so well or easily disguised herself as a hefty constable nor give the commandant such a mighty hit on the head. It wasn't the work of the poor who were his audience in the mosque, for they didn't use cunning. They were too stupid. They used only open force. Nor was it the rich who could purchase anyone's courage for money, since they'd none of their own. Not them, because they'd have gained no profit from it, and that disposed of any suspicion of them. If one were to think that someone was involved who knew how to forge seals, write letters to commandants, issue orders, and knew in whose name to issue them, again one would be wrong, for it was against such people that Ramiz had spoken most bitterly. Why would they do something against themselves? And so, considering everything and examining all sides of the question, one might conclude that the rescue had been carried out by nobody. And were it carried out by some thing, then he was unqualified to comment, since he didn't believe in the supernatural.

They were quite intelligent young people, but to me they didn't seem too honest. They didn't care much about Ramiz's escape, but they weren't on his side. They weren't even on the side of their own superiors. They laughed at their incompetence in the name of their own competence, which was not allowed to express itself. Had they had the power they should have, Ramiz would never have gotten out of the Fortress. They didn't say this directly, but this was what they meant. These young old men, who would add to their rapacious desire for prestige all that they'd learned from their elders, would ensure us a happy future. The present powers allowed us to weep, these would not, and so we'd have a happier life. The present powers allowed us to be dissatisfied, as long as we kept it to ourselves; this lot would quietly forbid us even this, and so we'd live more happily, since dissatisfaction is the greatest misfortune.

I remembered the dinner at *hadji*-Duhotina's once again, who knows for how many times, and left the room, so I'd not say something I shouldn't. The present ones beat you up, these would castrate you.

I passed by Osman without looking at him.

"What's the matter, can't you see me?" he asked with a laugh.

"You didn't see me."

"Don't be childish! I didn't want to recognize you because of Zafraniya. He's a nosy bugger."

"I know."

"And we were having an interesting conversation. Do you know what I asked him? How could they let a thing like that happen in the Fortress? And why had they made such a fuss about Ramiz? And he just looked at me, swallowed, and was silent."

"And why didn't you let Mahmut into the house?"

"What Mahmut?"

"He was with you last night in Zayko's inn."

"Oh, that one! What could I do with him in all this, for God's sake? You saw how many people there were. Who wasn't here! The *kadi*, the *muselim*, the *mufti*, and the *defter-dar*. I sat them all down together. I know they hate each other and backbite like a lot of mad bitches. Let's see what happens, I said to myself. And they sat there on the settee, one beside the other, smiling sourly, even saying the odd word to one another, so people wouldn't see what was between them, as if everybody didn't know! The *muselim* was the first to give in. He got up, took a polite leave, I must admit, and dashed off. The *kadi* stayed a bit longer, but then he, too, left, pale in the face. No matter, I can't tell you how much I enjoyed it!"

He also enjoyed, he said, that they all had to come to Shehaga, even though they knew Shehaga couldn't stand them. And they came because they were afraid of him. They knew he was at the *vali*'s yesterday. They knew he'd be going today to wish him a happy Bairam, and who knows what could be said along with good wishes. They were dying of fear in case he did them some harm, so they smiled politely, even though the sight of him turned their stomachs. They feared Shehaga because of the *vali*. The *vali* didn't need much excuse to turn against them. As they hated each other, they all hated the *vali*. And the *vali* them. If it weren't for this, God help us! If they held together, they'd eat us to the last bone. What saved us was their mutual hatred, may God bless it! So it was always and everywhere. Ordinary folk somehow managed to save their heads while theirs hung by a thread. Shehaga had a lot of influence, so much so they shivered at the thought. Was Shehaga the *vali*'s friend? Not on your life; there was no friendship between the powerful. They both claimed they were friends, they had to, but they weren't. To be a friend was something different, he didn't know what, but it was not this. The *vali* was in debt to Shehaga. He was a great spendthrift and came here without a sou, and Shehaga helped him, offered him money so he'd not be short. And he wasn't! In no time at all he'd borrowed a hundred bags of ducats! What did he spend it on? To begin with, he spent a lot because it came easy, and then he hadn't spent it all. He'd take it back with him to where he came from. Such people came with light luggage and went back heavy, laden with a whole caravan of goods. It was strange how no one with a position ever preserved their honesty. Or did they fear to offend the system and the resulting dismissal, for one had to live even after that? Or the position was such that it was impossible not to take until you were replaced. Afterward they could even be honest.

Neither Shehaga nor the *vali* ever spoke about the debt, the *vali* because he didn't wish to return it, Shehaga because it didn't pay for him to get it back, for, with the debt, the *vali* was less than he was and Shehaga greater than he was. Without the debt, the *vali* would have been mighty as a rock, but lighter by a hundred bags of ducats, which was quite a fortune, and he'd rather have remained with less dignity and more money. So one could see the value of money, for if power were a disaster, greed made it more bearable. How did Shehaga not fear that the debt would cost him his life, for then the *vali* would be freed from an aggravating obligation? But the point was that it wouldn't help him. Shehaga was clever and knew what game he was about. He'd been careful to get the *vali*'s receipt, confirmed by all possible stamps and seals and authorized by the court. He made sure that the *vali* would repay the entire debt in favor of the foundation that would bear Shehaga's name, and toward helping the *medrese* and the library, should anything happen to Shehaga, no matter how or for what reason. They both knew very well what this meant, so that the *vali* wished Shehaga a long life, just as he did himself, and would do everything to shield him from all dangers. So the ducats he'd lent had become a miraculous talisman that guarded him from an evil fate.

"And do these ducats guard you, too?"

"Indeed they do."

"Then you're not such great heroes."

"Who said we were? And who cares for heroism these days?"

I asked him the same question I'd asked Shehaga: Where was Ramiz?

He laughed. "He's not in the Fortress anymore."

"That tells me a lot."

"That's all you need to know."

I left with the unpleasant taste of Osman's tale of hatred. What a life these people led! What an unremitting strain, the calculation of every step and of every word, the fatiguing consideration of the possible moves of an opponent! What a torment, what a waste of life! What little time or opportunity for normal human thinking and feeling, for caring for anything beyond oneself and one's danger! We saw them exercising power, force, in all their might, but didn't realize their unease, their fear of everything, of themselves, of the other, the greater, the lesser, the more intelligent, the more malicious, the more skillful, of the secret, of the shadow, of the dark, of the light, of taking the wrong step, of the sincere word, of everything and everybody!

Was it any wonder they were evil!

Would I have involved myself in such devilish entanglements had I, by some miracle, taken their path? Certainly! And I would not have been aware of the misery I was in, for they didn't know that one could live in any other way.

But one could! Sometimes without bread, but without hatred, without constant anxiety, without fear. I could afford the luxury of mad thoughts, of unreasonable happiness, of strong feeling, of thoughtless words. I always had time for my commonplace self. And I was preparing myself, taking my time about it, admittedly, for a human life in peace.

Ever in their thoughts was that other whom they didn't like and who hated them and that possible one, known or unknown, who was laying a trap for them. They were constantly at war, and only death would save them from their torment.

But my thoughts were occupied with the woman I loved (why was she angry?), and in my heart was a childish joy at the sight of the first snow. I looked at it with delight, as if it were for the first time, falling in dense flakes, covering the town in white.

Meaningless thoughts, meaningless sensations, yet how much richer was I than they! And, it would seem, the only value these possessed was that they separated me from the darkness of the great.

Mahmut was sauntering down the street, sloshing his worn shoes on the wet snow.

"Where are you going?"

"Nowhere. I'm just walking. It's snowing."

"I've been talking to Osman about you. He says he's sorry. There were so many people in the house, he didn't know what he was doing."

The poor chap took heart, once again!

"What about my dropping in there now?"

"Don't, it's still packed. I saw him only for a moment in passing. I managed to ask him only what I've just told you."

"Then what about tomorrow?"

"That would be better."

My poor Mahmut, tomorrow you'll still be "that other." Even tomorrow, the servants won't let you in. Still, at least you can live in hope till tomorrow. Though you've no need to hope. We're not for them, and I'd say thank God!

And once again I turned to my happy thoughts, which Mahmut had interrupted.

The first snow, the sweet story, the madness of childhood happiness, as flimsy as a spiderweb, the dream of beauty. I'd take Tiyana out. We'd go for a long walk down streets that the snow was steadily burying. I'd tell her about my childhood. No, I'd tell her how much I loved her and what joy I had in life. We'd wander without purpose. We'd rejoice, we'd laugh without reason, for the only, single reason that we were alive and loved each other. And what better reason could one find!

She'd just returned from somewhere, carrying some of the dishes sent by Shehaga.

"Where've you been?"

"I've given everything Shehaga sent us to the neighbors' children."

"You've done right."

"Sure I've done right. I don't need charity."

Today was her day for being angry, it would seem. She clearly hadn't got over it.

"It wasn't charity," I said quietly. "It's the custom."

"I hate customs that humiliate me."

"What's the matter with you today?"

There was nothing the matter with her, she said in an icy voice. Rather, what was the matter with me? She was always alone. She'd no one to talk to (I knew it all by heart!), and she, too, was a human being, she couldn't be forever talking to four walls. And what had she done against God that he punished her so, and what had she done to me to deserve such treatment? She'd given up everything that she was, forgotten her family, put aside everything to which she was accustomed, lost contact with friends and acquaintances, and all for my sake. I'd given up nothing. I could go out, I had my own friends, my own worries that were not hers, since I hid them. I was away all day, heaven alone knew where I was and what I was doing. I kept and observed all my customs. I hadn't forgotten Bairam, while she would forget all hers and would end up as empty as a field of stubble.

Last Wednesday was her saint's day, Saint Nicholas. For twenty years, she'd always spent that day together with her family, and last Wednesday she'd sat alone and wept and not because of the family saint's day, but because of her fate. Why hadn't she said anything? Did she have to say everything? Couldn't I see for myself? I cared about Mahmut, about Ramiz, about Shehaga, but I didn't care about her.

She noticed every change in me, every shadow that crossed my face, while I saw nothing that happened to her. I'd got so used to her attentions that I didn't even notice them, but it was her fault, she'd spoiled me, she'd hidden all our troubles from me, our lack of money, even her own misery, simply so I'd not feel their burden. If I only saw this, she'd not complain. Other husbands danced attendance on their wives, pleased them, spoiled them. She didn't ask for this, she was just saying what others did. And how did I treat her? Had I ever taken her out? Never! Had I ever surprised her during those last two years with anything nice? Never! As if she were a servant and not a wife. Men were coarse and selfish, loving only at first, till they got used to it. But when a woman grew ugly, as she had, then they avoided being at home. She knew all that. No one needed to tell her. She could see I didn't love her anymore, and she wouldn't be surprised to hear that I had a mistress. But she wouldn't put up with it as other women did. She'd leave. She hadn't anything or anybody, but she'd go away, anywhere, be a serving girl, but she would not put up with humiliation.

So she told me off, both for things I was guilty of and for things she imagined I was guilty of, accused me of the sins of all men, dead and alive, blamed me for the vices of our grandfathers and great-grandfathers and for the general male viciousness that required no proof.

At first I thought it funny, then I was hurt, then I got angry, and, in the end, I didn't know what I was saying anymore than she did.

Hang on, look at the snow, I said. And then: What the

hell's the matter with you! And then: Have I deserved this from you!

Angrily, I reminded her that I'd told her everything honestly when we first met, who I was and what I was. I didn't hide anything. She knew she could expect poverty, and now all I could do was pity her for not marrying some merchant or craftsman. She'd have been a prominent and respected wife by now. (It was anger, not reason, that spoke, and I went on at her like mad Muyo beating his drum.) I could offer her neither wealth nor position, only love. But that wasn't enough for her. Much she cared for my love. I could stick my love where I liked. And what did she want from me? Where should I take her? Should I take her around the Bashcharshia for the young men to stare at? And as for her saint's day, how could I know when I didn't even know my own? I wouldn't even have known about Bairam if Shehaga hadn't invited me. She said she'd spoiled me. I could see how she'd spoiled me when she scolded me until I didn't know what I was doing. It was I who'd done the spoiling. I'd let her have her own way so much that soon I'd not dare to put a foot out of the door. She'd soon be chaining me by the leg.

Later I was ashamed of having talked such nonsense, and even more for having shouted at her, but what could I do, anger gets the better of one.

And while the sparks were flying, because of her injustice, my unrecognized goodness, my unappreciated love, as I foamed at the mouth, pitying myself and cursing her, into the room came Mahmut Neretlyak.

He stopped dead, blinked bloodshot, sleepless eyes, and then gave a nod, as though apologizing—Please, carry on!— and quickly left the room.

His comical confusion and clumsy wave of the hand that told us not to let him interrupt cut off my anger, took away its force and keenness. In a second it vanished, melted, faded away, and all that remained was embarrassment. Mahmut was taken aback, surprised at our quarrelling, and then tried to put things right by encouraging us to carry on where we stopped, doing what all others did.

He was amazed and comforted at the same time, perhaps disappointed that we were as we were, perhaps glad that we were no different from others. Or perhaps he pitied Tiyana, for he came just as I was shouting and she was crying, so that in his eyes I appeared the aggressor and she the victim.

Still, what did it matter!

I knew I was wrong. I'd flared up too hastily. Couldn't I have kept quiet, laughed, made a joke of it, taken her out into the snow? But I couldn't restrain myself, hurt by her unjust accusations. She was angry with someone else and was taking it out on me. It wasn't fair. Yet perhaps she was really unhappy with our life. Then she didn't love me.

"It looks as if you don't love me anymore," I said reproachfully.

But my reproaches were not harsh, for her sake. She was sitting on the trunk, huddled with her chin on her knees, completely absent. I'd have preferred her to be furious.

"I wish I didn't love you," she whispered to the floor.

"Then what's the matter?"

"I'm sad. I can't tell you how sad I am."

"Why?"

She gave a scarcely noticeable shrug of the shoulders. Truly sad, genuinely miserable.

There was nothing wrong with her, she'd have told me for sure. How then could she be sad for nothing? Perhaps due to memories, the past, a moment of insecurity, the onset of sad thoughts? I understood somebody being sad because of something real or something that might happen. But there you are, we were not all the same. It seemed I should have to get used to sadness without a reason or with a reason that was not visible, due to thoughts that wandered in their own internal spaces, weary, God knows why, sad for who knows what reason.

I was sorry for her. I couldn't bear to see her so lost.

I sat down beside her and put my arm round her, gently, not to upset her anymore. I sensed the storm had passed, but she was profoundly unhappy. What was the matter with her? Why had I been so hard on her?

"Look, it's snowing."

She didn't answer. She didn't even turn to look. There was something stronger and more pressing.

"I'd thought of going for a walk together. It's white all over."

She still said nothing. All right. I'd wait till our bodies grew closer. We'd drawn apart while we were shouting at one another.

Then she said something I didn't understand. Her voice was too weak.

"Why are you whispering?"

"I think I'm pregnant."

"Are you sure?"

She nodded.

"Thanks be to God! Bless you for such good news!"

"I'm afraid."

Her voice was unsure, scarcely audible. I guessed what she meant.

"What are you afraid of?"

"I don't know. Everything."

Why should she be afraid, I said. It was pregnancy; all women get afraid. (I didn't know whether all women got afraid, I just said it to calm her down.) When she was carrying last time, our life was hard and full of stress. Her nerves couldn't stand it. Now it was different, life was more peaceful. It could be better, but it wasn't too bad. It could only get better. And what happened before was my fault, but it was over. I'd never repeat such madness, I promised. I once thought it was dishonorable to remain silent. Now I kept silent and didn't feel it dishonorable. For her sake. She was more important than anything else, even honor. She was all I cared for and all my happiness. I'd behaved badly, but why hadn't she told me earlier? Why had she kept quiet, when she knew how pleased I'd be?

I wanted to calm her and so didn't tell the whole truth. I, too, feared her pregnancy and her fear. What would that new worm bring her, the worm that was growing inside her? Would it bring her only pain and torment? Would he feed her on doubts and terrors?

That was the cause of her disquiet, the secret of the conception of this new being within her, the fear lest what had happened before be repeated, only now, perhaps, with more serious consequences. Who knows how she'd suffered, thinking of the unthinkable, for it was hidden and unknown, feeling herself truly alone. She'd attacked me, perhaps not realizing the real reason for doing so, blaming me for her sufferings. Unfortunately, she was right, because some understanding on my side, had I not been blind, would at least have lessened them, if not banished them.

She'd been thinking of her pregnancy, I of Ramiz, and we'd shouted at one another, venting our accumulated bitterness. It wasn't her fault. The guilt was mine.

But no matter, it was all over and done with. I felt a bit ashamed. I loved her dearly. We'd forgiven one another our harsh words, which were ridiculous in any case. We felt the pleasure and warmth of bodies brought close, the joy of her secret and of my ready repentance. The heat of the baker's oven belonged only to us. The snow hovered in heavy flakes outside the window to make us feel our warmth. We were no longer sad or unhappy, even though there remained on her face a faint shadow of anxiety.

■ □ ■ □ ■

CHAPTER 14

THE POWER OF LOVE

FULL OF GOODWILL, FOLLOWING THE CONTROVERSY THAT I'D begun with a joke, continued with anger, and finished by feeling ashamed, I was careful not to leave Tiyana on her own. She needed my help.

A pregnant woman is a different being, unknown even to herself, a being that's beginning to sense hidden mysteries. All that has been repressed awakens, emerges from the remote corners of the soul, imposes itself, demands to be recognized. And it acts, unconsciously but powerfully. She can't cope with the mass of new and unfamiliar feelings, neither shame nor willpower are capable of suppressing them. Her jealousy is fear of ugliness; her impulsiveness is the need to be free of an internal pressure; her anxiety is a sign of the storm within her. Her blood circulates different-ly, her glands secrete differently, her organs act in a different way, her brain works differently. And it all happens in spite of her. She's at the mercy of something stronger than her will and is unable either to stop it or to change its direction. Because of the mystery inside her, the world itself becomes a mystery to her, and insecurity gives rise to thoughts of death. "If I die," she'd say, rather as one might say, "If I catch cold."

"If I die, how will you manage?"

"If I die, will you think of me?"

"If I die, would you marry again? I'm sure you would.

The pain felt at losing a wife is like hitting your funny bone, it's sharp, but it doesn't last long. Everybody gets married again."

"Stop talking like that, for God's sake," I said, trying to calm her.

"Will you get married again if I die?"

"I won't," I would answer, feeling I had to, ridiculous as it was.

"Have you been so unhappy with me that you'd never marry again?"

"I'd die of grief, I love you so much."

"No, you've burned your fingers once, and that would be enough. But perhaps you would, not long after my death."

"And wouldn't you marry again if I died?" I said jokingly.

"Please, don't make a joke of it!" (Her face was deathly serious.)

"Why? Our chances are equal. But stop it. Why think about things that are fifty years away?"

"It'll be sooner, much sooner. I feel it. And I'm afraid."

It was useless to try to talk reason. Her revived fears were more powerful than reason. I calmed her with affection, the only remedy that could help her. I tried to humor her, petted her, spared her every strain; I did what I could and what I couldn't, turning myself into a well-intentioned but clumsy nanny. My attentions touched her and made her cry. She laughed at my clumsiness, but slowly grew calmer, since she no longer felt deserted.

In the evening, I'd take her for a walk. She wouldn't go out in daytime, because she felt her pregnancy already made her look ugly. I got the impression that she preferred to go out when it was dark, because she could freely lean on my arm, which she'd have been ashamed to do in daylight. In this way she felt more secure in the dark and in a space that was not her own.

"You're the best man on earth," she would say lovingly, moved by God knows what sentiment.

"The other day I was the worst."

"Now you're the best."

Mahmut told me cautiously that I was making a mistake. Tiyana was a very good wife, but there was no point in exaggerating. If I accustomed her to so much attention, what would I do afterward? You could put up with anything in life for a short time. You could be good, brave, and attentive, but life wasn't short, and nothing could be worse than a burden you put on yourself in a moment of weakness and sentimentality. You'd be ashamed of giving it up. It would be hell to carry on. And you'd have nobody to swear at, because you'd have done it yourself. But then, it was well known, sickness does not only exhaust, it destroys. Pregnancy wasn't an illness, true, but I was coddling my wife, as if she were on her deathbed—which God forbid!—I'd pay for it, God grant he was wrong, she'd ride me into the earth. Women love to dominate, with love or without it, no matter. He wasn't denying that a man should be nice to his wife. If he wasn't, others would be. And even if they weren't, she'd be better off living on her own than being treated like a dog. But a bit of discipline never hurt. For he who could manage it, of course. Some couldn't, but then he was talking in general, without reference to anyone in particular, just saying what would be best, not what was. But as far as he could see, and as far as he knew, for me, it would go on like this forever and that wouldn't be easy to put up with.

When, in justification, I told him Tiyana wasn't feeling well, he offered to bring his wife. She'd have a look at Tiyana, so we'd know whether she was all right or not. When she was fitter, she used to help women giving birth, and, even now, people came to her, begging her, saying it was easier for them with her, and she really knew everything about such matters, like a doctor.

We agreed, since even if it didn't help much, it wouldn't do any harm, and so Mahmut brought his wife, whom we'd never met till then. Whether Mahmut was ashamed of us or of her, or of himself left alone with his wife, Tiyana, and myself, I didn't know. Perhaps he'd lied to his wife that we were more important and richer than we were. Or his wife was so ugly and impossible, as he'd told us, that he hesitated to show her to us, for the ears bear ugliness better than the eyes do, so that it's less unpleasant when talked about than when seen. Or he was afraid to let us see how much his wife despised him?

Which of these was true, I didn't know, but I took an instant liking to his wife. She scarcely walked on swollen feet, was completely breathless, and could hardly speak from fatigue, but she spoke, looking at us merrily through small eyes sunk in fat. She began by saying that she'd often heard from Mahmut how good and attractive Tiyana was, so she'd thought she must be ugly and bad-tempered, since he always got it wrong. And he had. He was mistaken as usual, for Tiyana was not just beautiful, but very beautiful. And she was good, for sure, since there was nothing sharp or mean about her, no guile. Her laugh was sincere and open, such as she hadn't heard for many a day, and she'd have liked to have met her every morning, so her day could have a good beginning. She'd say, judging by her, that I couldn't be bad either, since a woman with a bad husband became a shrew. But perhaps Tiyana would have been as she was even if I were bad, for Tiyana's eyes told her she was good for her own sake and not for the sake of others. And then again, a husband who wished himself well would do what his wife told him. Men were children, even when they grew old. Women were more reasonable. They knew exactly what was good for the family. They were never too hasty. They thought three times before acting, especially if they had children. For only a woman knew what it cost her to bear them and bring them up. Men thought women liked it and rarely helped, not because they were bad but because they were stupid. But what could one do, she said with a merry laugh, they were mad, but they were ours, bless them whatever they were.

Mahmut squinted through his nearsighted eyes and gently rubbed his legs, not looking at his wife nor at her two teeth that gleamed white from the hollow of her mouth.

Was she talking about him? Even if she were, she'd said nothing to hurt him, and there was nothing nasty in her cheery speech, not even a hint of complaint.

Then she told us both to go and get some fresh air, and we went out onto the narrow veranda, hopping up and down to avoid the damp cold.

"Just listen to her! She will talk!" Mahmut said, absent-mindedly.

"She talks, but what she says makes sense."

"I'd like to see you having to put up with her sense from morning till night."

"You're never at home from morning till night."

"The bit I do hear is enough for me."

We were silent, he thinking of some worries of his own, I thinking of Tiyana. What would Mahmut's wife say?

What could she say? What did she know? She'd helped the local women in childbirth, casting spells and leaving all to God's will, and they either died or recovered, depending on their luck.

What did I care what she'd say!

"She's taking her time," I said, nodding toward the room, stamping my feet to warm them.

"She hasn't been long. You're just worrying."

"So, I'm worrying."

"You've no need. Women are like cats."

When Mahmut's wife called us in, the first thing I did was look at her face. What was its expression, happy or falsely comforting? I saw it shone with relief. All's well, then, I thought happily. And she's a wonderful woman and really knows her job.

Tiyana had an embarrassed smile.

"It couldn't be better, touch wood," Mahmut's wife said proudly, as if it were all her doing.

"Tiyana's worried," I said, seeking some word of encouragement.

"Every woman worries. But she has no reason. And you, my love, have nothing to worry about. God willing, you'll have it easily, I could tell straight away. Naturally I saw it. How many times I've been a midwife, I couldn't tell you myself. And I've had four, so I should know."

"Four?" I asked, surprised.

"Two alive, two dead."

I looked at Mahmut. Hadn't he mentioned only a daughter?

He didn't reply, but his wife did. "Our son's in Mostar, learning to be a goldsmith. There's just the two of us here."

She looked around our humble room and, as if a thought had just struck her, said, "You haven't much room here, my children. What do you say, Mahmut, why don't they move in with us?"

"It'd be a pity for them to leave here in winter. You see how warm the bakery keeps them. Sometimes even I come here to get warm."

"It's better for quarrelling when we're alone," I joked, not thinking how Tiyana might take it. Luckily, she laughed.

Mahmut's wife laughed, too. "As far as quarrelling goes, we won't get in your way. Nor you in ours. Quarrel away, it makes love all the sweeter afterward. All right, we'll wait till spring. You'd find it hard here with a kid. How are you fixed for money?"

"We're all right."

"Not all right, that's for sure. If you need any, Tiyana, you come to me, and we'll manage something. Mahmut picks up a bit, and so do I. We never have much, but neither you nor we need a lot. And come and see me, anyway, so we can have a good talk. Don't stay here on your own."

"I'm not alone. Ahmet's with me."

"Then chase him out. It's no good having a man hanging about the house. So, you come!"

I was long to remember, with pleasure, that determined woman who seemed to take life so easily. For her, everything was simple and jolly. Your flat's no good? Come to us! We'll share what we have! You want to quarrel? Why shouldn't you! Do you want to make love? Why not!

I'd known such women. They used to come to see my mother, always happy, interesting, sure, the most balanced creatures on earth. These ordinary local women had discovered the secret of tranquility, without looking for it. Everything delighted them, nothing surprised them. They didn't ask for the impossible. They were kind, until you trod on their corns, sharp if you hurt them. They gossiped, but without much envy. They had big mouths, but they'd help anybody in trouble. They knew life was hard, but they didn't cry about it, and they'd always dig out something of beauty in it, and, for them, what was beautiful was simple: the garden in blossom, a picnic on the hillside, a wedding, and conversations, long conversations when they'd all talk at once, in chorus, most often finding what was funny in things and people. They were thrifty, because they weren't rich. They knew how to enjoy themselves, since they weren't poor. They were like the cherry tree. They blossomed only when it was not too cold and not too hot. If they were poor, they were sullen, malicious, vulgar, and scolding. If they were rich, then they were cold, detached, always in fear of genuine humor and genuine happiness, never simply at ease.

Tiyana was charmed by her, too. Heavens, what a nice woman, she said delightedly, how jolly, how happy. Lucky Mahmut to have found her.

Tiyana was different. She'd experienced pain, loneliness, and insecurity too early. My mother was different, too, forever thinking about my unreliable father.

Had I met Tiyana by chance, or had I unconsciously sought my mother's likeness? Without thinking, I was driven by some internal sense toward what was not visible externally. I was returning to my beloved childhood, it would seem.

Mahmut's wife was a gift from God, but I didn't know whether I'd have been happy if Tiyana had been like her. Perhaps the very simplicity would have got me down. Perhaps Tiyana's sensitivity was both a sign and a sickness of a fuller thought and a more vital feeling. Pain and thought deprive us of carefree laughter.

But I didn't believe that Mahmut's wife knew nothing of pain and thought. It would seem that there are people, rare though they be, for whom neither pain nor thought can destroy their cheerfulness and simplicity. They even make them better. I don't know how they do it, but I wish I did.

Her straightforward question to Tiyana whether we needed anything took me by surprise. When Mahmut was angry because she wouldn't give him money for drink, he'd purposefully borrow whatever he could from acquaintances, to shame both himself and her, to spite her, to force her to untie the money bag that she kept hidden in her bosom, since he'd have spent it all. Tiyana had answered her that we had all we needed and had no need to borrow. Mahmut's wife believed her, or pretended to believe her; nevertheless, the two of them became inseparable.

One morning Tiyana said she was going to visit Mahmut's wife. She'd be a couple of hours and would be back by midday to make lunch.

This surprised me, and I was even a bit annoyed. So, I was not enough for her, and I'd wasted my time promising myself and her that I wouldn't leave her on her own. She'd leave me. She was gradually making a life of her own. Still, reason prevailed, and I realized that it was for the best. She'd get out, which would do her good, talk, cheer herself up, find something to do, and not think about fear and death. We'd have less reason to quarrel.

But what should I do? I'd wanted to be free, and now I didn't know what to do with my freedom. I felt no urge to go to the coffeehouse. People were always talking about the same things, while I kept quiet.

Should I wander the streets, like a fool? It would be stupid and pointless.

To go to the river and watch the water didn't even occur to me. Because it was snowing, because I felt no need, because I was not escaping from anything? I was no longer empty. What I was, I didn't know, but empty and desolate I was not.

Books occurred to me. They were not the whole man, but they were what was best in him, the man at his best moments. With that nonexistent yet living man one could converse, enjoy, without having to thank him. You could even argue with him, and he hadn't the ability to answer anything other than what he'd already written. You could air your own intelligence, telling him stupidities, and he'd patiently listen. You could leave him and go to another, and he'd not be angry. He'd welcome you, should you return, always ready to reopen the conversation.

I didn't go to the library to have that conversation.

I thought of Mula Ibrahim. I'd go and see him to find out what he knew about Ramiz and to tell him that I'd achieved nothing with Shehaga, to talk of any sort of ordinary things, but not of the eternal questions, not today. I needed people, and he, such as he was, was the closest. He'd helped me while he dared and wanted to help me even when he didn't, and it was not his fault that he wasn't the man I'd have liked him to be. That he wasn't different from what he was was more a matter of sorrow than anger.

Shehaga was in the shop and waved to me. Mula Ibrahim didn't even do that. He was listening thoughtfully and seriously to what Shehaga was saying. Shehaga stopped only for a second to look at me, somewhat dissatisfied that I'd intruded on their confidences, born of some agreement between them, of some climate, some need, and now they had to adapt it to a third party. But it seemed that a great army of words was drawn up behind his forehead, and he'd had to let them out, for they were impatient. So far, he'd said too little and had to continue for his own sake and not for that of Mula Ibrahim or me. He wanted only understanding and silence. With Mula Ibrahim, he'd find both. I'd just be silent.

Man desired power (he said, looking at Mula Ibrahim, who was listening patiently). Because he was alive, moving, encountering people. And he wanted to leave something behind him, to create something, not merely to have existed like a tree. And he had the illusion of having achieved something, of being strong and important. But God so arranged it that he'd suddenly gain insight and perceive not with these eyes, but with those others, more perceptive, that he was only a grain of sand in the immeasurable desert of this world, tiny and insignificant, like an ant in an anthill. Did ants desire power? Did they want to be stronger and more significant than others? Did they have their worries, their sufferings, their sleepless nights, their despair? We didn't know, and we didn't care much. They were too small for us. Might it not be possible, then, that somebody greater than we might exist, for whom our worries and troubles would seem of no importance? We didn't see him, since he was inconceivable to our thought. We felt him only when in something he revealed his will. The ant didn't see the whole of a man. Due to his size, the man didn't exist for the ant. It saw only his finger, or the twig, if one put it in its way. It would feel an earthquake if one destroyed its anthill. But man was tinier than an ant when compared with the universe.

And why should only man exist and only his method of thinking? The world had existed before us. It existed regardless of us, it would go on existing without us. Would everything disappear if man died out? No. Everything would be the same, what we knew and what we didn't know; only we would be no more. There were many mysteries that we couldn't even approach, never mind explain. And perhaps the greatest mystery of all was death, a mystery and a horror. And when we were not thinking of it, it was thinking of us. It waited for us on a corner, when we least expected it, and everything that was, was no more. We'd travelled this earthly path in vain. In vain we'd hoped, sorrowed over losses, rejoiced at success. All in vain. Death made nonsense of life and of all that was done in life. And beyond that, dread fate, an unknown darkness. We knew the end, yet knew nothing about it. One couldn't be reconciled with it, yet one could change nothing. It didn't take place according to our will, for few would wish to die, but according to an all-powerful will of which we knew nothing, save that it was inexorable and completely consistent. Perhaps it was some universal spirit, utterly different from us, but unknowable, since it was outside our experience. The fact that we couldn't know it did not mean it didn't exist. He imagined it not in human guise, but as a supernatural force and mind that coldly balanced both the visible and invisible worlds. It was useless to pray to it, to implore it, for its standards and reasoning were not human and what they were we couldn't even begin to understand. He himself said "it" and "its," since we didn't know it, nor was our language capable of expressing something our thought could not fathom. And if it were so, and it certainly was, it was impossible to imagine that that universal spirit was playing an unworthy game with people, leaving them to run through life, emerging from nothing and irreversibly departing into nothingness. That would be a senseless waste of so much energy. It was far more believable and more logical and less offensive that the body should be mortal while the soul was immortal. The soul was a particle of the general universal energy given to us, temporarily lent to us at birth, which would live its unknown life even after the body's death or else settle into a newborn entity to carry on its eternal circulation. Not a single drop of water was lost. It merely changed. How, then, could everything human be lost? It had to be that life existed according to some higher principle and not simply by the absurd, the evil, the mad!

I listened, not believing my ears. For this was a final breaking of what had appeared to be a strong man! He no longer believed his own eyes, his own reason, not even his own experience. He'd lost faith both in himself and in people. He lacked the strength to go on struggling with the pain that gnawed at him. Was this due to his son's death and to his own inability to save him from disaster? He found this death too cruel, too senseless, and, therefore, sought its reason in a will outside and above our own and his own consolation in the inevitability of what had occurred. He was too proud to admit defeat at the hands of people. Let it be at the hands of the gods, of a universal spirit, or of anything incomprehensible! And it was cruel, yet it was in the framework of a certain happening that possessed its own laws and its own purpose, which we could not discover. And if his son's body was dead, his soul was immortal and his tragic end was simply an insignificant moment in eternal duration. They would laugh at it, when their souls met!

Had we been alone and had he been speaking only to me, I don't know how I'd have answered him. Perhaps, horrified, I'd have knelt in front of him, begging him, at least, to hang on to his reason. Or, shedding tears, I'd have bowed my head before his torment. It was greater than I'd thought.

But he wasn't talking to me. I was only a chance listener. Would Mula Ibrahim say anything, or would he remain silent? For what could one say to a despair that sought its consolation beyond human logic?

While Shehaga was confiding his acute suffering, apparently speaking calmly, Mula Ibrahim listened with bowed head, as though he were asleep. Yet when he began to speak, I saw that he'd listened attentively. Judging by what I knew, it would appear that they'd lent one another their convictions, and Mula Ibrahim used words I could have expected from Shehaga and Shehaga words that, in my opinion, could have been those of Mula Ibrahim. The one, a powerful man, spoke of human helplessness; the other, helpless himself, spoke of man's duty to be a man! What did that mean? The one lessened his sorrow by seeking for it a higher meaning that he would not ultimately accept. The other rejected his own weakness, praising manly courage that he would never apply!

Their rejection of themselves was sad to hear.

Mula Ibrahim agreed with Shehaga that men desired power, but this was no bad thing. Without this, people would be worse off: submissive, downtrodden, reconciled to their fate, the slaves of everybody. Nor was every desire for power the same. One thing was the desire to rule people, to make them submit, to instill fear into them, to drive them to acts that they would never have committed without compulsion. That was a demand for silence, for nonresistant obedience according to the law of some force. Such a desire for power was immoral. It degraded both the oppressor and the oppressed. The man was to be pitied who'd felt this on his own skin. (Was he saying this about himself and about me? He was humiliated by another's oppression; I was harmed by his humiliation. He complaining, defending himself, accusing!) Totally different was the desire for power that consisted of helping people, that conquered through love, that encouraged understanding. That was a great power that all people would do well to learn and that rendered evil impossible. With such power, man was not a grain of sand, not without significance. Whether some supreme being existed or not, he couldn't say, perhaps it did, but he was certain that no one would bring order to our human affairs if we didn't do it ourselves. To await salvation and seek comfort in some supernatural power, which people had been doing in vain for thousands of years, meant, in fact, to admit one's own helplessness and to do nothing to improve matters. The world had existed before man and would exist after him. But what was that to us? Let whatever creatures who'd live then worry about it. We couldn't leave our worries to be solved by somebody else. We had to learn the power of love, if we were not to turn life into a torture chamber. As regards the soul, he, too, had had his thoughts on the subject, since it was difficult to avoid the fear and anxiety at a short life and at a disappearance into the unknown darkness of eternity. And in thinking of this, it had seemed to him that the existing order of human growth and development was unjust. Man was born like an innocent child that knew nothing of itself, of the world, of sin, of humiliation, of prestige. Everything was new to him and fresh, everything was wonderful, because his spiritual life had not yet developed. Afterward, living, he gained experience over a long time and with great effort and, the moment he matured, the thought of death appeared to him. He died weak, exhausted, desperate, oppressed by thoughts of the guilt he'd imposed on himself, dissatisfied with what he'd done in life, since most often it was not by his will, dissatisfied at what he'd not done, since this he'd only desired and not dared to accomplish, frantic at the absurdity behind him and the impenetrable mystery in front of him. Scared to death, without any support that might assure him that he'd lived according to the decisions of his own pure conscience, he thought in desperation of an eternal soul, of endless duration, of the possibility that somewhere and at some time he might discover a sense for being. So he ended his life ingloriously, utterly defeated.

How much better it would be were we to be born as old men and then gradually become middle-aged, forgetting, by degrees, our first fears of death, and then liberated young men, sufficiently flippant not to think of anything too seriously, and, last, carefree children, to die as newborn babes, unaware of anything, innocent embryos. What a wonderful and free death that would be! But since this was impossible, salvation lay in the victory of love and humanity. In that way, both life and death would be easier. He was not interested in what would happen to him after death, whether his soul would rot together with his body or retire to rest and rejoice in idleness, or whether, besmirched and soiled, be given to some newborn child, which would be a great injustice toward an innocent being. But what did interest him, and very much so, was that after his death he should leave to people or at least to one man, a good name and a favorable memory. In that way, he'd certainly lengthen his short life. Such a wish obliged a man during his life not to do evil and even sometimes to do good. The concept of an eternal soul involved no obligations, for this was the worry of some higher power, irrespective of what a man had done or how he'd lived, so that the soul of a hardened evildoer might settle into the body of an innocent newborn baby. The concept of humaneness was more just and more human. And the brevity of life was no problem to him, as long as it was pure. If it were not, then it would only be adding to the evil. And what if life were longer? What would one do with immortality? It would be the greatest disaster that could happen to a man. Akhasver was the most unfortunate of men, horrified at the thought of life without end, without final peace, without fear but also without joy, without love, since it was senseless in that endless duration. Indeed, the fear of death lent a beauty to all things, to everything that we experienced. One had to live everything, taking the joy of pure life and the beauty of love for people in this brief transition between two mysteries.

"But where are those people?" Shehaga asked vehemently. "The people we live with are worse than wolves. They'd tear you to pieces the moment you put a foot wrong."

Mula Ibrahim shook his head in disagreement.

"Not all people are like that. The bad ones have come to the fore, they're too easily seen and felt, which is why we think all people are like them. But they're not!"

Then he glanced at the street. His two assistants were strolling up and down in front of the shop, with heads and shoulders covered in snow.

He'd sent them out because of Shehaga's presence. He wouldn't have done it for me! Everything he did was the opposite of what he said. Why did he bother to say it? Both he and Shehaga? Do people acknowledge and value what they lack? Do they deceive others or just themselves? Or is their thought divided into what they desired and what they were compelled to do?

Speaking as he did, Mula Ibrahim certainly wanted to live like that, but then everything got in the way of his wanting. All that remained in his soul was an empty memory of himself as once he was, with good intentions, preserved in words that would never be transformed into actions. But what remained behind was good, albeit a ruin. I don't know whose thoughts he was repeating, but they seemed to me more valid than anything I'd ever heard, though I was troubled by an uncomfortable doubt whether cowardice and humanity could exist together in the same man.

Excusing himself, Mula Ibrahim went out onto the street to talk to his assistants, to keep them away from the shop for a little longer.

Thoughtfully, Shehaga followed him with his eyes.

"He's not right. He's intelligent, but he's not right."

"What he said seemed all right to me."

"Because you lack experience. If you knew life as I know it, if you knew people better, you'd not talk so. Why doesn't he live by his own ideals?"

"God knows what's prevented him."

"You find excuses for everybody."

"How did you get into such a strange conversation?"

"I came to help you, to get him to take you on again. But I forgot. I don't know how I started this conversation. It just happened. Or perhaps it didn't. Sometimes a man feels the need to speak about the things he doesn't know."

He'd come for my sake, but their conversation was hardly about me! I was touched that he'd thought about me, but I'd have liked it better if he hadn't forgotten.

"Isn't it better to worry about the things we know?"

He shook his upright and refined head: He'd had enough of what he knew, he'd had it up to here. But his cold gray eyes were not as determined as his gesture. In his thoughts, they were fixed upon his irreparable suffering. He couldn't easily put aside his experience and earthly existence. Why then did he speak like that? Did he want to justify his weakness, unforgivable before others, by a superhuman will? But if he couldn't be reconciled with human cruelty, how could he accept some other cruelty, which was unknown? Surely not just because it was unknown and inconceivable? He was like a desperate victim, a terminal case who'd lost faith in doctors and sought help in soothsaying. The trouble was, he had too much common sense to believe in a miracle. And he couldn't accept Mula Ibrahim's remedy to be at peace with people, to accept love, rather than hate, as a law. He felt it easier to blame God than men, yet hatred of both God and men remained in his embittered heart, and his grief for his son would remain with him, together with his angry bewilderment at an incomprehensible fate.

I didn't know whether he expected me to say anything, but I was too taken aback. I was forever discovering my complete failure to understand people. What they said was not what they did, but was it what they thought? Perhaps they didn't know themselves. And what could I tell him that he didn't know, with which he'd not wrestled through many a sleepless night? I was silent, too, because of his hands, clenched in a spasmodic knot of fingers. He wasn't thinking, he was suffering.

I was sorry for him and amazed at the persistence of his sorrow. Had not time healed it at all? Or had he done his son some injury during life, and his son's death had removed forever the possibility of putting it right? If that was so, then he'd learned what hell was, here, on earth.

And while I stood silent, wondering whether it was the final misfortune or an unrealized nobility that made people forever question how to live, a man who lived without giving such things a thought entered the shop—Osman Vuk. He came in together with Mula Ibrahim, laughing and dusting the snow from his shoulders with his cap.

"It's not half coming down!" he said cheerfully, as though nobody could see it for themselves and as if it were the most beautiful and important thing in the world. And as though happy to be able to bring someone the good news that he brought, he smiled at Shehaga. "It took me a while to reckon you might be here. I've got something to tell you."

"Go on!"

"I'd rather tell you on our own."

Shehaga looked from him to us, intending to be magnanimous and show that there were no secrets between us, but this noble thought was short-lived. Once more he belonged entirely to this world.

"Excuse us!" he said with a smile and went out of the shop with Osman.

I got up. Their secrets didn't interest me, and we'd not be resuming our conversation. It was time I went home. I'd be there to greet Tiyana, if she'd not already returned.

But Shehaga opened the door and called me outside.

"Listen to this! Tell him, Osman."

Osman showed no surprise. They'd obviously talked it over, and he told me how, a short while ago, he'd had a visit from Zayko the innkeeper. He told him that Avdiya, the son of Omer Skakavats, had come into his inn, somewhat drunk, and got even drunker, and had begun to boast that he knew who'd rescued Ramiz from the Fortress. Luckily, the only other person in the inn was Muyo Dushitsa, the porter. He'd been sopping *rakiya* all morning, and didn't know what he was saying, never mind what others said. Zayko served Avdiya more drink, and he was now fast asleep in the inn. He'd managed to turn Muyo Dushitsa out. He thought it was his wife kicking him out of the house, so he made no protest. Zayko told his servant to keep watch on Avdiya and not to let anybody else in, while he hurried off to tell Osman.

"So there you are," Shehaga said calmly. "If the young man really knows something, there could be trouble. Someone should tell his father, but we don't know whom to send.

For Osman to go would look suspicious. Zayko can't, because of the inn and, in any case, it's nothing to do with him, and it would not be wise to involve other people."

Their playing hide-and-seek with me offended me. They'd already made up their minds that I was the one to go, but they wanted it to look as if it were my decision. And they hadn't told me the whole story. They were hiding something. Why had Zayko gone to Osman? All the same, I'd do what they expected of me, or they'd think I was afraid. I'd show them I wasn't.

But I was afraid. My heart fluttered as I made my decision. And perhaps this was why I said, "I'll go."

"Do you know where they live?"

"I do. At Byelave."

"Then you'd better go at once."

"Why did Zayko go to Osman, in particular?" I asked suddenly, not knowing that I'd do this even the second before I spoke.

Shehaga laughed. "I thought you wouldn't notice that gap in the story. Avdiya said that only he and Osman Vuk knew who'd carried out the rescue."

This time I laughed, too. "It's some gap! And what am I to say?"

"Tell them to go and collect Avdiya. And tell them to talk some sense into him. Don't worry. If it were dangerous, I wouldn't send you."

"Do I look afraid?"

I played the hero, which I certainly wasn't, but my fear had passed. They'd helped Ramiz, now I'd help them. It wasn't much, but it wasn't little, either.

"Don't be in a hurry. Pretend you're just having a walk," Osman advised me.

Would I meet the *serdar*-Avdaga on the street? Happily, I didn't. I felt as if the secret I carried in my brain stared out of my eyes, that its shadow was on my face, that I expressed it in the way I held myself, in my gait.

They'd held me at a distance, concealing everything from me. Now they'd revealed a part of their secret, because they needed me.

And the snow was falling determinedly, like everything that has just begun. It stuck to my shoulders, clothing me in white rags, cooling both my nose and my excitement.

Had Shehaga and Osman done it all through others?

Somebody had clearly gone to old Skakavats with a proposal that he and his sons should carry out the rescue, agreed on a price, and paid him. Now my task was to prevent any possible complications.

But who'd fixed the commandant?

With the Skakavatses, it was easy. For them it was just a job like any other, perhaps even simpler than stealing horses in Posavina and Machva, which, it would seem, was their main occupation. They could either have agreed or not, and that would have been the end of it. They'd no liking for interviews with the authorities, be they long or short.

But who'd had the courage to suggest to the commandant that he betray his duty? Had the commandant refused, that unknown person would have been in trouble. He'd have surely found himself in the dungeons along with Ramiz. No matter who he was, he'd have had to have known the commandant well not to frighten him with such a dangerous proposal. Was it Osman who'd have been prepared to kill if things had gone wrong? Or was it Shehaga himself, whose denial would carry more weight than the commandant's accusations? Or was it a third person, someone I couldn't even imagine nor had seen the like of among the people I knew. He'd have to have qualities that were hard to find in one person: honor, so one might have faith in him as one would in oneself; wisdom, to enable him to approach the commandant without frightening him into refusing; bravery, so as not to fear the consequences of a possible failure. Who could that man have been?

If they'd happened to offer the job to me, I'd have refused

even to think of talking to the commandant. I wouldn't have got involved in it for anything. To me it would have been like signing my own death warrant.

Going to the Skakavatses I dared, for it was really not dangerous. I'd drop in, like one who'd happened to be just passing, lured outside by the first snow. I'd deliver a message from somebody else, as though ignorant of what I was saying. I couldn't be suspected in any way, even if it came to be known. That was it, every job found the right man to do it. My suitability was for small matters, like the one in which I was engaged. And that was fine as far as I was concerned.

I saw the old Omer Skakavats at once, from the street. He was forking hay from a stack. He was tall, thin, and muscular, his shirt open, showing his bare chest, in a sheepskin coat that kept getting in his way and that he constantly pushed back onto his shoulders with regular movements.

Two lads, who must have been his sons, were carrying the hay into a stall from which came the neighing of horses and the nervous stamping of horses' hooves.

When I approached him, the old man regarded me coldly, with sharp dark eyes, dangerous and distrusting, threatening like the point of a knife. I'd not have liked to be in front of them when they flashed, when the fire burst from those embers beneath the white eaves of his thick eyebrows. And everything about him was alert, the eyes, the hands that gripped the hay fork, the muscular legs set astride, the outthrust, bony chin, the pursed lips.

He didn't ask why I'd come, what I wanted, who I was looking for; that he left until I'd said my piece. Be it trivial, important, dangerous, he'd meet it all alike, and do what was most favorable to him.

His silence was menacing. Until I said what I wanted, I was the enemy. So, without being asked, I blurted Zayko's and Osman's message in a single breath.

The old Skakavats heard me out with the same threatening calm, only a deep furrow appeared between his white eyebrows, and he angrily called his sons.

They came running out of the stall, gripping their hay prongs and looking at me threateningly.

"Take a horse and go and get that fool out of Zayko's inn. He's drunk and shooting his mouth off."

His sons, clearly disappointed that I was not the culprit, turned round at once and went into the stall for a horse, and the old man continued dragging the hay from under the snow. He didn't even give me a look, nor as much as a thank you. The conversation was at an end. I'd done what I had to do, and he'd done what he had to do, and the job was completed. I could go.

And I went, mumbling a good-bye which he neither heard nor expected and walking backward so as not immediately to turn my back on him, scared by the old man's silence and the hostile look he gave me before I turned away, as nervous as if I'd just been in a robbers' den.

Once I got out onto the street, I sighed with relief.

God save me from meeting these Skakavatses on a narrow path in a deep wood. They wouldn't have had to draw their knives, I'd have died of fear, stabbed by their murderous eyes.

What horrible people Osman had to deal with in order to save one good man!

Could there be no good without violence?

Damn you, you'd give me nightmares! Thank God I hadn't any serious business that forced me to have dealings with these or any other Skakavatses.

Long live my poor dear Mahmut, whom not even a cat could be afraid of.

■ □ ■ □ ■

CHAPTER 15

FATHER AND SON

AND WHAT OCCURRED THREE DAYS AFTER THAT VISIT convinced me that each should keep to his own path and not wander onto another's. Admittedly, I didn't know what my path was, but I knew what it wasn't.

Avdiya Skakavats, Omer's youngest son, died suddenly and was to be buried that day. He wasn't ill. He was as healthy as a horse. He was taken suddenly, poisoned by drink to which he was not accustomed.

His father and brothers laid him out, washed him themselves, wrapped him in linen, and summoned three *hodjas* to read prayers for his soul. All day and all night, old Omer stood over his dead son, who, covered in a white sheet, lay stretched in the middle of the room.

Osman invited me to go with him to the funeral, which started off from the Begova mosque. He told me all about Avdiya.

"But they killed him," I said, horrified, remembering Omer Skakavats's murderous look.

"I don't think so. He probably really did die of too much drink."

But the way he dismissed my suspicion was unconvincing. He said it just for something to say, without much insistence.

No, they'd killed him, for sure. Osman knew that, too. He'd made me think it himself, by the way he spoke.

They'd beaten him to drive some sense into his head, but, instead, they'd driven his soul out of his body, without intending to. Their savagery, bad enough without the Avdiya affair, became worse when faced with his stupid actions. For the young man had made a great mistake, breaking their law of silence that protected them, like a wall, and which was their fortress. They didn't like to boast of their deeds nor did they seek recognition for them. They drew no attention to themselves. Avdiya had opened his mouth and put the family at risk. They wanted to make him realize, make him remember, make him learn, once and for all, that the family's security was sacred. And when they'd concluded that they'd beaten enough sense into him, for words were of no help, when they'd agreed that for the time being he'd had enough of their harsh teaching, and it was hard to know what for them was enough, when they'd left him to sleep, Avdiya had fallen asleep forever, cured of stupidity and well taught never again to open his mouth, persuaded not ever to bring the family into danger.

They'd killed him, and I was the one who'd taken them the news of his guilt. So I was to blame for his death!

The thought took me by surprise, stabbed me like a knife. It got to me so that I at once began energetically to defend myself.

I was not guilty!

How could I have known that such people existed! How could one kill a son and a brother just for the sake of one's own security? I could have imagined they might have cursed him, threatened him, even struck him, but this I could never have imagined, not in delirium. And then I was of no importance in all this. If I hadn't gone, another would, and it would have been the same.

I was not guilty!

I was not guilty, I repeated desperately, no way was I guilty. But I couldn't stop thinking of the lad whom, drunk, his father and brothers had beaten and trampled on, mad with rage at his unforgivable crime. Or had they waited for him to wake up the next morning and only then abused him? Perhaps he'd said something that had angered them and made them begin the execution of their family justice?

What had taken place in some locked room, in some dark cellar, in their hearts, in their minds? He probably kept silent, for, after all, he was a Skakavats, too, and this was what finished him. He wouldn't admit his guilt, and this may have looked like defiance. Perhaps he did defy them, by dying. Had he been conscious of every blow that racked his innards and ruptured his veins? Did he see the bloodshot eyes that burned him like fire? Perhaps this was why he refused to submit and ask for mercy.

Morbidly, I imagined the battered man, choked with internal bleeding, saw how, with his last remaining strength, he lifted a broken arm to defend his head, still perhaps in hope. Or without hope. Or without thought. Or thinking that what they were doing to him was just, and that was why he kept silent. It was their family business, and therefore he dared not utter a sound, lest anybody hear. It was their business and nobody else's. He, his father, and his brothers were in the power of a law stronger and superior to them.

Or was it perhaps his rebellion against the cruelty of such a law? It's all the same both in small and large communities.

I was sickened by these imaginings, by the multitude of feverish images, movements, horrors, blood that stuck to maddened fists, bones that were quietly crushed, heavy breathing from the effort and exertion, right up to that final silence whose name is death. And what sickened me more was that through this imagination I increased my sense of guilt. It was no use my awakened conscience yelling at me that all this would have happened without me. It had happened with me, and there was nothing I could do.

What sort of a life, what sort of a world was this in which I did evil when I intended only the best!

And I did evil even when I did nothing, leaving both

good and evil in peace. I did evil even in speaking, because I never said what I should have said. I did evil even when I was silent, for it meant that I was living as though I didn't exist. I did evil because I was alive and didn't know how to live.

I was present in life by chance, and nothing I did was mine.

I'd killed a man because I'd moved, because I'd spoken. I didn't know him. I'd never seen him. Yet I knew I was guilty for the fact that I never would see him. And I didn't think about him, why he'd broken the law of the family fortress, whether he was bored with being silent, whether he wanted to say something good, something meaningful about himself. He was too young. He needed more than action. He needed to speak of action, perhaps to speak of anything, if only to express himself. I thought rather about myself, why I'd agreed to interfere in another's life, without thinking, wishing to show courage I didn't possess so as, partly, to be on a level with people with whom I could never be equal. And I asked myself what I'd said that had so angered old Omer. Had I let some harsh words escape me, had I appeared angry at the young man's behavior, had there been anything offensive in my movements? No, none of this was true. I'd been confused, somewhat scared, somewhat offended at the old man's looking at me as an enemy, at the fact that he scarcely listened to me. I'd thought only of myself, not of what I was saying, nor of the lad about whom I was saying it. And this had been his death sentence. The mere fact I'd spoken, no matter how. The fact that I was there, no matter why. Because I'd taken another's path.

Osman was talking, I didn't know what about, laughing as ever, as we approached the mosque. I was looking at the tracks in the snow, thinking of my guilt. The snow was no longer pure and white. It had become an ugly slush. I noticed this unconsciously, in passing. From a cookshop came the heavy suffocating smell of melted butter. Osman's laughter was as though he were jeering at my torment.

"Will you stop laughing!"

Osman was genuinely surprised. "What's the matter? What's wrong with my laughing?"

I didn't answer, angry with myself. Was I at the point where even laughter irritated me?

For a wonder, he wasn't angry. He asked me good-humoredly, "Are you in a bad mood? You look like a wet week."

"Leave me alone. If you cleaned my boots, I'd kick you in the face!"

"So I see, only I don't know why. Have you had a quarrel with the wife?"

"Of course not!"

"Have you got bellyache? Have you eaten something that didn't agree with you?"

"It's not that, either. I was thinking of the poor lad whose funeral we're going to."

"What do you want to think about him for, for God's sake?"

"If I'd not gone to old Omer Skakavats, the lad might still be alive."

"Oh, that's it, is it? Honestly, don't take offense, but you really are mad. If you hadn't gone, someone else would."

"Then I wouldn't be guilty."

"Just fancy. Shehaga said you weren't up to the job. Why shouldn't he be, I said. We could send a child, never mind him. But, there you are, Shehaga was right. You really are bloody useless!"

"I wish you'd sent a child. I'd have known nothing about it, and my conscience would have let me alone."

Osman gave me a pitying look, as though I were mentally retarded, or a spoiled brat who knew nothing of life. He stopped laughing, grabbed me by the arm, turned me toward him, and said roughly, "And now let me tell you something! You wouldn't have known, you say? Are you sure? If you hadn't gone to old Omer, another would, and it would have all been the same, only you'd have been clean, you'd have known all about it, only you wouldn't have been worried by your imagined guilt. But if we hadn't found anybody, or if we'd found the wrong man, who'd have been scared and gone to the *serdar*-Avdaga instead of to Omer Skakavats, what would have happened then? Come on, give that egghead of yours a shake! This is what would have happened: That idiot Avdiya would have been arrested and certainly dead, just as he is now. They'd also have arrested Osman Vuk, who's laughing now, and he'd have had no time for laughter. They might even have arrested Shehaga Socho, because he'd listened to you and saved your friend. And the Skakavatses, all three of them. And they might, God forbid, have arrested even you, because when a man's tortured, he doesn't know what he's saying or whom he's naming. And how many dead men might there have been? A fair few, I'd say, 'cause once disaster starts to roll, it's not easy to stop. And it can start from nothing, like choosing the wrong man for a simple job, for instance. This way, there's only one dead, and it's no one's fault, no one's! It was just as if he'd drowned, got out of his depth and been swept away. Is that clearer now?"

I said nothing. The stark truth can be very convincing.

"There, that's how I see it," he said, and again gave a laugh. "And you hang your bollockless prattle on your prick. Shall we go in? And don't look either sad or happy at the funeral, but just ordinary and serious. And don't think of the lad. That was his fate, and if you want to know the truth, better that way than another. Worse for him, but better for us."

"How can I not think of him?"

"Easily. Think of your lovely wife. She sure is lovely!"

"Cut it out!"

"Why? We're just talking. But I'll tell you frankly, if we weren't friends, I'd take her off you."

I winced, as though he'd stabbed me.

"And I'll tell you, once and for all: I don't like this type of conversation."

"Nor I." Osman gave a muffled laugh, since people were beginning to come into the courtyard in front of the mosque. "I just wanted to make you think of something else and forget about the lad. Better to think of your living wife than of dead Avdiya."

There was nothing you could do with him. He'd hit you and caress you, anger and calm you, all in the same moment. He was the smiling Satan, heartless, but with a brilliant mind, cold and accurate as a clock.

In front of the courtyard stood *bayraktar* Muharem, begging without stretching a hand or saying a word. I felt my pocket, knowing it was empty, and asked Osman to lend me a few coins. He pulled out a whole fistful of coins, without counting them.

"Give them to the *bayraktar*."

He held them out to him, and Muharem took them, without a word of thanks.

"Cunning old devil!" Osman said cheerfully, as we went in.

Could anything touch him? Was he unmoved even at such injustice?

"Who are you talking about?"

"About the *bayraktar* Muharem."

"Aren't you ever sorry for a man when he's down and out? It's not his fault."

"But I am sorry the old hero's been left on the street."

"And is that funny?"

"And forced to end his life begging. Not to die of hunger."

"And isn't that the truth?"

"Of course it's not, man. What do you mean? It's not. Shehaga gives him more than enough every month."

I was surprised.

"I'd heard that he begged out of protest because he hadn't got what he wanted, but this I didn't know."

"That's it, out of protest. And if he'd got what he wanted

he'd be like all the rest, perhaps worse. Now shut up, it's starting."

We stood at the back of the queue that had formed behind the *hodja* and the dead man on the stone bench in front of the mosque. While the *hodja* recited his prayers, I thought about Osman.

Was the world as he saw it simpler or more complex than the world I saw? It would seem more complex, for he knew that there were two sides to everything: the appearance and the essence, the bark and the core. For me, the *bayraktar*'s begging was his misfortune and our shame. For Osman, it was an old man's foible and a petty vengeance. I saw everything as fate and lack of communication between people, for which there was no cure. He put everything into a human framework, into human categories, favoring neither misfortune nor violence. Misfortune was the unavoidable, violence what was possible. For him yes and no were so mixed that one could scarcely tell the one from the other. Evil and good were inseparable and often went hand in hand. Crime and punishment were weakness and power. Life was the intriguing arena in which some fell and others won, not because the ones were more stupid or the others more intelligent, but because some were clumsy and others more cunning. There was no need to feel sorry for the clumsy; they'd be as cruel as the others, were fate or chance to give them the power. You should let nothing disturb you, and, best of all, laugh at everything, while making sure you were not the victim. If you didn't wish to be on top, then make sure you were not on the bottom, and live as you please. He didn't hate people, he simply didn't take them seriously. Rather, he despised them, for they spent their lives in quarrelling and worry, like madmen.

This superficial philosophy, which both repelled and attracted me, strangely brought together both independence and a considerable knowledge of people. With me, on the other hand, there was a union of sensitivity for every action and a great ignorance of people. And I thought more simply than Osman did, despite his superficiality. For me yes and no were summer and winter. Good and evil were two different sides of the world. There were more punishments than there were offenses, and they lacked any causal relationship. Life was a pitiful battlefield on which there were few executioners and many victims. The ruthless prospered, the weak went to the wall, and all was so pathetic that it was easier just to weep and not to think.

My view was that of a coward and a weakling, unacceptable to a man of action. His view was cruel and egoistic and unacceptable to a man who thought. What view then was acceptable? Ramiz's? His attitude for me was the closest and at the same time the furthest removed, for it was the most unselfish but at the same time the most dangerous. But I'd not think of him now.

In that silent and muddled self-examination, I'd forgotten the old prayers that I knew, which everyone knew, yet were helpful for every new mortal, for every ending is the same, as is the mercy we ask of God. This ever similar human fate and the ever same beseeching forgiveness for sins are what make funerals so exhausting. And when the *hodja* turned toward us and began to ask what sort of a man the dead man had been, had he been good and honest in life, and had he deserved the heavenly kingdom, I woke up to reality. I looked at old Omer Skakavats. I saw him out of the corner of my eyes. His wrinkled face was set and tense, his white brows overhanging deep-set eyes like the wings of a white bird. What was he thinking, as we were replying that the dead man had been good and honorable? Did his heart ache, or did he still hold grief at a distance? He had raised his head, wrestling with himself, or defying his pain, and then bowed his head more and more, till his chin touched his chest. A tear dropped from his lower eyelashes and, slowly rolling down his rough face, vanished in the heavy wrinkles. I nudged Osman and nodded toward Omer. Osman merely gave a sign that he too had seen it. And then, with a forceful movement, the hardened old man raised his head and stood there staring into a window of the mosque, above the earth, above the stone bench, above the dead man. Alone with himself, ashamed of his tears either before himself or before others. Would he be overcome by grief and repentance when night fell, the night that separates and isolates us and the darkness that brings us face to face with ourselves? Or would he justify himself by the young man's offense and the sanctity of the endangered family? Now he stood before us as the victim of a merciless fate, and people were sorry for him, sorry for a murderer, while the real victim lay on the stone bench, covered in an olive-green cloth, motionless and silent, an eloquent reproach only to his father and brothers. Yet still, knowing everything, both regarding father and son, I was sorry for them. They were both victims.

When I went up to Omer to express sympathy, like the rest, his stony face contorted, and his hand in mine was still and cold as ice. He recognized me and recalled that day when his son was still alive. Both for him and for his son, I'd been the harbinger of evil. I withdrew my hand and held it, limp and hot, shaken by the old man's senseless hatred.

"He'll go on hating you and me and his sons and the whole world, anything to escape thinking of his own guilt," Osman whispered to me, as though guessing my thoughts.

I'd paid no thought to my guilt. I feared its tormenting me as I looked at the lad's covered corpse. I'd thrust it aside while studying the secrets of his father's frozen face. But as my thoughts about him scattered, growing pale and tired, like the image that remains in the eye after the eyelids are closed, I began to feel a strange discomfort. Why, I didn't know. For a moment I'd forget it, only for it to return, like a vague shadow and an intimation of something unpleasant. It was not the old man nor his son. What was it then, and why? I knew this came from old buried fears, some ancient forebodings, past premonitions, especially those from the war, as I had crawled through a forest barely suppressing the fear of a heart that sensed the proximity of an enemy soldier. I sought these fears, tracked them in myself, and extracted them, apparently dead, only to come across them again in some cranny of thought, in the center of some reasonless terror. But now I was unable to discover this old, unrecognized sense of unease, although I recalled all that I knew, summoning it gently, as a fakir draws snakes from their hiding place with his pipes. My call was unanswered. The snake-dread remained, even though I couldn't define it.

And then I turned, suddenly, for no reason, and my eyes met those of the *serdar*-Avdaga.

There was the source of my unease!

Perhaps I'd seen those eyes somewhat earlier, without being aware of them, forgetting them while my thoughts were engaged in something more important. Or perhaps I hadn't, but rather, fixing his glance on the back of my neck, he'd warned me of his presence before I caught sight of him. I'd sensed him, as I did the enemy soldier.

We stood there, like a bullet and a target.

As I was going up to Omer Skakavats, I'd seen Osman talking to Avdaga.

When I rejoined him I asked, "What were you talking to Avdaga about?"

"I was asking him whether he knew Avdiya."

He was mad! Or was he flying like a moth round a candle?

Reproachfully I warned him, "I once knew a soldier who got dreadfully scared the moment battle began. He'd charge into the thick of it rather than suffer the waiting. He was soon killed."

"Yes, but I'm not that scared soldier of yours. Avdaga wanted to ask me the same question, but I got in first. He asked me only later. 'You and I know everybody,' I said. 'You because of your business, and I because of mine. Only my acquaintances don't hide from me.'"

"He was looking at me all the time."

"He was looking at everybody, that's his job. What do you care!"

I asked him to go with me to Mahmut Neretlyak, who had his shop quite close by, in the Kuyundzhiluk, to give him a few words of encouragement, since he still hadn't forgotten or got over the fact that at Bairam the servants hadn't let him into the house.

"That Mahmut of yours is a fool. What's he hanging on to me for?"

"His one ambition is to have a friend who's an important man."

"And am I that important man?"

"He's been talking for days only about you."

Osman began to laugh, as though it were a great joke. "Huh, he's a bigger fool than I thought."

However, he did agree to meet Mahmut, although not understanding my reasons and thinking I was a bit mad or hiding something. He didn't know what pity was. He considered it insulting, both for the one who gave it and for the one who received it. He pointed out that he hadn't much time and didn't know why he was wasting it on stupidities. But, anyway, he'd say a couple of silly words and then back to work. He'd lost enough time as it was.

Mahmut was in his shop. We saw a young man coming out and then going in again, as if someone had called him or he'd forgotten something.

As we approached, we heard a thin and tall lad talking, holding on to the knob of the open door, as though adding some final remark before he left. But when we heard what he was saying, we stopped, looked at the half-open door, and then at one another, not knowing what to do. I didn't know, and I didn't think Osman did either. I guessed at once that it was Mahmut's son, the goldsmith from Mostar, come to have a talk with his father. But God, what a talk! For it was no talk, but a furious snarling in which Mahmut, from time to time, timidly inserted the odd word.

"That's his son," I whispered to Osman in embarrassment. "Let's go."

"Hang on, I want to hear!"

He stood to one side of the door and listened attentively, with an ugly grin, murmuring something I couldn't hear.

"You say it's shameful my talking like this? What's shameful is what you've done all your life! Since I can remember, I've been ashamed because of you. I used to cry for days on end, because my father was a thief. You ruined my childhood. I say father. Alas, you are. That's why I left the house, because of having such a father. I was an exile, like you, only I was innocent. And now, when I want to start a new life, I've the right to demand my share."

"Here's the shop, here's the house. Bring your wife here and we'll live together."

"I'd sooner jump into the River Neretva than come back here."

"Wait a bit and I'll find the money."

"I won't wait, and you won't find the money. Sell the shop, sell the house. What do you want such a large house for? Get a smaller one."

"Not in my old age, son! Can't you wait till we die? It won't be long."

"I can't wait. I need the money."

"Have you talked to your mother?"

"I'll talk to the *kadi*. I'll go to the court for my share. And I'll take mother with me to Mostar."

"She's happy here with me."

"No one can be happy with you."

Osman gave a brittle laugh, showing his teeth, and began to kick his feet on the threshold to shake the snow off his shoes, so they'd hear him.

I grabbed his arm to stop him, but he pulled away.

In the shop there was a silence.

"Don't let on that we heard what they were saying."

He went in. Was he going to spoil everything? Mahmut

was a bit of a fool, but he had his pride. He'd even hidden the fact that he had a son! He kept quiet about him, so no one would know they didn't get on.

"Have we come at a bad time?" Osman asked, looking at the young man.

"No way!"

Naturally we hadn't come at a bad time. Help couldn't have reached him at a better time.

But still he looked from side to side.

"Who's this, Mahmut?"

"My son."

"Fine lad."

Mahmut looked at us in confusion, not knowing whether we'd heard what he and his son were saying.

I hastened to reassure him and change the subject, since Osman was furiously beating his right fist into his left hand, and it was quite possible that soon his own hand would not be enough.

"We just dropped in to see you."

"Thanks," Mahmut stuttered.

"And to apologize for Bairam," Osman added, in an unnaturally friendly tone. "I'm sorry we didn't see each other. As I told Ahmet, I was up to my neck."

"I know. Ahmet told me."

The young man turned to his father. "I'll be off. I'll be off, but we'll meet again, or you'll hear from me soon!"

It sounded like a threat!

And he went out, without giving us a glance. Either we'd not made much of an impression, or perhaps he'd given us up, as soon as he heard we were Mahmut's friends. I was sorry for Mahmut, but I couldn't blame the lad, either. His life couldn't have been easy.

Mahmut hastened to excuse his bad behavior. "He's getting married and doesn't know whether he's on his head or his heels. We were just talking a while ago about my selling the shop, so he can buy something in Mostar."

Oh, the troubles of parents!

"Sell it," Osman said decisively.

"I don't know. Selling is not so easy. When you sell, everything's cheap, when you buy, everything's dear. And anyway, I'd be sorry. I come here and sit and feel as if I'm doing something."

Something suddenly occurred to Osman. "And why do you sit in this empty shop pretending you're doing something? Why don't you really do something?"

"Old age, dear Osman. What could I do?"

"Do you know Shehaga's warehouse where we store the grain? Could you note how many sacks you receive?"

"Of course I could!"

"Then, get yourself a brazier and come for the keys! Dedo's leaving. He's opening his own shop."

Mahmut swallowed hard, his Adam's apple taking some time to slide down his skinny neck. He looked at me, as if asking whether it was all a joke. He went up to Osman and stood there in utter confusion.

Was he going to roll his eyes? Wave his arms? Faint?

But no! Mahmut held on bravely. He was excited, but he held on!

And I was excited. What had happened to Osman?

"If you're serious," Mahmut said in a trembling voice, trying to appear as if nothing had happened. "If you're really serious . . . then of course, I agree. How could I not? If you're serious . . . and I don't know how to thank you!"

"Why should I not be serious? And what have you got to thank me for? I'm not making you a mufti. And as for the shop, sell it!"

"I will. I'll go and tell the wife. I will. At once! And what about the house? Shall I sell it too?"

He'd lost his head!

"Why sell the house?"

"It's big. What do we need such a big one for? I'd like to buy a smaller one."

"And what about when your son brings his wife? You won't have enough room."

"You're right! Indeed, we wouldn't."

Later we walked through the town in silence. Osman was shaking his head, as if in amazement and anger. I told him what I was thinking. "You surprised me. I wouldn't have expected it of you."

"That idiot made me angry."

"I was scared you were going to hit him."

"I nearly did. It was one of two things, either hit him or do something stupid, one or the other."

"You did nothing stupid."

"Like hell, I didn't! You'll see what a mess there'll be in the warehouse. Mahmut's no good for anything."

"Don't let him handle money," I said reluctantly, but it was only fair to tell him, only fair to Mahmut.

"Is that how you talk about a friend?"

"It's better not to put temptation in his way. Opportunity makes thieves."

Osman laughed. Laughter was his remedy, it would seem.

"And thieves create opportunity. Of course, he'll be tempted. And he'll give in. He won't have any money, because I deal with the accounts, but he'll pinch a couple of kilos from every sack, and that'll be enough for him. That's what Dedo did, and, you see, he's opening his own shop. And anyone would do the same, even a saint. What of it! Every good merchant provides for wastage, taking human weakness into account. It would be a good idea if we provided for wastage in everything in life. One knows that's the way things are and doesn't worry about it."

And so, for the first time, I saw that even Osman had his weaknesses. And for the first time, he was mistaken about Mahmut.

Mahmut turned the warehouse into his own kingdom.

Aired, cleaned, and whitewashed, it had become pleasanter

and lighter, and the little room in which he sat had been turned into a comfortable den. In the middle there was a brazier full of red-hot coals. Along the walls were comfortable settees. The floor was washed, the walls white, and Mahmut was happy.

"It's nice here," I said, knowing that would please him.

"It didn't used to be nice."

"I can believe it."

"When I came here first, it made me sick. It was filthy, dark, repulsive, you couldn't bear to go in, let alone stay there. 'Where could I receive friends?' I thought. But I persuaded Osman-*aga*, and we had the workmen whitewash it, and I and the wife cleaned and scrubbed it, and we brought these things from home, and now it's as you see it. No doubt you're surprised at all these settees, Osman-aga was surprised, too."

"And who's Osman-*aga*?"

"Osman-*aga* Vuk. These settees are for the neighbors, merchants, and craftsmen. They were here this morning. Yesterday I visited them and invited them to a housewarming."

"Is that the first thing you did?"

"The first thing I did was to clean, and only then I invited them. That's the way with businessmen."

"Are you going to advise them?"

"Oh, no! That's not the thing in business. Except if you're asked. And I've enough to do as it is."

"I can't even smell any *rakiya*."

"I don't drink here, it's not done. I have a drink at home, but only a little one and then to bed. One has to come to work early and leave late."

"Here, hold on! Have I come to the wrong place? Am I talking to somebody who's Mahmut's double? Is there nothing left of the old Mahmut?"

"I've come to my senses, that's the only change. For the better, I hope. And it's time you settled down, too."

What had happened to Mahmut? While he was unemployed, he was a chattering magpie; now he was a wise owl. Once he used to break all the rules, like an immature boy; now he knew the ways of the town, like any other minor merchant. What had Osman made of him? Had he pulled off the butterfly's wings and left a worm that crawled on the earth? Mahmut used to be interesting, now he was a bore. The tree that had been full of sap was now a dry twig. Once he was the one and only; now he was just one of the many. Was that what they meant by "coming to one's senses"?

"Do you still dream of becoming rich?"

"I don't dream," he answered seriously. "Why lie to myself? This way is more secure, and it's better and easier. The work's not hard, and I haven't yet discussed pay with Osman-*aga* . . ."

"Who's this Osman-*aga?*"

"Osman-*aga* Vuk, man! As I say, we haven't talked about wages, but if I get what Dedo was getting, I shan't fear poverty in my old age. And they'll not be less, for sure, and I believe they might be even higher. Osman-*aga* knows what it was like before me and what it's like now. Have you seen the cats in the warehouse?"

"What cats?"

"I brought four cats from the neighbors. They make a bit more work. I have to change their water and clean up after them, but they're useful. They catch mice."

"That's very sensible of you!" I said, not bothering to hide my sarcasm.

He took it seriously. "It is sensible. I saw we had a whole army of mice. The sacks were gnawed, and the grain eaten, a great waste. I reckoned it this way: Say there are two hundred in the warehouse, in a year there'll be two thousand; in ten years, twenty thousand."

"But what have they been waiting for up to now? Why only two hundred of them?"

"There must have been only two mice last year; a male and

a female, and they breed like hell. And so there'll be two thousand of them. So, say one mouse eats only twenty grains in a day, two hundred mice will eat four thousand grains in a day, in a year almost a million and a half grains. Let's say that in every *oke* there are two thousand grains, that's seven hundred and fifty *okes*. If as many neighboring mice come to visit, and certainly more than that do come, how many loads of grain is that? Loads! Osman-*aga* was open-mouthed when I told him."

"Who's that . . . oh, I know! I can't get used to that Osman-*aga*."

And Osman-*aga* certainly must have gaped when he heard how many loads of grain Mahmut was going to take from the warehouse, blaming it all on the mice!

But not even that was the truth! I, too, gaped as did Osman, and for the same reason, for Mahmut was no longer Mahmut. He wouldn't take a thing!

"We've bunged up all the holes, brought in the cats, and now there'll be three loads more in the warehouse."

Open up, ye heavens! He was cutting off his own retreat!

"Did you work out for that Osman-*aga* of yours how many mice the cats would kill?"

"I did. If each one catches only ten mice a day, four will catch forty."

"And annually, so many and so many, all right, and so in this battle between the cats and the mice, the mice will win, I hope."

"They won't, because, you see . . ."

"I see. Have you sold the shop?"

"I've several buyers. I'm waiting for the best price. It's in a good position."

It all made me very sad. This was no longer my Mahmut. Mine was a poetic liar. This one was a petty calculator. My Mahmut tried to catch the clouds, this one caught mice. My Mahmut was daft and dear, this one was boring and hateful.

How could such a change take place in such a short time? He hadn't, then, been a dreamer of the impossible, but just a cheat, simply waiting for the chance to become what he really was.

Perhaps my thoughts were unjust, for the poor chap had got what he dreamt of, rather less, rather more prosaic, but he was settled. Why had I imagined him a dreamer who had no desire to realize anything? This way was more natural. But in life it meant there was one interesting man less, and that was an irreparable loss. It was no loss when one of the many disappeared, that was the fall of a human leaf. But if the one who stood out by his freshness died, it left a terrifying void. The more gray people in a gray life meant that life was grayer and sadder.

A poet, no matter how good or bad, had died, and just another merchant had been born.

Perhaps he never existed. Perhaps I'd imagined him. Perhaps I'd singled him out through no fault or virtue of his own. And then again, I was the loser. His eternal longing for happiness, imagined though it probably was, was a dream that would never be achieved, and for that very reason beautiful. His futile versatility, his scatterbrained character, his cheerful helplessness, his naïve lying, his inconsistency, his fear and insecurity, his muddled chatter, all that was human. This was all too normal. To this man, I'd have nothing to say. And he'd be glad when we parted. I, as I was, was of no further use to him, as he was. Nor he to me.

And while, with some bitterness and much sadness, I was burying one man who no longer existed, with no desire to make a friend of his replacement, I was thinking how I could leave without offending the one I'd known, for the present one was of no concern to me.

And then the *serdar*-Avdaga came into the warehouse. It neither pleased me nor the opposite. I thought I'd find it easier to leave without any explanation.

But I didn't leave. It would have looked as if I were running away.

Mahmut got up, put his hand on his breast, and bowed,

lower and more humbly than would the old Mahmut, but with much more dignity. Once he'd have faced Avdaga, miserable and scared, unable to think of his posture; now he was calm, assured, protected, aware of what he should do.

He even said something, I can't remember what, but I know it was polite and appropriate, he was glad, he was honored, or something of that sort. And for this very reason, I decided not to get up, angered by Mahmut's behavior, by the pitiful change in him that was to be seen in everything he did, embittered by his apparent humility and actual self-assurance, which for me was the least acceptable of anything Mahmut could have invented—not invented, but become. Henceforth he was unlikely to be inventing anything. And then it occurred to me that my behavior was out of place and was no defiance of Mahmut but of Avdaga, and without any sense or reason, and I rose hesitantly, then sat, rose again, and sat down again while Mahmut led Avdaga to the settee, as though he were leading a bride. Both my own and Mahmut's behavior had spoiled my mood, and my ridiculous rising to my feet convinced me that in minor things it's better to do what others do, lest one do what others do not do.

It was a pity I couldn't leave at once. It would be embarrassing, rude, and perhaps again I'd start to leave and change my mind several times, just as I'd kept sitting down and getting up. The worst thing a man can do is, because of some trifling error, to string a number of others to it, like a string of beads. Nothing hates being on its own as much as does a mistake.

The safest way to avoid further errors was to keep quiet.

The *serdar*-Avdaga was silent, too.

Luckily, Mahmut was full of talk. He said what he'd said to me, even using the same words, not caring that I was listening (he'd never have done that in the old days), about the whitewashing, about the scrubbing, the furniture, the mice, the amount of grain in an *oke*, of the losses, the cats from the neighborhood, and of their value, which even Osman-*aga* himself had recognized.

I could hardly keep from laughing when Avdaga asked, "Who's this Osman-*aga?*" Only he didn't ask with bitterness and sarcasm as I had, but because he really didn't know who Osman-*aga* was, for nobody ever called Osman that.

Mahmut's talk was silly and trivial as before, perhaps all the less bearable because I was hearing it for the second time. And those walls would hear it every day, but I'd heard it for the last time. But then, such as it was, this boring claptrap made some sense, served a purpose by filling an uncomfortable silence that might have come over us.

I avoided Avdaga's eyes, pretending to be listening to Mahmut's chatter. And when I did look at him, I saw he was listening in silence. He was keeping silent rather than listening. His glance was fixed on the glowing brazier. His silence was heavy, burdensome, tortuous, full of malice and, for a wonder, sadness. Yes, sadness!

How did there come to be sadness in the heart and on the face of this man who'd not regretted even his murdered brother, who had no one of his own, because he needed no one, for whom his service was wife, children, love, and happiness? And yet, sadness and misery stared out of his eyes, out of his attitude, out of his every feature, the same as with any other man.

But as the torment on his face grew greater, his head fell lower, and when it looked as if he were about to go to sleep, he suddenly raised his hand in the middle of Mahmut's talking, interrupting him without waiting for the end of the sentence about cats and mice.

Mahmut obediently stopped talking, neither flustered nor frightened, and calmly waited for him to speak.

Avdaga asked quietly, "Why did Osman give you this job?"

"He knows I'm honest and a good worker. That's why."

"And why didn't he give it to him?" he said, pointing to me. "He doesn't like working any more than you do, but he's more honest."

"It's not fair to bring that up, Avdaga. When one's young all sorts of things can happen, and I paid, more than enough. Why don't you judge me not by what I was then but by what I am now?"

"As for that 'now,' I don't know. Neither does Osman. For the 'then,' I do know. And so does Osman. So why did he give you the job? You're not even a merchant."

"You know what, Avdaga," Mahmut said, in the tone of any reputable man whose honor had been impugned. "Why don't you ask Osman-*aga* rather than me? He should know best."

"Perhaps I will. But now I'm asking you. Why did he give you this job?"

"To tell you the truth, I find your question offensive."

"I don't know whether it's offensive, but it's necessary."

They were both silent.

Mahmut began to rub his bad leg. Fear and hurt always made him do that.

Avdaga looked at Mahmut with sad, dead eyes, no doubt regretting that Mahmut's head was not made of glass or that he couldn't smash it so as to find in his brain the answer to the question that had brought him there.

Neither the one nor the other, it seemed, knew anything. Mahmut was certain that luck had come his way, that someone, at last, had discovered his business abilities and given him a job. Any other explanation, no matter what, and he couldn't imagine one, was insulting. Avdaga, on the other hand, thought that only a madman could for no apparent reason take on Mahmut. Osman was not mad; so there had to be some reason for such foolish behavior. What was the reason? Was he under some obligation? Was this payment for some service? Mahmut's services were always doubtful, this Avdaga knew well, in which case there'd been some wrongdoing, and it needed to be found out.

Did he always start his inquiries like that, in the dark?

He kept silent; this was a method of upsetting a man's calm.

Mahmut rubbed his bad leg with trembling fingers more and more strongly, silenced by Avdaga's reticence concerning his vague suspicion, upset by Avdaga's insistence, for which he knew no reason. Perhaps he was thinking: Surely not obstacles at the very first step? Surely they're not trying to prevent my good luck? In his misery, he began to look to me like the old Mahmut.

It could have been interesting if it hadn't been painful.

Avdaga's silence filled his victim with fear for what he didn't say or reveal, leaving the victim time to think of his possible crimes and to lose heart. Or perhaps it was just a case of economic firing, due to a lack of ammunition. If all there was was suspicion, the attack couldn't last long. They'd be turning in the vicious circle of the same questions and the same answers, and the suspicion would be no nearer confirmation.

But Avdaga still had some resources; he began to weave an ever-narrowing circle around his victim. He asked, "Did you know the commandant?"

"What commandant?" Mahmut asked, sly in his helplessness.

"The commandant."

"Ah, the commandant!"

"Yes, the commandant."

"I knew him."

"Well?"

"Only by sight."

"Did you often talk with him?"

"Never, not often. I've never spoken a word to him in my life."

"Try to remember!"

"I'm sure."

"Could you swear to it?"

"I could."

"And what about when you were in the Fortress?"

"Oh, that! I don't know, he may have asked me my name."

"And your crime."

"I've forgotten."

"And what else have you forgotten?"

"I don't know what you mean."

"When did you last talk to him?"

"I told you. Then, in the Fortress."

"You didn't say that, I said it. But now, recently?"

"Never since then. I swear by my children."

"I've seen what your oath's worth."

"Ask the commandant. He'll tell you."

Once again silence descended like a cloud.

Mahmut convulsively denied that he'd ever spoken with the commandant, as though this in itself were suspicious. He'd have denied in the same way that he'd been for a walk by the river, or had stuffed cabbage for lunch, that he'd five instead of four cats, if Avdaga had asked him, for who knew what might be suspicious and dangerous.

And it was only then that it dawned on me. Avdaga was carrying out this interrogation because of the rescue and was thinking that Mahmut had talked to the commandant! As a reward for this service, Osman had given him the job.

I was sorry for Mahmut. I knew he hadn't been mixed up in anything, yet I couldn't help him. How could I say to Avdaga that Osman Vuk hadn't known that Mahmut existed. They'd met for the first time on the night of the rescue.

Why Osman had given him the job, I didn't know. He'd surprised both me and Mahmut, perhaps even himself, with that moment of weakness, which would not be soon repeated.

Avdaga couldn't understand human inconsistencies nor sudden decisions. He saw only cause and effect, service and reward. He was thinking that someone had persuaded the commandant to let the rescuers into the Fortress; after that, Osman Vuk had given a job to the incompetent Mahmut. Why? Because Mahmut had persuaded the commandant. According to Avdaga's logic, it was so clear that even Mahmut's muddled denial was a sure proof.

And he was sad because he couldn't prove Mahmut's

316

guilt. He needed proof. He was too honest to punish a man without it. He had to have a witness, a confession, and where were they? There were none, as yet, but he would not leave Mahmut alone until one or another of them faltered. He'd pursue him as a hungry wolf pursues an old stag. Both would stumble, fleeing and chasing, panting from fear and sensuality. Perhaps the victim would give in, perhaps he'd agree to suffer, if this meant the end of his fatigue.

And for no reason, for a suspicion that wrongly linked certain facts. And I listened in silence, not daring to say, "Leave the man alone. He doesn't even know what you're talking about, and that will make you suspect him even more."

And if I'd said it, it would have been of no use. Avdaga was addicted to his calling. It was his only passion. He lived to chase and take people, as others lived to comfort and cure them. Only Avdaga, in his calling, more often experienced the joy of success.

But why did he suspect Osman? Or was I attributing to him suspicion of Osman because of my knowledge, while he was not even thinking of him? But perhaps he was thinking, If Osman's given Mahmut this job, then it was in payment for something. He was suspicious of the entire world. He lived with suspicion, he dreamt suspicion, and not always without reason. Crimes took place every day. If the culprit was not caught, then all people were possible culprits. He knew well that no one could swear that any man alive would not do evil. Avdaga tracked, Avdaga suspected. That was his fate, his duty, and his satisfaction. And it was not easy, for most often crime was clothed in darkness, and the real culprit would pass by him, look him in the eye, quietly go about his business, laugh, perhaps even sit with him, and he only sensed, scented, felt, perhaps got close only again to lose the tracks, assured but not sure, happy when he found a track, despairing when he lost it, and only his death could force him to give up the chase.

For he knew, were he to give up, grow tired, were he not

to catch and punish the criminal, crime would dominate the world, darkness would fall upon the earth, and the day of judgment would come.

In the case of Mahmut, Avdaga was on a thin thread, but all the same, he had grasped it firmly. The greatest pity was that it was Mahmut's good luck that was the cause of Avdaga's suspicion. And Osman's generosity, for which he himself repented. Some people are born to be unfortunate. So many people have succeeded in life, without intelligence, without ability, without honesty, and no one turned a hair. And poor old Mahmut, by the mere fact that he'd got into his dark warehouse full of mice and their droppings, thinking himself to be free of the fear of a hungry old age, had immediately become an object of suspicion. He'd never had any luck. How could he expect to settle down now! Osman hadn't given him the job because of his pretty face.

And honestly, why had Osman given him that job? It was nasty of me to ask it, but, honestly, why? I was glad when he did it, but why did he?

How should I know! I'd asked Osman to take him to the inn that evening. I'd asked him to say a few friendly words to him. It was my fault that we'd overheard the quarrel that had made Osman angry. I knew all this, but all the same, why had he? Surely not just because the son had been insolent to the father? Worse things than an ordinary quarrel would have had no effect on Osman.

So you see how another's suspicion is infectious, how it undermines one, even when one knows that the object is innocent.

If he is innocent.

But what if he isn't, what if the experienced hunter Avdaga was on the right track?

The thought defeated me.

It was impossible, I knew it was!

But I could no longer get rid of the thought that, against

my will, crossed the boundary placed by my liking for Mahmut, drawing the whole of me into the abyss of imagined possibilities.

If this were the case, then it was easy to put everything together, and everything became clear.

Osman had sent Mahmut to talk with the commandant. He was the best man for it, since if Mahmut had betrayed him, no one would have believed it. Afterward, Mahmut had stubbornly insisted on meeting Osman, in order to receive payment for his services. Osman had refused, so it would not look suspicious, while Mahmut's unfortunate situation with his son served as a good excuse to give him his promised award.

It all added up. Only what didn't was that it made me look a fool, but this wouldn't have worried them. They'd pretended, skillfully concealing everything, and I'd served them as a link and shield.

It all added up, exactly as Osman might have planned it. For him people were only a means. Why should I be an exception?

But Mahmut? Would Mahmut have been capable of such pretense? I thought I knew everything about him. I believed all sorts of things of him, but I also thought that he was incapable of keeping a secret. He'd appear to hide his own worthless secrets, keep silent about them for a day or an hour, only to reveal them in public, freeing himself of them with relief, as if casting off a burden. For me he'd been a chaotic, overgrown child with a good heart, which was why I was fond of him. But if he'd had a hand in this dirty game, then he was a stinking old rascal whom I'd best forget. I'd parted with one Mahmut, the present one. Was I to part, then, with that past Mahmut, who no longer existed?

I looked at him, suspiciously. And he looked at me, uncomfortably, as though he guessed my thoughts and as though seeking defense in repentance. He looked helpless, as he used to look, and once again I missed my Mahmut, but this one I couldn't forgive. Anyone had the right to deceive me, except for a friend.

Avdaga sat silent, stirring the dying embers with a pair of tongs. What was he waiting for? Why didn't he leave? But perhaps neither he nor Mahmut would leave. They'd, both of them, sit beside the brazier, grow cold like the embers, remain silent, dying before saying a word. The prosecutor would remain without proof, and the accused without punishment.

But the half-dead Avdaga, still alive, unfortunately, straightened his powerful shoulders and looked at me.

Was it my turn now?

His voice was quiet, tired, and sad. I'm bitter and irritated. Neither you nor I feel like talking, so what do you want of me?

But he was on duty and took no notice of fatigue.

He asked me, "Why didn't Osman give you the warehouse?"

"What would I do in the warehouse?"

"You're looking for something better?"

"I'm not looking for anything."

"What are you living on?"

"I steal, I mug or kill, as I happen to feel at the time."

"I saw you at Avdiya Skakavats's funeral."

"And I saw you."

"Why were you there?"

"I didn't know it was forbidden."

"What were you talking about with old Omer Skakavats in his yard?"

It was lucky I had thought of this earlier. Osman had warned me.

"I heard he had some good tobacco, and I was asking him to sell me some."

"Did you buy any?"

"No. He hadn't any."

"After that his sons took a horse and went to fetch Avdiya."

"That I don't know."

I remembered Osman's advice that sometimes it was best to shoot first. I asked, "What did the lad die of? They say he was healthy."

He looked at me more alertly and attentively than before, and I regretted my sally. Perhaps he wasn't all that intelligent, but he didn't let himself be made a fool of. He didn't answer, which was perhaps the worst answer he could have given, as though he'd said, "Why do you ask me?"

He sat a while longer, his eyes fixed on the brazier, and then got up slowly and, without haste, left the room.

Mahmut unenthusiastically and without his former confidence saw him out and returned with a worried look. As soon as he'd closed the door, he turned to me. "Why was he asking me about the commandant?"

"He asked me about Omer Skakavats."

"But why?"

"Perhaps he'll tell us tomorrow."

"Do you think he'll come tomorrow, too?"

"For certain."

"Man, the way he looks, the way he sits there without a word! It fair makes you shiver."

"Why be afraid, if you're not guilty?"

"What do you mean guilty, for God's sake? And for what?"

I got up to take my leave. I couldn't bear to stay with him any longer. The possibility of his treachery had hurt me deeply.

My departure and perhaps my coldness frightened him. Once again he looked like the old Mahmut, but my hurt didn't allow him to be resurrected.

"Stay on a bit," he pleaded.

"I've got to go."

I left him alone with the mice and the cats and his fear. Once on the street, I realized I shouldn't have done it, but I didn't go back.

CHAPTER 16

THE EPITAPH

THE NEXT DAY, AT NOON, WHEN I CAME HOME, TIYANA TOLD me Mahmut had been looking for me.

I told her why he was looking for me, that he felt himself alone again, because he couldn't discuss his fears with the merchants. It seemed he'd got involved with Osman about something and the *serdar*-Avdaga was suspicious.

I put it to her gently, not to frighten her, but she scarcely listened, as though bored by male stupidities. She'd more important things than our intrigues and falsehoods. She showed me a scarf that Mahmut's wife, Pasa, had given her, done on silk with a fine needle, with tiny chains of yellow and blue flowers in the middle and on the edges. Wasn't that better than our poor efforts?

They'd formed a close friendship, if not more than that. They'd become necessary to each other. If Tiyana didn't go to Vratnik, then Pasa would come to her, and they'd immediately resume the talk of yesterday, which would be continued on the morrow. Their main topic was the child Tiyana was bearing. They were preparing to make baby clothes, guessing whether it would be male or female. They tried out countless names, from poetry, history, and life, usually ending up by choosing the very worst, just as they'd do on the day the child was born. The new person would have to carry that impossible name, like a burden or an object of shame, for the rest of its life. Pasa indulged her inexhaustible maternal feelings (her own children were not enough, she wished she'd had ten), and Tiyana pushed aside her fear and dread in those joyful worries, seriously occupied with trifles, amazingly preoccupied with a feeling of happiness and pride.

She'd rather forgotten me, put me aside as not being so important as formerly. All her attention was focused on that living, yet unborn, creature, more alive than I and more important than anything else on earth. No matter what she said, I knew she was thinking of it. When she asked whether I'd any hope of getting employment, it was for its sake. If she remembered her father, it was no longer with that deep sadness that used to frighten me, but with regret that the grandfather wouldn't see his grandchild. Even our room was no longer any good, for its sake. We had to find something better in the spring, without cockroaches, without heat, with more room. Everything she did, said, or thought had one reason and one reason only. She already loved this embryo, this future child. She even asked me, irrationally, whether I loved it, and I had to say I did, so she wouldn't think me a monster, for she wouldn't understand that a mother loves the very thought of a child and that a father begins to love a living creature, perhaps only after its first smile. I knew nothing of it. It was strange and distant. She constantly felt it as part of herself. I thought of it as a source of worry, for her and for the life that was about to change. She thought of it as the meaning of everything, and, for her, it was natural that life should be adapted to it and to its happiness. I was uneasy, fearing what would happen were she to miscarry, as she did the first time. She was calm, everything within her and around her was ordered, nothing in the world was out of line, nothing was empty or without meaning. The child inside her had brought sense and order into everything.

I'd watch her preparing lunch and suddenly stop, taken by surprise, with wide-open eyes, smiling happily, and sit on the settee, calm and upright, solemnly, gently touching the roundness of her belly.

"It's kicking," she would say, delighted. "I felt its little foot."

No joyful news, no gift, no riches could have given her such happiness as that silent kick of a living being within her. She would wait for it to be repeated, like a blessing. She'd dream of it, as she might have dreamt of love.

Touched by her delight, which I could not entirely understand, I went to her, ready to be as solemn as she was, took her by the hand, and told her I loved her. Gently she pressed my fingers, grateful that I'd come to her because of it, that I loved her because of it, that we existed because of it. Generously, I accepted her injustice, suppressing my dissatisfaction at becoming of secondary importance, overcoming my sorrow at losing her, hoping that the birth might return her to me.

I missed the fact that we no longer discussed everything, that I didn't tell her everything that happened to me and everything I felt, be it joy, fear, or anger. Now I had to bear it myself. For her, it meant nothing. She listened without interest and without attention. She replied unwillingly and without sympathy. She left me alone with my thoughts, perhaps sure that I was experiencing the same feelings as she was.

The *serdar*-Avdaga had been looking for me, too. I was glad he didn't find me. Not having found me, I was sure he'd gone to lean on Mahmut, scaring him stiff, as he'd done the day before.

They were looking for me. I went to look for Osman Vuk. He wasn't at home. The servants knew only that he'd gone off somewhere on horseback, and that was all. Shehaga was not at home, either. No doubt they were busy. Osman had mentioned a deal in wool. Or Shehaga might have gone shooting, for he left business matters to Osman.

It was only on the third day that I found Osman and told him how the *serdar*-Avdaga had questioned Mahmut and me. He waved the whole thing aside as being of no significance, and laughed when I told him Mahmut was under suspicion of having talked to the commandant.

"Mahmut, for God's sake! Who'd rely on Mahmut in such a matter!"

"Then who did?"

"How should I know!"

"How do you know it wasn't Mahmut?"

"I don't think he's up to such things. He's all right sitting in a warehouse, measuring grain. And he's better at it than I thought. Did you know he'd got some cats to deal with the mice? He's laughable, but he's all right for that sort of work."

He turned the conversation, refusing to talk about his own affairs. He did this openly, keeping me out of it, perhaps for my own good. What I didn't know, I couldn't tell.

I told him I had the impression that he and Mahmut had hidden everything from me and that the *serdar*-Avdaga had revealed it all. I was scared that he knew so much. For this reason, I'd spent three days looking for him, Osman, to tell him.

He hadn't been there, he said, because of the wool purchase and because of Shehaga. He'd looked for him, but once again couldn't find him. Several nights ago, before dawn, he'd gone off on horseback, and nobody knew where he was. His wife was mad with fear and hadn't slept a wink, waiting for him to come back. Poor woman, she either mourned her son or feared for her husband. And he, Osman, was worried. It had been snowing, and the nights were cold, and, since Shehaga didn't know what he was doing when he was drunk (that was why he drank), anything might have happened. And it was all rather suspicious. He'd asked him for an account of his dealings and a list of his debtors, despite the fact that he'd done this two months before, and then he'd sent for Mula Ibrahim. It looked as if he wanted to change his will. For this reason, Osman had kept a close guard on him, but, nevertheless, he'd got away while Osman was asleep.

"What will you do now?"

"Nothing. I'll just wait."

And there was something else that had made him wonder. The day before he took off, Dzhemal Zafraniya had been to see him and had asked for Shehaga's help, both for him and for the *kadi*. The *kadi* was about to become mufti, and Zafraniya *naib*. But then there'd been that trouble over Ramiz's rescue, and their enemies were blaming both of them and doing all they could to hinder their promotion. But were Shehaga, whom they deeply respected, to say but one word, the *vali* would listen to him. Both he and the *kadi* would be grateful for the rest of their lives and would know how to return a favor. Were they hinting at something, were they suggesting knowledge of something else? Osman didn't know, but it would seem to have infuriated Shehaga. He jumped on Zafraniya, which for him was quite unusual, since he avoided offending anyone without cause, and told him that in fact what he was really asking was that he would not stand in their way. Why lie to one another? He wouldn't help them. He'd prevent their promotion, if at all possible, since he considered they didn't deserve the positions they held, never mind higher ones. Let them rest easy and hang on to what they had, for better and more honest people than they were walking the streets without work or were in fear of the two of them. And they'd better watch what they were doing. People were complaining, and the cries of the poor carried far. Why should he help them? In what way had they deserved it?

Osman was surprised at Shehaga's speaking like that. He could have promised and done nothing, and it would all have been the same. But Shehaga was already in one of his moods and saw in Zafraniya that unknown and nameless judge who'd condemned his son to death, or who would condemn another, and could not restrain himself from venting his hatred and sorrow. Zafraniya had come out, looking pale and supporting himself on the wall, and Shehaga had gone to the *vali* to prevent a promotion that did not concern him. Had he met Zafraniya at a better moment, when he was not poisoned with hatred, perhaps it would have been the same, but more politely done. But Shehaga was no longer in control of himself. The older he got, the worse it was. He was tormented by the thought that nothing would remain of him, not even his name. And so, here we were, in open war. No matter, indeed, whether it was open or secret, but one needed to be on one's guard, for they, too, were no angels and would return the blow, if ever they had a chance.

"And you'd better watch yourself," he said with a laugh, "for you're on our side."

"Is that why they sent Avdaga to question me?"

"Avdaga's the stupidest and most honest of the lot of them. He's honest, like a wild boar. He attacks without malice. Perhaps they did send him. They're looking for proofs. Without them, they daren't move against Shehaga. But the problem is where to find them."

"Will the Skakavatses say anything?"

"If they're involved, they won't say a word. You've no need to fear."

"I've no fear and no reason to fear."

"Thank God for that. Fear is the worst traitor there is."

He was a strange man, Osman. He spoke calmly about everything. He saw everything, but he was never afraid. He even seemed to enjoy himself in this free-for-all. His common sense and coolness made him respected. It was as if he were armored with Shehaga's power, strengthened by his own intrepidity, by his superior disdain of people, his insolent cunning, and his unscrupulousness, his readiness to act and be silent, for it was the act that interested him and not the fame of it. He was loyal to Shehaga, it would seem, because he respected his power, because he needed his protection, because he did what he wanted. And perhaps, in some ways, they were similar. They'd been together for years. They'd no secrets from one another, nor could they have, knowing each other so well. They were equally merciless, equally dangerous, equally removed from people, only each in his own way: Shehaga with a burning hatred, Osman with a cold contempt.

Leaving Osman and thinking about him, I noticed the *serdar*-Avdaga, only too late, and was unable to change my direction. He might have been there by chance or waiting for somebody else or, perhaps, he knew where I'd been, but no matter what ill chance had brought him there, we couldn't pass each other without a word. Enmity, like friendship, imposes its obligations. He looked at me, like someone who shared with me a dark secret, or like a close acquaintance who expected me to stop and have a word, no matter about what. Perhaps he'd seen by my attitude and sour expression that I wasn't exactly pleased at our meeting and would have happily passed by if he hadn't stopped me.

He asked me in a dead voice, as though it were of no importance, "Where have you been?"

"For a walk."

"You were with Osman Vuk."

"Why ask, when you know?"

"Did you tell him what we were talking about?"

"I did."

"And what did he say? I bet he laughed. He's always laughing."

"He laughed and was surprised at your questioning me."

"Then he knows whom I should have been questioning."

"I asked him, 'What does the *serdar*-Avdaga want?' He didn't know."

"And what else did you talk about?"

"About Shehaga. He's left home again."

"What have you got to do with Shehaga?"

He was patient and stubborn, like a hunting dog that never lets go once it has its teeth around anything, even if its jaws are broken. Would he go on clicking his teeth around my throat until one or the other of us gave in? He was circling me like a wild beast uncertain of its leap, but once sure of not missing, he'd break my back.

He knew Mahmut and I were the weakest links in the chain and that was what he was getting at. He wouldn't let go.

My heart grew cold at the thought of such a happy future, and my brain turned to a jelly without a single thought of anything. It lasted only a moment, a long and painful moment. I forgot to breathe, from fear and anxiety. In my thoughts, I began to look around me, blindly and terrified, ready to run anywhere to save myself from that moment and from that terror.

But as the vacuum rose in my brain, as I felt the fear in my heart, suddenly and without reason I felt anger, like a rush of blood after a sudden stop, like shame at a humiliating fear. And as the anger broke out, I was aware that it wouldn't help, but it was too hot to be stopped. I was angry at myself for my cowardice. What could he know about me? If he really did know anything, why didn't he look in the right place? He was gnawing the rope where it was thinnest, going for me because I was defenseless.

Having found a prop, both my anger and indignation became real and assured.

"You ask what have I to do with Shehaga," I growled provocatively, wanting to humiliate both myself and him. "Don't you know how long I've been unemployed? I dance attendance on Shehaga, I look into his eyes adoringly, I say whatever he wants to hear, anything for him to find me some work, no matter what, anything to stop eating my heart out because they've cast me aside, like a dog! That's what Shehaga means to me! It's a wonder I haven't joined Bechir Toska's bandits. What do you want from me? It's easy to play the fool with poor folk, Avdaga!"

"What are you angry about?" he asked calmly. "What have I said?"

"That's why I'm angry. You keep going round me, feeling for something, looking for something. Why the hell don't you say openly that you're looking for such and such? I'll tell you all I know."

"What were you talking about with old Omer Skakavats?"

"I wanted to buy some tobacco, I told you. If you don't believe me, ask him."

"I did. He said the same."

"There you are! What more do you want?"

"That's what's suspicious, that you both say the same."

So there it was! I laughed helplessly. "Forgive me for saying this, Avdaga. You're older than I am, but you're really weird! What to anyone else is proof, to you is a reason for suspicion."

"To me, everything's a reason for suspicion. And why are you so angry?" he added reasonably. "Anyone with a clear conscience answers calmly. It's the one who is guilty that gets angry, because he's disturbed."

"But what am I supposed to be guilty of?"

He didn't hurry to reply. He was silent, looking at me with his serious expression, pityingly, hurt, sadly, God knows how to say it, as though he saw right through me and was both angry and aggrieved that I refused to confess. Sorry, but I won't, I thought. I'll hold out, grit my teeth, wait for you to pass by, like any other storm.

But what if it didn't pass?

When he'd gazed his fill, as if lusting after me, he resumed his gnawing.

"You say it's easy to play the fool with the poor. But who isn't it easy to play the fool with?"

"I know my own troubles. Others don't concern me."

"Do those others have a name?"

"Avdaga, I'll tell you again: I don't know what you're looking for. And what you're saying sounds to me as if you're casting a spell, as if you're trying to bewitch me."

He treated me once more to one of his kind looks, enough to make the birds freeze as in front of a snake, and slowly went off down the street.

It was a good job, for I was already feeling sick, as though he'd had me by the throat, and I'd lost my breath.

I remembered the story my grandmother told me long ago about Karandzholoz, the black demon who, at Christmastime, waylaid people on dark crossroads and, heavy and stinking, climbed on their backs. The man carrying him and stumbling under the weight would be almost dead with fright, but Karandzholoz would ask, "Am I heavy?" The man would groan and say what he thought, "You're heavy." Karandzholoz would become still heavier. The following morning they'd find the man dead. But whoever answered "You're not heavy" was saved, for Karandzholoz immediately disappeared, and the man was free. Due to this word of courage, this word of defiance. Later I used to think it was a story about life: If we complain that things weigh heavy on us, we give in; if we say to life, I'll hang on, you won't break me, the pain grows less.

At a certain crossroads of life, I'd been met by the Karandzholoz Avdaga, and he'd climbed on my back. My breath grew short from his weight, as though I were carrying a mountain. I wouldn't say he was heavy, but then I wouldn't say that he was light, either. We'd go on with our game, and I'd not be free of him till I felt freedom inside myself. As yet I didn't feel it. Fear prevented it.

Even when I forgot the reason, fear and anxiety were inside me. "What is it?" I asked. "Why?" I asked. And then Avdaga's image emerged from the darkness, like an answer to my question.

And what about Mahmut? If he knew nothing, he'd be terrified at Avdaga's suspicion. If he did know something, how could he help but tell? He'd confess, just to put an end to his torment. He'd jump into the abyss rather than die of fright. And perhaps he was really innocent. Would Osman have been so calm if Mahmut had known anything? Mahmut was like a torn sack, and everything would fall out of him immediately, yet Osman dismissed it. In that case, the *serdar*-Avdaga had roasted him for nothing. I'd go to him. He was sure to be lonely and unhappy, and I'd behaved like a silly schoolboy. And even if he had hidden everything from me, I'd no right to leave him alone when things were going badly.

But the warehouse was locked. He'd gone somewhere, running from his fear and from Avdaga, leaving his unfed cats to chase an indestructible army of mice. His joy at being a merchant had been short-lived.

His neighbor, the grocer, told me Mahmut was at Zayko's inn. He had a slight stomachache and had gone to drink some herbal *rakiya*.

And that was where I actually found him. He was sitting alone in a corner, his chin on his skinny hand, looking absolutely beat, the picture of misery.

When I approached him, he looked up, and his face immediately brightened.

"Thank God!" he said with relief.

And he got up, took me by the hand, as though I might run away, motioned me to sit down, keeping his eyes on me, feeling my shoulder, my elbow, the seams of my sleeve, the better to convince himself of my presence.

"I've been looking for you. I've even been to your home." His voice was quiet, weak, as if he was getting over a bad illness.

"Anyone seeing you so down would swear you had something troubling you."

"More than that. I think I've had it."

"They told me you had a bad stomach, and you'd gone to get some herbal *rakiya*. That's how I found you."

He ordered two *rakiyas*, one for me and one for himself and drank both of them.

"I'm glad you've come. I left you a message. I knew you'd be looking for me. And my stomach really is aching. *That one* came to see me again."

"Is that why you've got a stomachache?"

"Yes!"

That one meant Avdaga. It was as if, like the devil's, his name should not be spoken.

"He came to see me, too."

"When he came to the warehouse the first time, I got the squitters like I'd eaten too many crab apples. I calmed it with coffee and mint tea, but the moment I thought of him, my guts boiled and poured out of me like out of a tap."

"From fear."

"Yes, from fear. And I told myself not to think about him! And I began to think about the business, about all the troubles I'd had, about other people. But whoever I thought about, it turned into his eyes, his face, his voice. And my stomach again: whoof! And only this herbal *rakiya* helps."

"Because it makes you forget."

"I forget and I don't forget, but it's a bit easier. I was sitting here. To tell you the truth, I'd left the warehouse to get away from him, and I was thinking, 'How have I sinned against God to deserve all this?' I'm guilty for those copper coins and for a few other little matters, but what interest is that to God? And I don't think God's so petty as to torment me just out of spite. But that's my fucking luck. And then, why should it always be my fucking luck? It's not fair. I've never done anyone any harm, so why? For years I've dreamt of getting something like what I've just been lucky enough to get, and I haven't even got used to the smell of the warehouse and there has to be this trouble. Why, tell me?"

His voice was tearful, poor chap. He'd gone through many things, as I knew well, but I'd never seen him so distressed. He'd been irresponsible, ever ready to cheat, full of hopes, and now everything looked black. All of a sudden, he'd had a bit of luck, only to see that luck was not for him, nor he for it.

"What does Avdaga want with you?" I asked, to see what he'd say.

"If I knew what he was after, I'd feel easier. What's getting me down is that I don't know."

"Have you done anything, anything at all, that he might want to know about?"

"I've gone over and over it till my head's bursting. It's no good. But I can see he suspects something. He can't prove anything, so he won't say what it is, and I can't tell him he's wrong, because I don't know what it is."

"Why should you worry! He won't get any further than suspecting."

"He will, Ahmet. Alas, he will. I can see it's something big. He wouldn't waste all that time on nothing, and somebody's going to get it in the neck. And who but me? If they can't find the right man, then anybody'll do them. Perhaps it'll be Mahmut. Nobody'll protect me, nobody'll even be surprised, nobody'll be sorry for me. I'll be their scapegoat. I can see it. Some are born lucky, some for the devil. I'm a scapegoat."

Tears began to ooze out of his narrowed eyes, fear and the *rakiya* had made him maudlin.

"Don't be a fool!" I said sharply. "You're innocent. They can't do anything to you. What scapegoat? What devil? Do you think Avdaga suspects only you? He suspects everybody."

This seemed to help, just because I didn't show him any pity.

"Do you think so?" he asked with hope.

"I don't think, I know. But if you go on drinking and snivelling like this, you really will look suspicious."

"Do you think so?"

"Yes, I'm sure. Go back to the warehouse and do your work. If he comes again, just ask him politely, 'What are you looking for?' And get used to him. That's what I do. If he goes on asking the same thing, then you go on answering the same thing! In the end he'll get bored."

"Do you think so?"

Three times he'd asked the same thing, without contradiction, hoping I was right and wanting to be convinced. He didn't like being sad, and this moment of weakness was a short-lived self-pity and wouldn't last long. Already he looked more cheerful, more assured, back to his old nonsensical chatter, as if looking into friendly eyes gave him strength, even if false. For him it was real and welcome. It crossed my mind that this silly man would die if he had to live alone, without friends or without people he thought were his friends. My empty words had pulled him together just because they suited his irresponsible nature and because they were spoken by a friend.

"You're right," he said boldly. "When he comes, I'll say to him, 'What are you sniffing around me for? Get off my neck!'"

But then, perhaps, in his mind's eye he encountered Avdaga's face, and his courage faded away.

"Or perhaps I won't. You dare, I don't."

"To tell you the truth, I don't dare often. But when a man's really angry, he thinks, 'To hell with it. Do what you like, a man only dies once!'"

He didn't like this sort of desperate bravery, nor such mad and senseless defiance.

"But that's just the trouble, my dear Ahmet, a man only dies once. If it were twice or three times, one wouldn't grudge one death. But this way, you've got to be a hero or a fool not to fear. I don't think I'm boasting if I say I'm not a fool, and a hero I couldn't be, even if I wanted. I haven't the guts. . . . There, you see, the very thought of him. . . . Wait and I'll be right back."

And he dashed off to the toilet.

I laughed at his discomfort. It was inconvenient, no doubt, but one couldn't help laughing. He talked of his fear like a child, openly and directly, without any self-consciousness. Fear is ugly when we see it in another.

I wouldn't have it like that! I'd said, pretty insincerely, trying to encourage him, "A man dies only once." But now I really thought that way. It wasn't courage but shame at being humiliated. Fear was the worst traitor, Osman had said. But it seemed to me that fear was the greatest shame in this world and man's greatest humiliation, raised above him like a whip, pointed at his throat like a knife. Man is surrounded by fear as by flame, drowned in it, as in water. He fears fate, the morrow, the law, a stronger man; and he isn't what he wants to be but what he has to be. He fawns before fate, prays to the morrow, blindly follows the law, smiles humbly at the man in power whom he hates, reconciled to being a monstrous creation made up of fear and obedience.

If man was sometimes sad, it was because he recalled himself as he was in his dreams, as he could have been, were he not as he was. And if the world were not what it is.

I wouldn't have it like that!

I said, I am not afraid of you, fate! Nor you, tomorrow! Nor you, powerful man! But this I said to myself, and I said it with fear, half free, split down the middle. One part isolating itself because it couldn't accept, the other silent because it didn't want to suffer.

Then I was a coward, too, like Mahmut. Only in a different way.

Freedom lay in action, and this I never achieved.

My powers were weak; there was little I could do. I didn't know even what I should do, without becoming either a useless victim or a silent malcontent. There was so much evil, and the scope of my powers was limited.

Why then was I thinking of the act of my freedom, when it was unrealizable?

Should I state this once and for all, and then be silent?

Should I act once, never to act again?

Should I remain silent, satisfied that I was alive?

And if I were to agree to be a victim, for what I didn't know, how could I be certain that I wouldn't injure somebody?

I'd moved to save Ramiz and had destroyed Avdiya.

Should I then do nothing, leave the world to go its way, since, in any case, I could change nothing?

All reasonings said this was the best. Only one form of reasoning gave me no peace: that of conscience. I didn't know where it came from; I didn't know what use it was. It stood in the way of my living, yet I couldn't rid myself of it.

Leave me alone, I told that uninvited conscience, stop bullying me! And it crouched there in some corner of me, sometimes drowsy, sometimes awake, but never leaving me. You're so damn useless, I told it, it's funny. I'm not glad that I have you. I don't feel any satisfaction at having you inside me. You're not my nobility, but my downfall. Why didn't you find somebody powerful and strong, fearless and honest? If you couldn't find anyone like that, it's hardly my fault. You've taken refuge in me, like an orphan, and you keep silent, like an orphan. You ask for nothing. You give me no advice. You leave everything to me to decide, and it's all right while I forget about you, but I feel ashamed the moment I remember you. I don't know why, I don't owe you anything. I don't even know what you are: a formless presence, a silent warning that takes no heed of reason, an invisible signpost pointing in an invisible direction, and it's left to me to find it. How am I to find it, and how am I not to wilt if I do? You're unreasonable. You couldn't care less for the harsh experience of another. You despise danger, you lead one down perilous paths, and you don't consider this a brave action but merely the fulfillment of duty. And why do you think I owe you anything? And why me, anyway? Go and find somebody more suitable, you're just wasting your time with me.

And it crouched there, silent, waiting for its moment. The moment of my inspiration, or madness. It could be that it wouldn't find it. There was ever less likelihood that it would.

When Mahmut came back from the toilet, interrupting

my chat with my conscience and ordering yet another herbal *rakiya* to quiet the pains in his stomach, he said that, excuse the expression, while he was there he'd been thinking about me and come to the conclusion that I was right. Sure, it wasn't worth being afraid. But it wasn't easy not to be afraid. Yet, it wasn't worth it. Man's life passed in fear, and it was as if he'd never lived. What was the point of living then? But again, there was no point in being hasty, and the best thing would be if I were to have a talk with Shehaga and see if he could take Avdaga off our necks.

I told him he'd chosen a fine place to think about me in and that he hadn't wasted his time. That about Shehaga was a good idea, only it was a pity that Shehaga had gone away. But we'd wait, given that Avdaga would wait. All honor to courage, but better without it. It was good not to fear anyone, if it was possible, but still better if the question didn't arise. Courage lasted a minute, fear a whole life, and there was more sense in worrying about one's whole life than about a minute. Better to take fear beforehand, lest one take fear when it was too late.

I said whatever came into my head, not worrying whether it made sense, for that was not important, and Mahmut listened respectfully because he didn't understand what I was saying, and, comforted, went back to work. And at that moment, he remembered to tell me that Mula Ibrahim had been looking for me. And he added that they'd arrested the woman Ramiz had had lodgings with. This told me that his own worries were somewhat abated, so that he'd managed even to think of me.

This news concerning an unknown woman was devastating. Another disaster for which I was guilty!

Now I had two reasons to go to Mula Ibrahim, one because he was looking for me, the other because I needed to see him.

I wanted to ask him whether we could do anything for the arrested woman. I hadn't even known she existed, yet I'd plunged her into trouble. Perhaps they'd have arrested her even if Ramiz had not escaped, but that supposition was too shaky to free me from a feeling of guilt. It wasn't all that bad. It was rather as if I'd dislodged a stone when walking on a mountainside, and it had hit somebody walking below. I was neither directly nor consciously guilty. I'd neither known nor seen the person hit, but it was I who'd started the stone. And here I was, trying to help. And later I'd think of the strange situation in the world in which, doing good, one often did evil. And what was the point of good if it couldn't be done without evil?

I wasn't thinking of the aim as much as of the man and, for that reason, my every step was uncertain.

I knew Mula Ibrahim would refuse any talk about the woman, but I would insist, if only to assure myself, yet again, that even honest people had little will to help others. Sometimes it was no bad thing to know that there were worse people than ourselves. My conscience would reject such an excuse as being dishonest, and would warn me that each must answer to himself. Still, it would be some sort of consolation, even if only momentary.

I found Mula Ibrahim in his shop and told him I'd come because of the woman. I told him this in a whisper, so that others wouldn't hear that I was asking on her behalf, yet I'd have liked to say it aloud, so others might hear his refusal.

He refused his help and even to talk about her, silently, with a shake of the head and a wave of an arm.

The fact that I'd guessed right didn't please me. Was there really no one who'd help her?

I told him it was a disgrace. No one was willing to offer help.

My word was worthless, but he could do something. He knew the *kadi*, he knew Zafraniya, knew all the people in the court and the police. They ought to let her go. She sure- ly didn't ask Ramiz what he thought and what he was doing when she rented him the room. She had enough troubles of her own. Her husband was confined to bed ill, the neighbors visited him out of charity, but human charity is short-lived; it lacks endurance, and the poor man would be left alone and helpless. And she, too, was ill. What did they want of her?

Mula Ibrahim simply shook his head, but I was as insistent as a wasp, all the more stubborn as I was the more certain that he'd do nothing. I'd known it from the start, although I'd have been glad to have been wrong.

But my tormenting him was useless. He was too afraid to do anything. No doubt he'd have been glad to help the unfortunate woman, for he was a good man, but he was afraid of arousing somebody's suspicion. Who, at that time, took the part of people who'd been arrested? Even to intervene for them was dangerous. Would it not have been showing a lack of trust in the court? Disagreement with the court's measures? Or did it hide some ties with the accused? And they could have thought that he was an acquaintance of Ramiz's. And this was enough to make any form of generosity step back in fear. It wouldn't help the woman, and it could do him great harm.

Last, he said that if she was innocent, they'd certainly let her go, and, if she was guilty, there was no point in talking. This was an excuse, as old as the earth, not to interfere, even though he knew it didn't hold water. It was a lie that they released the innocent, and he was well aware of this, but he called on the principle of a nonexistent justice in order, with a clear conscience, not to be involved. And, faced with what might happen, he was helpless anyway.

And so both he and I said what we wanted, what we could, what we dared, and nothing was changed. For a while we played with our consciences, although I was truly sorry for the woman, but then Mula Ibrahim told me he'd been looking for me regarding a job. The relatives of the murdered imam from Zhupcha were going to put a headstone on his grave and were looking for someone to compose an epitaph to be carved into the stone. And he'd remembered me. I'd certainly do a good job, and it wouldn't be for nothing. Peasants paid well for death, just as they did for appeals and complaints.

I thanked him, thinking that, instead of affairs of the spirit which brooked no solution, we'd completed practical matters, the things by which one lived, instantly and without trouble. These were the one and only things people could still agree on.

When I told Tiyana that I was off to Zhupcha next day, she shrugged her shoulders and laughed. "I never thought a husband of mine would be writing epitaphs on headstones."

"They offered me to become a mufti, but I refused."

"Just as well. What sort of a mufti's wife would I be?"

Early the next day, I set off for Zhupcha. I walked slowly, bemused by the gleam of the snow in the sun and by the view that opened up on the mountaintops, forgetting the fatigue of legs unaccustomed to long journeys on foot, free from yesterday's troubles in the silence of the wide spaces and the powerful sense of the mountains. We were constricted, we jostled one another in stuffy towns, we hated each other, got in each other's way, while here was the peace of an erstwhile world, pure and untouched, the ancient law of a forgotten beauty, and a mighty peace penetrated the circulation of the blood. From there, everything down there in the valley seemed small and of no importance, in a lower world. Yesterday I'd gone to another unfortunate, to free myself from thoughts concerning the arrested woman, and returned bitter that I'd failed to deceive myself. Today, I'd almost forgotten her. And even if I hadn't, it all seemed easier.

In Zhupcha I was warmly greeted. Mula Ibrahim had warned them of my coming. The imam's brother gave me food and drink and wanted to show me where I could sleep. He was taken aback when I said that I'd not be spending the night and that I'd finish the task right away. He was also somewhat disappointed, since he disapproved of haste in anything and especially in things done for eternity. I calmed him by saying that I'd already planned everything at home and that I'd discussed it with Mula Ibrahim and other learned people and therefore carried several epitaphs in my head, from which we'd choose the best.

I wanted to make everything sound as solemn as possible, in case he thought I was too young and not sufficiently serious for the job. I hadn't a single completed epitaph in my head. All I had was a mass of words of every shade, but I didn't know which might suit the dead imam. As concerned the dead man, of course, it didn't matter. He'd agree to anything I wrote. But I had to satisfy his relations, their vanity, perhaps even their pain, and this was not easy. I'd be safest if I said only the best, but I didn't know what his relatives thought the best was and what they wanted to be recorded.

I asked them, in order to avoid responsibility. But the imam's brother, a hardheaded peasant, slow of speech and impenetrable of thought, made my job all the harder.

"Did he like people?" I said, starting with what I thought was the easy part.

His unexpected reply took me by surprise. "He liked some, he hated others. Like everyone else."

"Did he know what was waiting for him, if he opposed the sultan's order?"

"No way! If he had, he'd never have got mixed up in it. Who'd ever have thought it could have cost anyone their head! No way! How could he have known! We'd agreed, if they pressed, we'd give in."

"But he was certainly a brave man."

"That he wasn't. He was scared of everything."

"Why then was he against supplying the army?"

"What do you mean why? Everybody's against supplying the army. We don't want war, and we haven't anything to give. He only said what everyone else was thinking."

"Then he was a good man."

"It's easy to be a good man. It's hard to remain alive."

"Did he hate authority?"

"God forbid! Why should he hate authority?"

"And you?"

"I what?"

"Do you hate authority? It killed your brother."

"A rock falls and kills a man. Do you hate the rock?"

"These were people, not a rock."

"They weren't people, they were authority."

"Shall we say that the stone has been raised by his brother or by the family?"

"Why write that? Who else would raise it?"

"So what shall I write?"

"Ah, that I don't know."

At a loss, with no idea what to write, bereft of the self-assurance I'd felt earlier, I wrote and crossed out until, apart from the date of birth and death, there remained only a single sentence: "He was a good man and died innocent."

Not even this pleased him. The imam was a good man, that was true, but why mention that he died innocent? Everyone dies innocent. Guilt is only while one's alive.

We agreed, with difficulty, to leave it as "He was a good man and died without guilt. May Allah grant him eternal bliss."

As regards the last sentence, we knew neither what it meant nor what purpose it served, but it sounded solemn and fitting, and it pleased him.

He thanked me, paid me fairly, and I prepared to set off home. But he'd something he wanted to say. I'd already noticed this, but he kept suppressing it, and I thought he'd never say it. Such people were more likely to keep silent than to speak up. All the same, he said, "Do you know Halil Kovachevich?"

"I can't remember ever having heard the name."

"His brother works for Shehaga Socho. He looks after his house."

"I think I've seen him. A tall, thin man."

"Halil would like you to call on him. It's not far, the third house from mine."

"Why?"

"Some man was asking after you."

"What man?"

"I don't know."

I thought that the lost Shehaga had hidden himself in this mountain village and the peasants wanted me to take him home, in order to be rid of him. It was six days since he'd run away.

I immediately recognized Halil Kovachevich. He looked exactly like one of Shehaga's servants. They were as like as two peas.

"I'm Ahmet Shabo. Why did you ask for me?"

"I didn't. We were talking about you, and I wanted to see what you looked like."

"You must have had a reason then."

He looked at me and then at the house. I felt he was hesitating, that he'd made a decision and then changed his mind, still uncertain.

"I'd no special reason," he said smiling sourly as though unaccustomed to it. "I was just talking."

"The imam's brother said there was somebody asking after me."

"Who?"

"How should I know!"

"Ah, yes, so he did, just by the way."

"What did he want?"

"I've no idea."

It seemed he'd changed his mind. He wasn't going to tell me.

"OK," I said. "You've seen me. You've seen your fill, and we've had a good talk. Now I must be off to reach the town before dark."

"Yes, it's a winter day and gets dark early."

I set off down the hill.

"Shall I come part of the way with you?" he asked. And he joined me.

"You wanted to say something and changed your mind." I came straight to the point.

Halil laughed. "Yes, I did, but it didn't seem very important."

"Perhaps it is."

"No."

"Who was it who was asking? Was it Shehaga?"

"What Shehaga? What's he got to do with it?"

"Then who?"

"Who? I don't know. I don't know either who he was or what it was about. He turned up today, quite by chance, and had probably seen you, for he asked, 'Is that Ahmet Shabo?'"

"Was he young, swarthy, skinny?"

"Yes, that could be him."

"Was it Ramiz?"

"I don't know. It could have been."

"Did he ask you to bring me to him?"

"Who? That young man? No, he didn't, he just left straight away."

"Where did he go?"

"I really didn't see."

"OK. If you see him, give him my greetings."

"I don't think I will."

"Look here, Halil, next time, think what you're going to say before you ask someone to call on you. And now I'll be on my way alone, and you go back home."

"And how are things down there, in the town? I mean, generally."

"Generally, they're going here and there, making inquiries, looking for Ramiz. That's how things are."

"And why are they looking for him?"

"I've no idea why they're looking for him, but it'd be just as well that they don't find him."

He remained behind on the hill, lit from without by the sun but retaining his mystery within him, while I hurried toward the town that was wrapped in a gray mist.

This man had got me down, wanting to tell me something and then hiding it. And then he tried to get out of me what had happened, without letting on. I was sure that Ramiz was hiding in his house, had seen me when I entered the village, perhaps even knew that I was coming, and had told him to bring me over. Perhaps at first he'd refused, then agreed and waited for me in front of the house, thinking it over, and, when he'd thought it out, changed his mind and spoken in hints, made sure I recognized Ramiz, but kept himself out of it, passing it off as a chance meeting: He'd arrived, he didn't know from where, asked some questions, and then gone off somewhere or other. I was certain that Ramiz had wanted to see me, but Halil had concluded that it was better this way. Better and safer both for him and for Ramiz. He'd promised Ramiz to bring me to him, stood on his own in front of the house, so Ramiz might see us; now he'd tell him any old lie, that I was in a hurry to get home, that I was scared, that I didn't want to come, and he'd be satisfied with his scheming. He was right. He'd hidden Ramiz to please Shehaga, or his brother, or, perhaps, for the sake of the money he'd received, and he was sufficiently scared at harboring a runaway rebel in his house. All he needed was to start talking about him to all and sundry!

I'd be in the wrong with Ramiz. He'd be hurt.

Then I remembered Mula Ibrahim. Why had he sent me to Zhupcha? Did he know where Ramiz was and had sent me in that direction, without saying a word? Or had Ramiz got a message to him, asking for me to come, why, God alone knew? It would be no use asking. Mula Ibrahim would merely shake his head, deny it, surprised how I could ask such a question, for he knew nothing and didn't want to know.

The cautious Halil had cut all the threads, and a part of the secret remained with many people.

Did I want to see Ramiz? I didn't know. Perhaps I'd just be loading myself with a new danger and a new fear lest someone learn of our meeting. I'd seen it before: one step and numberless consequences.

All the same, I was sorry we hadn't met. I could have asked him many questions about people and about life. I knew what his answers would have been, but perhaps I'd have believed in his goodwill and firm optimism. I needed to believe. I'd have preferred to live with false hope than with certain hopelessness.

But in town Mahmut met me with bad news. He'd been to the house of the arrested woman, to see her sick husband and to take him some food. And he'd walked into a tragedy: The woman had died, in the prison. Who knew how? Of fear, of her illness, or from torture?

Ugly news and a senseless death.

It didn't occur to me to wonder how Mahmut had found the courage to visit a house that was under suspicion. And was his need to help others even more unfortunate than himself really so strong?

■ □ ■ □ ■

CHAPTER 17

THE ETERNAL TRACKER

OSMAN VUK CERTAINLY KNEW EVERYTHING ABOUT THE mystery. Shehaga knew as much as he wished to know, and the *serdar*-Avdaga as much as he'd managed to unravel. And, unfortunately, he'd unravelled a great deal, as though the devil himself had prompted him.

I'd never thought that Ramiz would ever mean more to me than just another man against whom I'd brushed in life, whom I'd noted and pushed to the back of my mind. He'd just passed by, like a friend whom we'd met gladly only to part from without regret, like a woman whom we'd loved and then forgotten even her name. (I said this not from experience, either about the friend or the woman; I'd known few of either. This was what I'd heard Osman say, and I remembered it, surprised by his cheerful cynicism.) Yet, I was bound up with Ramiz's fate to such an extent that I could think of nothing else.

This had been forced on me by the *serdar*-Avdaga.

Time was passing, but he'd not forgotten the rescue. At first I thought his zeal was due to his superiors, but I was mistaken. They had enough on their hands with Shehaga. He'd returned from his wanderings, without saying where he'd been. He arrived without money, horse, or coat, thin, silent, making no reference to his absence. He'd caused them so much trouble, they were so afraid of his hatred that, thinking of their own necks, they'd certainly forgotten both the student Ramiz and the *serdar*-Avdaga. All because of Shehaga's desire, expressed to the *vali*, that they go to hell. I didn't know whether it was exactly expressed in this way, or as a plea, on behalf of the people, in whose name both good and evil were done, to put an end to their tyranny. Anyway, there was a rumor that the *kadi* was to be transferred to the poverty-stricken district of Zvornik, and Dzhemal Zafraniya to Srebrenitsa, and they would both remain there for some time, one like a clapped-out *kadi,* the other as an elderly scribe, that is, unless they were saved by the good fortune of the *vali* being either killed or dismissed. Such cases were neither rare nor unusual, but till now there'd been no sign that this might happen in the near future. Their legs dangled like those of a hanged man as they walked about the town, green with woe and resentment. They wrote letters of protest to Constantinople. They cornered people with threats and supplications to appeal to the highest authority to allow them to remain in Sarajevo, for better servants and greater friends of the people (as if the two could go together) had never been, nor ever would be. They looked for allies and protectors, but all in vain. From Constantinople there came no replies, for no one thought of helping them. They found no allies or protectors, because they'd not sought them when they were strong, but only after they'd gone downhill. And so they baked on the hot fire of Shehaga's hatred and froze in the frost of general indifference, hoping for the impossible: that the hatred and the indifference would turn to favor while they awaited what was inescapable, namely to bow their heads and move off into the dense darkness of a small town, as though into exile.

Shehaga had drowned them like kittens, for no special reason that concerned them, because of ugly things that he'd heard about them, because of their arrogance and belated leniency, and certainly, most of all, because of his hatred of all bureaucrats. For him, these were the worst people on earth, the most harmful and the most corrupt. They supported any power; they were power. They sowed fear without mercy, without any scruples, cold as ice, sharp as knives. Like dogs, they were faithful to any state; like whores, they were unfaithful to every individual. They were the least human of all people. While they were there, there could be no happiness on earth, for they would destroy everything that was of truly human value.

They'd felt Shehaga's hatred and enmity many times, but always at intervals. He'd forget them for long periods, only suddenly recalling their existence when, as it would seem, he remembered his own sufferings. And he'd revenge himself mercilessly on any one of them. For him they were all guilty, all the same, like snakes. Now chance had it that it was the turn of the *kadi* and his chief scribe, and nothing could save them. Everyone knew that the two of them were finished, the moment Shehaga mentioned their names.

The *vali* obeyed Shehaga, because Shehaga made no mention of the *vali*'s repaying what he owed him, leaving it as an earnest for future influence, and because, apart from those in his immediate vicinity, the *vali* took little care for the fate of his officials. What did he care for a *kadi* or a scribe who'd become a nuisance? He'd find hundreds like them, some better some worse, no matter, but there was only one Shehaga.

The *kadi* and Zafraniya were no different from all the others. What set them apart was their bad luck that Shehaga remembered them in one of his dark moods. He remembered them and put his finger on them. Perhaps by chance, like the thunder striking a tree that happens to be five inches taller than the others. And perhaps they'd made a mistake not to have thought earlier of such a possibility, always present and dangerous, like a volcano, and that they'd not tried, by some good word or deed, to avert Shehaga's attention from them, so that this dread man, in a moment of venting his fury, might think of one of their friends and not of them. They'd have been ready to divert his undesired attention even to their own fathers, if only it would pass them by. But there you have it, power had blinded them and robbed them of their senses through a feeling of invulnerability, and Shehaga was only a distant cloud on the horizon. When they realized that this vast, dark cloud carried within it a storm, it was too late.

They defended themselves, even a drowning man does that, flailing his arms on the water that's pulling him down. That they'd written to all sorts of people, begging for help and mercy, even going so far as to reveal the reason for Shehaga's influence, fateful even for the best people (they were hinting at the *vali*, although they didn't consider him one of the best people), merely made matters worse. All bureaucrats, when threatened, write letters, seeking the justice that they forget when they're handing it out. Already under suspicion for seeking mercy, they made an even bigger mistake in presenting themselves as angels and others as devils, for everyone knew they weren't angels, and those devils were usually people of importance that it's unwise to call so, until the time when their position begins to be shaky. Then one may safely call them even vampires. Before that, no way. Now these two were stumbling and becoming objects of ridicule. It was the time of defenselessness, of loneliness, of helpless hatred. Everything they did was wrong, and the murky water carried them away into oblivion. And once again, nothing would change. In their place would come other gray people, and hardly anyone would notice that they were not them. But if, by any miracle, they should rise from the dead, they'd become monsters of cruelty. The human species contains none worse.

Now they were on the slippery slope, these two, taken up by themselves, stunned and offended by the misfortune that had befallen them. And it was no wonder that they could spare no thought for anything else.

But the *serdar*-Avdaga could: without orders, without profit, urged on by an inner need, like a scholar, an artist, a scientific researcher, for the sake of the thing itself, from a

sense of duty, from something for which it would be difficult
to give a rational explanation. His estate was going to wrack
and ruin, while he was unselfishly chasing witches. This was
not an obstinacy called forth by some bad experience, some
misfortune, some hatred that had its root in his life, and this
made it all the harder to comprehend. If anyone would be
praised for what he was doing, he would not. If any were to
receive an award, it would not be he. If any were to gain promotion, he would not. His reward was the contempt and
fear that others bore him. His reward was the pure satisfaction of honestly doing what he had to. He didn't hate those
he pursued, nor had he any clear idea where their guilt lay.
And I thought, what a pity it was that stupid people were
also extremely stubborn. Were he to dig the earth with the
same determination, in a year he'd have removed half of
Mount Trebevich, so it would not hide Sarajevo from the
sun, and people would remember him for a good act. But he
considered it a greater good to catch criminals whose crime
he couldn't comprehend, yet he knew that they'd offended
against the law. He was a fanatical believer in law and order,
whose sense he never questioned, rather as religious believers
never question the meaning of God.

In the name of his faith, he diligently hunted people.

He'd particularly come down on me and on Mahmut.

Every day, in Mahmut's warehouse, he sat silent, watch-
ful, or asked always the same things. Mahmut grew thin,
turned yellow. There were bags under his eyes. He looked
about him like a madman. His hands shook, his legs hurt,
the diarrhea went on, and every few minutes he had to run
out of the warehouse, leaving Avdaga in midsentence, and,
returning exhausted, would obediently take his place in
front of the *serdar* and wait for his torture to be resumed. He
took it all as his fate, as his punishment for his many sins,
even though his atonement was all too severe.

But for some of his sins Avdaga, too, suffered. If he was
killing Mahmut with his suspicion, which Mahmut rejected,

that same suspicion would kill him, too, by the mere fact that he could not establish it.

It seemed as though he'd neglected everything else and forgotten all other criminals, so that the real thieves could only wish for yet another escape from the Fortress. He spent all his time and attention on Mahmut. And on me. Or was it only my impression, namely, that we were the only center of his attention, simply because his presence had become a burden? Tirelessly, he circled by the same paths, spoke with the same people, put the same questions, hoping that in a moment of luck, when the stars were favorable, when God moved one of us, he would find the right stitch by which all would easily be unravelled. He sought real evidence. Having gone over to the Fortress, he'd chat with the ex-commandant and then with the Skakavatses and then with Mahmut and then with me.

He didn't always approach me. He'd come into the coffee-house and sit opposite me, always alone, silent, always deep in thought, never taking his eyes off me, as though he might find in me the thing he needed. Or I'd suddenly feel him behind me, by day or by night, like my shadow, like a lover saddened by unrequited love. At times I'd stop and wait for him, annoyed by this shadowing, always at the same distance, feeling as though I were dragging a weight behind me. I preferred conversation, even if painful. But he, too, would stop, calmly waiting for me to go on and then continue following me. In front of my yard gate, he'd stop, and then I'd hear him slowly striding in front of the house and then departing.

Sometimes he'd come up to me, either talking or standing silent. But he never uttered a single word that didn't touch on Ramiz's rescue. I got used to his following me and questioning me, but in no way could I get used to the same repeated words, the same questions, the same expression on his face. He's sick, I thought. It's an obsession, madness, he can think of nothing else, he lives and dreams it. As I dream of him and his sad, accusing look. Perhaps it was his method of wearing down his victims, yet it had brought him no advantage, because I was always ready for him. But still I didn't find it easy.

I kept changing the time of my going out and my route, but I couldn't avoid him. He'd smell me out, as though I left a scent behind me, and meet me on the street, or await me in some ambush, asking gloomily, "Why were you at Omer Skakavats's? What did you talk about?"

My reply was always the same, just as was his question, but it didn't anger him. He'd keep his eyes on me, as though wondering that I could so stubbornly go on giving the same answer, or he'd lower his eyes, as if ashamed at my lying. And he'd then leave me without even saying good-bye.

I'd become a necessity to him, and for me he was a habit, and I was disturbed if for a whole day I didn't see him. What had happened to my shadow? Had he got on to something else? His insane insistence was not without danger, but I'd grown used to it, and his repetition of the same words and approaches calmed me, being, as yet, without repercussion.

But the town spun around my head when he told me he knew everything concerning me and the Skakavatses.

Had somebody told him?

I replied that it was the first I'd heard of it, and that I was surprised that anyone could think up so many lies, but later I thought with horror that I might have given myself away by fear, by some careless word, by some unawaited weariness and resignation such as when, possibly, one abandons the struggle. But this was only the distorted memory after the fact, the relived fear of utter surprise, the momentary loss of breath at this change of customary method.

I took immediate control of myself, refusing to submit.

But how much did he really know?

He kept me wondering for some time, and then, one morning, he met me on the street and asked me to go with him. We walked through the town in silence, without exchanging a word, he because he didn't wish it, I because I didn't dare. His silence frightened me, and I was afraid he might sense my fear, were I to ask where he was taking me and why, or were I to begin any general conversation. This new tactic of his, the purpose of which was unclear, disturbed me.

I grew cold at the though that he might be taking me to the Fortress, and I was relieved when he took me to his room.

I'd been there before. Everything looked like him, oppressive, silent, repellent, dangerous, only now it seemed both colder and harsher.

He sat down opposite me and, for some time, looked at his clutched fingers. And then, without preamble or superfluous words, without looking at me, he stated that he knew everything and was disappointed that I refused to confess. I'd taken part in a crime, and he would have had me arrested, but he'd then have respected my honesty and sincerity. (I thought I'd rather he didn't respect me than that he'd have me arrested.)

When I asked what this crime was, of which I knew nothing, he shook his head reproachfully and gave me a complete account of the rescue from beginning to end.

My legs gave way, and my stomach surged, as if I were Mahmut.

What he said was the following: Osman Vuk, himself or with Shehaga's knowledge, more likely the latter than the former, had planned Ramiz's rescue. He didn't know why they'd done it. Perhaps because they agreed with Ramiz or perhaps in order to spite authority, but this didn't matter, and was none of his business. They'd bought the services of old Omer and his three sons, no doubt for a considerable amount, to get Ramiz out of the Fortress. They'd sent Mahmut to the commandant with the money to bribe him to let the Skakavatses into the Fortress. They'd got in without trouble, through the open gates, beat up the guards, and carried off Ramiz on horseback in an unknown direction. Unknown only for a while, because Ramiz would give himself away. He couldn't stay quiet. After the rescue, Omer's youngest son got drunk in Zayko's inn and began to let everything out. He boasted that he and one other knew who'd rescued Ramiz. The porter Muyo Dushitsa didn't exactly remember whom the young man had mentioned, but when he was asked whether it could have been Osman Vuk, he replied that it could have. Zayko had reported this to Osman, and Osman had sent me to the old Skakavats to tell him about his son. The two younger Skakavatses had immediately taken a horse and fetched their brother home. He didn't know what had taken place between them. All he knew was that they'd killed him. We were all at the funeral.

Not believing my ears, I listened to the true story of the rescue. There were a few unimportant gaps, but we were all there in the right places.

This was what he'd put together, piece by piece!

"Isn't that it?" he asked almost cheerfully.

"I've no idea," I replied, my head buzzing. "I can only speak for myself and say it's not. I've told you a hundred times that I know nothing about it."

"And a hundred times you've lied."

"Look here, Avdaga, it's none of my business, but to me your story sounds very doubtful. The porter doesn't remember, nobody knows anything, there are no witnesses, yet you speak as if you'd seen it all yourself."

"I've been twenty years in this job. I know people, and I know who can do what."

"All right then, Avdaga," I said angrily, "why don't you have us arrested, if you know everything?"

He raised his thick eyebrows, regaining his former gloom. "I know everything, but I can't touch you. I've no real proof. The Skakavatses won't talk. Muyo Dushitsa doesn't remember. Mahmut goes dumb at the mere mention of the commandant. You're keeping quiet. And not even the *kadi* will do anything against Shehaga. He's still hoping he won't be driven out of Sarajevo. But is it right that a crime should go unpunished?"

"Do you know what Ramiz did?"

"I know that he spoke against the authorities and that he was arrested. The rest doesn't interest me. But I know who got him out of the Fortress. That's a crime. And if crime is not to be punished, then the world's at an end. I've nothing against you, but against what you've done. And I'll find proof. And then I won't help you, because you haven't helped me. I'd have told the *kadi* that you knew nothing and that you served them as a messenger, without knowing what you were doing. This way, I won't."

"Do what you conscience tells you. But I'm not going to lie."

"I'll tell you this: I'll soon have proof. One of Omer Skakavats's sons has already begun to talk. And if the *kadi* agrees to arrest all three of them, together with you and Mahmut, we'll soon get to know everything. And he'll agree, because that'll help him."

"I've told you once, it's easy to strike at the poor, Avdaga."

"If those poor people talk as they should, and they will, then I hope no one will remain unpunished. No one! I know what you're thinking, and I'm not afraid of anyone's name or position. All I care about is justice."

"Looking for justice, you may commit an injustice!"

He made no reply. He merely gestured for me to go.

I left on wooden feet that fell hard on the uneven cobble-stones. I was struck by his openness. Was he so certain that caution and cunning were no longer necessary? He'd got to the truth, and he'd even get to justice. His justice. He was dangerous because of his stubbornness and the fact that he believed he could save the world. A determined tracker, he exhausted both himself and others, cruel but in no way petty, of limited intelligence but of strong will, honest in his way, without hypocrisy, without self-interest, pure in his unfounded devotion and terrible for the very reason that he was such. He knew not what he served, but he served it well. He knew not why he punished, but he punished severely. Maybe he'd grown accustomed to one law, but he'd have scarcely noticed had it been replaced by another. He was born long ago, aeons ago, and would be born again in every time. He was eternal. And his passion, through the centuries, was ever the same: to hunt down the disobedient, and if those disobedient came to power, to pursue the new disobedient. And I wondered, for his sake, whether the man was honorable or dishonorable if he employed honorable means to evil ends. And was he honorable or dishonorable if he employed dishonorable means to honorable ends?

I thought about all this later, but at the time all I felt was fear, both defined and undefined. Were Avdaga to find what he was looking for, and he certainly would, my skin wasn't worth a ram's fleece. But over and around this direct hazard, like fog and darkness, I was encompassed by an incalculable menace. It was as though a hundred shadows and a hundred pairs of eyes were around me, inescapable and unbearable, their circle ever narrower, their proximity ever more oppressive, as though I were revolving in helplessness, seeing neither a way out nor salvation. And all these innumerable eyes and shadows were Avdaga's. He'd grown a hundredfold, become an army of specters. And it was this feeling of helplessness that was worse than what I knew, than what I could easily think about. Such a stroke of fate is not for thinking about; one bears it as a weight, as a sickness.

I'd experienced that panic before, in the war, in the darkness, in the open, in the dense forest. I'd seen no one, heard no voice, but the danger was everywhere around me, and I could not determine its form, or its proximity, or its intention, and this made it all the more terrible. Faced with the terror of an unknown foreboding, the reason is powerless to soothe, as is the eye in complete darkness.

And who knows how long I'd have gone on indulging in

cowardice, had I not grown disgusted with myself and spat on my womanly weakness. To hell with this imagined fear! I was a man, not a dead target awaiting a bullet. I could not face misfortune on my knees: for my own sake, for my shame, for the others who had faith in me and who would be disappointed.

I'd done little, but what I'd done, I'd done intentionally. Why should I besmirch even that little?

I'd not tremble nor would I fear!

And did the worst really have to happen?

Avdaga knew everything, but was doing nothing (I thought more calmly), and was leading me to confess to make his own job easier. Yes, but I wouldn't confess, nobody would, and Avdaga would follow me to his dying day, repeating his questions ever more faintly. He was the one who'd die from frustration, rather than I from torment.

Or would Shehaga do something to stop him? He'd remember him when his hatred piled up in his heart, as poison accumulates in a viper, and so another's vengeance would bury both the *serdar* and our guilt.

Bringing this danger down to earth, among ordinary people, I could look at it with more courage. It was not without significance, but it was in perspective. I realized its range and its threat, but I no longer felt desperate.

Avdaga was trying to destroy me, but I'd fight to preserve my skin intact. It wasn't worth much, but it was all I had and served me well, and it would be of no use to him. He was preparing my ruin, and I could only wish him to fail. Considering our powers, mine negligible and his unlimited, it would be well if he weren't to gain anything and I to lose nothing. It was an uneven bet. I was betting my all, he not a thing. For him, failure meant only defeat; for me it meant the end of everything. So, better he suffer defeat than I experience the end. My life meant something to me, his failure meant nothing.

Relieved by the desire to preserve my life and the determination not passively to wait for a knife in the back, I went to find Osman Vuk. I'd thought of him the moment I decided for self-defense. If anyone could stop Avdaga, it was he.

I found him in Mahmut's warehouse, which was full of wool that I hadn't seen before. He was supervising the baling.

Mahmut was limping about, testing the strings, quite unnecessarily, but clearly trying to show his expertise and keenness in front of Osman. To be honest, he'd more keenness than expertise, so Osman rechecked everything, making sure all was firm and tight.

"The wool's for Venice," Mahmut informed me, as it seemed to me, in a tone of regret. "Osman and Shehaga are going there."

"Why didn't you ask them to take you with them?" I asked, realizing that he was unhappy.

He shrugged. Who'd take him!

And he went off to jerk the string on the bales.

"Where have you been? You could have been helping." Osman laughed.

"I wanted to talk to you."

"Let's just finish this."

"I'd like to now, at once."

"There's a lot of things I'd like to do, too."

But he led the way into Mahmut's little room. I followed him and closed the door.

"Will it take long?"

"As you will."

"Then cut it short! I'm busy."

"I've had a talk with Avdaga."

"Well, well! It's not the first time!"

He could joke now. He'd be more serious when I told him what I had to say.

"Avdaga knows everything. It's given me a shock."

Mahmut came in, regarding us humbly, gripped by curiosity. He'd have given a year of his life to know what we were talking about.

"Do you need anything? Would you like some coffee?"

"We don't need anything," Osman cut him off rudely, "we're talking."

Mahmut left, dejected. Our talk was the reason he'd come in in the first place.

I told Osman what Avdaga had said about the rescue, leaving nothing out. He listened without interrupting me, but with a sardonic attention that surprised me. I'd expected him to be considerably more worried.

He even laughed aloud when I'd finished, which I certainly didn't expect.

"What did he say? Mahmut had a talk with the commandant! A lot he knows. He's miles off!"

"Then who had?"

"A little bird!"

"Why are you keeping everything from me? You surely don't think I'd tell anyone."

"I don't, mate, you're not mad enough. It was Muharem-*bayraktar* who dealt with the commandant. Does that make you feel any better?"

"Why him?"

"He hates them all. And he knows the commandant well, they were together in the war, one old, the other young. Now they're both old."

Muharem-*bayraktar!* And poor Mahmut had shat his guts out, for no reason at all! And what about the rest? Was he wrong about them?

"He wasn't wrong about you."

"Avdaga's dangerous and is getting more so."

"I know."

"What are we going to do?"

"Put our hopes in God."

"If that's our only hope, we've had it."

Osman laughed, giving me a friendly pat on the knee. "Not even the devil's as black as he's painted."

And cheerfully, without the least sign of worry, he went off to supervise the men binding the wool into bales.

On my way out I saw Mahmut talking to Osman and giving me a sorrowful look, because he hadn't been able to ask me what we were talking about. He couldn't bear secrets, his own or other people's, and what irritated him most was when he came upon a secret by chance, without knowing what it was all about.

But what could I have told him? That he was innocent and that Avdaga was mistaken? This he knew better than anyone, and it didn't help him much. While to tell him that he was suffering because of the *bayraktar* Muharem never even crossed my mind. He wouldn't be proud that they'd replaced him with the heroic *bayraktar*, and he might wish to get rid of his diarrhea and to get rid of the *serdar*-Avdaga by telling him the real name of the person he was looking for.

I didn't know. Perhaps it would have been right for him to be freed of an unjust burden, or perhaps it wouldn't. But there it was, it depended on me whether Mahmut should be the guilty one or the *bayraktar*. Were I to tell him, I'd relieve Mahmut of a torment that was beginning to get him down, but I'd then have destroyed another unfortunate. What was the better? What was the worse? If I were to tell Mahmut the truth, and he didn't keep it to himself, the *serdar*-Avdaga would grasp with both hands the proof he'd been looking for, for so long, and would begin to unravel the entire business. The *bayraktar* would either die under torture or confess. God alone knew how many people would suffer. But this way, Mahmut would be linked with us all, unjustly indeed, but the danger would be less. Better leave things as they were! Mahmut would know nothing and could give nothing away. Anything else would make matters worse.

But this decision did nothing to calm me. No matter how wise my decision might be, it was not right. It meant I'd left an innocent man to suffer and, by this very fact, perhaps condemned him. I comforted myself that, if everything came out, I'd tell the truth about him, and so save him at the last moment. But my feeling of guilt toward my friend was unabated.

To decide the fate of others was hard. I was bad at that fashioning of justice, which always contained at least some small measure of injustice, no matter to whom. I'd never wanted to have to judge between people, for in that there was no justice.

And now I was forced to judge and felt like a leper: guilty before myself and others.

And I was worried, too, by Osman's behavior when he heard that Avdaga knew everything. He'd laughed unconcernedly and left it all to God's mercy. It was all right for him to put his faith in a divine mercy in which he didn't believe any more than I did when he was protected by the broad umbrella of a Shehaga. Did it mean that he was leaving the rest of us to our threadbare luck? I couldn't believe in such ruthlessness, although from him anything might be expected. But, equally, I couldn't believe that he was thoughtless, since it would go ill both with him and Shehaga were the whole truth to come out.

Why, then, had he received my news so carelessly? Especially since he himself knew that Avdaga was becoming increasingly dangerous?

I spent three uncomfortable days, saying nothing to Tiyana. Like all the others, I, too, became a closed and besieged fortress, frowning and mute. What could I have told her? I'd have only upset her unnecessarily. To share our anxieties would have been no help. At least let her be spared.

Indeed, in her presence, I tried to appear as cheerful and free of care as usual. But, as usual, I failed to deceive her. Be it that worry lent an artificial set to my smile or that I simply was no good at pretending, she noticed that I was not as I usually was.

"What's the matter?" she asked me worriedly.

"What should be the matter? I'm all right."

The first time she accepted my denial, but that evening she was more decisive.

"Why don't you tell me what's the matter? You're hiding something."

"I'm not hiding anything. Why should I?"

"You haven't fallen in love with another girl? And you won't tell me, because you're sorry for me."

Do women explain everything by love?

I laughed bitterly. That love of mine bore the name of the *serdar*-Avdaga!

"What do you mean, woman, falling in love? Get away with you!"

"If it's happened, don't hesitate to tell me. I'd rather know than be left in doubt. I'd not be surprised. I've grown ugly, I can see for myself."

"You've grown more beautiful, not more ugly. And I've never loved you so much."

I said this with feeling, for it was the truth. She was my only shelter, but she, too, was under threat together with me. What would happen to her if they arrested me?

She grew calmer, accepting my word.

"Then what's the matter with you? There's something wrong, for sure."

"I'm fed up because I can't find a job. I'm hanging about, like the lowest lout. How long can we go on like this?"

She accepted my explanation cheerfully, reproaching me for lack of faith and consoling me that I'd certainly find a job. For the moment I'd no need to worry. With the money we had and which she would make go a long way, we could live for a whole year, if we had to. Not well, but still we'd live. We were young and healthy, what more did we need! If that was our only worry, then it was the least.

Of course, it wasn't the least of her worries, but she bravely suppressed her anxiety for my sake, to calm and console me, not knowing that this was not my greatest worry either.

She'd failed to cure my real ailment, but her loyalty touched me. She was a cure in herself and as lovely and dear as love itself.

And then, when I no longer needed to, I told her all about Avdaga.

She became rather thoughtful, but that evening she'd seemed determined to preserve her courage to the end. She belittled my guilt at the onset of danger. She would have increased it by calling it a merit had they been offering rewards for such a role.

She found it easy to defend me. "You don't even know what really happened. How can you be guilty?"

Her reasoning was not particularly convincing, but at least it helped me to go to sleep more calmly.

But then the whole thing was solved by an event that no one could have foreseen.

The third day after our uncomfortable conversation, the *serdar*-Avdaga was killed by the Dariva Bridge, sometime after evening prayers. It was said that the bandit Bechir Toska waylaid Avdaga, while he was returning from the commandant's through a dark gorge, and shot him dead.

I learned about it the next morning from the workers in the bakery and, forgetting even to buy the bread, hurried to find Mahmut.

He met me full of excitement, almost beside himself with joy.

"It's true, it's true!" was his delighted reply to my question. "I was coming here this morning and wondering whether the *serdar*-Avdaga would come again today, when there was Abaz the joiner. 'Have you heard?' he said. 'The *serdar*-Avdaga's been killed.' For a moment I could scarcely speak. I wanted to ask about it, to say something, to be surprised, but all I could do was to wheeze. And Abaz said he was killed by the Dariva Bridge, shot, they say, by Bechir Toska, who killed him and then calmly returned to the mountains. The commandant had heard horses' hooves just at that time. That was what Abaz said, and I listened, getting a grip on myself, wanting to laugh, wanting to put my arms round him. I'd never been so happy since my son was born. Then I hurried to the warehouse, locked myself in, and began to walk up and down between the sacks of grain and the bales of wool. I laughed, saying to myself, 'He's gone!' Just that: 'He's gone!' As if I'd gone mad with happiness. And then I remembered and knelt down here on the settee and thanked God: 'Oh merciful God, I thank thee for croaking that monster! For years I've neglected you, forgive me, but thou art generous, unlike some heartless people. Thou sawest how the brute was torturing me, and thou leapt to my aid, just when I needed it. You took your time about it! And if you'd been a bit longer, I'd not have needed anybody's help, not even yours.' There's no doubt, there is justice in the world, dear Ahmet!"

"I heard it at the baker's, and I haven't taken it in yet."

"I was just thinking of coming to you with the good news, and here you are! And good luck to both of us!"

"And how did Bechir Toska come to be so near to the town? And just at the time when the *serdar*-Avdaga was passing!"

"I don't care. That's not important. What's important, more important than anything else on earth, is that I shan't ever have to look at the door and die every time somebody touches the handle. Now let anyone come who wants to! Come in, everyone! Today I'm a new man!"

As my thoughts were wandering over how strange was this world, where a man could rejoice over the death of another, be liberated by it, Osman Vuk came into the warehouse. He looked serious.

"Have you heard about the *serdar*-Avdaga's death?" he asked us both.

"We have, thank God for it!" Mahmut replied happily.

"It's a bad thing to rejoice at another's death," Osman reproached him. "No matter what he was in life, he's dead now and all one should say is 'May he rest in peace.'"

"I'm glad that I can say 'May he rest in peace!' Ahmet asked a moment ago, 'Who killed him?' And I said, 'God's mercy.' He was a curse to God and men."

"They say Bechir Toska killed him. How did Bechir turn up just at that time?"

Osman gave me a quick look. His eyes were gray and cold. He said, as though it were a threat rather than an expression of resignation, "It was God's will. Or Avdaga's misfortune."

And then, at that moment, I was sure that it was he who'd killed Avdaga. I'd wondered before, now I was certain. It was his words, common enough, but not his, the menacing warning I sensed in his voice, the cold gleam in his narrowed eyes, the thought that arose in me without a shade of doubt. It was as if two beams, one from my brain, one from his, had met and crossed as we thought of the same thing. Between us there were no more secrets.

And, immediately after this, he told Mahmut that there would be several loads of wool coming that day and that he should prepare ropes and binding.

I looked after him, to see what a killer looked like in peacetime (in the war, we called them heroes). And I saw nothing unusual: handsome, calm, businesslike, engaged in the affairs of today, untouched by yesterday. I didn't know his inner state, but I wouldn't have said he was disturbed, or that he was thinking of the man he'd killed. If he did think about him, then he did it with satisfaction: He'd completed an important business, removed a serious obstacle; danger no longer hung over his head.

If ten such ruthless men joined together, they could rule the world. The great majority were weaklings, like me. What could we do against them?

Mahmut looked cruel, but wasn't. He was as direct as a child. He was almost dancing with happiness, brought to him by another's misfortune, and thanked his forgotten God for freeing him from a misery against which he was incapable of defense. Osman put more faith in his own skill than in the mercy of God. He didn't wait helplessly for chance to aid him; he cruelly cut the knots that were being woven around him and calmly went on his way.

He hadn't done the killing himself, but it was his doing. Who knows how many were the go-betweens between him and the death he desired? Between his intention, which had arranged that death, and that last man who'd pulled the trigger, there was a whole chain of unknown people. That last man had probably never heard of Osman. But, without Osman, Avdaga would still have been alive. Osman was his evil fate.

As I was going, he called after me. "Shehaga wants to see you. He said you're to come at once."

I went out onto the street and walked with my eyes on the ground, avoiding people, so as not to hear the talk about the dead Avdaga. I'd rather not have thought of him, but I couldn't stop.

No more would he appear at the end of the street, tall, gaunt, with grim eyes that saw everything. Never again would he intercept me to ask what I'd talked to the old Omer Skakavats about, nor would I awake sad because the day would bring me an encounter with him.

But I felt no joy. I only thought: Was it I who killed him?

I wanted to be free of fear and danger, but I hadn't wished for his death.

Fearing later repentance, I mercilessly inquired of myself whether, nonetheless, in my subconscious I'd not expected just such an outcome? For could it have been otherwise? Could Osman have convinced him, bribed him, or frightened him? Certainly not. Avdaga would have rejected any of it with contempt. What then was there left to the ruthless Osman Vuk? To put his faith in luck and the mercy of God, as he had said sarcastically at the same time as he was planning murder? No, that wasn't Osman. He found the solution in what he'd done; there was no other. Neither for Osman nor for Avdaga. Had Avdaga been more intelligent, he'd have been scared. Had he been less honest, he'd have taken the money. Had he been less diligent, he'd have given up. But he was what he was, and only death could stop him. And that death only Osman could have planned.

And I knew all this, just as I knew both of them. What did I want then, what was I thinking?

I turned it over in my mind, raked and ransacked, seeking that hidden intention, and not finding it, certain that it had not existed. There could have been no other solution. I could see that now, yet I hadn't thought of it even for a moment. I could have thought, but I didn't.

How could a man so completely hush his conscience? How could one snap off one's thoughts, like a thread, and forbid oneself from thinking of the consequences, not wishing to be aware of them? It would appear that one could. Instinct defends us with complete oblivion, to save us the torture of responsibility. I'd left everything to others, in this case to Osman, for him to solve, without me, without my participation!

If this was so, and there was no other explanation, then man was a somewhat unpleasant creature, even when he was not aware of what he was doing. Because he didn't want to be aware!

But cunning instinct had succeeded nonetheless, for though I felt rather bad about it, still I didn't feel responsible. I couldn't be responsible for something that was neither my conscious idea nor my decision. I even thought that it could all have happened without me (how often it had!), for Osman knew all about Avdaga. It was most unlikely that he was waiting for my warning and only then made up his mind.

Thus did my partial thinking, my faithful defender, seek new ways of relieving my conscience. And my conscience seized upon this defense, indeed, with a shade of vague doubt and with some discomfort, for the sake of honor, but was well on the way to being completely pacified.

When I told Tiyana about Avdaga's death, she said bitterly, "How stupid people are! They do evil, and so they get it back."

Once she'd said, "How unhappy people are."

Now she believed that every evil should be punished. She couldn't and had no wish to think differently, when she was creating her own family unit.

And so, one death and so many opinions about it. And nobody cared about the death, only about their thoughts concerning it.

Shehaga Socho invited me to go with him to Venice, since a young man should see some of the world, since then he, Shehaga, would not be on his own, and because he wanted to take me into his service. Should I not want to be taken into his service, even though it was high time I got myself a job, the journey would do me no harm. It would make it easier to face life in this misery. He'd leave me money for Tiyana, and she could either go on living in our present flat or move into his house. This latter he considered to be the best. She'd have her own room and servants, no worries, and could chat with his wife when she wished and if she wished. The two of them would get on well. Of Tiyana he'd heard the very best (From whom had he heard? From Osman?), and his wife was an angel. If she wept for her son (she could never forget him and spoke with him as if he were alive), let Tiyana comfort her or leave her alone, she'd not hold it against her. And he'd feel easier to know she had someone they knew with her. If Tiyana liked it there, we could stay, it would be better for the child. The yard was spacious, the house large, and there was another smaller one, next to it, where we could live. We'd be no trouble to him or his wife, nor they to us, he hoped. Nor would the child trouble them, when it was born. Let it cry and scream, anything was better than an empty house.

He referred to his son as if he were the subject only of his wife's grief, but I knew he couldn't forget him, either. He was taking me in his place. Somehow he linked us together. We were in the same war. We were the same age, born in the same month. We'd committed the same madness, only with different results. He'd tried to subdue his grief with hatred; now he was trying to soothe it by caring for others. He'd not succeed, I feared. Perhaps his sadness might grow even harder at the sight of our happiness, but he was looking for a cure, like a terminally ill person who'd nothing to lose.

I'd not let him come to hate me when he was disappointed, seeing that the cure didn't help. I'd remove myself before it came to that, but, for the time being, I couldn't refuse.

I was touched by the sadness that he tried unsuccessfully to conceal and by his seeking for a peace that he couldn't find. Nor would he find it now. I couldn't be someone else, nor that which he held in his memory, and the shadow of his dead son would always be dearer to him and better than I, living. But I'd be a relief to him, if only for a short time. And that was at least something.

So, let it be, I'd set out on that journey of hope. I'd simply be there, and the rest would be up to him. He'd make of it what he needed.

CHAPTER 18

DEATH IN VENICE

SHOULD I HAVE SET OUT ON THIS LONG JOURNEY? I WENT almost unthinkingly, without any special desire or need, for the sake of another. And perhaps I'd gain from seeing this strange Frankish world. I say perhaps, because I didn't believe it. Apart from merchants, travelling was only for those disturbed people unable to remain alone with themselves, who chased after the new sights that an unknown world offered to their eyes while their hearts remained empty.

What would I see there, happiness or monstrosity? I couldn't take a single morsel of happiness with me, and no alien monstrosity would console me for the monstrosity in which I lived. Still, perhaps.

But the further I got from Sarajevo and from Bosnia, the more I was gripped by an ever greater sense of insecurity, almost a fear, particularly at dusk and at night. There was no visible reason for this. I feared nothing definite; yet my apprehension constantly increased. It was as though everything inside me had been displaced, as though I were suffering from some unknown illness that consisted not of pain, but of fear. I felt empty inside, a sadness. Everything was foreign. The country was sad, the people cold, the sky distant, the world unsafe, my thoughts disturbed.

All that I saw was not mine. It was shut away, unreachable. I grew more and more perturbed.

I remember well that, at moments of extreme insecurity, the most ordinary things caused me disquiet. We were approaching the coast. The Bosnian snow was some two days behind us, harsh but dear to me, now that distance had melted it. The gray rocky ground made me feel sick, and then, on a hill, I saw a typical house with a flat stone roof, a pathetic yard, fenced in by a wall of stones, and the dark figure of an old woman standing out on the background of a cloudy sky. She was shouting to someone I couldn't see, alone, in the desperate expanse of rocks. In different circumstances, I'd have thought she was calling a neighbor or one of her household, about cattle or whatever. But then, it was a picture of despair. I looked at her, saddened, unable to resist the onset of apprehension and horror: the last man, alone on earth, all else had turned to stone, crying his misery to the sky.

What was I doing here, I wondered in panic. What was anyone doing anywhere?

Later, I grew accustomed to this feeling of sadness. When our armed escort left us at the coast, I envied them, thinking them the happiest people on earth, because they were going back to Sarajevo, which I was leaving ever further behind. And I felt more and more insecure, as though I'd pulled up the root that held me to one place. I was no longer anywhere.

I thought of Tiyana with a painful longing. The distance between us, the empty time spent without her, tormented me. I'd been alone and lost until I found her. It was a lucky star that had led me to her. I was lifeless, and she gave me life, more generously even than to the child she was bearing. I'd been shaken by the war and by life. She'd given me security, but limited to the time when I was with her. She was the earth that nurtured me with its juices, she was the air I breathed, the sunny side of my life.

Why had I parted from her?

I thought of silly old Mahmut, who'd wept seeing me off, perhaps because he wasn't going to Venice, or perhaps because we'd not see each other for a long time. And I thought of the dead *serdar*-Avdaga, who'd not allowed me to feel empty or bored, and of the good and frightened Mula Ibrahim, who was delighted at this journey, not knowing how hard it would be for me. And I thought of my ugly room, which now seemed to me to be the finest place on earth, of my downtrodden alley with its leaning fences. I thought of everything that was mine, worthless yet dear to me.

I thought, and I was sad.

Luckily my back ached from riding, my stomach rose from the heaving of the boat, the high waves and the wide open sea frightened me, and so the torments of the body mercifully saved me from those of the spirit.

Shehaga was braver and more resilient than I. He was more accustomed to the doubtful beauties of travel, and in any case he was a different character. I never knew what to expect from myself, while he held himself in control and did only what his pride allowed him, save when sadness took over. Indeed, I didn't know whether his face was a true reflection of his inner feelings, but his pleasant smile and calm gray expression revealed to me a new Shehaga, as if the journey had changed him. He was animated, interested in all he saw, politely and cheerfully dealing with people, complaining neither at lodging nor food, strangely enlivened, as though expecting something particular from this journey.

He would meet me with the kind smile of a friend. He didn't speak of unpleasant things, nor mention his hatred. Nor was he excessively withdrawn. He spoke of his son and of his grief for him, briefly and restrainedly, it is true, but for one of his reluctance to reveal himself, quite unexpected. He also spoke about me, about my future with many children, advising me not to gamble with fate by having only one, with an occupation that would absorb me, and with a loving family that would serve me as a fortress where I could withdraw from the world. Nothing was more important than one's peace and the happiness that one created for oneself.

Hence, one should guard it, that happiness, encompass it with entrenchments and allow none to threaten it. Let me take no care for others. Life was cruel, people evil, and one should hold them at a distance. Keep them as far as possible from what was yours and what was dear to you!

I didn't agree with his ideas, which rose from experience that gave a man wisdom when it was no longer necessary. Wisdom and experience are a burden rather than an advantage.

It would stop you at every stride, spoil your every attempt, offer you numberless proofs that it was better to remain silent, to do nothing, to ignore what went on. All wisdom and all experience would refute the actions of the student Ramiz. But Ramiz offered people hope. Wisdom was both cowardly and desperate. Experience was valuable only for crawling through life. It rejected what is, yet put nothing in its place. Only lack of experience and madness lent man wings. He who neglected the experience of others would crash to earth, that's true. But he would have flown— risen above the clay and left a memory that wouldn't die. Were there more of that courageous madness, perhaps the ancient experience would have ceased to frighten us.

I said nothing to him of what I thought, for his own experience was too painful, and it would have been cruel to have contradicted him with empty assertions of principle, which I myself did not follow in life.

On the boat I noted a change in Shehaga. Suddenly he withdrew into himself, staying alone more than before. He spoke less and without his former confidence, almost as if he were afraid, occupied with something deep inside him. Or he'd stop in midsentence, eyes wide open, startled, as though he'd recalled something painful or as though listening to some voice that only he heard. It would last only a moment. Later, I doubted whether it had even happened, but my own disquiet assured me that I was not mistaken.

I thought that this was due to his memories, from which he couldn't escape. If it were so, it would have been bad for me and for him. We'd have become unbearable to one another. But whenever he came out of his gloomy isolation, he was as pleasant as ever, and I threw off doubts. I lacked both strength and courage to have him look kindly on me beside the dead son, newly brought to life in his heart.

And perhaps his momentary absences were merely the result of physical discomfort, due to a heavy sea. We had a south wind all the way and the boat heaved from stem to stern.

Slightly worried, I asked him, "Is the sea always like this in winter?"

"Usually."

"Why do you come every year?"

"I love Venice. It's jolly, especially now, in the carnival season."

Why should the carnival appeal to him?

"But what about when there isn't a carnival? I bet it's as boring as it is at home."

"It's always boring at home."

"Don't you like Bosnia?"

"No."

"Then why don't you settle in Venice?"

"Perhaps I'd come to hate it, too. It's better as it is."

Was this pilgrimage of his to a foreign land a mere habit, a repetition of what he'd always done, an escape from himself and his sadness? This I didn't know. Or was it because of some love connection that, be it only temporarily, freed him from his constant tension? His preoccupation with this foreign city seemed to me out of place, because exaggerated, as though out of spite.

Venice, he said, was like a piece of lace, made to be looked at, created for enjoyment; there one was free to be oneself. Open to everything human, it was a city of mature people who were neither ashamed nor afraid of what they did, who accepted human weakness as reality and regarded human nobility as a welcome addition. They had few laws, but strict and just ones, and they knew that the more laws there were, the more criminals they'd have. They had few rulers, and therefore few gluttons. They punished, but only for real crimes, and without prejudice and without unnecessary cruelty. Everyone cared for the state, and all gave taxes according to their ability and paid special attention to schools and to the beauty of their city. There were rich people, but no paupers. There were injustices, but no violence. There were prisons, but no torture chambers. The citizens elected the government, but they replaced it at least every three years. They consulted about everything, which was why they were powerful. They hadn't created a paradise, but they had arranged life as well as possible.

Could such a place be? I thought in surprise.

It was my nose that told me about this, Shehaga's paradise. The canals into which the filth of this strange city was poured unmercifully stank to high heaven, and over the still water hung a mist that bore a stench of moldiness, as if the wind never blew through this human settlement with so much water and so little land.

Somehow, Shehaga's paradise seemed rather doubtful. Perhaps he'd linked this ideal picture of life, as he imagined and desired it, to this city, without any justification, from a pure wish that such a place should exist, so he might think of it when faced with our poverty, be consoled when regarding our misery. And perhaps it was a part of his vengeance: See how they can do it in Venice! And perhaps it was something more than this: a belief and a desire that somewhere there might be a city, a country, where life was not torment and injustice. And if it could be in one place, why not in another? This imagined city was the product of a desire that it should be. It didn't exist, but he refused to accept the fact.

This journey, so it seemed, was a pilgrimage to his beautiful dream.

"Isn't it beautiful?" he said, as I watched old porters huddled against the walls of the houses, sheltering from the wind.

Did they care about the state or about a piece of bread?

Did they believe this was paradise? Were these wondrous palaces built for their enjoyment? Was it they who replaced governments? Were they consulted when affairs of state were discussed?

There were the rich, and so there were the poor.

It was easy to desire a city of dreams. It was hard to imagine it in reality, even harder to retain one's faith in it.

How had Shehaga managed to preserve the picture of what he desired?

I'd ask him later, when I myself understood what it was I wanted to ask him.

We were met on the quay by Osman Vuk, who had already arrived with the wool. He wanted to start talking business right away, but Shehaga interrupted him with a tired wave of the hand: Later!

Osman Vuk led us to a hotel on the Grand Canal. Shehaga's room was large, with a hall; mine was smaller and next door to his.

I unpacked, had a wash, and went to Shehaga to discuss how we should spend the day. I was surprised to find him lying on his bed, fully clothed.

"Aren't you feeling well?"

"I think I'll have a little rest." He smiled. "Age forgives no one. There was a time when the journey was nothing."

"Try to sleep. I'll come later."

Osman was sitting in a small lounge on the first floor. He knew that Shehaga was lying down, but seemed more disappointed than worried. When I said that Shehaga was tired from the journey, he shook his head doubtfully.

"If that was all, he wouldn't have lain down. A man doesn't come all the way from Bosnia to Venice just to go to his room, does he? I don't like the look of his face. I don't like it at all."

He repeated this when we went into my room. Why should this happen to him now of all times, he complained. And it didn't take much to get out of him that he'd arranged with some Greeks and a Herzegovinian to play dice that evening. And there you are, he wouldn't be able to, and this meant he'd lose quite a lot of money, for the simple reason that Shehaga would definitely need him, if he'd caught cold or a stomach infection, and, another thing, he'd got the money for the wool they'd sold on him, and one didn't carry that amount of money with one at night, especially in Venice. That's just what happens when one's poor and unlucky. And last night he'd lost on purpose so as to draw the Greeks on for tonight.

"What do you mean, you're poor? You earn enough. What do you do with it?"

"I've a hole in my pocket, and money just vanishes the moment I get it."

"What do you spend it on? Women?"

"What don't I spend it on!"

"And what if tonight you lose?"

"Are you thinking of that man from Brchko?" he said with a laugh. "That was a different matter. The man from Brchko was a master gambler, but these are just merchants. They've just sold two boatloads of olive oil. As far as I could judge of their ability last night, one of those boatloads is mine."

"Is it honest to take people for so much money?"

"They'd do it to me if they could."

"All right then, I'll stay with Shehaga. You go off and do your dirty work. Leave the wool money with me. Make a note of how much it is."

"I don't like to trouble you so much. You'll probably have to sit up all night. I really wouldn't want it."

"I know you don't mind it one bit. You're just making sure I'll do it. That's why you were saying all this, just to get me to take your place."

"To tell you the truth, I did," he said with a laugh. "Thanks, I owe you one."

"What do you think is the matter with Shehaga?"

"An upset stomach, I'd think. I'll ask them to make some chamomile tea for you to give him. And he probably won't even need it."

Now he was belittling the danger, justifying his intention to spend the night gambling rather than at Shehaga's bedside.

"Why does Shehaga come to Venice every year?" I asked this man who knew all secrets.

"He was here with his son before his son went off to war. His son spent a wild evening. You'll see. Tomorrow Shehaga will visit all the places where his son went."

Good God! There's more sorrow in the truth than in anything we imagine.

That evening the noise of the carnival approached our hotel, and Shehaga got up to look, but stumbled as if his legs were of clay. I scarcely stopped him from falling. Scared by this strong man's weakness, I begged him to get undressed and lie down, and said we'd watch the carnival the next day.

Weak as he was, he let me help him lie down, and he closed his eyes. He didn't open them even when the noise was right under our open windows.

I looked down onto the street. Hundreds of men and women, clad in the most outrageous costumes, crowded in an indescribable chaos. Their voices merged into a mighty noise in which no single voice was audible. The light of torches and lanterns was reflected in the quiet water of the canal.

I looked in bewilderment at this multicolored throng that rocked and twisted, that moved and halted as one, yet each person was doing his own thing, leaping, dancing, singing, as though competing for who should commit the greatest madness. I felt giddy at this strange rejoicing that bordered on hysteria. It was not joy, it was escape. Come on! Let's go! Yesterday was misery and repression, and tomorrow it will be the same. Grab what you can of this day of freedom.

"What do you see?" came Shehaga's voice.

I went over to him.

"How do you feel?"

"What did you see on the street?"

I told him in three words.

"You don't like it, it would seem."

"I don't know. They're in a hurry to have a good time, as though they were going to jail tomorrow."

"You're not in it, that's why it looks strange. If you were with them, you'd enjoy it."

"Perhaps."

"This is a holiday for everyone. All you need are a few rags not to be what you are every day. With a mask on your face to hide your true self, so as not to be shamed of any madness whatsoever. Because they're all doing it. It's a wisdom where all agree: Come, let's play the fool! Everything's allowed, nothing's ugly, nothing's sinful. It's not the act of an individual, to spite all, to stand out. But it's everybody. And then there's no sin and no reproach. For several days and nights to be what you want to be, to take a rest from everything, from restrictions, from orders, from lies, cruelty, shame; it's a cure for the soul. We don't have it in us."

"And then?"

"Then back to the old ways, until a new catharsis comes along."

No, that wasn't what was worrying him, and I didn't dare ask him what it was.

I told him I was relieving Osman Vuk and that he'd gone to play dice with some Greeks. I gave him the money Osman had left with me, and he put it under his pillow without as much as a look.

He smiled. "That rascal will spread our fame throughout the world. People will think we're all like him. Sometimes I envy him his character. He's all right, wherever he is."

"And I can hardly wait to go home."

And I knew instantly that I'd made a mistake. I shouldn't have said it.

Without replying, Shehaga turned his head to the wall.

Silent, I listened to the roar of the carnival, its shouted

obscenities, a hundred songs begun and unfinished, loud laughter. I listened, as did Shehaga. I looked at his white-haired head. I felt sorry for him, perhaps all the more so for the fact that he said nothing and concealed his pain. There was nothing I could do to help him.

When we were on the boat, he'd enjoyed my talking about people, half sadly, half jokingly, as it is in life. I'd talked about my comrades at Chocim and about others whom I'd known: the bookbinder Ibrahim, who went off to war to escape his three wives and who would have fared better if he'd fought with them rather than with the Russians; about *hadji*–Husein Pishmish, who took refuge from his debts in the distant Ukraine, but who paid the heaviest interest on them; about Avdiya Suprda, who was not killed by war but by a crooked pear tree; about Salih Golub and his abysmal luck; about Rabiya-*hanuma* and her late love affair; about Mahmut's fear and the squitters—about people and things that one sees most clearly when one laughs at them through tears.

I asked him now, "Do you want me to talk to you?"

"I was here with my son four years ago," he said suddenly. "We spent the whole night on the street, wearing masks."

The words came involuntarily.

I asked nothing, I said nothing, leaving him to say what he had to.

"In the eighteen years that I saw him grow up in front of my eyes, never had I seen him so happy. I planned we'd come every winter. And then he went off to the war. I don't know. . . . I don't know why he went. Perhaps he didn't want to leave his friends. I don't know."

His voice was dry, repressed, quiet.

He said just this, and then turned once more to the wall.

I went to the window for some air and to arrange my thoughts.

The street was empty, silent, the noise had retreated to another part of the city.

I felt a sudden shiver. Was it a groan I heard? Or was it a heavy sigh that turned into a sob?

But when I went to Shehaga, he was lying in the same position, breathing quietly.

Late in the night, when he'd fallen asleep, I went out onto the street. It was empty, littered with all the discarded rubbish of the carnival, strangely quiet after the noise that had shaken the stone buildings.

I stood on the edge of the canal, above the quiet water, alone on the street, drowned in the silence, as though in the motionless waters of the canal, enshrouded in the shadows of another's darkness, sick with a sadness for which I could find no reason.

I'd fled from that strange night, and from my unknown self.

I found Shehaga on his knees in front of the bed, leaning his head on the bedside, trying to raise himself on strengthless arms.

I lifted him and placed him on the bed. He looked like a man close to death.

"Shall I call a doctor?"

"No!" he whispered.

I gave him some chamomile tea, and he soon grew calm. He even fell asleep.

The next morning, he awoke almost recovered. I got him to stay in bed and not to smoke, since the heart was no laughing matter.

"You think it's my heart?"

"It looks like it."

"Good, I'll do what you say. But don't call any doctors! They'll stick leeches on me, and I'll lose even the little blood I've got left."

"Perhaps it wouldn't hurt."

"My God, how easily people agree to letting the blood of another."

He was joking. He began to discuss how we'd make up

for this lying about and idling. He'd take me and show me the beauties of Venice that would take my breath away.

"The sooner I turn my back on its beauty, the better I'll like it," I said frankly.

"Why? What the hell do you want to hurry back to that misery for? The longer we stay, the better."

Osman Vuk returned late. The game hadn't gone well. When things started to go badly, the Greeks began to cheat. He'd warned them, but they just went on, and he'd jumped up and knocked the hell out of them. The police arrived at the sound of their cries and took Osman and the Herzegovinian to jail. In the morning, they'd released them, but only after they'd paid a hefty fine. So Osman remained both without his winnings and without even the money he'd already had.

"Do you always have to cause an upheaval?" Shehaga laughed. But a sudden pain interrupted him. He writhed, sitting up in bed, his chin on his knees, then sat up straight, was silent a moment, his face white, and said to Osman, "You play me!"

We were surprised.

"How can I play with you? Where would I have the money?"

Shehaga drew the money from under his pillow. "If you win, it's all yours. If you lose, that'll be your punishment."

"It's not fair, Shehaga."

"I know you play well. But no cheating!"

"God forbid!"

"All right, sit you down!"

Osman drew a table up to the bed and sat down in bewilderment.

"Your hands are shaking," Shehaga said. "Calm down."

"How can I be calm with all that money at stake?"

"Shall we leave it till later?"

"Let's do it now."

"Your throw!"

I watched that extraordinary game between a skilled gambler and an eccentric. For one, it was as if his whole life were at stake; the other was laughing, or wishing to help but not wanting to give. One was shaken to the core; the other was enjoying watching his torment. One was on hot coals, horrified at the unexpected fortune; the other was simply amused, caring nothing whether he won or lost. Osman threw the dice with a shaky, almost paralyzed hand.

"What's the matter with you?" Shehaga scolded him. "I can't bear to watch you. You can't lose. All you can do is win."

"I can lose a rare chance."

"There are hundreds of chances in life. You can't grab every one. Your chance will come. You're like a bird of prey, you want to kill us all."

"I don't. What do you mean!"

"You do! That's why I'm fond of you. And I'd like you to win. Why should you spare anyone?"

"And I'd like to win, too."

But fortune turned its back on Osman when he needed it most. He seemed to have shrunk. He was sweating. His eyes had grown sad, and his expression was one of despair.

He lost every game.

Each game was short, in all ten throws. For me it felt drawn out, like an illness.

"Fate is not on your side," Shehaga said in a serious voice.

"So I see."

Osman got up and threw the dice out of the window into the canal.

"Never again!" he said despondently.

"Swear it! Not on your soul, not on your word, but on your luck!"

He did, as if accepting a punishment, and left the room. I was sorry for him.

"What did you do that for?" I reproached Shehaga.

"I was testing fate: If he'd won, I'd have won, too. It seems both of us have lost."

"In what way? I don't understand."

He waved a hand, not wishing to reply.

I saw that his momentary alertness had passed. He moved his hands weakly over the bedcover, lacking the strength to raise them. His face was pale and covered in sweat, his lips clenched.

I was afraid. Was this death?

"Shehaga, what's the matter! Shehaga!"

I lowered his head onto the pillow, for he had begun to lean to one side as though about to fall out of the bed.

For several moments he lay still and then slowly raised his eyelids, exposing blank pupils, almost dead. He even managed a smile, telling me not to be afraid. He was stronger and braver than I'd thought. He wouldn't let me go for a doctor.

"This is our thing. Don't let's involve foreigners," he whispered.

I didn't understand.

And when life again returned to his pupils, he gave me a long and penetrating look, as if he were seeking something behind my forehead. Why didn't he ask? I'd have told him everything. I might have.

"Don't be afraid," he said quietly, but firmly, like a threat. "I'm not going to die. I haven't done all I have to do. I have to pay them for the evil they've done to me. A man mustn't die in debt."

"Why think of revenge? What happiness is there in vengeance?"

"There's no happiness in living, but I live."

"Vengeance is like drink, one never gets enough. But why think of this now?"

"And what would you have me think of?" he cried angrily. But he quickly stopped, grasping the edge of the bedcover with a terrified movement, and began to pull it toward his out-thrust chin with a cry of pain, as if from an acute cramp in his stomach. For a wonder, he soon grew calm and pushed aside the towel with which I was wiping his sweating brow.

"No need," he said quietly. "Where's Osman?"

"I don't know, he's gone out. What do you want? Tell me."

"You're not up to it."

"Up to what?"

"Perhaps I've expected this, but at another time and place. Not here, not like this."

"What are you talking about, Shehaga?"

I felt a sick excitement at the sight of him, at his incomprehensible talk, at the music and merry voices from the street, at the sad room, at the mystery that scared me.

The pains came more and more often, twisting his face into a painful grimace, and his body grew steadily weaker.

He was nauseated, as if at any moment he might vomit. He breathed deeply through his wide-open mouth, struggled to keep his breath, yet never took his eyes off me. The sickness seemed about to dim the light of those gray eyes that people feared.

"Do you know what's wrong with me?" he asked in a whisper, when the spasm of pain abated. "It looks as if I've been poisoned."

"Poisoned, for God's sake! What do you mean?"

"My insides are on fire. And my throat. And my head."

"Who?" I cried. "Who could have poisoned you?"

"Who couldn't! Perhaps you did. Or Osman. But, no. You're too weak to do anything like that. Osman wasn't with us, and I began to feel the burning on the road. Perhaps it was one of the servants."

"Why didn't you tell me? You've always kept everything to yourself, but why this?"

"It could have been some stranger, who'd been paid to do it, at one of our stops or in an inn. But the real culprit's in Sarajevo."

"Damn their eyes!"

"Tell Osman to come, and leave me alone with him."

"I know why you want him. Don't, I beg you. Don't think of revenge! You'll recover!"

"Get Osman!"

I couldn't move. I couldn't collect my thoughts, nor did I know what to do. The man might be dying in front of me, poisoned, and I wasn't thinking so much about his misfortune as about his cruelty, and the cruelty of those who'd poisoned him.

"They've caught up with me, they've won, that's all," he whispered through blue lips. "I've been let down somewhere by somebody. It was inevitable."

Was it better not to obey him and let him die reproaching me, or obey him and let his hatred go on?

"Shall I fetch the doctor?"

"Get Osman!"

I went out into the corridor.

Osman was talking to the proprietor, an Italian, in some strange nonexistent language that seemed to worry neither of them. The landlord was inquiring in worried tones about the sick man, fearing lest a traveller might die in his hotel, which would put off the other guests. Osman was hesitating between a desire to frighten him with this very fact and his own fear of tempting fate by doing so, so merely shrugged his shoulders and made do with some general, philosophic remarks (it's all in the hands of God), and pointed to the heavens while the proprietor, following Osman's gaze, looked in bewilderment at the flaking ceiling.

I told Osman that Shehaga was very ill and was asking for him.

"What's the matter with him?" He sounded worried.

"I'm going for the doctor."

"Is it that bad? Or perhaps you're just panicking. You see what bloody luck I have! I'm not fated to stand on my own feet, to enroll in the human race."

"Go to Shehaga!"

"Right away. But to tell the truth, there's something strange about that illness of his."

It was as if he scented murder.

The proprietor came to my aid and explained to me where the doctor lived: the third street left and then the second right, and up and down and right. I scarcely found the doctor, but the rheumatism that had afflicted him that very day enabled me to catch him.

I remembered Mahmut's sick herbalist who cured others but couldn't cure himself, but I'd no choice. I managed somehow to persuade him to visit the patient. The ducats, which I didn't spare, succeeded in lending movement to his creaking bones. It was the ducats that convinced him, for he didn't know my language nor I his (all the words I'd learned had gone from my head, and I remembered only the words for "please" and "patient"), and I thanked God that there were some things common to all people. I didn't know how good a doctor he was, nor did I need to, for fate had prescribed him for the unlucky Shehaga. Clearly, he knew little about rheumatism, but then Shehaga wasn't suffering from rheumatism, and in his illness luck might serve him better than any doctor. I couldn't go for luck, but for this limping fat man I could. If Shehaga could have any luck, then perhaps he'd be his luck.

When we arrived at the hotel, we saw the proprietor and his wife standing in Shehaga's hallway, desperate at the misfortune that had overtaken them through this foreigner's illness, yet nonetheless stunned by what was going on in the room. They stood as if rooted and simply explained briefly to the doctor that one of Shehaga's servants was trying out a spell on the sick man.

Without turning round, perhaps unaware of their presence, Osman Vuk was kneeling by Shehaga's bed and holding his limp hand, slowly pronouncing his well-known litany comprised of the names of Bosnian villages, but not cheerfully and sarcastically, as he usually did, making fun of our poverty, but softly and absentmindedly, as though performing an arduous task.

In the hotel room, over the Grand Canal that flowed

through the city of Shehaga's dreams, amidst the deafening noise of the carnival, could be heard the grim words denoting our poverty:

"Luckless, Blackwater, Mudville, Thornystake, Burnt Ash, Hunger, Wolfsden, Thorny, Misery, Snake-hole . . . "

Shehaga suddenly began to writhe, twisting into a knot from invisible pains, blue in the face, and threw up a gob of ugly liquid onto the towel that Osman was holding. He began to foam at the mouth.

The doctor approached the sick man and examined him carefully, without touching him.

"Do you know what's wrong with him?" he asked shortly, and I thought I heard fear in his voice. If we didn't know, then he'd pretend not to know, either. The last thing he wanted was to be involved with the courts.

I shrugged my shoulders. Let's leave it that we didn't know.

"It's the heart," said Osman, pointing to the left side of his chest.

The doctor nodded. That's what he would write: Death due to heart failure.

It was all the same to him and to us. It was all the same to Shehaga.

This isn't their thing, Shehaga had said. Perhaps we'd nothing to boast about, but it was too late now.

Shehaga grew slightly calmer. Only his hand moved weakly, seeking Osman's.

Osman turned. "He wanted me to sing our songs, which I did. He wanted to hear the sound of our speech. So I spoke. What more could I do?"

Shehaga's hand still beckoned, quietly, limply.

Osman took hold of his fingers. They tried to grip. He wanted something.

Osman looked at me.

I nodded: Say anything!

Gently, leaning down close to Shehaga's face, which was

increasingly deathly pale, save that there was a dark blue circle around his clenched lips, Osman Vuk, in a voice hoarse with emotion, began to recite numbers!

"One, two, three, four, five . . ."

Over the dying man's pale cheeks passed something like relief. His face took on a shade of sad fulfillment, and, from under a closed eyelid, slid a tear. He was still alive, still holding Osman's hand, still wishing for that speech, that hidden love.

Suddenly, I grasped it all, and a shudder went right through me. Osman Vuk, the scoundrel, the gambler, the killer, was performing the most merciful act in life. A need for the warmth of home had arisen in Shehaga, here in a foreign land, before the final alienation that inevitably awaited him at any moment. Or a need for human speech, for a human voice that softly fell on ears that heard less and less, so he would not be alone before the great loneliness, so that all would not be utterly silent and empty before the great emptiness.

His hatred of people and of his native land had been due only to his hurt. And when thoughts of vengeance had paled before the proximity of death, there had emerged of itself the hidden essence: love for the root and a longing for human intimacy.

What thoughts, what final thoughts, were passing through the dying brain? What pictures, what sadness, or, perhaps, joy? Was he thinking of his native country, from which he'd fled, fleeing from himself? Was he seeing the people he'd loved? Was he regretting not having lived differently? Did the last vestiges of memory cling to the native skies of childhood, which none of us ever forget?

> In the beginning love,
> In life hatred,
> At the end memory.

Love, after all, is stronger than anything.

And then a cold sweat took me at the thought that flashed, like lightning, through my brain. But what if I was mistaken? What if that last pressure of a half-dead hand was merely a call to vengeance?

No, I'd not think that way. I'd no right to be cynical. He himself had asked that the sound of our speech, no matter what, should be the last thing he heard. In his last moments he'd forgotten vengeance and remembered his love, which he'd concealed.

Or he'd remembered it only after communicating his desire for vengeance to Osman, at peace, certain that the debt would be ruthlessly paid.

I never learned. They were both silent, one dead, the other living but distrustful. Yet I wanted to know. Rarely had I ever wanted anything so much, as though that knowledge would have opened to me many secrets concerning humanity.

I'd seen the death of a powerful man, killed by grief. I'd seen what was perhaps murder from a distance. I'd seen human hatred, but I was obsessed by only one thing: Was his last thought vengeance or love?

It seemed as though my entire life depended on it.

I decided for love. It was less realistic and less probable, but more noble. And better: This way everything had more meaning. Both death . . . and life.

■ □ ■ □ ■

CHAPTER 19

THE FORTRESS

FULL OF SADNESS, I LOOKED AT THE EVENING STAR, IN A foreign night, in a foreign country.

And I thought, feeling lost,

Oh, familiar star,
I know thee not.

I recognized everything, including myself, when I got home.

I hid my tears on sensing the familiar smells of my beloved country.

I whispered to myself, excitedly, as to a beloved woman: Without you I feel like a leper. Without you my heart cries out in isolation. Without you my thought is crippled and wingless.

I thought the same when I embraced Tiyana, her closeness a balm to my fears, her smell freeing me from all that was alien.

I gave no thought to the evils and suffering in that land of mine. I thought of the good people I'd known and of our dear native sky. Perhaps for the very fact that an unhappy man had hidden how much he loved it.

I'd been sensitized by a foreign land and by a strange death. A fever had begun to shake me already on the way home.

I took to my bed the very day of my return. A high temperature shut me off from Tiyana, from my friends, from the whole world, from my very self.

I thought I was lying in the old room above the bakery. I thought I was lying in the bakery furnace. I'd no thoughts. I burned like a log. My body was bursting with the onset of sickly images and voices. Wild horses rushed down on me, rearing up over me. From the darkness emerged the tiny distorted images of my comrades from Chocim, armless, legless, headless, transforming into vast monsters. From endless empty spaces, I heard maddened cries, at times human, from the fear that dominated the earth. All was red, burning, all was a deep abyss, all was an expanse bereft of frontier and boundary. And then everything would return to normal human dimensions, distorted, yet recognizable. As in a dream, I felt a tiny hand on my swollen forehead, and I knew that it was Tiyana's. I heard her whisper, and Osman's laughter. I saw their heads drawn close together. "No!" I cried. "I'll kill you!" I cried out, and when the high fever had passed, I felt a heavy tiredness in my body that was drained of strength.

"Did Osman come?" I asked Tiyana.

"Yes. Every day."

"I heard him laughing."

"I never realized what a good man he was."

He'd been there all right. It was not a delusion brought on by the fever. Had I rightly remembered all the rest of it?

It was impossible, it was a creation of my fevered brain, in its fear. Impossible! Yet I didn't dare to ask.

And Mahmut had been coming, too, only I didn't remember him. I'd no fear of him. On the third day, when I came to myself, he shed tears of relief.

"Thank God, thank God," he whispered.

He looked at me reproachfully for having gone away, and delightedly that I'd recovered. And what would I be doing in a strange world? People are people, and houses are houses.

And what matters to a man are his friends. He felt empty and sad without me. He'd go out onto the road or into the fields, though he knew we wouldn't be coming. It made him feel better. He felt closer to us, and when I fell ill, he sat with me all the time, feeling angry. What made me go looking for trouble in foreign lands? There was enough here. If I were to die, he'd thought, what would he do? And what would my poor wife do, who'd wept her eyes out, and he and Osman had spent hours comforting her? Indeed, it was easier for her, she was young and beautiful. She'd soon get married again, but what would he do? A good friend wasn't easy to find.

"Whom would she marry?" I thought. "Osman?" No, I was sorry, she wouldn't have a chance to marry anybody. I was alive, here, and here I'd stay, alive.

For himself, Mahmut said he'd not remain in his present job. He'd only been waiting for Osman to return to hand over the warehouse. He couldn't stand it any longer. He'd had enough of sitting in one place like a block of wood or a stone. It was bad for his legs. He should have more exercise, and he liked to see people.

What was this?

This funny dreamer preferred insecurity in his dreams to security in loneliness. He was enchanted by the thought of outstanding actions, and all that he got were the most usual and boring. He'd ended up feeding cats and chasing mice, he who, in his imagination, had soared above the clouds, and felt himself betrayed, more than if he'd remained to vegetate in poverty, cherishing his hope of the unattainable.

Now he was thinking of breeding canaries. It was a nice occupation, clean, pleasant, interesting. Canaries made love, sang, and bred. They bred so much that he could make a good living by selling the young.

And then he fell silent, passing a hand over his thin face.

"You're keeping something back," I said.

"What am I keeping back?"

"I don't know. I'm asking you."

"I've told you all that matters. The rest is unimportant."

"What do you mean unimportant?"

"Well, I gave grain on credit, and Osman got angry."

"Why did you do that?"

"Why? It was a bad winter, and people had no cash, that's why. They'll pay, when they can."

"Have you noted their names?"

"I have, almost all."

No, of course, he hadn't noted a single one. How could a generous magnate, as at that moment he really had been, note down the names of those who owed him?

I didn't know what led him to such unpredictable actions. Was it a desire for gratitude and respect? Or was it a wish to stand out: No one would do this, but he would. Or perhaps it was just out of kindness of heart?

"And what are you going to do now?"

"I'll sell the house."

"How often have you been selling it?"

"This time I'll really sell it."

He cared only for the present. He forgot what had been and spared no thought for the future. He ruined himself with everything he did, be it good or bad. He told Osman he'd sell the house and make up for the loss, hoping that Osman would not agree. But Osman was no Ahmet Shabo, who had more sentiments than sense. Much Osman cared for sentiment! He agreed at once and even demanded its immediate sale. Mahmut's wife agreed, scolding Mahmut affectionately: Will you never grow up? It's not your fault!

"It's easy to be generous with somebody else's cash," Osman said and calmly took the money, but his thoughts were elsewhere.

He told me how they'd buried Shehaga. We'd set off with him alive and returned with him dead, in an ironbound oak coffin.

A lot of people came to the big house to view Shehaga, invisible, ironbound in his coffin. The only people to see him were the *kadi* and his scribes and witnesses. He did this honor to the dead Shehaga by this last visit, which for him constituted a considerable satisfaction, for a dead enemy was surely to be preferred to a living friend. He looked serious, but his heart was singing like a lark.

Zafraniya also came with the *kadi*. Perhaps he believed those who'd seen the body, that it was Shehaga and that he really was dead, but, to be safe, he pushed his way close to Shehaga's yellow face, to be certain, to smell the corpse, as if it were a flower.

They all expressed their condolences to him, Osman, and requested that he pass on their sympathies to Shehaga's wife, who had taken to her bed at this final tragedy. Osman had thanked both Zafraniya and the *kadi* most effusively. He even told them how Shehaga, on his deathbed, remembered all his friends and begged them to forgive him if he had offended any of them, as he forgave them.

Hard luck on those he'd mentioned, I thought. I knew only too well Osman's wolfish nature.

"Are the *kadi* and Zafraniya to blame for Shehaga's death?" I asked Osman.

"How could they be to blame? Shehaga died of grief for his son," he replied reproachfully.

"He himself said he was poisoned. He called you to make you swear to avenge him."

"For goodness' sake, what do you mean avenge him? He called me to discuss business."

He said this with an icy, spiked smile, ever on the watch, ever defensive: a closed fortress.

I said this to him, and he laughed. "Like everyone else. And thank God. Why should we remain defenseless? The enemy's all around us."

Had Shehaga left him the task of vengeance?

If he had, this apparent peace would soon be shattered.

Which of them would be the quicker? Who would be the first to accuse Bechir Toska of yet another crime?

Nevertheless, I'd ask Tiyana about what I thought I'd seen. It was impossible, but still I'd ask. I was mad to think of it, but still I'd ask.

I put it off, till my fear abated.

All I wanted was to leave that house as soon as possible.

Meanwhile, in my beloved country, the banners of war were once more unfurled, and new taxes were levied. The people cursed all wars, but they paid the taxes and went to war.

Only the peasants of Zhupcha rebelled. They drove off the sultan's officials and refused to give either taxes or men.

It was not for nothing that Ramiz had taken refuge in Zhupcha.

My good Mula Ibrahim, terrorized by the cruelty of people, spoke only of the weather and of his health, and quietly and carefully at that, for anything could sound suspicious, whether you said the weather was bad or whether you didn't feel well. But he'd not forgotten me. He found me a cheap lodging and a job as a children's teacher. I'd have accepted no other. I taught children to read and write. I tried to teach them to be kind, in the hope that some of my naïve words might remain with them.

And among the children there sometimes sat Mahmut Neretlyak, his pointed knees folded under him and, silently, rubbing his bad leg, he listened, nodding his head. I didn't know whether in doubt or in agreement.

He shook his head with special sadness when, after having seen off ten people from Zhupcha in shackles to the Fortress, we'd returned to the children, as though I sought consolation among them. Beside the prisoners marched the ex–Austrian prisoner of war, the cheerful Ferid, with his guards. He'd taken over the dead Avdaga's work, but not his habits. He'd regained his property, settled in the house, and driven out his wife and his replacement with their five children, become a chief of police, and now repaid the justice he'd received with cruelty.

The Zhupcha people marched between armed guards, looking surprised, wondering why they'd been arrested and what they'd done.

Their wives and relatives followed them at a distance in silence.

And, from the square, soldiers were already setting off for war.

And they, too, were followed by fathers, mothers, sisters, girlfriends, who were weeping or keeping a stunned silence.

Salih the barber from Alifakovats stood to one side. Had he learned the truth about his sons, or did he still live in hope?

Of those who were going, who would be killed? And where? In the Danubian marshes? In the forests of Bessarabia? In far foreign fields?

I looked at them in sadness. Was there among them an Ahmet-*aga* Misira who became an *aga* and who would pay for it with his own death and that of others? Where was the angry town crier Hido who was fleeing from poverty? Was there another Ibrahim Paro escaping from his wives? Were there the sons of some other Salih the barber from some other Alifakovats? Was there a Husein Pishmish, a Smail Sovo, an Avdiya Suprda?

No matter what their names, their fate was the same.

No matter whether they were sad or falsely cheerful, they'd not return. My comrades hadn't returned. They'd perished to a man.

And would my children tread the same miserable path when they grew up?

Would they live as stupidly as their fathers did?

In all probability they would, but I refused to believe it.

I refused to believe, but I couldn't free myself from apprehension.

GLOSSARY
AND REFERENCES

aga: Originally, an officer about equal to a captain; later, a gentleman or landowner.

Al-Azhar University: A prominent Muslim university in Egypt, still extant.

Alifakovats: A hilly district of Sarajevo.

Ali-pasha mosque: A mosque of Sarajevo well known for its beauty, still extant.

Allahemanet: Goodbye (Turco-Arabic).

ayan: A local government official; usually, a member of a distinguished family.

Bairam: One of the two most important Muslim religious holidays. There are two Bairams in the year: one following the fast of Ramadan, and the second the so-called Kurban or Hadzi Bairam, which occurs two months and ten days after the first.

Bashcharshia: A district of Sarajevo with shops and markets surrounding the Begova mosque.

bayraktar: Literally, a standard-bearer; generally, a rank in the Ottoman army also used as a title of rank in civilian life.

beg: A high-ranking official in provincial service; in Bosnia, often a title of respect, regardless of the occupation of the person so addressed.

Begova mosque: One of the main mosques in Bashcharshia, still extant.

Begovats: A village near Sarajevo.

bezistan: A covered market, usually specializing in craft goods and haberdashery.

Birgivi: Muhamed bin Pir Ali (1522–73), a Turkish religious scholar.

Brchko: A town in Bosnia.

Brezik: A village near Sarajevo.

brothers Morich: Between 1747 and 1757, Hadji-Pasho Morich and his brother Ibrahim-*aga* Morich led Bosnian Muslims in Sarajevo in rebellion against the sultan. The brothers were executed in Sarajevo in 1757.

Chocim: A fortress town on the east bank of the Dniestr and the scene of famous battle, in 1621, during which Poles and Cossacks defeated the army of Sultan Osman II. In 1769, the Turks, who had occupied Chocim, tried unsuccessfully to raise the Russian siege of the fortress.

Crni vrh, Berkusha, Bjelave, Koshevo: Four of many other districts of Sarajevo, centrally located.

Dariva: An area of Sarajevo upstream of the Milyatska River.

defterdar: An officer of finance, the accountant-general of a province.

Dniestr: A river in today's Ukraine.

Dubitsa: One of several battles fought between the Ottoman Empire and Austria.

dzhemat: A Muslim parish.

effendi: A title of respect; initially used for government officials and members of learned professions, it was later used as an equivalent for "sir" or "master."

Glasinats: A small town in Bosnia.

Gorazhde: A town in Bosnia.

Goritsa: A hilly area of Sarajevo.

groschen: Small coins; small change (German).

gusle: A one-stringed fiddle, usually made of maple wood.

hadji: A title of honor given to one who has made a pilgrimage to Mecca.

hafiz: A title of honor earned by one who knows the Koran by heart.

Hamzevian Order: A term for an heretical school of dervishes.

han: A shelter for travellers.

hanuma: A title for a well-to-do wife or, more generally, a term of respect equivalent to "lady."

haznadar: Turkish for a government treasurer.

hodja: A Muslim man of religion; a teacher.

imam: A prayer leader.

inulin: Greek helenion, a plant from whose roots a medical starch was made.

janissary: A soldier in an elite corps of Ottoman troops. Before the sixteenth century, those destined to be janissaries were usually taken as small boys from Christian families and raised as Muslims.

kadi: A Muslim judge who interprets and administers the religious law of Islam.

kasaba: A provincial town (Arabic).

kolo: A Balkan ring dance.

Kozya chupriya: A bridge over the River Milyatska outside Sarajevo (to the east).

Kuyundzhiluk: A street in Sarajevo known for its gold- and silversmiths' shops.

lokum: A sweet cake.

Machva: A region in present-day Serbia.

medrese: A Muslim religious secondary school, a theological seminary.

merhaba: A Muslim greeting meaning "hello."

Mevli: An Islamic poet.

Milyatska: The river running through Sarajevo.

muderis: A high-ranking teacher in a *medrese.*

Mudzeliti: A street in Sarajevo, originally a street of book-binders.

muezzin: A man who proclaims the hour of prayer from a minaret.

mufti: The highest-ranking religious official in a province.

mula: A title for anyone qualified to teach religion, even at the lowest levels.

muselim: The chief executive official in a district.

Muyo: A common abbreviation of the male given name Mustafa.

naib: A deputy assisting a *kadi* (Arabic).

Neretva: The river running through the Herzegovinian town of Mostar.

oke: A unit of measure equal to 1.283 kilos.

pasha: A military and civil rank equal to that of general.

Podrgab: A village near Sarajevo.

Posavina: A region in present-day Bosnia.

rakiya: A type of brandy, often made from plums.

Ramadan: The ninth month of the Muslim calendar, during which a solemn fast is observed daily from sunup to sundown.

Sari-Murat: A partisan who fought with the Morich brothers in their rebellion against the sultan.

Sava: One of the major rivers in the former Yugoslavia.

serdar: A title given to a high-ranking official in military and civil service.

shagiye: A stringed musical instrument (Arabic).

sheitan: The devil (Hebrew).

sherbet: A refreshing cool drink made from sweetened water.

Siyavuz-*pasha*'s Jewish quarter: A courtyard in Sarajevo built in the sixteenth century to accommodate poorer Jews from the town center. It existed until the end of the nineteenth century. Unlike occupants of a true ghetto, residents had freedom of movement, and outsiders could readily gain access to the quarter.

Smederevo: A town in Serbia.

Srebrenitsa: A town in Bosnia.

sûrah: A chapter of the Koran.

tamburitza: A small stringed musical instrument.

third brother, the: A reference to the proverbial third brother of folklore and fairy tales; usually the third and youngest brother, although considered a fool, ends by marrying the princess or attaining some similar good fortune.

Trebevich: A mountain to the south of Sarajevo.

ulema: A Muslim learned body, a gathering of learned men.

vaiz: A Muslim preacher.

vali: The civil governor of an Ottoman province; the term is here used synonymously with "vizier."

Valyevo: A town in Serbia.

Vishegrad: A town in Bosnia.

vizier: Here, the sultan's deputy, governor of an Ottoman province.

Vratnik: A district of Sarajevo, above Bashcharshia.

Vuk: A common male given name, meaning "wolf."

Zhupcha: A village in Bosnia.

Zvornik: A town in Bosnia.

Death and the Dervish
The Fortress
MEŠA SELIMOVIĆ

Fording the Stream of Consciousness
In the Jaws of Life and Other Stories
DUBRAVKA UGREŠIĆ

Angel Riding a Beast
LILIANA URSU

Ballad of Descent
MARTIN VOPĚNKA

The Silk, The Shears, and *Marina*
IRENA VRKLJAN